Braking Kane
The Struggle to Stop

by Laura L. Dell

To my good
friend,
may it serve the
purpose...
Laura L Dell
LAURA L DELL
MAHOPAC, NY
10-22-16

COVER PHOTO BY: Richard Thornton/ Shutterstock.com

ISBN-13: 978-1503322905
ISBN-10: 1503322904

DEDICATION

This book is dedicated to all the young ones, who, like their older counterparts, shall remain anonymous, and who, along with their families, continue to struggle.

ACKNOWLEDGEMENTS

Thank you to all my friends who were kind enough to read the various revisions of this work and to offer their criticisms and suggestions.

And very special thanks to all those in the fields of substance abuse treatment, youth services, and law enforcement, and those who are, themselves, in recovery, who gave me an invaluable education, (during four decades), in exchange for little more than my sincere compassion for, and interest in, their very sacred work. May it serve the purpose!

And, finally, thank you to all those who helped me to learn to navigate the new publishing business!

--Laura Dell

DISCLAIMER

This is a work of fiction. Due to the somewhat predictable nature of the disease of addiction, some readers may identify with some of the events described, either from their own experience or from that of someone they know. However, any similarity to any real-life persons, places, events, or entities is purely coincidental.

This book is written "for entertainment purposes only". The author is not offering any professional services or suggestions, and both the author and publisher specifically disclaim all responsibility for any liability, risk, or loss, which might be incurred by the reader, for the real-life application of any information or techniques suggested by this fictional work.

The disease of addiction is difficult and dangerous to treat. The reasons for use, and the pathway to recovery are unique to each individual and each family. Treatment is best done in a professionally supervised program, specifically chosen for the client's age, gender, and type and level of use.

(For those who wish to learn more about the author's interest in this field, please see "About the Author" at the end of the final chapter.)

1. Arrivals

It was just after Christmas when I got the phone call. It was a Monday night. My own kids were all out, enjoying the Christmas vacation. I had actually thought that, for once, I would have a whole night to myself. I really should have known better.

When the phone rang, I just knew it would be one of the kids. My youngest was eight and was sleeping over at a friend's house for the first time. The parents were taking them, the next day, to a Broadway show and dinner, and then Hannah would sleep over until Wednesday morning. My seventeen-year-old, Dana, had gone with her school to Washington, on a four-day trip.

The boys, David, twenty-one, and Daniel, twenty-four, were adults, and mostly on their own. David had been in and out, visiting friends home from college, but he had just left to stay with his roommate's family, at their ski lodge, for a few days. I called to thank them personally for the invitation, and to see if we could repay them by sending up some groceries or something with David. They were very gracious people and knew exactly why I had called. They assured me that it was, indeed, a family vacation.

And Danny, the eldest, was safely back in New York, ready to go back to work. He had just called me. It was supposedly to thank me for the visit, but he knew how I worried about him getting home safely. I was touched that he was finally old enough to remember to call on his own.

I loved my kids. They drove me nuts, but I wouldn't have missed raising a family for the world... even if it hadn't worked out quite the way I had planned it. My husband had passed away just after Hannah was born. But we did okay.

So, anyway, when I got this phone call, I assumed it was going to be one of the kids. Somebody had undoubtedly forgotten something. They would probably just need me to tell them that, whatever it was, they didn't really need it.

"Hello?" I said, as I picked up the phone.

"Yes, hello. Is this Tara Wilson?"

"Speaking."

"I work for Trans-Ten Airlines, Mrs. Wilson, and we have a situation here that we're hoping you can help with."

I thought quickly. None of my kids was flying anywhere. "What is this in reference to?"

"We have a boy here who's in pretty bad shape, and we think you may know him."

"Okay..." I was a little suspicious, but I was thinking that maybe it was a student who was afraid to call home. I had been teaching in a junior high school, in Connecticut, for a number of years and was on a year's leave. I'd worked with thousands of teenagers and had run interference for kids before. I was also thinking that I was probably being really stupid. I usually hung up right away on anything strange on the phone. But, I had to admit, I was curious.

"Well, we don't have a lot to go on, so we'd really appreciate any help you can give us. According to the stewardess, this young man, he seems to be about fourteen, got on the flight by himself in San Francisco. Shortly after takeoff, she noticed that he was sound asleep. She covered him up, and he slept the whole flight. She tried to wake him once for a meal, but he didn't respond. She figured that he was just really tired and let him sleep. However, when they arrived in New York, and she tried to awaken him to deplane, she couldn't rouse him. She called for assistance and, after the other passengers had deplaned, they managed to finally awaken him. But he was still very, very groggy, as if he had been drugged or had been drinking very heavily."

'Or both,' I thought to myself. I could tell that she was choosing her words very carefully. In fact, it sounded as if she were reading from a report. Also, I assumed that she didn't want to scare me away or put me on the defensive. But I had been in that situation myself, trying to alert parents who, I suspected, might be in denial. I recalled the old joke where the teacher calls the parent and says, 'Is your child on any kind of medication?' (…the old stand-by line when the kid was coming stoned to your class every day…) And the parent says, 'No…but he smokes pot, and he drinks a lot!'

When I didn't give her a negative reaction, the airline woman went on. "They called for a wheelchair, but they had to carry him down the aisle of the plane to get to it. He could barely hold his head up and was still not responding to their questions. They brought him here to the First Aid Station. He seemed in no immediate danger, so we decided to just let him sleep it off. We searched his bags for some clue as to his identity... Are you still there?"

"Yes, I'm still listening. Go ahead."

"Well, he had identification and a letter giving him permission to travel to the home of his aunt, in New York."

"You do realize that you're calling Connecticut?" I asked.

"Oh, yes. But your name was not on the papers we found."

"Okaay...." Now I was even more intrigued.

She continued. "We tried to track down the aunt mentioned in the letter, and the parents, whose signatures are barely legible, and any information on the boy himself. All the names appear to be bogus."

"And I come into this, how?"

"Finally, we found a small piece of paper in the boy's backpack..."

"Don't tell me. My name was on it."

"Your name and this number. Do you live in Wellmore?"

"Yes, as a matter of fact." I began to think. "Wait a minute. Where did this kid come in from?"

"San Francisco."

I started to say that I really didn't know anybody in San Francisco, but all of a sudden I could feel an enormous 'Uh oh' welling up inside me.

She was speaking again. "Are you still there?"

"Yeah. Listen. How old did you say this kid is?"

"He looks about fourteen."

I was searching in my wallet for one of those school pictures that my sister sent every year of my nephew, Kane. My sister and her husband live in California, and I don't get to see them very much. They're a two-career family. They have the trophy house in a posh suburb of L.A. You know… the kind of house that people buy to show other people that they've made it big. And I always suspected that Kane was the trophy child. It was like everybody else had one, so my sister had to have one too. When he was born, I strongly suspected that she had no idea what it meant to give up her life, or at least a large part of it, for a child.

I finally found the photo that I was looking for, and I realized that we hadn't gotten a new picture of Kane this year. I studied the one I had and checked the age on the back. His birthday was in March, so in last year's fall picture he would have been twelve. "Does this kid have dirty blonde hair, kind of shaggy and curly?"

"Yes, he does. In fact, it's very long, almost to his shoulders."

"You said fourteen. He could be thirteen?"

"Well, yeah, I guess. I really don't have much to do with kids this age. He could be thirteen. I feel sorry for him though, whatever his age is."

"You feel sorry for him?"

"Lady, you sound really nice, so I have to be truthful with you. This kid is stoned out of his head. He's obviously a runaway. He's like 3,000 miles away from home. I'm guessing he didn't *earn* the money for this plane ticket. And, apparently, the person he was counting on as a last resort, if I may be so bold, doesn't even really *know* him."

I resisted the temptation to defend myself, or blame my stupid sister, and tried to concentrate on how lucky this poor kid was to find this lady. "Look, before I jump to conclusions here and open myself up to a potentially dangerous coincidence, can you describe this kid a little more?" I asked.

"Sure. Listen. I'm sorry. I didn't mean to lay a guilt trip on you. It just makes me sick to see kids like this."

"It's okay. I'm a teacher. I see a lot of it. I just didn't think that it might be going on in my own family, without my knowing it. You just caught me a little off guard here."

She described the boy she had in front of her, and the evidence began to mount. My mind was racing. This was so preposterous, and yet, with that slim chance, I couldn't *take* a chance.

"Look. Can I call you back?" I asked her. "I need to call my sister in Los Angeles."

"Sure. But you will call back, right? Otherwise this kid goes to Juvie. I really hate to send anybody there...Wait a minute. He's coming around. Do you want to try to talk to him?"

I took a deep breath...how to handle this. "Okay." I could hear their voices in the background.

"Hey! Wha' is this place? Who're you?" He did sound a little out of it...and nasty!

"Sit up! Somebody wants to talk to you." For someone who didn't know the age group, she sure knew enough not to baby him.

"Hullo?"

I couldn't get anything from one word, but I figured I'd go for it. "Kane? What are you doing here?"

"Aunt... Aunt Tara?"

Okay, *now* what was I going to do? "Are you straight enough to know what I'm saying to you?"

"Yes, ma'am."

Whoa. 'Yes, ma'am.' I never heard that in my neck of the woods. He had to know he was in trouble. "Are you sure?" I was using my most commanding, no-nonsense voice.

"Yes, ma'am."

"All right. Then listen carefully. Do you have any idea how much trouble you're in?"

"I'm not sorry I did it. I hate my parents. I'm not going back there." Well, *his* tone changed in a hurry. We were obviously dealing with a little bit of emotion here.

"Well, here's the deal." I knew, from some limited experience, that I had to be really careful here. I wanted him to be safe with me, and not in the hands of the juvenile authorities. But if I were going to have any hope at all of helping him, he was going to have to want it more than I did. I went on. "I'll take you in until you get yourself straightened out, but only if you wanna be here. My house. My rules. No crap. Or you're outta here. Your other choice is to go with that nice lady there. She'll call the police, and they'll book you as a runaway. They'll lock you up overnight, and your parents will be out here in the morning."

"My parents don' know where I am."

He was making a power play. I knew so many kids who had lost faith in their parents' ability to act like parents. These kids started talking to all adults as if they were equals. I had to 'up' the authority in my voice. I had to try to stay 'above' him. He had to trust that I was the adult and that I knew what I was doing…even if I didn't!

"Hey! How long you been gettin' high? Is your brain fried?! I'm givin' you five seconds to make your decision. It'll take me another five seconds to call your parents. Unless you killed them before you left, they're gonna have the news real quick."

Despite the serious tone that I was determined to maintain for my nephew's sake, I had to smile at myself. It had been about twenty years since I'd done volunteer work in a local drug program. But I could immediately hear myself slipping back into the way we used to talk to the kids in those days. The 'g' in my 'ing' words was always the first thing to go!

While I was waiting for his reply, I was hoping that he had come down enough, and that he was scared enough, that I could get through to him. Of course, if he was still high, it wouldn't work. You just can't reason with anybody when they're high.

"Don't call them." He tried to sound tough, but I could hear him start to break down on the other end. I had to be strong. I had seen this before. It could so be part of the act.

"Give your answer to the nice lady, and then put her back on the phone."

"Hello?" The airline lady came on again.

I told her what I had said to him. "He's going to tell you whether he's coming with me or letting you send him to Juvenile Hall. He sounded like he started to cry. Does he look remorseful over this, or is it an act? One… remorseful. Two… an act."

"I'd say 'one', but given the priors here..."

"Gotcha. Well, what's his answer?"

"He's curled up on the cot again. He's still pretty out of it."

"Oh, great. Well, jerk him back to reality, so we can get going on this."

She turned away from the phone and said, "Hey, kid! What's it gonna be?"

I could hear him in the background again. "I don' know!! I don' wan' my parents to know where I am."

"They're gonna find out either way." She was doing the best she could, but this poor airport lady certainly didn't plan on an evening like this. At least she didn't try to make it easy for him.

Although I hadn't seen my nephew in years, he had been an adorable little boy, and I was guessing that, even as a punk, he was appealing. I had seen more 'cute little boys' get into trouble that way. Teachers, counselors, even mothers, couldn't resist the temptation to give in to them. Adults failed to discipline them, and that undermined their character development at a young age. It was hard to turn them around after that. They had, in effect, been 'taught' how to manipulate themselves out of every potential character-building situation...But, then again, who really understood anything about human beings? I knew I didn't.

I could hear silence on the other end. I didn't know whether she was giving him time to think or whether he had passed out again. She had left the phone open so that I could hear. Finally, I heard him again. "I don' wan my aunt to see me like this." He was still slurring his words.

"Aww... He's good!" I thought. I couldn't believe how cynical I felt. I usually had more compassion. I guessed that I was frustrated that this was happening in my own family. Again. And, besides that, I was getting a little impatient.

She was talking to him. "So, then it's settled? I call the police?" She was getting impatient too.

"No! No. I'll go to my aunt."

"Okay." She turned back to the phone. "You heard?"

"Yeah. Thanks. You did a good job. Okay. This is what I'm going to do. I'll give you the number of a limo service that covers our area. If you would call them and tell them exactly where to pick him up, and then have them call me, I'll give them my credit card number. If you could call me when he's left there, then I'll call my sister and let her know what's happening. Sound good?"

"Sounds okay to me."

We took care of the details, I thanked her, and I hung up. While I waited to hear back from the limo company, and then from the airport, I had time to think about what I was doing. I had no idea what I was doing. But, obviously, it was falling to me, once again, to have to do *something* about this.

2. Running Away

When I knew Kane was safely in the limo, I called my sister.

"Hello?" My sister's voice was very anxious.

"Sis!" I greeted her.

"Tara? Is that you?"

"Yeah, what's up?" I was going to let *her* tell *me* what was going on.

"Oh, Tara! You can't imagine. Something terrible has happened."

"What?" I wanted so badly to put her out of her misery, but I needed to know some things first.

"Kane has run away. We can't find him anywhere. Apparently, he's been gone since Friday night. He went to a friend's house to spend the weekend, and when he didn't come home last night, we called, and the mother said that he hadn't been there at all!"

"You mean she never called you when he didn't show up on Friday night?" I knew what had happened, but I wanted to see if she'd say it.

"She didn't know he was coming. Apparently the boys cooked this up together."

"You mean your child told you that he was going to spend the weekend at a friend's house, and you never called the mother to make sure that the parents would be home? That there would be 'no sex, no smoking, no drugs, no drinking, no crime, no gambling'?" Despite the seriousness of the circumstances, I had to smile. It was a litany that my husband had made up, and that my kids knew by heart...and pretty much respected...but made fun of at every possible opportunity!

"Tara! I know you haven't seen Kane in years, but he's still a little boy!"

"Oh, really? How old is he now?"

"Well, he's just thirteen."

"Sis, thirteen is no 'little boy'. But, tell me. This didn't happen out of the blue. What's he been up to?"

"Oh, you know, the regular kid stuff."

"No, Sis. I mean what's he been *up* to?" For some reason, I could hear Arlo Guthrie's voice in my head.

"You know something, don't you? My God, Tara! Is he there with you? Please say he's there with you. Oh, what am I saying? He couldn't be. My God, how could he get across the entire country!? I'm sorry, Sis. I'm going crazy here."

"He should be here in about an hour." I finally told her.

"What?! You've heard from him?! Where is he?"

I filled her in briefly on what I knew, but I really needed to know what I was facing. I asked her to give me a rundown of the events leading up to this.

"Oh, Tara. I didn't want you to know. I feel like such a failure. What did we do? Our lives are so busy. He just started to slip away from us..."

My sister went on and on, filling me in on recent events in their lives. The first she had noticed that something was wrong was when Kane had mingled among the guests at last year's Christmas party and had gotten into the punch. He carried on and embarrassed them royally, wouldn't go to his room when he was told, and slammed out of the house in front of all the guests. He was still twelve.

He sneaked back in the house, early in the morning. (I couldn't believe that they didn't break up the party and go out looking for him... or weren't, at least, sitting on his window sill when he climbed back in the next morning!) She said that they had tried to punish him, but he refused to comply. He was sneaking out on a regular basis and, eventually, fell in with the ever-available, 'bad crowd', which, of course, is who is out there at all ends and hours of the night.

Yes, he'd been drinking, and she guessed that, yes, he'd probably experimented with drugs. I resisted quipping that, in more than a year, he had probably passed experimenting and was on his way to a Nobel Prize. But I was good. I just listened. But one thing kept bothering me, and I had to say it.

"Katy, I can't believe that, after all this, you just, a few minutes ago, referred to him as a 'little boy'."

"Oh, Tara. He'll always be my little boy. I love him. I just can't control him any more."

"You know, when a boy reaches the age of five, that mother-love has to take a back seat to Daddy's kick-in-the-pants once in a while...actually, most of the time. Where's Paul on all of this?"

"He's down at the police station, right now, filing a report."

"No, I mean, what's he been doing with Kane? Does he have a relationship with him? Do they talk? Does Kane respect him? Does he teach Kane what it means to be a man? Do they talk about drinking and sex and right and wrong?"

I could sense my sister's pain on the other end of the phone.

"Paul loves Kane. It's just that our lives are so busy." I could hear her start to cry.

"I know, Sis. I actually understand. I see it happening all too often. Children are a twenty-four-hour-a-day job, and there just isn't enough time for them in our culture."

"But *you* did it! You raised four of them... by yourself."

"But, Kate, remember, I have no life. My big night out, once a year, is Parent Night at school. Other than that, I would rather stay home than leave the kids with a sitter... especially a teenager, which is what's available around here. I teach teenagers. I know that they think they can handle the world, but I also know that if anything really tragic happened, and they felt responsible for it, it would destroy them.

"And, Kate, remember that my job requires that I live a kid's schedule. It happened to work with child rearing. I know, with your job, and with Paul's, you have no choice. And raising the kids by myself actually made it easier in some ways. My kids had one voice, one set of rules, and one person making decisions for them.

"But enough of that! What are we going to do about Kane? He doesn't want you to know where he is, and he doesn't want to go home. I only got him to come here because they threatened to send him to Juvenile Hall."

"Oh, my God!"

"Yeah, Sis. This is big time. Kids are not allowed to do this. And you, as parents, are not allowed to let them. You realize that I'm saving you a flight to New York City this evening."

"Oh!" I could tell that my sister was beside herself.

"Look, Kate. Listen to me. I'm going to hang up. You find Paul and tell him that Kane is okay, and that we know where he is. And let me make this offer to you. If I think I can handle him...I'll know in a day or two...I'll keep him here with me for a while. That will give the two of you a chance to talk this out and decide what you want to do. You may want to look into some counseling for yourselves and maybe a treatment program for Kane."

"Counseling? Treatment? Tara, I can't handle this."

"You have to handle it. You're a grown-up! And this is not a piece of exercise equipment that you just realized you shouldn't have bought. This is your child, for God's sake!"

"I can't. I can't."

"Look. Just talk to Paul."

"I can't. Paul's not here."

"You know what I mean. When he comes home, the two of you will give each other strength and encouragement and ideas. You know."

"No, I don't know. And Paul's not coming home. He left me."

Oh, duh. I should have definitely seen that coming. How come you never recognize a classic plot when it's happening in your own life? Anyway, that's what I was thinking, but what came out of my mouth was, "What?! What do you mean he left you? You said he went to the police station."

"Well, he did. When I told him what happened, he said he would go and report it. But, Tara, Paul moved out in July. We were having some problems, and neither of us could seem to work it out."

"Let me guess. You didn't have time to work on the relationship. What were you thinking? You and Paul were good together. No wonder Kane's screwed up. Don't you know that kids his age always feel responsible when this happens?"

"We talked to him. We explained things!"

"Look, Kate. I'm glad we had time to talk before I saw your son. You know that I'm not working this year. I'll hold on to Kane for as long as I can. Take a break. Think about what you have to do. Decide what you're going to do about your marriage and about your child. Kane needs strong, committed adults in his world right now. You and Paul both need to slow your pace and sit down and discuss what's important. You need to put your little daily tasks in perspective, and get on with the business of being adult humans with a child to raise!"

"Thanks, Sis. I know we blew this."

"I have to go," I said, finally. "We've been talking a long time."

"Can you call me as soon as he gets there? I want to talk to him."

"No. Absolutely not!" I told her. "The last thing he needs right now is a full-grown adult looking to him for support. I don't think you should speak to him until you've made a grown-up decision as to how you're going to handle him. And you can't do that until you've made a grownup decision about how you're going to handle your own life."

"I guess I deserved that," Kate said.

"I'm not saying it to be mean. I love you and Kane dearly, and I want the best for both of you. But I'm afraid that, right now, the best for *both* of you is not *either* of you."

"What will you say when he asks you if you spoke to us?"

"I don't lie to kids, Kate. But I also don't think they have to know everything, especially when it's obviously not in their best interests. It's going to take a lot of work to get him back on his feet. Anything I can use, including manipulating him, and his love for you, is fair game. You have to promise me that you won't interfere, until I tell you how and when."

"You got it. I love you."

"I love you, too. Bye, Katy."

I sat down to ponder what my sister had said...and to pray for wisdom. Boy, did I really, really lack confidence on this one!

3. Reunion

I had barely begun to relax a little, when I heard a car pull in the driveway. I took a deep breath and went downstairs. I opened the garage door to see the driver getting out of the limo. He came over to me with the credit slip, and then he proceeded to take the bags from the back seat.

"Can't he do that?" I asked.

"I don't think so, ma'am."

"Why not? Is he sleeping? We'll wake him up. Surely he's sober enough by now." I was surprised at the tone of annoyance in my own voice. I had planned to be in much better control.

"I don't think so, ma'am." He calmly put the bags in the garage. "Do you want me to help you carry him upstairs?"

I looked at him and then made my way to the side door of the car. "Kane! Kane! Wake up!"

"Is he yours, ma'am?" the driver asked.

"No, thank God. He's my nephew. He ran away from home…from Los Angeles! Do you believe that?"

"No, ma'am. When I ran away from home, it was just to the corner. I didn't have money for the bus."

"Do you see that shed back there?" I pointed to the back of the property, dimly lit by the garage light. "I made it about that far. Then my mother called me for lunch." We both smiled.

"Ma'am, you seem nice, so I'll tell you. I think he took somethin' before we left the airport."

"'Something'? What do you mean?"

"Well, the airport security lady let him go to the bathroom by himself, just before we left. She didn't have any male personnel to take him, and I certainly wasn't going to put myself in that position."

"No, of course not. I don't blame you. Go on."

"He didn't look too bad when he went in, and he seemed all right when he first came out, but after a little while, by the time we were gettin' in my car, he could hardly walk. We practically dumped him in the back seat. That lady looked real glad to be rid of him. I watched him in the rear view mirror all the way up here. He never woke up. To tell you the truth, I was scared he might have overdosed. He *is* still breathing, isn't he?"

I stared at the driver, processing this new information. I was beginning to feel real sure that I wouldn't be keeping this child in my house for very long.

I leaned in to get a better look at my nephew — and to make sure that he was still breathing.

The driver went around to the other door, put the overhead light on, and prepared to help me get Kane out of the car. I shook him again to see if I could rouse him. This time he stirred a little. He was way too big for even the driver to have to carry upstairs. He did look much older than thirteen.

I always felt sorry for the ones that matured early. Adults always began to treat them a little more standoffishly and to expect more from them, while their undersized counterparts still had their hair tousled and got away with murder. And, in spite of the fact that he was a total mess at the moment, he was also very good-looking. This kind always had the girls on their case, even the girls two to four years older, before they were anywhere near ready to handle all that. What looked like nature's blessing could make life incredibly confusing for a young adolescent. I did not envy this child what he was going to have to go through. The 'tunnel back' can be dark, long, and scary.

I shook him again and spoke to him. He began to open his eyes. He looked up at me, and then at the driver, and seemed to be putting things together. Then he started to cry. He closed his eyes and the tears ran down his face. Then he started to sob uncontrollably.

I looked at the driver, and he shrugged his shoulders. "Whatever it was didn't keep him under quite long enough. Either he cries when he gets loaded or you have one sorry kid there."

I would have liked to think it was the latter, but I figured that the kid had just loaded his nervous system with so much junk in the last twenty-four hours that he just couldn't handle it.

The driver helped me get Kane up into the house and onto the bed in the spare room. I gave him a generous tip. I'd bill my sister later. I saw the driver out and then headed right back inside to check on my nephew.

This recent turn of events had confused me. I thought that he would want to be at his best to see me, seeing as how I had his 'head in the noose', as it were. I guess he thought that postponing the inevitable for as long as possible was a better idea.

I sat down beside him to see if he would awaken again. He seemed to have fallen back to sleep as soon as he hit the bed, but I wasn't sure that this wasn't just an avoidance technique. I decided to talk to him, like they say you should do with people in comas. I needed to make him feel safe, but not too comfortable.

"Kane. You're safe here for now. I'll take care of you and make sure that you have a place to sleep tonight, and that you have something to eat. I don't allow drugs in my house, so if you have anything on you, I expect you to turn them over to me."

I was not stupid enough to think that that would work, but I was hoping that he was still young enough, and off balance enough in an unfamiliar place, to do what he was told. He didn't stir. He was either really out of it or just 'playing possum' and listening.

"Kane. I'm getting really tired of sitting here, apparently talking to myself. So if you can hear me, I want you to let me know. If you don't feel well, I'll let you go back to sleep, but I want to know that you're all right."

I was getting tired. It was late. So much for my 'night off'! I closed my eyes for just a moment and rested my head in my hands, waiting for some idea of what to do next.

"I'm okay." It was faint, but I heard him. I looked up quickly. His eyes were still closed. Then he started to cry again. I tried to ignore that, since comforting him was not a good role for me right then.

"Can you sit up? I want you to take off your hoodie." He nodded his head, and I helped him to sit up on the edge of the bed. I kept thinking how I was treating him like some homeless stranger, rather than the sweet little boy that I remembered from not so many years before.

How fragile children are. And how quickly they learn to put up a hard shell to protect themselves when they feel threatened. I was praying that his 'shell' wasn't totally impenetrable yet.

I helped him take off his sweatshirt and a pullover sweater. I thought that it was smart of him, a California kid, to layer up for New York in December. Then I remembered that he came in from San Francisco, and that San Francisco is always chilly. But *then* I remembered that he *left* from Los Angeles! So then this adventure was well planned! This boy sure had a 'lot o' 'splainin'' to do.

As I removed the sweater, he started to fall forward. Thinking he was going to pass out again, I instinctively put my hands on his shoulders to sit him up. Then, grasping his chin in my hand, I tilted his face up to see if he was still awake. As I did so, I noticed immediately that he was burning up. I put my hand on his forehead and guessed at about 102°.

"Lie back down." I took off his shoes and socks, but there was no way I was going to undress him any further. Even if he was family, I had no idea what this kid was up to. "Can you hear me?" He nodded. "Empty everything out of your pockets, and turn your pockets inside out." He did as he was told. There was nothing I didn't recognize. "Turn over and do the same with the back pockets." He had a little more trouble doing that, but I was satisfied that he was clean. Of course, I couldn't check the waistband and inside the seams of the ragged jeans that he was still wearing. But I was now more concerned that he was sick than that he was high and possibly holding.

I was afraid to give him any medication for the fever. I decided to hope that it was just from his emotional state. Maybe, as he calmed down and felt safer, it would go away. When my children were little, they always ran high fevers right before anything very exciting, or when they were very nervous or anxious. My older girl ran 104° the night before we left for a week at Disney! I was hoping that this was the case with Kane, although this was definitely not going to be any 'trip to Disney', for either of us.

I covered him over and told him that I would be nearby. If he felt bad or needed anything, he should call me. I went down the hall, where I could still see and hear him, but where, if I talked very quietly, *he* couldn't hear *me*. I called my sister again.

"Kate? It's me Tara. I have him. He's sleeping, but I think he has a fever. I just wanted to run that by you to make sure there isn't anything else that I should know about. And I should know whether he's allergic to any medications."

"Oh, Tara. Thank you for calling. No, he's probably just so stressed out. I always just gave him Tylenol. He was never really sick very much."

"Has he had all his shots? How about childhood diseases?"

"I know he's up-to-date," Kate assured me. "His schools were always very on top of that. And he had Chicken Pox."

"Did he have a flu shot this year?"

"No, his doctor didn't recommend that for him. Kane's always been very healthy."

I resisted the temptation to mention that his doctor seemed to have no clue that this kid was self-medicating, and that Kane had probably, by now, ruined a good portion of that natural good health.

"Okay, listen," I said. "Write up a medical release form and fax it to me, with a copy of your insurance stuff, just in case I need it at some point. I'm going to hang up now. Remember our deal. I'll call you when I think the time is right. Don't try to contact him. I'm not going to give him any medication, because I don't know what he's already taken, and I don't want to overdose him."

"Overdose! Oh, my God!"

"Hey, take it easy, Kate! I'm not gonna tell you anything if you're gonna go berserk!"

"I'm sorry. I don't know what to say. Thank you for taking care of him, Tara."

"Sis...I'm assuming you've seen him like this before, so you've gotta know, I don't know if I can do this."

"Please try, Tara. I don't know what else to do."

"I will. I've gotta go. I don't want to leave him alone too long."

4. Bottom

The nonchalance of boys who are sure of a dinner and would
disdain as much as a lord to do or say aught to conciliate one is the
healthy attitude of human nature.

- "Self Reliance", Ralph Waldo Emerson

I put on my nightgown and pulled the bedding off my bed, all
the time listening. I went back to the spare room where Kane was still
sleeping. I had removed all his stuff from the room earlier, so that if he
had anything in his bags, he wouldn't be able to get at it.

I made myself comfortable in a big chair and tried to rest. I
must have just dozed off for a short time, as it was not much later on
the clock when I heard Kane start to stir. He was moaning and sobbing
very softly and calling for his mom and dad. Some big tough stoner! I
listened and watched him carefully for a while, and then he went back
to sleep.

When I awoke again, it was late. The sun was up. Kane,
thankfully, was still asleep. I was so grateful to have been able to sleep
through the night. We, no doubt, had a difficult day ahead of us, and I
didn't want him, drugged or otherwise, to have had a more restful night
than I did.

I stood up, and stretched, and went over to look out the
window. It was starting out a glorious day. I prayed that the day
wouldn't be *too* difficult. I went down the hall and grabbed some
clothes, dressing as quickly as possible. I didn't want to leave him
alone later while I dressed, so I thought I'd better do it now. It
reminded me of when my kids were toddlers.

On the way back to his room, I grabbed a thermometer. It
turned out that I had plenty of time. This kid seemed to spend a lot of
time out of touch with the world. Maybe he was depressed. I had come
to believe that a lot of people who did illegal drugs wouldn't have to if
they could get a proper diagnosis and get the correct drugs. But then
again, maybe it was the drugs that *caused* the depression. What did I
know?

I sat and watched him for a while longer and then remembered
the baby monitor. I thought that I had left one in this room when
friends were visiting recently. I found it in a dresser drawer and
quickly set it up. Then I went downstairs to make myself some
breakfast. I took my food back upstairs and had plenty of time to sip
my decaf tea before Kane finally began to stir.

I always found that the worst part of working with kids like Kane was that you had to put on a persona, an attitude, that wasn't who you really were. People who care about kids are usually loving, nurturing, and supportive people. But when you're working with kids like this, you have to be careful not to appear to care about *them* more than they care about *themselves*. And since they're obviously at a point where they don't care a *bit* about themselves, you've got to be pretty rough. I had learned, on many occasions, that it was not something I enjoyed, but then neither was tending to bloody cuts or cleaning up vomit. 'A mom's gotta do what a mom's gotta do!'

I pulled a chair over to the side of the bed. I wanted to be right in his face from the minute he came around. I had no idea what he was going to be like when he wasn't so heavily medicated. Some of these kids were brutal. I didn't know if I would be able to handle him. But I was going to give it my best shot, for his sake. I sat back and waited.

He woke up slowly and rolled over on his back. He didn't open his eyes for a long time. I continued to wait. Finally, he rubbed his eyes, opened them, and stared up at the ceiling. He looked awful, and as he began to remember the events of the day before, and to realize where he must be, his face took on an even more pained expression. He covered his face with both his hands and winced softly to himself.

"Remembering?" I said quietly.

He jerked his head around quickly, seeing me for the first time. A look of mixed emotions crossed his face. "'You my aunt?"

"Maybe... Maybe your worst nightmare."

"Look. I'll do whatever you say. I don't want any more trouble right now."

"All right. Stand up and tell me how you feel." I pushed my chair back so he'd have plenty of room.

He pulled back the covers and sat on the edge of the bed. He sat very still for a minute. Then he tried to stand up. It took him a while, but he finally got to his feet. "Whoa. I guess not so good."

"Why? What's the matter?" I asked him.

"I don't know." He put his hand to his face and looked like he was going to lose his balance. I stood up quickly and grabbed his shoulders. He closed his eyes and swayed.

"All right. Sit back down. Open your mouth. I'm taking your temperature." He did as he was told. I was right. Even after a night's sleep, it was still 102°. "Okay. Lie back down. Did you know you have a fever?" He shook his head, lay down, and closed his eyes again, obviously glad to do what he was told. "I can't give you anything for it until you fill me in on everything you did yesterday."

He looked at me quickly. "What do you mean?"

"You know exactly what I mean." Actually, a little Tylenol probably wouldn't have done any harm at that point, but I wanted his story. And it worked. At least, I got *a* story. Whether it was the truth or not, I had no way of knowing.

He admitted that he had drunk a lot of alcohol before boarding the plane. A 'friend' had given it to him. His friend told him that if they couldn't wake him up on the plane, they couldn't ask him any questions. He had hitchhiked from Los Angeles to San Francisco, so it would take them longer to find out who he was, if they caught him. And his plan in New York? If anyone asked, he was going to his make-believe aunt. If not, he would get a job in the city.

Yeah. I knew what that would be. But I didn't say anything. New York City had a way of making use of young runaways. It was no place for a young kid alone.

I tried not to show any emotional reaction when I spoke, so that he wouldn't try to impress me by playing down, or exaggerating, what he had done. "But you overdosed and didn't wake up in time to get off the plane by yourself," I concluded for him.

"Hey!" he protested. "I didn't overdose!" I just looked at him. "Okay...okay. I guess I did...a little."

"Let me get this straight. You drank quite a bit before you got on the plane. You passed out and must have slept for, what, about six hours?" He nodded. At least I knew he was following me. "And then what did you take in the bathroom before you got in the limo?"

I took a chance. I figured it was worth a shot. If I was wrong, it would weaken my image as the all-knowing one, a role I actually had to try to play right then. If I was right, and he didn't own up to it, I would also be in a bad position. It would not be good for him to get away with anything right now. This just had to work.

He looked at me like he had no idea in the world what I could possibly be talking about. I stood up and walked across the room. Then I turned and looked at him.

He continued to stare at me. He was going to try to hold back on this one. I waited. Nothing. This was important. I waited some more. Still nothing.

Finally, I walked over and stood beside his bed. "Get up!"

"But I'm really sick!"

"Get up out of that bed before I rip every hair outta your head." I could feel an anger welling up in me that even surprised me. He knew I meant business. He got out of bed and stood in front of me. "Now get your stuff and get out of here."

"What? Why? I'm sorry. I'm sorry. I - I'll tell you. Please give me another chance. I have no place to go, and… and… I… I feel really bad."

"Oh! And if you had some place else to go, you'd stand here and defy me and hold back on me? ... after I take you into my house?! You make *me* sick."

"No! No. I didn't mean that. Honest. I didn't tell you because... because...it's really bad."

"Oh, cut the crap. Like all of the rest of this stuff isn't bad? You didn't tell me because you wanted to see if you could hold out on me and get away with it. Well, I'm tellin' you right now, you answer me, and you answer me straight, or you're out of here, sick or not!"

"Okay! Okay... I – I – I took some sleeping pills."

"Same friend?" I was still in attack mode. I wasn't even really thinking about what he had said.

"Yeah." He hung his head.

Being careful now to control every move I made, yet still give the appearance of being outraged, I took a hold of the hair on the top of his head and lifted his face. "Are you even remotely aware that that combination could have killed you?"

No longer being able to look away, he just closed his eyes. He didn't answer. All of a sudden it hit me. Oh, my God! He knew exactly what he had done. That was why he didn't want to tell me. He had attempted suicide. At least he thought he had. God knows what was actually in those street drugs.

Now I knew I was in over my head.

Again, I had to play this one carefully. *Really* carefully! I never felt so under-qualified to do anything. I knew that you just didn't fool around with suicide cases. My intention had been to just scare the devil out of him, so he'd be afraid to mess with me.

All this went through my head very fast. Something told me that if I reacted the way he was afraid I would, he couldn't handle it. I just didn't think it was a good idea right then for me to acknowledge the seriousness of what he had done. I needed to *under*-react.

I continued in my same tone, which wasn't easy, considering the humongous lump in my throat. "Open your eyes and look at me!

I'm asking you a question. Didn't you just learn not to 'dis' me by not answering?"

He opened his eyes and stared at the ceiling. "Yes." He was fighting back tears again. "Yes. I knew what I was doing."

And this was the moment to diffuse this with a down play. 'God, give me the words to help this child,' I prayed silently. I let go of his hair. He was trying really hard to stand up and not cry. I lowered my tone and in a quiet and steady voice said, "Look at me." He looked at me with a mixture of shame, defiance, and desperation. I was surprisingly glad to see the defiance. Ironically, I knew that I had to keep that alive. It would have to be controlled, but it might be the only thing that would bring him through this. I continued, "So, rather than come and face me, you were gonna *kill* yourself? How do you think that makes *me* feel?!"

It was the best I could do. In any other context, it would have been funny. It wasn't funny. I was fighting desperately for him. I had to take the horror that he felt, at what he had done, and help him turn it away from himself. I had to take his act and redefine it as a personal affront to my hospitality. It was absurd, but it had to work. I put him in a position to have to apologize for offending me. I thought maybe if I could reroute his emotions, I could get him a little better stabilized.

"I- I'm sorry."

"Sorry for *what*?!" It wasn't a question. It was a demand.

"I'm sorry for hurting your feelings." I could barely hear him.

"You're what?!" I was practically shouting at him.

"I'm sorry for hurting your feelings!" Much better.

I stood quietly for a moment. I was wiped out. I was thinking to myself, 'Your father walks out on you. Your mother is too busy with her work to even know you're gone for three days. You're so desperate that you take drugs from a guy who gives you the means to kill yourself. Then you attempt suicide because you can't face your family, the only people in the world who care about you, no matter what...And you're apologizing to *me*!?' But I just stood there.

He looked at me in utter confusion then shook his head. "What do you want me to say? I'll say anything. Just don't kick me out. I really feel bad. I know I messed up."

I told him he could lie down. As I watched him drop down, totally drained, I wanted desperately to say something that would help him. He was so young. And his thinking was so screwed up. I wished that I could find the words to help him see himself in a better light. But that was going to take a lot of time. Maybe a lot more time than I would have with him.

And at this point, I'd be wasting my energy. He didn't need a lesson in philosophy tonight. 'First things first.' Right now *he* needed to go back to sleep, because *I* was exhausted!

5. Support

While Kane slept through most of that day, I went through every inch of his clothing and other belongings. It was understood, in my house, that there was no such thing as privacy when it came to the kids' personal possessions. If you have something you don't want me to find, don't bring it into my house. I went through my children's rooms regularly, as part of my cleaning and deglutting. And I asked them about anything that I found that I thought might jeopardize their well-being or that of our family.

They knew full well that I wasn't particularly interested in their notes and diaries and magazines and such. I was looking for anything that might be illegal or dangerous. After all, as an adult, and as the owner of the house, I would be the one held legally responsible for anything illegal found *in* it.

We had long discussions on not only what was right and wrong, but why. Granted, it was only my opinion. But, as a parent, in my house, with my kids, my opinion was what they were going to get. And it was certainly going to be better than anything they got in school, or from friends, or on the street! I had to teach them what worked for our family. Who else was going to be able to teach them that? And besides, I would be seeing my kids for the rest of my life. I wanted them to grow up to be people that I liked...and respected.

I monitored Kane throughout the day. His fever finally broke, and he slept a lot. I gave him a little soup and toast. About three in the afternoon, he vomited up what little he had in his stomach. I figured it had to be mostly toxic waste, so I guessed it was a good thing. I cleaned him up, and he dozed off again.

Well, so much for Mom's Day Off. This was the first time, in the past twenty-four hours, that I had a chance to feel sorry for myself. Well, maybe I could, at least, watch a movie on TV. I took the baby monitor and went back downstairs. Of course, there was nothing on. And I was not going to watch The Little Mermaid for the umteenth time. I tried reading. I tried exercising. I couldn't go out. I decided to call a friend.

My best friend, Karen, was home and also feeling trapped. Her son had a playmate over. And she had to be there, of course.

"Hey! What are you doing home?" she asked. "Aren't these your big two days off?!"

"Funny you should mention that," I replied.

"No! What happened? Is Hannah sick?"

"No."

"Well, what happened?"

"You won't believe it. My nephew showed up."

"Which nephew? Tom's kid?"

"No. Kate's son."

"Kate? Isn't she still living in California? What do you mean, he 'showed up'?"

I proceeded to tell her the whole story, with all the gory details.

"Well, when are you sending him back?" Karen asked me.

"Not now."

"Why not? You don't need to deal with a kid like that. What about Hannah? You don't need that influence in your house."

So I proceeded to tell her all about my sister and her marital problems, ending with "...and I can't send this poor kid back into that. He'll never make it. We'll lose him. I've seen this too many times before."

"So you're about to raise child number five."

"I don't know. Can I raise this kind of child?"

"He *is* just a child. He's only thirteen." She was playing devil's advocate for me.

"Yes, but on the other hand, he's already *thirteen*. It's a little late, no?"

"Tara, you'd never give up on a kid that came to you. Remember, this kid made the *decision* to come to you."

"True...although he was drunk at the time...and deathly sick. And don't forget, he never intended to actually arrive here *alive*."

"Minor points, minor points," she joked.

We laughed; we discussed; we hashed this one over, from top to bottom. It's so good to have a friend, somebody to discuss things with, to bounce things off. We talked for hours.

"So, where is he now?" she asked me.

"He's been sleeping all day."

"You're sure he hasn't sneaked out?"

"No, I have the baby monitor on. I can hear him breathing. Besides, I told him he wasn't allowed to get up without asking me first."

"Oh, yeah, right! Like he's really gonna do that!"

"If he was in Juvie, he'd be doing it. And they probably wouldn't even let him get up. 'Make him pee in his bed."

"He has to ask your permission to go to the bathroom?"

"From the little bit I've learned about this kid today, he's gonna have to ask my permission to breathe!"

"Do you really think you can exert that kind of control over a kid that age?"

"He needs me to do that, at least for a while. He is acutely aware of what happened to him when he tried to take care of himself. I need to get him *back* to taking care of himself, as soon as possible. But right now he needs somebody to re-pattern him. He needs to be walked through the steps of what's okay, and what's not, until he learns that all over again."

"Tara, this sounds like an enormous job. Is this how you're going to spend your leave, re-raising somebody else's kid?"

"He's family. And besides, I'm not going to force him to stay here. There are no bars on my windows. If he doesn't play by my rules, he doesn't play at all. I have nothing to lose, and he has everything. At some point, he's going to decide that he can't take this, and he's going to bolt... at which point, my job is over. He's out of here."

"Can I predict what's going to happen?" Karen ventured.

"Sure. Why not?"

"You're going to like this kid. You're going to ask your sister for guardianship, and you're going to raise him, through years of thick and thin, until he's a fine young man and out on his own."

"Yeah, right. I'll bet you he's gone by Thursday!" We laughed. Who knew? Then we decided we'd been talking long enough.

"You know, you might want to get him up for a while, so he'll sleep tonight," my friend suggested. "You don't want him to take off, or do something worse, while you're asleep."

"You know, you're right. Isn't it amazing how similar this is to taking care of a little one?"

"Well, you know," she said, "as you, yourself, have told me before, when a kid starts using drugs, he stops growing up. He may get older and taller, but he doesn't mature. So this thirteen-year-old is back to like, what, ten or eleven, in his character development."

"Yeah, and he acts like he thinks he's twenty-one! And now I'd better get going. I think I hear him stirring. Wish me well!"

"Believe me, I do. You be careful."

We hung up, and I went upstairs. I looked into Kane's room and saw that he was not in the bed. But I could see the bathroom light on and could hear him in the bathroom.

"Kane?"

"Yeah?"

"Are you using the toilet?"

"Nah, I'm done."

"Then open the door." He opened the door and looked at me. "Did you forget what I told you, or are you just defying me?"

He looked genuinely confused. "No, I- I just, I just had to go to the bathroom."

"I told you. You don't make a move without asking."

"Oh, okay. I forgot that. I -I guess I've been pretty out of it. I didn't see you anywhere."

"All you have to do is call me. The house isn't that big. Now, as long as you're up, wash your hands and face." As long as he was acting as if he wanted to comply, I would give him something to do.

I watched him carefully as he turned to the sink. He was still unsteady, but he looked much better. He washed his hands, and I gave him a washcloth to wash his face. As he straightened up again, he looked at himself in the mirror. He stopped suddenly, and then looked down again.

"What's the matter?" I asked him.

"I look like shit."

"We don't use that word here."

"Sorry." He took a deep breath. "Sorry I keep doin' everything wrong...and I'm sorry for all the trouble I've been. Hey! I'm sorry for my whole fucked up life!" He was starting to get upset again. He composed himself and took another deep breath. "As soon as I can stand up for longer than five minutes at a time, I'll leave. I'm okay with bein' on my own."

I didn't want to get angry with him, but I was also not going to let him think that what he had said was acceptable. And I was certainly going to straighten him out on who would be calling the shots from here on in.

"We don't use the F-word either." I told him. "Actually, you look much better than you did last night. And you won't have to be sorry, 'cause I'm gonna be tellin' you exactly what you're gonna be doin'. And if I'm not tellin' you, you're not doin' it, so there won't be anything to be sorry about, get it?" He stared down at the sink for a minute, apparently mulling this over. Then he nodded his head. I continued. "Oh, and as for leaving, don't get any ideas. Unless you're ready for even more trouble than you're in right now, you'll be leaving when I tell you you're leaving. And, believe me, it won't be alone. Now get back to bed, and don't get out again unless I tell you to."

"Yes, ma'am."

He needed that. He needed an emotional anchor. I stepped aside and let him go past me. He made his way back down the hall, holding onto the wall as he went. I noticed for the first time how thin he was. He threw himself down on the bed and buried his face in the pillow.

I made myself a light supper. He didn't want anything. I watched a little TV and then headed to bed to read for a while. I was tired from the night before. I checked on him before I turned out my light. He was still lying on top of the bed, as I'd left him hours before.

"Covers!" I called out. It was cold that night. He rolled over and covered himself up.

I headed back to my room and set the baby monitor on my night table. I could hear him crying again. He didn't know that I could hear him. It killed me not to be able to go and sit with him, and cradle his head, like I did when my own kids were in pain. But my kids never did anything like this, at least not this young, and I knew that rewarding what he did with nurturing was not appropriate. It was sometimes over-nurturing that got kids in this shape in the first place. Eventually, he cried himself to sleep. And I went to sleep.

It was three a.m. on my alarm clock, when I awoke with a start. One of the kids was calling me. A mom wakes up in an instant when she hears her child calling. It took me a second to open my eyes and look toward the hall. The kids always called softly from the doorway.

"Hannah?" There was no answer. Then I remembered that the kids weren't home. My heart began to pound. I thought maybe one of the kids might be in danger and that I was receiving some kind of psychic message! Then I remembered the baby monitor. And Kane. I listened more carefully.

"Mom... Mom... I'm sorry. I love you...*and* Dad. I never meant to cause you so much trouble... please come and get me. Please... please..."

I couldn't figure out whether he was talking in his sleep or whether he was trying to see if I could hear him. I still didn't trust him. I listened for a while longer, but I didn't hear anything. I kept thinking that I was alone in this house with a complete stranger who had dealings with the criminal world!

I got up very quietly and stood where I could see straight down the hall, through the crack in my door. I didn't raise four kids without being a little sneaky.

I couldn't see anything from my room. So, finally, I walked quietly down the hall and into his bedroom and stood beside his bed. He appeared to be asleep. I didn't want to frighten him, but I wanted to be ready if he was planning anything.

When he heard me, he rolled over and looked up at me. "Aunt Tara?"

"Are you all right?"

"Yeah, I guess."

"Did I wake you up?" I asked him.

"No. I guess I've been sleepin' too much. I was just thinkin' about stuff."

"What stuff?" I was used to being very direct with my children. With other people's kids, you had to wait until they felt comfortable enough to tell you what was on their minds. But with your own kids, you just couldn't afford to wait. For right now at least, Kane was one of mine.

"Just stuff."

"Kane. Night or day, you're still dealing with *me*. I have a pretty good idea. But you need to say it."

He was quiet for a few minutes. But he knew by now that he'd better come up with something. "I can't believe I did this. I can't believe I'm here with you, and you're treating me like I'm a criminal. Not that I don't deserve it. You're right not to let me get away with anything." He stopped. I felt that he was being somewhat honest, but this was not critical material. I wanted to push him further.

"Keep going," I said.

"That's about it."

"Not by a long shot, Buddy. Keep talkin'. Tell me about your parents."

"Do they know I'm here? My mother must be a wreck. Can I call her?"

Nice try. I didn't even address that one. "You said you hated your parents and you never wanted to go home."

"I was wasted!"

"According to your parents, you've been wasted for over a year. What makes you think that they're not glad to be rid of you?"

"Did they say that? Did you talk to my mom?"

"You're avoiding again."

"I don't know what you want me to say." He obviously didn't.

"By the way," I pressured him, "how come you keep asking for your mom? What about your dad? Don't you think he's worried about you too?" He didn't answer. He rolled face down again and buried his face in the pillow. I put my hand on his shoulder and gently pulled him back. He didn't pull away. "I asked you a question. Look at me, and tell me how you feel about your dad."

"He left us." His voice was hard.

Bingo.

"Really. Did he divorce your mom?"

"I don't know exactly. I just know that he moved out." He was controlling the emotion in his voice.

"Because of you?" Kids always believed that. And apparently Kane did also. He turned away from me again, and this time I let him be. I had gotten him to the place where he needed to be, in order to start facing his feelings. And this would probably be just about when he would go and get high.

I waited for a long time. I thought maybe he had gone back to sleep, although I was hoping that he was awake and was thinking this through. Finally, I made a move to leave, to see if he would say any more. I was satisfied that we had made a start.

But he heard me get up, and he looked at me again. "It *was* because of me. It was my fault. I've been doin' shit...uh, sorry...I've been gettin' high since I was really young." He was still working hard not to show any emotion.

"How young?"

"Twelve."

"Try eleven," I said. I took a chance that this had been going on for a long time before he got caught.

"Yeah. Eleven," he admitted.

Hmm... so now I was guessing that he had really started at ten. "And you think your parents split up because you started doing drugs?" He nodded his head. He was so miserable. I could see that this was really hard for him. "Did it ever occur to you that maybe you started doing drugs because something else was going on at home... something that was making you feel bad?"

Kane stared at me. He was somewhat sober now and seemed to have gotten over being sick. He was thoughtfully processing what I had said. I had a feeling that he hadn't had a lot of these lucid moments in the past couple of years. Finally, he spoke. "Maybe.'"

I wanted to say, 'Look, kid, I know you think that your behavior has your parents all focused on you, but the truth is that your parents are too busy with their own problems to give you any real attention at all… and *that's* why you're sittin' here, 3000 miles away from them, and royally screwed up.' But all I said was, "Now, do you think you have the guts to stick this place out another day?"

"I'm not gonna run, if that's what you mean."

"Is your word still worth anything?"

"You don't trust me, do you?"

"Nope. Right now, I don't think you can even trust yourself… am I right?" I didn't expect him to respond. "I hope I'll see you in the morning. Remember, you stay in bed until I tell you that you can get up. Good night." I shut off the light and started down the hall.

"Aunt Tara?"

"Yeah?"

"How did you know what I was thinking about?"

"I didn't."

"Yes, you did."

"Good night, Kane."

"Good night."

I reached my room and switched on the monitor again, just in case. As I did so, I heard him saying, "Thanks for taking care of me."

I thought better of calling out 'You're welcome'. Maybe he was actually praying. 'Oh, cut it out, Tara,' I thought to myself, 'you are such a Pollyanna!'

At any rate, I still needed to maintain what I called 'adult distance'. We had a really long way to go. He hadn't even been downstairs yet. Could I possibly imagine this kid in a public junior high school? How could I keep him here? What was I thinking?

6. Hannah

I got up early the next morning, took a quick peek at my 'ward', got washed and dressed myself, and then went back in to wake him up.

"Kane! Get up! I'm leaving clean clothes for you. I want you to take a shower and then come down to breakfast." He blinked his eyes a few times and stared up at me. "Repeat what I said."

"Uh...clean clothes, shower, downstairs."

"I'll expect you in fifteen minutes."

I chuckled to myself as I set out breakfast. He reminded me of a time when I was traveling in London with a group of students. We had gone to see the rock musical, Hair. Near the end of the performance, the guide came over to me and carefully explained that the actors were going to invite the audience to go up and dance on the stage during the finale. But that we couldn't do that because we had to catch the train back to the suburbs, and, being that it was the last train of the night, we couldn't miss it, because then we'd miss the bus back to the school where we were staying. I turned to the student next to me and repeated, almost verbatim, what the guide had told me and asked her to pass the word on down the row. I heard her turn to the student next to her and say, "No dancin' on the stage. We gotta split early." Now why didn't I think of that?

My daydreaming was interrupted by the sound of a car in the driveway. My Hannah was home. I was so happy to see her. I opened the back door and welcomed her in. I waved to her friend's mom, who indicated that all was well but that they had to run.

"Hannah! How was it? Did you have a wonderful time?"

"Oh, Mom! It was great! The show was amazing. And we had this great dinner and, well, we just had so much fun. Mom, can I have a sister?"

"You have a sister!"

"No, I mean a sister near my age."

"How about we just have Macy sleep over *here* sometime?"

"Oh, could we?"

At that moment, Kane appeared in the kitchen. Hannah was startled to hear someone behind her. She had been thinking that she was going to have her mom to herself that day. Then, realizing that she didn't recognize this person, she backed up against me.

"It's okay, Sweetie. This is your cousin, Kane, from California. Remember? He's Aunt Kate's son. We always get a picture of him at

Christmas."

Hannah was a really sweet child, and when she recovered from her surprise, she was quick to make her cousin feel welcome. "Oh, hi! I didn't know you were coming to visit. Mom, why didn't you tell us?"

"I didn't know he was coming, either." I quickly changed the subject until I could think of how I should explain this to Hannah. "Kane, you sit here. Can you keep down some eggs?" He nodded.

Hannah went bubbling on. "Oh, what a great surprise. Can Kane come to the birthday party with me?"

"Yes. Kane will be coming *everywhere* with Mom."

Hannah looked at me sharply. She knew that phrase. She looked back at Kane.

"Mommy, is Kane grounded already? He just got here. Can you ground other people's kids, too?"

Kane looked at her sweet little face in surprise and then up at me. I shrugged. "She has three older siblings."

"What did he do, Mom?" Hannah continued.

"Kane, do you want to take this one?" I asked my nephew.

"What do I say to her?"

"The truth. My kids expect people to tell them the truth."

"But she's only a little girl."

"I'm eight, and I'm in the third grade! I know a lot of stuff."

"Not this stuff, I hope." He was half talking to himself. Hannah looked up at me.

"Hannah, Kane doesn't have any sisters or brothers, so he's not quite used to talking to little girls. Why don't you go up and put your stuff away and get ready for the party? We'll all talk later."

Hannah left the room, and Kane went on with his breakfast. I didn't say anything. He knew that I was going to, though. He was a smart boy and had to be catching on to how things worked around here.

Finally, he spoke. "What was I supposed to say to her?"

"I *told* you. The truth."

"What? ...about drinkin' and gettin' high? She's a nice little girl from a really nice family, and she doesn't need to know about that."

"Whoa, whoa. Wait a minute. You were a nice little boy from the very same 'really nice family', and, just maybe, if someone had talked to *you* when you were eight, we wouldn't be having this conversation *now*, way after the fact. Besides, she knows about everything already."

"About me?"

"No, not about you. Who knew about you?!" He could sense that I was getting annoyed with him and that he was making me angry. I sort of did that on purpose and then watched as he backed off. Interesting. I wondered if he would have backed off so fast if he were high.

But I didn't want to know that. In fact, I had no idea where all this was heading. I just figured that every hour that I could keep him out of trouble would give my sister that much more time to come up with a solution to this. After all, he was not my son.

"Listen. If you stay here, you're going to have to tell your story at least four times," I told him. "You might as well start with Hannah. She's a sweetheart. She might even feel sorry for you." What I really meant was that Hannah kicked butt better than any of my kids, but I guess it just didn't come out that way.

"What if I don't stay here? I thought you said it was up to me."

"Oh, feeling better, are we?"

"I'm sorry. I didn't mean that."

"It *is* up to you. But whether you get to stay or not depends on how you behave and what you do, and don't do, when you're given a directive."

"So you're telling me to talk to Hannah."

"You got it...Come on. She's a baby. You can do this."

He took a deep breath and blew it out.

I went on. "One thing though. She knows that there's no excuse for drinking or using illegal drugs. Don't try to blame your actions on anybody, or anything, else. I wouldn't want her to get the wrong idea." And, besides, I thought to myself, she'll tear your story to shreds and spit it back in your face so fast you won't know what hit you. "Ready?"

"No...but if I have to..."

I was going to be very interested in this conversation.

"Hannah! Hannah! Could you come down here?"

"Sure, Mom. I'm just about ready."

"No, Sweetie. It's still too early for the party. Your cousin just wants to talk to you."

"Okay! Coming!"

Hannah bounded in the door again, ready, as she always was, for anything. She plopped herself down at the table, next to Kane, and propped her chin up on her hands... "Okay, I'm ready! Shoot! What did you do?"

I hid a smile by turning to tend to the pan in the sink.

"Well, uh, your Mom is helping me out 'cause I did something really stupid." He paused. I hoped he didn't think she was going to let him off that easy.

"Go on," Hannah encouraged him. Even with my back turned, I knew she was still staring up at him, with her big brown eyes, chin in her hands, listening in 'awe and wonderment'. On the few occasions when her brothers stepped out of line, when she was little, I used to make them 'confess', as it were, to her, as well as to their other sister and brother. I told them that we were a small family, so, it was really important that they didn't keep secrets from each other, that they learned from each other's mistakes, and that they supported each other...

The boys always told me that they hated talking to their sisters the most, not only because they were embarrassed that they hadn't been good role models, but also because the girls were merciless and always looked so disappointed in them. They admitted, as they got older, that there were many times when they were tempted to go along with something, but didn't, because they didn't want to have to explain to their sisters that they had done something wrong.

"I can't do this." Kane was speaking to me, but I ignored him.

So Hannah explained, "Look, all you have to do is sit here and start at the beginning and, in your own words, tell me what happened." I hid a grin, as she continued. "Hey! I'm a good one to start with. My sister's worse than I am, and if you're still here when my brothers get back, well, all I can say is, you're gonna need some practice. So you might as well get started."

I turned around because I had to see the look on his face. He was staring at her in amazement. She just had a way about her.

"Okay! Okay! Here goes," Kane started, reluctantly.

"And remember," Hannah interrupted him, "I'm just a little kid, so don't lie to me. It's not right to lie to little kids."

7. Kane's version

I listened with interest as Kane told his story. When I felt that it wouldn't distract him, I went and sat down across the table from him and Hannah. This is what he said:

"My parents haven't gotten along, for as long as I can remember. Everybody says, that when grown-ups split up, the kids always think it's their fault…and that it's not. Well, with my parents, it was. They didn't need a kid. My mom's a great lawyer, and my dad's a CEO."

"What's a CEO?" Hannah asked.

"It means he has all the responsibility for his whole company."

"Oh."

"Well, they both have jobs that they love and that take a lot of time. And they have lots of friends, and people to meet with, and go out with. And, well, I think they realized too late that a kid just ties you down."

"Wait a minute! My mom isn't tied down. My mom likes being stuck with kids. Don't you, Mom?" Hannah asked. I nodded my head and shrugged my shoulders. "See?" she said, turning back to Kane.

"Well, my parents didn't. They didn't like packing my lunch every night, and making sure my uniforms were clean, and sitting through my games. And they really hated that they had to stay home for supper, and that my mother had to cook and buy groceries, just because I had to do homework and go to bed early.

"They started leaving me with sitters a lot. At first, it was just really lonely. Then, when I got older, they hired teenagers who would play video games with me. Sometimes this one girl would come over, and, as soon as my parents would leave, her boyfriend would come over, and they would get stoned together and forget about me completely."

"What does 'get stoned' mean?"

Kane looked at me, and I shrugged. "Tell her." I knew that she already knew, the little imp. They were both just warming up.

"It means they used drugs," Kane explained, a little awkwardly.

"Like from the drugstore?" Hannah asked.

"No, illegal drugs that you buy from people on the street."

"And you didn't tell your parents?"

"I didn't know if they would believe me, and I didn't want to get anybody in trouble."

"Kane..."

"Yes, Hannah?"

"Did you ever buy illegal drugs from somebody on the street?"

Geez, she was good. 'The moment of truth.' I thought he was going to die, just to avoid the question.

"Yeah, Hannah, I did." Then he quickly added, "But I was wrong to do that." He glanced over at me, and I nodded in approval.

"You're tellin' me! Is that why you're here? Are you hiding from the police?" Hannah asked him.

"No! ...No. I just ran away from home. I couldn't stand my parents fighting and ignoring me any more."

"That's it? You just ran away from home?" Hannah had this wonderful way of downplaying, so that your guilt didn't just eat you alive. But then you felt like you had to defend yourself. It was actually kind of amusing. I could see Kane starting to buy into it and then realizing what he was saying. He was a smart boy for all his recent stupidity.

"No, Hannah. First of all, it was wrong to run away. But it was worse than that. I stole five hundred dollars, from my parents. I bought alcohol and drugs from some guy that I didn't know. Then I got myself good and drunk and got on a plane to come to New York. Only, when I got here, I was too wasted to get off the plane, and I got caught."

"Well, thank God for that!"

"God and some annoying lady who worked for the airline. She went through my stuff and kept digging until she found your mom's name and phone number. I could hear her making phone calls and checkin' out all my stuff. And I wanted to stand up and tell her that I could take care of myself, and that I just wanted out of there."

"But you couldn't," Hannah said.

"Right. Have you ever seen somebody so drunk that they couldn't even stand up?"

"I didn't mean you couldn't stand up. I meant you couldn't take care of yourself. You're just a kid. My sister is older than you, and Mom just started letting her shop at the mall by herself. Don't you ever see on the news about what happens to kids who run away to the city?!"

"Bad, huh?"

"The worst! Just watch the news on TV tonight!" At that point she looked at me, and I shook my head. "Sorry, I forgot. No TV for you, I guess. So, is that it? She called my mom, and here you are?"

"Yeah, that's it." He looked over at me, and I raised my eyebrows. He changed his answer, "No..." This was the hard part for him. If he could get through this, I'd be more than satisfied. "No. There's more."

"I'm listening."

"You know you're a lot like your mother?" He was stalling. He was trying to lighten this up. "Okay...." He took a deep breath and then started again. "By the time the airport lady got through to your mom, and your mom figured out who I was, I was comin' around. I knew I was in deep sh... trouble. I had to decide whether to let them put me in a jail cell somewhere or let your mom see me like that."

"Oh, tough choice!" Hannah sounded genuinely concerned for poor Kane.

"It was. Even though I hadn't seen your mom in a long time, she always sent me presents, and I thought that if I ever needed anything, that she would help me. But I thought that if she saw me like that, that she wouldn't have anything to do with me."

"Oh, Mom's not like that. But it *was* a tough choice. I don't think you know my mom real well." They both looked at me, and I tried not to smile.

I spoke up then. "Okay, Kane. Finish up." I knew that we had this birthday party to get to. We were going to have to put his crisis on fast forward.

But Hannah wasn't done. "What else happened, Kane?" I could always count on that girl.

"When I realized I had no choice and that your mom was gonna see me whether I liked it or not, I..." He stopped. He could go either way with this. "I didn't want to think about it any more, at least not all the way up here. So I took some... a sleeping pill." I closed my eyes and massaged my forehead with my fingertips. Come on, Kane, the whole truth. We all sat there for a few minutes.

Then Hannah spoke up, "You just wanted to go to sleep?"

"'Yeah. I just wanted to go to sleep."

"Wait. Didn't you say that you were drinking alcohol?"

"Yeah, I told you that."

"Mom, didn't Dana say that if you mix alcohol and sleeping pills, you could die?"

I was afraid to breathe. I nodded my head.

Kane looked at her. Then he looked at me. I looked him right in the eye.

"I was drunk," he said. I didn't answer. No need to explain it to *me*. He turned back to Hannah then and said, "I was drunk...I was drunk, and I was afraid, and I was all alone, and I didn't know what was gonna happen to me."

"So you tried to kill yourself?!" Bless her heart. She always got right to the point.

"Yeah...yeah... I tried to kill myself!" With that, he pounded the table with his open hand, stood up and left the room.

Hannah looked at me. I patted her on the back. "Good job, Sweetie."

"Is he gonna be okay, Mom?!" she called to me, as I took off after him.

I turned back and gave her a 'thumbs up' and whispered, "Stay here!" as I followed him into the living room.

He was just on the other side of the door, doubled over, sobbing and trying to catch his breath.

I put my hands on his back and his chest, and I helped him stand up straight. "You 'done good'. She's the worst." I was trying to lighten things up a little.

"I-I" he was gasping for breath. "I don't want her to see me crying."

"Okay. Go upstairs and wash your face. We have to be out of here in ten minutes." He started for the stairs. I thought of something and called after him. "Kane!" He turned. "It's over. You did it. You talked about it, and it's over. 'Got it?"

He nodded. I wasn't sure that I'd convinced him. I'd have to work on that. After the confrontation, the support is crucial.

8. Reassurance

I went back to the kitchen to talk with Hannah. "Hannah, did you understand what Kane said?"

"I think so, Mom. Did he really try to kill himself?"

I didn't want to frighten her now, so I chose my words carefully. "See, this is what happens when kids drink alcohol. They lose the ability to make good decisions. Kane made a decision, under the influence of alcohol, that could have cost him his life."

"So then he didn't really *mean* to kill himself?"

"I don't think so. I don't think that, now that he's sober, he wishes he were dead. But, because he wasn't thinking straight last night, he did make the decision to mix together two drugs that could have killed him."

"Why didn't they, Mom? Remember, Dana was telling us about what she learned in her class?"

"Well, now, there's *another* good lesson in this. When people buy street drugs, they really don't know what they're getting. It could be anything, and it could be any amount of anything. You just don't know…"

"So, Kane was really lucky then."

"Kane was extremely lucky. And I think he knows that now, and that's why he's so upset."

"Why would he even do that, Mom?"

"As he said, he had drunk a lot of alcohol, which, instead of making you feel *better* about what's going on with you, winds up making you feel *worse* about everything. Kane was already feeling bad about himself and about what he had done. He just wanted it all to go away.

"Maybe if his parents were spending more time with him, they would never have let him get into a position to feel so bad. Maybe if they had been watching him and talking to him and correcting and encouraging him right along, that pain wouldn't have built up so much to where he couldn't handle it.

"Or maybe there's something else going on with Kane that we haven't figured out yet. Sometimes kids hide things, and their parents are the last to know that there's a problem. Whatever's going on, somebody needs to pay a lot more attention to him... and right now."

"You know, Mom. If I do something wrong, I sort of feel better after you find out... It's like I don't have to worry any more about getting caught."

"You are an amazing child, Hanny!" I couldn't help but smile at her. "You're right. If you do something wrong and you get away with it, the guilt builds up until you can't stand it any more. You were right when you said that Kane's not old enough to be taking care of himself. From what I'm hearing, he's done a lot of things wrong in the past couple of years. I think that he just decided to punish himself."

"So, you think he just made a mistake, because he was drinking alcohol?" Hannah, obviously, still needed reassurance.

"Yes, I do. And because he's too young to be away from his parents so much and to be allowed to do what he's been doing."

"Why did he get so upset when he talked about it?"

"Because it was a terrible mistake…a terrible, terrifying mistake. And he realizes that now. And, of course, it's just adding to the list of things that he feels he's done wrong and that he can't make right. I'm sure that he feels really bad, and guilty, and afraid of what he might do next."

"Mom, can't you punish him, so he'll feel better?"

I had to smile. "While he's with us, I will treat him like I would treat any one of you. But it's not just about punishment, Hannah. Kane is not using drugs because he's a 'bad boy'. People use drugs because they're in pain. Kane needs a lot of help figuring out a better way to deal with the pain he's feeling...whatever it's coming from. But I'm not his parent, and I don't know if I'm qualified to help him."

"But you love him, don't you, Mom?"

"Of course I do."

"Then I think you're qualified."

"Thank you, Hannah. That makes me feel much more confident!" Again I had to smile.

"Besides, Mom, I think you're the only one he has, except for us kids."

"And you were terrific. You really got him to spill his guts. You know that talking about painful things, even when it's really difficult to do that, makes them less painful. You're going to make a great mom someday."

Hannah threw her arms around me and gave me a big hug. Her affection was always so spontaneous and genuine. Even if I couldn't help my nephew, I had to use every opportunity to teach my own kids about surviving all the snags and pitfalls of life.

"Come on, we've got a birthday party to go to."

9. Birthday Party

The birthday party was fun. I loved watching the kids and chatting with the other parents. This was how I learned about the kinds of families that my kids' friends came from. And this is where I had always picked up parenting tips and learned about what was going on in the social lives of my children and their peers.

Kane said that he would wait in the car, and I made it clear to him that *that* was not going to happen, and, besides, Hannah would want to show off her good-looking cousin to all her little girlfriends.

Even in the midst of all his angst, Kane looked at me when I said 'good-looking'. "Really?" he said, skeptically.

"Oh, come on, you are to die for! You are not going to deprive my daughter of the chance to steal the center of attention from the Birthday Girl!"

I knew that the way to a young man's will was through his ego, and, without my having to pull rank, he was out of the car, being dragged by Hannah to the front door of the gym.

I called out to her. "Hannah! Wait for me!" Still, at eight, she sometimes forgot and ran ahead.

"I wouldn't go in, Mom."

"Remember, Kane is not Dana or David," I reprimanded her, as I approached.

"Sorry."

We went in and found the Birthday Girl and her mom. Hannah introduced us and then asked, "Mom, can Kane come with me and meet my friends?"

"No, Hannah. He can meet them while you're eating. Now they want you to get ready for the gymnastics class."

The Birthday Mom appeared at that moment and chimed in, "Oh, that's quite all right. Let him go. They won't be starting for a few minutes."

I really hated it when other parents tried to change my directives to my own children. Like they thought my kids should listen to them rather than to me! Or like I didn't have a good reason for telling my children what they needed to do. But I assumed that she was just trying to be nice. And I was probably overreacting, being extra tired and under the stress of not knowing what was coming next with this boy.

"Thanks. But this one needs to stay with me."

"Is this your son? I didn't know that Hannah had a brother."

"Oh, no, he's not my son. He's my nephew. But Hannah is the youngest of four. She has two older brothers and an older sister."

"Oh, how nice. Well, listen. Please feel free to order some coffee from the snack bar. The other parents are around somewhere."

"Thanks. I see several people I know."

Kane and I made our way to the snack bar and sat with some other parents. After a few minutes, I told him that he could go and watch the kids from some benches on the sidelines, closer to the action. "I expect you to stay where I can see you," I told him.

"Yes, ma'am."

One of my friends came up at that moment and sat with me. We shared some news about the holidays and caught up on some personal items. Finally, she said to me, "Is there some reason that you're not making eye contact with me today? I know the kids are adorable and all, but surely you can take your eyes off Hannah for a few minutes."

I started to giggle. I was way too tired and overstressed. "I'm sorry."

"What's so funny?"

"Nothing, really. It's just that I've had an unusually stressful couple of days, and it feels good to laugh. It's nice to be able to sit and visit with friends."

"Well, I'm glad I can provide such merriment. What's been going on?"

"Look, I don't really feel comfortable going into all of the details right now, but I'm not watching Hannah. I'm watching that boy over there with the red shirt. He's my sister's kid. To make a long story short, he's in big trouble, and I'm trying to help him out."

"Who's he in big trouble with?" she asked.

"Well, himself, mostly."

"I hear ya! I'm so happy that my two are through puberty. I didn't think I was going to make it. And you, with four of your own and no man around! Girl, are you nuts?! Where are his parents?"

"California."

"And they sent him to you?! I tell you, some parents these days. No offense, of course."

"Believe me. I am not offended. If my sister and her husband don't get their act together and start raising this child before it's too late, I'm going to go out there and personally wring their necks."

"You go, girl. You give it to them."

"By the way, they didn't send him to me. He's a runaway."

"Across the country?!"

"I don't know how long I'm going to be able to control him. Apparently he has quite a history. The reason I'm watching him like a hawk is that he's feeling better now, and I think he'll probably run again soon."

"Wait a minute. History? Feeling better? Run? Should I guess here?"

"No need. I'm sure you can figure this out."

"Aren't you worried about your own kids?"

"Well, a little. But I'm also worried about him. I just don't know how much I can afford to care. So far, he's been very compliant. But if he brings 'stuff' into the house, or starts making 'new friends' out here, I'm going to have to either turn him in or send him home. Either way, we're going to lose him. Permanently, I'm sure."

"That serious?"

"I think so. I hope not. But I think so."

At that point, the party began to move to the food room. Hannah came over with Kane in tow, and she asked if he could go with her.

"Go ahead, Sweetie. I'm right behind you." I turned to my friend, "Listen, call me when you can, and make sure I'm surviving."

Hannah truly stole the show with her cousin Kane, who was actually very good around the children. He helped the 'Ruling Mom', as my friend used to call the birthday child's mother, to serve and clean up. I was pleasantly surprised. He did okay. And all the little girls adored him.

Everything was about picked up, the goody bags were given out, and Hannah was just saying goodbye to her friends, when the Birthday Mom asked me if Kane could help carry the gifts to her car.

I hesitated. Kane looked at me, waiting for an answer. And then, as if reading my thoughts, he said very quietly, "I won't run. I promise."

It was a really tough moment for me. I sure didn't trust him, and I knew he couldn't possibly trust himself yet.

"If it's a problem, I understand," said the Birthday Mom. "We can manage."

I'm sure this woman thought I was a control freak. I looked at Kane again and then back at the woman. "If you can wait a minute, until my Hannah's ready, we'll *all* help you, and we can make it in one trip! We have to leave anyway, to pick up my daughter from her Washington trip."

Kane looked at me with an unreadable expression. Then he proceeded to round up Hannah and the gifts, and we all left the gym together.

Once back in the car, I expected to hear all kinds of complaints. 'You embarrassed me!' 'You don't trust me.' 'Blah Blah Blah.' But he never said a word. I couldn't decide if that was good or bad. It certainly wasn't normal. I knew. I had been through it on countless occasions.

As a single parent, especially of more than one child, you can't ground your child by keeping him in the house. That only works if you have a two-parent family, in which the other parent is free to go out and get the groceries and take the other kids where they have to go. When a kid is 'grounded' in a single-parent family, you can't leave him home alone, so the best you can do is to 'tie him to your apron strings', so to speak.

It's actually more powerful than a stay-in-your-hi-tech-room grounding, because it's so much more public. But it's also so much more humiliating. I never liked doing it, and my kids hated it. But, fortunately, I had good kids, so it didn't happen too often. And when it did, they tried to be as compliant as they could, because they knew that I wouldn't hesitate to make a big scene in public - especially if it meant that I was 'building their character'. Of course, that didn't mean that they didn't protest vehemently when we got home.

I debated as to whether or not I should say something. It was so nice for me not to have to put up with any arguments, but, as usual, 'if it's easy for the Mom, it's bad for the kid.' I hated that, but I knew that I was dealing with a kid who got in trouble because he didn't express his feelings. He just buried them, covered them up, anesthetized them. So I had to do it.

"Kane?"

"Ma'am?"

"How did you feel when I wouldn't let you carry out the gifts?"

"I was okay with it."

"No, you weren't. I embarrassed you in front of that lady. And you were angry that I didn't trust you." He didn't respond for a long time. I glanced in the rear-view mirror, but I couldn't see his face. Hannah knew not to say a word. This was Mom's conversation.

"Kane? Are you angry with me?"

"No. I was just thinking. It's been so long since I felt anything, I don't know how I feel any more. But I don't think I'm angry."

"Maybe you should be."

"Really. I don't feel anything. I had a nice time."

I left it at that. Nobody said anything for a long time. It was a long ride back to my daughter's high school, from the party. And then it turned out that we had to wait a while for the busses to come in. Hannah fell asleep, and Kane and I were lost in our own thoughts. Through the rear-view mirror, I could see him staring out the window. We sat there in silence for a long time, as we waited for the busses. Finally, he spoke.

"Actually, I was proud," he said.

"What?" I hadn't really heard him.

"I was proud back there," Kane repeated.

"You were proud? Of what?"

"I was proud to have somebody who wasn't afraid to stand up for me... even in front of people... even when it might be embarrassing for them. Weren't you embarrassed, Aunt Tara? Weren't you embarrassed to have to stand up to that lady... and to be with a kid who you couldn't trust to walk out to the parking lot on his own?"

I thought for a minute. Whoa. Still waters. Finally I said, "Whom."

"What?"

"Whom. It's 'whom I couldn't trust to walk out to the parking lot on his own'." (Another one of my feeble attempts at downplaying!) "And, no, I wasn't embarrassed. I've been doing it for twenty-four years. It's my job... Here come the busses. By the way, Dana's easier than Hannah. But I'd rehearse your story anyway. She's had to do this for both of her brothers, for years. She doesn't have a lot of patience. And she has an excellent crap-detector, so don't even bother defending yourself."

We woke up Hannah and went out into the cold evening air. Kane had offered to stay with her while she slept. But I let him know that *that* wasn't going to happen either.

10. Dana

We stood in the cold air, searching the crowd for Dana. Finally, Hannah spotted her. "There she is, Mom. Can I go?"

"Wait a minute. I don't see her. Oh, okay. There she is. Be careful."

I let Hannah run ahead to greet her adored, older sister. They gave each other a big hug, and I could see Hannah telling Dana about Kane. She pointed back to where we were, and I waved.

"Come on." I motioned to Kane to walk in front of me. As we approached, Dana came closer and gave me a hug. Then she turned and hugged her cousin, as well.

"Dude! You're not a little kid! Who knew?" Dana was beautiful (even if I was a little prejudiced) and so smooth, socially. She always, instinctively, knew just the right thing to do or say. I often envied her that. She definitely got it from her dad.

"How was the trip, Sweetie? Did you see everything?"

"Mom, it was fantastic! Thanks for letting me go. We saw everything in Washington, plus we had a great time together. It was the perfect Senior Trip."

"Nobody got in trouble?"

"Not that I know of. Of course, we never hear about that until Monday morning, when the gossiping starts!" We laughed.

"As long as it wasn't you!"

"Oh, Mom!"

"Where are your bags?" I asked her.

"Oh, they're probably off by now. C'mon Kane, give me a hand." Kane looked at me and didn't say a word. Dana caught his glance and looked at both of us. The interchange had taken only a second, but Dana had caught it. "What's the matter?" she asked.

Before she could say anything more, I nodded to Kane that he could go. It was only a matter of twenty feet or so, and, after he took off with Dana, I sent Hannah off to join them.

Not wanting to add to the crowd, I waited where I was. I could see all of them clearly. And, in a few minutes, we were piled in the car, Kane and Hannah in back, and Dana up front with me.

Dana had a million things to tell, and she talked non-stop for the first few minutes of our ride home. I was so glad that she had had a chance to make this trip. We chose our family expenses carefully, but I always encouraged educational travel. My biggest concern was that the *other* kids on the trip were just going so they could party, away from their parents. Sometimes parents sent kids on these trips just to have a chance for a getaway for themselves, regardless of whether or not the kid deserved it. I couldn't help but think of my sister and brother-in-law.

I continued to listen to Dana's narrative for a while, asking questions now and then to let her know that I was interested. Then, I noticed that she had stopped talking. We drove in silence for quite some time. We were all tired. But, all of a sudden, she turned to face her cousin...I knew it was coming. "So, Kane. What's up with you?"

Kane had been staring out the window, but now turned to face Dana. "My parents are splittin' up, so I stole some money to buy a plane ticket out here. I got myself loaded on the plane, so they wouldn't bother me. But then I got caught when I got to New York. They gave me a choice: the police or your mother. So I got the brilliant idea to put myself to sleep... permanently." He stopped then, took a deep breath, and then went on. "Somehow, I made it to your mom, and she's been on my case ever since."

Dana just sat with her mouth open. She stared at Kane and then looked back at me. I could hardly contain myself. I think my Dana was speechless for the first time in her life. I glanced over at her, then back to the road. She was looking at me as if to say, 'You could have clued me in ahead of time!' But she composed herself quickly and said to her cousin, "That's my mom! On your case and in your face."

She turned back toward the front then, gave me a quick, 'Really, Mom?!' glance, and then stared out the front window. I checked the rear-view mirror and saw that Kane had his head back, on the headrest of the seat, with his eyes closed. I guessed that he was relieved that that was over. He didn't know, of course, that his very 'complete explanation' had only served to pique his cousin's curiosity. She'd be back, and she'd get every last detail of his life for the past decade and a third.

And I'd make sure that he gave it to her. As much as I was amused by Dana's reaction, I was also not pleased with Kane's rather flippant attitude. He was showing off for Dana and had not really done what he was supposed to. There was no way that I was going to let him get away with that. But this wasn't the time.

11. Premonition

When all the kids were in bed that night, I decided to call my sister again. Even though I was angry with her, I knew how I would have felt if it were my son, and no one would tell me anything.

"Hi, Kate. It's me."

"Oh, Tara. How is he? Is he all right?"

"He's fine. That's why I'm calling. He's so fine that I'm a little worried."

"What do you mean?"

"Well, he's been co-operative, and obedient, and he's opened up to the kids and talked to them about what's been going on with him. I know he hasn't told us a fraction of what he's probably been doing, but he's shared the part of the story that I know to be true."

"And...?"

"He's being too perfect. From what I've heard from you, and from him, you don't come out of what he's been doing and do a turn-around like this. To tell you the truth, I bet my friend that he wouldn't make it through tomorrow. I am truly shocked that he's still here."

"Well, if you want to send him home..."

"No, no, that's not what I meant. He's welcome to stay here as long as he behaves himself. I just can't believe that he hasn't run."

"Where would he run to? He has no friends there that I know of, and he has to be out of money."

"You are so naïve, mah sistah! Do you remember when I used to tell you about backpacking through Europe when I was in my twenties? And how there was always a network of young people, who would give each other directions and names of places to stay, and exchange money, and share books and stuff?"

"Yeah...?"

"Well, when I went back to Europe, just a few years older, I could never find that population again. I couldn't 'see them' from my age. Well, that's how it is with the drug culture. Even though *we* can't 'see them', all Kane has to do is walk to the nearest convenience store, or make his way downtown in the village, and *they'll* find *him*. And I'm sure he knows that. And, as for the money, if he stole from you, he'd certainly have no trouble stealing from me."

"So what do you want me to do?"

"Well, you know what I want you to do. Have you made any progress with Paul?"

"We got together the other night. We have a lot to talk about. At least we're not fighting. I think this thing with Kane has brought us to a whole new level of communication."

"Well, as predicted, Kane is convinced that it's the boring lifestyle, that you were forced into when you became parents, that drove you two apart. Translation: It's all his fault."

"Oh, Tara, I wish I could talk to him."

"It wouldn't help, and I don't want to chance it yet. He hasn't even been clean for a week yet! Even though I know there's no geographical cure for drug use, he seems to be somewhat comfortable here in 'Mr. Rogers' Neighborhood'… at least for today. Which is why I'm calling you. I have this feeling that he's going to test me soon."

"How?"

"Well, now, isn't that the million-dollar question?! Will he defy me and break all our house rules? Will he run? Will he bring drugs into the house? Will he sneak out and come home loaded? Will he go vandalize or steal something and get arrested? The possibilities are endless. Bottom line is what will *I* do? Will I give up on him? Will I kick him out? Will I help him *stop* this behavior, or will I enable him to *continue* it? He's going to want to know that before he buys into this relationship much further."

"Whew!"

"'Whew' is right! You guys let this go way too far. Do you see what happens if you don't overreact and get right on them when they're little? This kind of stuff starts when they're two!"

"Two!? He didn't do drugs when he was two!"

"It's not about drugs. Didn't you ever hear that what they're like when they're two and three is what they'll be like when they're twelve and thirteen? I watch your son and control his behavior like I did with my kids when they were toddlers. You don't let your toddlers run loose, talk back, and disobey you! You don't let your two- or three-year-olds put junk in their mouths.

"If you don't convince your preschooler that you are someone who loves him, and knows what's best for him, and can make him do the right thing, he's never going to trust that you know *anything,* when he gets older.

"This whole thing about *asking* your toddlers to make choices, for example, drives me nuts. You know, let them choose whether they want the blue sippy cup or the green one? They tell you that it helps the kids learn to make decisions for themselves. Ha! What it teaches them is that you don't even know what *cup* they should use! So how would you know *anything* about the *important* things in their lives?

"After they've spent time, lots of time, doing things with their parents, and under their parents' guidance, they should *naturally* be able to make their own choices. After a while, based on experience and example, they should pretty much know what's okay and what's not, and when they can choose on their own and when they need to ask!"

"Maybe you're right. I never thought about it that way…" Kate conceded.

I knew that I was just going off on my sister. I was just feeling so frustrated about all this. I knew that she really tried to be a good mother, and I was sure that, like all of us, she had her challenges. And, also, my sister knew me well, and I knew that *she* knew that I was just trying to 'talk this out', so as to better understand it.

"But, Tara," Kate continued then, "about Kane…how are you keeping track of him? I know you're not working, but, surely, he can't go *everywhere* with you."

"Well, there you go. That's why I'm calling you. I wanted to let you know how things were going while they were going well, because one of these days he's going to step out of line, and I have no idea what's gonna happen. I didn't want you to get bad news and think that I hadn't done my job here."

"Oh, Sis, I would never feel that way. This isn't your job at all, and Paul and I will always be grateful for what you've done for Kane already."

"Thank you, Kate. I want you two to work this out and not have to worry about Kane. On the other hand, *I'm* really worried about Kane, and I wanted you to know that, just in case."

"Well, have you thought about what you're going to do if he does any of those things that you mentioned? Because, truthfully, he's done *all* of them, and we never knew what to do. And, Tara, I didn't tell you this, but he was in a secure rehab facility for three months this summer."

"What?!" My first reaction was outrage that she hadn't told me that before, but then I realized that she was telling me now. It had to be hard for her to do that, so I wasn't going to say anything.

"Some boys that he was with were caught with drugs," she explained. "They were older, so they were punished more severely. But

Kane wasn't actually in possession. So, the judge thought he'd try to get him some treatment and teach him a lesson at the same time. Our insurance doesn't cover drug treatment. We had to pay out-of-pocket. It cost us a fortune."

"Oh, great! So, they put him in a school with experts!" I said. "Geez, no wonder he's so willing to comply and submit to my authority. I'm sure they taught him that. So, it's not really respect for me, or my rules. He's just playing the game, like he did in the lock-up. This puts a whole new spin on things."

"I'm sorry, Sis."

"No, I'm really glad you told me. I need to know everything if I'm going to have any hope of surviving this."

She paused, and then continued, "By the way, Tara, what about school?"

"What about school? The kids are on vacation."

"No, I mean, if he stays with you much longer, somebody is going to start asking questions, either here or there."

"This is true... Well... you tell them that he was sick over vacation, and that he won't be in this week. That'll give us a little more time to see what he's going to do. If he screws up, and I have to send him back to you, then you can decide if he goes back to school or somewhere else. If he seems to be doing okay here, then I could think about enrolling him here, although, with his history, I think we'd be asking for big trouble if we put him in our public school."

"Maybe you could home-school him."

"Yeah, right. I'm trying to *build* the relationship!" It seemed to me, that, at least for some people, homeschooling put a real strain on a parent-child relationship, especially if the child had already experienced, and enjoyed, the freedom of regular school. Even as a teacher, I didn't think I'd have the patience to do that.

"Well, I guess we'll just have to wait and see." Kate said.

"I guess. Well, good night, Kate, and Happy New Year."

It was only about ten o'clock, but I was really tired. We never bothered with New Year's Eve in our house. As far as I was concerned, and, thankfully, my husband had always felt the same way, it was just an excuse to stay up late and drink. These were both things which we did not enjoy doing and didn't want the kids to do. I did one last check of the house and then fell into a deep sleep.

12. New Year's

I woke with a start about one o'clock in the morning. I couldn't imagine what had awakened me. I listened but didn't hear anything. As usual when this happened, I couldn't go back to sleep. I started thinking about my conversation with my sister, earlier in the evening. What *would* I do when Kane finally, and inevitably, decided to test me?

I had thought that maybe I should confront him, before the fact, and tell him not to try any of the stunts he had pulled before. If he wanted our attention, he had it. All he had to do was ask, and the whole family would sit down and listen. That's how we did things. We tried to keep everything out in the open, so nobody's feelings had a chance to get out of control.

I also thought about just how bad his offense would have to be for me to give up on him. That would be the hardest. I had to protect my own kids, but I also didn't want to do something harsh, like send him away, when he was just testing my loyalty to him. After all, he would have to do that, if he were going to trust me. On the other hand, I didn't want him to think that he could walk all over me! The punishment would have to fit the crime, whatever that might turn out to be.

I hated this. My entire parenting experience had been geared to trying to avoid this kind of thing. I talked and listened to my kids. I spent time with them and did things with them. I nurtured them and taught them to nurture themselves and each other. I took care of them and tried to be sensitive to their needs and feelings. I gave them work to do, and responsibilities, as well as surprises and fun times. Raising my kids took everything I had - all my time, my money, my patience, my character, and my creativity.

Of course, that didn't mean we didn't have problems. My mother always said that kids did, and tried, things, at different ages and stages, so that parents had the opportunity to teach and correct them. My kids gave me a run for my money.

But, as they got older, things got easier. People say that 'the bigger the kid, the bigger the problem'. As the kids approached adulthood, their problems involved the world outside more than when they were little. But I don't think the problems were more difficult. They were just more 'public'. Just as the kids were beginning to feel a little freedom from *our* rules, they began to realize that they then had to follow *the world's* rules, laws, and restrictions.

It was a good thing that we had taught them cause and effect, and consequences, when they were little. It would have been very expensive, as they got older, if the *courts* had to teach them! Feeling the shame of a time-out was nothing compared to the grown-up equivalent— having to come up with bail money! And stopping a little one from punching a parent, who couldn't even feel it, was easier than trying to explain to a teenager the consequences of what is considered 'assault'. I could go on and on. Everything a child does, good and bad, has an adult version. Running and screaming during free play in the back yard, getting play clothes filthy in the sandbox at the park, and laughing hysterically at age-appropriate humor (even if Mom doesn't get the joke!), don't matter; other things do.

Knowing the difference and responding, or not responding, appropriately, is the greatest challenge of parenthood. Parents have to know what to correct, what to encourage, and what's not going to matter. A teacher-friend of mine once commented, 'If only we could know which ones really needed our help and which ones would come through fine without us!'

There are so many things to deal with, not only with individual kids, but also with individual issues that come up. After a few kids, you get your routine worked out for the common challenges of childhood and youth, but, every once in a while, they throw you a curve ball to keep you on your toes.

My oldest has Attention Deficit Disorder. It just about drove me crazy until I got some help. There's a lot of information about it available now, but when Danny was little, I thought I would lose my mind. He threw endless tantrums, which seemed to be related to nothing. He was oppositional and defiant on everything he had to do. Sometimes, I would demand, in no uncertain terms, that he do the *opposite* of what we had to do, just so I could get him going. It was bizarre.

When he was about ten years old, a teacher picked up on the problem and told us how to have him tested. We tried all the natural remedies and behavior modification. Then, finally, somebody told us to stop wasting our time and energy and to get him the appropriate medication.

My husband was very much against that at first, since *his* brother had had severe drug problems in his youth, and *my* youngest brother did also. But this person explained to us that ADD and ADHD

(ADD with hyperactivity) tended to run in families, and that people with these disorders often tried illegal drugs in an attempt to self-medicate. If we didn't help our son, he would probably start experimenting with various substances himself, trying to control the runaway thoughts (a common symptom of this disorder) that were racing through his head.

That convinced my husband. We went for the medication, and Danny got through high school. With the medication, Danny was also able to finish a training program and get himself a good job.

Listening to teachers and caregivers, and not getting defensive about your child's behavior, is really important. It can help to root out difficult problems that even your child may not want to admit that he's having.

Being tuned in to every aspect of your child's being, behaviors, and thoughts, is so crucial to helping him become what he's going to be. I couldn't begin to think how I was going to help my nephew. I barely knew him! And *now*, I had found out that the little bit of behavior that I *had* observed was a show, staged to impress me!

I looked at the clock again. It was one-thirty. Why any of us would ever want to be a parent, I thought, is beyond me! I closed my eyes and fell back to sleep.

*   *   *   *   *   *   *   *

"Mom! Mom! Wake up!" It was Dana.

"Happy New Year, Sweetie."

"Mom, he's gone."

"What? Who?"

"Kane! He's gone."

I started to jump up and then thought better of it. I didn't want to upset my daughter. I sat up and took a deep breath before I spoke. "I figured this would happen sooner or later, Dana. He has a lot of problems."

"But aren't you going to do something? We looked all over the house for him. Hannah went outside to look around."

"Tell her to come in and get warm. We'll take care of this in a minute. I just have to think about what I want to do. Meanwhile, you two should go get some breakfast." Funny, I thought, I had just told my friend Karen that I didn't think he'd make it past Thursday!

"But Mom, every minute counts, doesn't it, when someone is

missing?"

"Dana, you are such a sweetheart. Come, sit down here a minute." Dana sat down but was not happy about it. "Dana, honey, this boy is like no one we know. We've given him the very best here that he can get anywhere. If he walks away from it, he isn't ready for it. And if he's not ready to work on his own behalf, and to accept what we have to offer, then we're not going to do him any good."

"But, Mom, he's only thirteen! He's a baby out there."

"He's no baby, Sweetie. Once you've walked where he's walked, you grow old very quickly."

The philosopher in my head rambled on. I thought to myself, 'He's eaten the apple; He's stepped out of the garden; He knows good and evil. And, when that happens, human will has very little power. He may go a long time before good and evil stop battering him about between them. It would be up to *him* to decide to come 'home' and submit himself to someone else's control again.'

"What do you *mean*, Mom?" Dana shook me from my thoughts.

"I'm glad you don't understand. You've always been a good kid."

"Oh, Mom, I am far from perfect."

"Of course, that's normal. But the bottom line is that you have respected, and submitted to, my authority over you - my authority as a parent who loves you. Kane, obviously, hasn't given that authority to anyone. Either his parents weren't vigilant enough, or something in his character is way too strong, or circumstances have tempted him beyond his ability to resist.

"Whatever it is, it really doesn't matter, I guess. The best we can do for him now is pray that he makes it safely through every day, until he finds his way back on his own. And I really, really don't envy him the trip...*if* he makes it."

"Mom! What are you *talking* about?! You're really not going to just sit here and give up on him!"

I sighed. This really wasn't working for either of us. "No, Dana. Give me a few minutes. I'll make some phone calls. Don't worry. Go find your sister, and both of you get some breakfast."

I said a silent prayer, as I debated whether to call the police station first, or the hospital.

13. Police Station

As soon as I got myself up and out of bed, I called the police station.

"Wellmore Police. Officer Link."

"Tom! It's Tara Wilson. Happy New Year!"

"Tara! Happy New Year! How are you?"

"We're doing okay, thanks. But I do have a little problem."

"What can I do for you?"

"Well, my nephew, Kane, showed up on my doorstep a few days ago. He ran away from his mother in California. And, as of this morning, he's apparently run away from me."

"Is this Kate's kid?"

"Yeah, she and her husband have been having marital problems, and the kid is acting out; drinking, drugs, you know, it's a classic case."

"Oh, I'm so sorry. Okay, let me guess. He's been with you a few days, enjoying the good life - and I know you provide the good life for your kids - and now the honeymoon is over, and he's testing you."

"You got it," I said. Tom and I had gone to school together in a neighboring town, and, since I had come to Wellmore to teach, we had often worked together on youth issues. We pretty much saw eye-to-eye on a lot of things. I was glad that he happened to be on duty.

I continued, "Even though I think I know the bottom line on this, Tom, I don't want to give up on him quite yet. Kate and Paul really can't handle him right now, and I may not be able to, either. But he's only thirteen, and I would really like to give him another chance here, with me and my kids."

"You know, Tara, I just walked in the door when you called. Let me check and see if we picked up anybody overnight." Tom put me on hold, and I waited. I didn't know what to hope for. If they had him, what would I do? If they didn't, what would I do? "I've got good news and bad news." Tom was back on the line. "The good news is that we've got him. The bad news is that he's still sleeping it off."

"Well, just tell me what you know," I sighed.

"Seems he had a ball celebrating last night. The guys got a call from a house over on Melon Drive. They were having a big bash, lots and lots of people. The kid must have crashed the party at some time during the evening. There were many families, so no one noticed one more kid. When all the guests left, at about three-o'clock this morning, the hosts were checking the house before turning in. That's when they found this one, passed out on the floor, in one of the spare bedrooms.

"Fortunately, our men were able to wake him up. So they brought him back here to the station, instead of to the ER. They figured that, surely by morning, somebody would be missing him and come looking for him… And here you are!" he concluded.

"Oh, wonderful," I sighed again. "Okay, so now what do we do?"

"How about you let me handle it at this end, and I'll call you when he's ready to come home?"

"That would be great, assuming that he'll *want* to come back here."

"You seriously underestimate how wonderful your family life is, Tara, compared to what we see around here. Unless this kid is totally stupid, he'll want what you have to offer."

"Tom, you flatter me."

"I'm not kidding. You wait and see. Okay, so what's his full name again?"

"Kane Winter." I spelled the name for him and then added, "Don't be too good to him. He doesn't deserve it. He has a list of offenses a mile long. Kate says that he's been screwin' around since he was ten or eleven."

"Trust me, Tara. I've got this. 'Not my first rodeo."

"Thanks, Tom! I'll be sitting here waiting for your call."

14. Back-up

If I had one day when I didn't have to be all confused, and I didn't have to feel that I was ashamed of everything. If I felt that I belonged someplace...

James Dean as Jim Stark,
Rebel Without a Cause

Officer Link went back to the juvenile detention area. He entered one of the small, windowless rooms. These were used to keep juveniles separated from any adults who might be in custody at the same time. The room had one long table and two chairs.

Tom entered and looked down at the young man who was seated at the opposite side of the table. The kid was asleep, head resting on his arms. He was wearing jeans and boots, a tee shirt, and a hoodie, with the hood half pulled up. His long hair, under his hood, was dirty and matted. 'This kid needs a haircut, in more ways than one,' Tom thought to himself.

A 'haircut' was an old slang term, used in drug programs and therapeutic communities (called TCs for short). In most places, it meant a 'chewing out', an upbraiding, a severe reprimand. But, in some programs, it was an actual shaving of the head, letting everyone in the program know that the 'shavee' had been punished for messing up somehow. It was used as a consequence for everything from getting high to doing something irresponsible on the job or in the community.

"Okay, kid. Wake up!" Tom addressed him. When Kane failed to move, Tom raised his voice. "HEY! WAKE UP!"

The boy started to move. He half lifted his head, tried to focus his eyes, and then dropped his head back down on the table. "What do you *want*?" he mumbled.

"WHAT! Who do you think you're *talking* to? SIT UP!" Tom could really bellow when he wanted someone to show respect. At that point, Kane did his best to sit up and try to focus his eyes. A look of sudden awareness crossed his face as he realized that he was looking at a uniformed police officer.

"Oh, shit," Kane moaned, putting his head in his hands.

"Sit up! Take off your hood! And look at me!" the officer commanded. Kane tried to sit up straighter and do as he was told. "What's your name and where do you live?"

"I don' have a name. I'm nobody. I don' live near here."

"Don't get smart with me! What's your name and where do you live?" the officer demanded, once again.

"I have to go to the bathroom."

Tom was required to accompany the kid into the bathroom. He closed the door behind the two of them. The room was small, so Kane was able to steady himself by holding onto the wall. When Kane was done, the officer took him back to the detention room.

"Now! Name and address!" Tom began again. The kid shook his head and still wouldn't answer. Tom decided to try a new tack. He sat down at the table, across from Kane. "Look, kid. Whoever is responsible for you is probably out of their mind with worry right now. They're probably thinkin' that you're dead on the road somewhere."

"Nobody cares about *me*! You don' have to worry about *that*," Kane informed him. "Did anybody call you this morning looking for a lost kid? No! Right? Look, just send me wherever you need to send me. I really don' care." He slumped back in his chair, head back, eyes closed.

Tom continued to sit where he was. He didn't say a word. He just sat there. And waited. He wanted Kane to *want* to be helped, before he offered to help him. Tom was beginning to understand what his friend was dealing with. Apparently, this kid was a tougher nut to crack than he had thought. But Tom saw it as a challenge. He, too, didn't want to give up on this kid. Not yet. After all, even though he didn't know the father, he did know the mother and the aunt, and he just felt that there had to be a soft spot in this boy… somewhere! And, if Tara were going to have any luck at all with him, she was going to need for him to have respect for the local police.

Finally, Tom said, "Sit up straight!" Kane lifted his head at that, his eyes bloodshot, his face pale and pained, and sat up in his chair. Tom went on. "There *was* one call… It was for you. It was your aunt."

For a minute, Kane didn't know what to say. But he was still pretty high from something that he had taken at the party earlier that morning. And he was pretty brazen when he was high. "So, did she tell you to keep me here?" he said, sarcastically.

"Is that what you want?" the officer asked him.

"Isn't that what *she* wants?"

"She didn't say that."

"What *did* she say?"

"She said you're in big trouble."

"Yeah, so what else is new? So I guess she'll be calling my

parents now. I deserve it. I screwed up. And she's gonna kick me out. It was just a matter of time. It might as well be now, before I..." He stopped.

"Before you start liking the place?" Tom second-guessed.

"I wasn' gonna say that," Kane lied, lowering his eyes.

"No matter. I don't think that's what she had in mind."

Interested, Kane looked up at him again. "Whaddya mean?"

"If I know Tara Wilson, she's gonna have the cleanest house and the best cleaned-out garage in all of Wellmore. No, no, wait, let me see now...crashing a private party, drinkin' and druggin', wakin' up in the jail, hmm... make that in all of Connecticut! I'll bet she's linin' up *your* punishments right now."

Kane tried to laugh. He really did. He was happy that his aunt had called. He was happy and relieved that someone actually did care about him. And at the same time, he was devastated. How could he face these people again? They took him into their home, really treated him like family, and he almost blew it. He was such a screwup. His thoughts and emotions were spinning around in his head. He couldn't go back there. He just couldn't face his aunt in this condition again ...for the second time in a week! How messed up was that!

"I can't...I can't face her. At least not now," Kane said.

"Yes! You can!" Officer Link informed him. "You're lucky to have somebody who cares about you. And you will not blow this opportunity. If *she* thinks you're worth her time, then you better *also* think you're worth her time. I'm cuttin' you some slack here, because I know your family. But we're gonna be watchin' you."

"That's not fair!" Kane knew, right after he'd said it, that he shouldn't have. But he was a little short on self-control that morning.

Tom was patient with him, this time. "Well, it may *not* be. But now that I know who you are, I'll be keeping an eye on you. It's our job to protect the people of this town. And you've got a reputation with us now. So, like it or not, and regardless of how big-hearted your aunt is, we know who you are, and you'd better keep your nose clean."

Kane tried to sit tough, but he really felt bad. He was afraid he was going to be sick. He wanted to put his head down. But the officer had told him to sit up, and he was afraid to piss this guy off again. In the shape he was in, Kane just couldn't handle any more trouble right then. And he still had to face his aunt and his cousins!

Officer Link stood up. He was 'all business' again. "So? Are you ready to face your aunt?"

Kane looked up and nodded slowly, thinking to himself, 'Anything to get outta *here*!'

"I didn't *hear* you!" Tom said, more loudly and sternly. He did *not* want this kid to forget this 'little experience'…*or* to *repeat* it!

"*Yes*, sir!" Kane said then, as clearly as he could, so that the officer wouldn't make him say it again. His head hurt *so* bad.

Officer Link left the detention room, and Kane heaved a sigh of relief. He was finally able to put his head back down on the table.

Tom went back out to the phones to call Tara.

"Hi, Tara! It's Tom. Yeah, listen, he's still a little high, but, unless he's an excellent con artist, I think he's embarrassed and ashamed, and ready to come home.

"Thank you so much! I'll be right down," I told him.

*   *   *   *   *   *   *   *

Tom was waiting for me in the lobby of the police station, and I followed him back to the juvenile detention area. Before we went into the room, Tom filled me in on exactly what had happened, and how Kane had behaved while in custody. I was grateful for his insight. It gave me another perspective on what I was dealing with.

Kane had his head back down on the table when Tom opened the door. But, this time, when he heard the door open, and saw the officer, Kane sat right up. And, when told to do so, he immediately stood up and moved toward us. He was still a little unsteady, but he managed to walk on his own.

He stopped in front of me, lowered his head, and said, "I'm really sorry. Thanks for coming for me." I still didn't know exactly how to treat him. I'd seen a lot of young boys master this 'penitent act', and I'd seen a lot of women fall for it. In such circumstances, it's always so much easier with a mom and a dad. They can do the good-cop bad-cop thing. Mom can do the, 'We're so glad you're safe', while Dad does the, 'C'mon, Son, we'll discuss this at home.' But, as a single parent, I always had to 'lay down the law' first. And, then, after I was sure that the kids understood that I meant business, *then,* I could be more supportive and nurturing. But the punishment would not be reduced, no matter how much we talked or how bad they felt. I always told the kids that, the *next* time, when they *didn't* mess up, *then* they wouldn't have to take the punishment!

It's so important to establish the adult-child relationship when the kids are young. Of course, you have to keep re-establishing 'adult distance' as the kids grow. But if the kids are also maturing, they will understand; as they get older, the limits *change,* but there will always be consequences if they go *beyond* those limits.

The parents who really seem to get into trouble are the ones who are, themselves, still like teenagers in their approach to what adulthood is all about. If the parents are still acting like adolescents, rebelling against growing up and taking responsibility, then their kids catch up to them really quickly. Then you've got 'big kids' (the parents) trying to act like grown-ups to 'little kids' (their children). And, believe me, the 'little kids' see right through it. And with no adult role models, they flounder. They get more and more angry (and hurt!) as *other* adults have to correct them, and even punish them, for things that their own parents should have taught them were wrong, or just 'not done'. It's embarrassing for them, and they get really upset when they're embarrassed.

I was thinking about all of this as I guided Kane out to the car. Tom went out with us to make sure that Kane didn't fall and that I could handle him.

The ride home was quiet. I sat him in the front, where I could watch him, and locked all the doors. He leaned his head back against the seat, but he kept his eyes open and seemed to be interested in what the town looked like. I found myself hoping that he was thinking about staying on... buying in… shaping up. But, he had to want that more than I did. And this little episode did not bode well for his future. I was still very aware of my own limitations, and I didn't dare get too hopeful.

Of course, the really scary thought in the back of my mind was that I also didn't know how far along Kane actually was in his drug use. Maybe he was already past the point where a relatively simple thing like punishment would deter his use. I didn't even want to think about *that* yet.

"Aunt Tara..."

"Yes, Kane."

"I know I screwed up. I'm sorry."

"Kane, although I appreciate the apology, 'sorry' doesn't excuse or erase anything. You can't just do whatever you want and then say 'sorry' and think that that makes everything okay. If that's what you're doing, don't even bother to say it, because it makes a mockery of apologizing. And I, for one, don't deserve that from you."

"I know. I expect to take my punishment."

"And what do you think your punishment should be?"

He shrugged, "I figured you'd know."

I didn't say anything. I felt like I was sitting next to a little wild animal that I was under the delusion that I could tame. And besides, I knew he was still high, so whatever I said didn't matter anyway.

He went on. "I just don' know if I can do it."

"Do what, Kane?"

"I don' know if I can stop gettin' high."

"Are you ready to get some help?"

"I don' know. I've already been in a TC. It didn' work."

"Were you ready for it to work?"

"I don' know... I don' know anything."

He sounded like he was still pretty much 'under the influence' but that he was starting to come down. I was anxious to get both of us home. I decided not to say anything more. If he stayed, we'd have plenty of time. If he split, what was the point?

But he obviously wasn't finished. "Look. I am really sorry I screwed up. I'll do anything you tell me."

I figured that if he felt like talking, I'd give it a shot, even if it didn't matter in the long run. "Didn't you tell me that once before?"

"Yeah."

"And then you went and did this?"

He hung his head. "Yeah." Then he looked up. "So you think I'm hopeless?"

"Kane, there is always hope. You can do it. It's just going to be very hard. And I don't know if you want it badly enough."

"I don' wanna be in trouble all the time." He put his head back on the seat and closed his eyes. He didn't look good. I debated as to whether I should say any more. But, as I glanced over at him, he forced himself to focus his eyes on me and seemed to be waiting for a reply. So I gave him one.

"Yeah, but you may not want to be in pain all the time either."

"Whaddya mean? I'm not in pain. Well, my head hurts a little…a lot actually. But, hey, it was New Year's Eve, right?"

"I'm not talking about physical pain. And, no, New Year's Eve is no excuse. Especially not for thirteen-year-old boys."

"Sorry." He shut up. I continued.

"People get high to feel better. That would mean that when you're not high you don't feel good about things. You have to be brave enough to explore that kind of pain and find some other way to handle it. That's not easy."

I could feel him looking at me. I could sense him thinking, 'I don't get it,' but he kept his mouth shut. Probably so he wouldn't put his foot in it again.

I went on. "The pain could be caused by any number of things. Maybe you have a biochemical imbalance, and you need nutritional support or a prescription drug to balance that out. Maybe your emotions are so 'screwed with' that you can't stand the way you feel about yourself, your parents, your future, whatever...and you need to explore how you really feel, and deal with it. Maybe you're just dying of terminal boredom. Maybe you need to just sit and be bored and accept that life is not always totally stimulating. Or maybe you need to develop a gift or talent that you don't have the courage or faith to recognize. Or maybe you have no gifts or talents at all, and you have to deal with that.

"Living life well can be really challenging, and when a kid's gettin' high, and gettin' in trouble all the time, that's a very common warning sign that something's wrong. Instead of spending so much time exploring the world of drugs and alcohol, if I were you, I would spend more time exploring the world of Kane. It would be a lot more interesting and a lot more worthwhile."

Kane was having trouble keeping his eyes open at that point. He rubbed his forehead with one hand, as he turned his head toward the window. I didn't say anything more.

*　　*　　*　　*　　*　　*　　*　　*

All the kids were in the living room when we got home. David had come home from his ski trip and had finished unpacking his stuff. He and the girls were watching a football game, but they shut it off when we came in.

"Is he okay, Mom?" Hannah was up and running to meet us.

"Ask him," I replied.

"Are you all right? We were all so worried about you."

Kane was taken aback by so much attention, but all he said was, "Oh, yeah. I'm jus' great."

"Why did you do that?" Hannah was really concerned.

"I don' know. Uh, could I like sit down?"

"Sure, come over here." David reached out and took Kane by

the arm. He helped him into a chair.

I felt that I needed to take a break and have some time to myself. "Listen, kids, would you stay here and talk to Kane for a while? I need to go upstairs and be by myself a little bit."

"Sure, Mom."

"Thanks." I really needed to get my thoughts together, and I knew the kids would make sure that Kane toed the line. As I went up the stairs, I could hear them start to talk to him. I knew he was still a little out of it, and we were probably all wasting our words, but I knew that they would say the right things to him. Peer support is always really important, as is peer reprimand. My kids would be good for my nephew.

"So, Kane. What exactly have you been doing?" David started the conversation.

"Yeah, Kane. What's with the low life? Our family doesn't do this," Dana joined in. "Are you trying to make us look bad in our own town?"

"Yeah," said David, "you have to clean up your act if you expect to have a life around here."

"Our mom is a great mom," Dana continued, "but we know she can't do it alone. If one of us screws up, it puts too much pressure on everybody else, especially Mom."

"Dana's right," said David. "We want you to stay here, and I'm pretty sure that Mom does, too. But she has to protect what we have. If you don't pull your weight, it makes it really tough on the rest of us. You need to be helping out, *not* getting in trouble!

Kane listened to his cousins. He'd never heard kids talk like this before. David and Dana were older than he was, but even Hannah nodded her head like she knew just what they meant.

Kane heard what they were saying, but defended himself. "But you guys don' un'erstand. I don' wanna do this shit… Oh, sorry… See what I mean? I just can' help it sometimes."

The kids were sympathetic, but skeptical. Their mom had brought kids home before, until she could get in touch with their parents. They all had a story and lots of excuses. And most of them were con artists, getting people to feel sorry for them, so they could get them off their case. But this was their cousin, and it looked like he might be staying for a while. That didn't make them any less skeptical, but it made what they said to him much more important.

David continued the lecture. "Mom will help you, but you have to buy into the fact that you have to do what she tells you. You can't, like, listen and then decide whether or not that's something you're going to do. You have to do what you're told, all the time, every time."

"Yeah," Dana added, "and you can't get high. Most of the time, you're expected to act nice and polite. But when you don't feel like doing that, you have to ask somebody if you can talk to them about how you're *feeling*. Nobody wants to hear you whine and complain all the time. And nobody wants to deal with you dumping your anger and stuff all over the place. Instead, you have to sit down and tell one of us what's going on with you. We try to make time to listen to each other ... and Mom will always make time for you."

"What if she's the one I'm angry with?" asked Kane.

"You can get angry with her," Dana told him.

"Yeah, right." Kane wasn't convinced. "I won't have to *fly* back to California. She'll kick my butt at least as far as Reno!"

"Then you come to one of us," said David.

"And what if I'm angry with all of you?" Kane asked.

"Then we all sit down and talk about it together," explained Dana. "'Cause chances are, if you're angry with all of us, at the same time, then what you're really angry about is something else, and you need to figure out what that is."

"'Cause if you don't," warned David, "you're going to go out and get yourself loaded again."

"How do you guys know so much about all this?" As bad as he felt, (in oh so many ways!), Kane respected his cousins, and he knew that they were being sincere in trying to help him.

With all the patience that he could muster, David explained, "Because, except for Hannah, we've all been on the planet longer than you have! Plus, our parents always talked to us a lot about this. Dad's brother and Mom's brother both had a lot of problems, so Mom and Dad were afraid it might be genetic in both sides of our family. And judging by you, it's looks like they might have been right! Anyway, they learned as much as they could and taught us. When Dad died eight years ago, Mom reminded us of Dad's concerns, and we decided that we could keep his spirit alive, at least in our family, by living like he would have wanted us to."

"And now maybe what we've learned will be useful to you," added Dana. "It's not hard once you know that you're loved and that your family won't quit on you."

Kane put his head down at that point and the kids all looked at each other. They knew they'd hit a nerve.

"Kane..." David spoke first. Kane looked up, blinking back tears. "Kane, we're sorry about what's going on with your parents. It's not right. Even though they're the grown-ups, they're not right in what they're doing. And I'm sure Mom has told them so. But *you* can't keep doing what *you're* doing. You can't keep hurting yourself. No matter what you think and how you feel, you can't keep destroying yourself because of what your parents are going through."

"But I can't help how I feel. Sometimes it just hurts so bad." Kane was fighting back tears.

"But you can decide how you're going to *act* on those feelings," Dana put in. "You can *think* about them, and *feel* them, and *talk* about them, and get angry, or cry, or scream, or *whatever*. You just can't get *high*. And maybe, eventually, you'll be able to turn the bad feelings around and use them to do something positive. Once you start filling your time with the right things, it will get easier."

"Wha' things?" Kane asked, warily.

"Oh, don't worry. I'm sure Mommy has a list a mile long already." Hannah piped in for the first time, allowing her brother and sister to explain the more complicated stuff that she didn't really understand yet.

Even Kane had to smile a little.

Hannah went over to him then and put her arms around his neck. "We love you, Kane. Please don't keep hurting yourself."

Kane's smile turned to tears at that point. He didn't know how he could feel so bad and so good at the same time.

David put his hand on Kane's shoulder, "It's okay, Bro."

Dana wiped the tears from her eyes and went to get Kane a blanket. She knew that he was going to be feeling worse before he felt better.

*   *   *   *   *   *   *   *

As it was New Year's Day, we spent the rest of the day at home. The kids watched the games on TV, and I caught up with my correspondence. Because he had sneaked out of the house while we were sleeping the night before, I wouldn't let Kane sleep at all during the day. He sat with the kids, watching TV, so that we could keep an eye on him. Every time he dozed off, we would wake him up. It was cruel, but I was desperate. I didn't know what else to do with him.

15. Family Weekend

I had to decide on Kane's punishment. I was beginning to suspect that his problem was not one that could be treated with discipline alone. But, until we figured this out, I felt that I needed to give him as much structure in his life as I could. And that included helping him understand cause and effect. If you do the things that we've learned don't 'work', then your life wasn't going to 'work' either. I had to reinforce that. I figured that the consequences for his recent behavior ought to involve training for his new lifestyle - a lifestyle that, hopefully, would be better than his old one. Appropriately, it was a lifestyle that included a lot of …work!

It was going to be a long weekend. It was only Friday. I wanted to have a fun time with my kids, but I didn't want to give 'this one' rewards for misbehavior. Of course, I rationalized, his new lifestyle would have to include healthy recreation. And I knew that I had to get out and have a little diversion myself. So I decided that Kane's punishment was going to have to wait. We were going to enjoy the weekend as a family.

I got on the phone and made some calls to the theaters. It was almost lunchtime, so I figured I'd treat the kids to lunch and the new Disney movie.

"David! Could you come up here a minute, please?"

David appeared in my room.

"Yeah, Mom?"

"How's it going with him?"

"He's doing some chores, but he's still hung over from yesterday." He paused, thoughtfully. "Mom, can we *handle* him?"

"I don't know, David. We'll have to pray a lot. Listen, I want to take Hannah to the movies today. She's been wanting to see the new Disney movie."

"Okay, I guess Dana and I can handle the kid."

"Oh, no! I'm not going to put you in that position yet. He's way too unstable."

"Okay, so, what do you want us to do?"

"Well, you don't have to actually go into the movie with us, if you don't want to, because I know Dana likes any movie. But I thought we could all go out to lunch and, then, at least the girls and I could take Kane.

"But isn't that like rewarding him for what he did?"

"Well, I don't think it's fair to the rest of us to have to stay home because of Kane's behavior. And, besides, when you all go back to school, he's going to be working his tail off."

"Okay. Sounds good to me. I don't mind going to the movies with the family! I want to see some friends tonight, but the movie shouldn't be over that late. I'll go tell the kids."

"Send Kane up to see me, please?"

"Sure."

* * * * * * * *

"David said that you wanted to see me." Kane stood in the doorway to my room.

"Yes. Sit down here." Kane made his way in and sat down on the edge of my bed. "How are you feeling?" I asked him.

"I'm okay. I mean... the kids were nice. I didn't deserve it."

"No, I really meant are you feeling sick?…because we're going out."

"I'd rather stay here."

"I know. But you're coming out with us. So, go get washed and change your clothes."

Kane picked himself up and headed for the door. When he got there, he turned to look back at me. "Don't you want to know what I did?"

"I know what you did."

"No, I mean don't you want to know what I took?"

"Would that make you feel really cool, to impress me with your knowledge of all the latest chemicals on the street?"

"No… I guess not."

"Well, good, because it's pretty much the same stuff that's been out there for the last thirty years. The only new stuff is there to replace the stuff that *killed* everybody. And, from what I'm hearing, now the *new* stuff is killing everybody. So, frankly, the drugs don't impress me. What *would* impress me is your having the guts to stay away from them."

Kane went to his room to get cleaned up. I figured that we'd all done enough talking to him for a while. We needed to give him time to process what we were all saying.

* * * * * * * *

Just as we were leaving for the theater, Danny showed up. He decided to come home for New Year's weekend. We turned him right around and piled him in the car with us. We were then a family of six. It was great.

We got a big booth at our favorite restaurant and enjoyed each other's company. I watched Kane out of the corner of my eye. He was still pretty hung over, but he knew better than to make an issue of it. I just kept watching him, in case he couldn't handle it all.

A few times, I saw a look of pain come over his face, but we pretty much ignored him. The boys knew what he was going through. Despite their lecture to Kane, they had each given 'adolescent rebellion' a brief try before they got their little tails pinned to the wall. And the girls were so wrapped up in spending time with their big brothers that they had all but forgotten about their 'new brother' and all his problems.

After lunch, we headed for the movies. Danny said he'd pass. It was expensive, and he needed to do some shopping in the same plaza. So, we set a time to meet after the movie. David knew that I was counting on him in case Kane surprised us with anything, so, although he would have liked to go with his brother, he came along with us as planned. I let him know how grateful I was.

We made a bathroom stop before we went in, so no one would have to leave during the movie. David took Kane. It just reminded me how hard it was going to be to take care of Kane when the boys left.

We got in and took our seats before it got dark. Hannah wanted to sit between Kane and David, so I put Kane next to me, then Hannah, then David, then Dana. We had him wedged in.

The movie was adorable. Hannah kept reaching across Kane to tap me when the movie had a part that she really liked. I was afraid that he was going to get angry and lash out at her, but he was slumped down, with his hood up over his head, seemingly resigned to his fate.

After a while, Hannah became engrossed in the story and stopped reaching over to me. The story was more than half over before she did it again. I leaned forward to hear her, but she put her finger to her lips and pointed to Kane. I turned to look at him and saw that he was sound asleep. I motioned to Hannah that we were going to *let* him sleep. He looked awful. The movie wasn't much longer, and it was still early, so he'd sleep through the night. I was still always uneasy about what he might do while we were sleeping.

When the film was over, everybody clapped. Kane stirred with the noise and began to wake up. We sat for a minute to let other people out and to give Kane time to come around.

"Hannah, did you like it?" I asked.

"It was great, Mom. Thanks for taking us!"

"You're welcome, Sweetie."

I stood up and helped Kane to his feet. He was still a little disoriented. We made our way out to the lobby and then decided to go to the store to look for Danny. We found him quickly and passed some time looking around. Kane was very good about staying right with us.

Back at home, everybody helped get dinner and then we cleared the table to play some board games. Since Kane was on a TV ban for his recent behavior, the kids used that as an excuse to pull out some board games that they used to like to play together. It was special for Hannah, too, since she didn't have siblings near her age, to play with, when she was growing up.

Kane tried to play for a while, but he soon asked to be excused. I told him he could sit out, but he couldn't go up to his room yet. He watched the kids play for a while and then started to doze off. Since it was getting late, I asked David to take him upstairs and for Dana to take Hannah. That gave me a chance to talk with Danny about what had happened in the incredibly long week since he had been home last.

*   *   *   *   *   *   *   *

The next morning being Saturday, the kids all had their chores to do. Everyone had to clean his or her own bedroom plus one common area, and all clothes had to be sorted and taken to the laundry room. When the kids were little, I used to take it all to the Laundromat and get six or eight loads done in a half hour. But, eventually, as the kids learned to do their own laundry, and as the older kids started to be away more, it was just too inconvenient. But we actually used to look forward to those Saturday morning trips. We would often go for donuts while the laundry was being done. Or sometimes the kids would bring their homework to do, and we'd save ourselves time later in the day.

Dana showed Kane where all the cleaning stuff was kept, and David and Danny showed him how I liked things done.

After lunch, we headed off to the ice rink. It turned out that Kane was quite a good skater. It also dawned on me that if he chose to take off while I was making my way around, holding on to the rink walls, I'd have no hope of going after him! I mentioned this to my sons, who were much better skaters than I, who assured me that they would be on alert. It was a fun day, and the exercise was good for all of us.

On Sunday, after church, everybody had to get ready to go back to school and to work. Danny left early. I wished he could get a job closer to home. And David left for school at about three o'clock, with a friend. The girls both had a little homework to finish up, and then they wanted showers and time to get all their things in order for school. Of course, I had lunches to pack, and Hannah's clothes to put out.

My most favorite thing about not working this year was what I called having 'a Sunday without a Monday'. When I was working, the weekend always ended at three o'clock on Sunday afternoon, and I had to start gearing myself up for the workweek. I had always felt like I stepped out on a tightrope on Sunday afternoon and didn't step off again until Friday night.

"Aunt Tara?"

"Oh, Kane. You startled me. Did you finish folding that laundry?"

"Yes, ma'am. What do you want me to do now?"

"Sit down here a minute. I'm just finishing Hannah's lunch for tomorrow."

"Yeah, I was gonna ask you about that."

"About Hannah's lunch?"

"No, I mean about tomorrow. Aren't I supposed to go to school?"

I looked at him. It was the very last thing I thought he would ask about. "Did you go to school at home?"

"Of course."

"What did you do there?"

He shrugged. "I went to classes." I guess he thought I was pretty stupid.

"And what else?" It then dawned on him that I wasn't so stupid after all. It just took him a minute to figure out what I was getting at. "Kane, do you really think you're ready to go to a public school with no supervision? Do you think you're even gonna make it through to, like, lunchtime without scoring something?"

"I been clean!"

"Yeah, for like seventy-two hours."

"But I don't know anybody here. How am I going to get anything?"

"Kane, I am old, but not *that* old. They're gonna see you comin', Babe. It's written all over your face. They're gonna spot you a mile away."

"That's crazy!"

"Trust me. You are not ready. And, frankly, *I'm* not ready."

"You're just embarrassed because you work there, right? You don't want anybody to know about me."

"Nice try."

"Aw, come on. What am I gonna do around here all day?"

That was the wrong thing for him to say. First of all, he was starting to overstep his bounds. I didn't like his tone. And, secondly, how dare he think that a house the size of ours, and a family the size of ours, didn't require constant, and I mean constant, work, to keep it running. I was going to work his little tail off.

He sensed that I was less than pleased with him. One thing I had always noticed about kids who were using drugs was that they were usually extremely sensitive people when they weren't high. I thought it might be the extra sensitivity that made them so vulnerable to all the hurts and stresses of life, causing them to turn to drugs for relief. But an old friend of mine, in recovery, explained that they were really just so self-centered that they thought that everything that people said or did was directed at them!

That made sense, I guess. If they had started getting high when they were young, and were still in that growth stage in which they considered themselves the center of the universe, then that would explain why everything was taken so personally.

Well, no matter what the theory, bottom line was that Kane had to learn to get through the day without using drugs, painful as it might be. And he needed to practice doing that without being exposed to a school full of 'salesmen'!

'Hearing' my silence and seeing the look on my face, he held up both hands in a gesture of backing off. "I'm sorry! You know best. My bad."

"You're right. I *do* know best. And I don't like your tone. And I want you to drop the street slang. It's not appropriate in my house."

I had stopped what I was doing while I said this, and it was designed to sound like a reprimand. His tone of voice was typical of his age group. The kids on TV talked like that to adults all the time. I just didn't like it, and I was not going to be spoken to like that. He got the point.

He nodded and was quiet for a minute. He changed his tone and went on. "So, what are we doing tomorrow?" he asked.

"Well, vacation is over for everybody. Tomorrow, we start you on your new life. So, if you have any ideas about leaving, tonight would be the time to go."

"I didn't say I wanted to leave," said Kane, a little confused.

"No, I know you didn't. I'm just saying. Just in case you can't hack daily life around here any better than you could at home, I just thought I'd let you know. We've been on vacation, and now it's back to business as usual. And it's dull and boring, like it is for everybody everywhere. So if you're looking for something else, this would be the time to leave. And if I don't see you in the morning, ready for daily life, remember...we love you, and we'll be pulling for you wherever you wind up."

Kane didn't expect me to say this. I took a chance. It was what came to my thoughts. I remembered reading about Chuck Dederich using a similar technique at Synanon, way back in the sixties. I knew that I couldn't watch this boy every minute. We had gotten him through a week, more or less, with everybody pitching in. But I couldn't do it alone, and I wasn't going to attempt a 'cat and mouse game' with him. If he was going to make it, he had to buy into it himself. I would allow him a few slip-ups; he'd need that. But, beyond that, he had to be working harder at this than he'd ever worked at anything else in his life… because I knew I would be!

Kane didn't say anything in response, so I decided to just keep things moving along. "Now, help me get supper ready."

"Again?! Didn't we just make supper *last* night?!"

I shot him a quick glance. I was about to give him a second reprimand on his attitude, when I noticed a smile on his face. He held up both hands. "I'm sorry! I was just kidding!"

"Here! Peel all ten pounds!" I tossed him the bag of potatoes.

"Yes, ma'am." He put his smile away, and I turned away from him so that he wouldn't see *mine*! This was going to be one, very challenging, young man!

16. Church

The first thing I did was to be sure that Kane got ten hours of sleep a night. Teenagers are supposed to get ten hours. So it was early to bed and early to rise. He was not allowed to watch TV or use any electronics within an hour of bedtime. The last hour was for getting ready for bed and reading. Sleep deprivation affects the brain and our ability to think and function. With the damage I was sure he'd already done to his brain, I figured we'd better give it every chance we could.

Secondly, I made sure I gave him the best quality food, low on sugar and white flour, and high on proteins, good fats, vegetables, fruit, and just a few whole grains. I knew that people with blood sugar problems, alcoholism among others, could not tolerate refined carbohydrates and were often grain intolerant. I also made sure that he drank a half-gallon of water daily.

Third, I made him wash himself every day and put on clean clothes, whether we were going out or not.

Then he had to exercise. We walked together every morning for a half-hour. And, every afternoon, I made him use the treadmill, or I took him over to the high school and had him jog the track while I walked or just watched him.

My plan, if he stayed on, was to have him evaluated by a medical doctor to see if he needed any special care. And I needed to find out what physical, academic, and psychological testing my sister had already had done on him. I realized that I had less information on this child than I had on most of the *students* that I'd taught!

Every day, he had to help me clean and pick up and do laundry. We went through the entire house, cleaning, repairing, and unpacking and reorganizing closets and shelves.

I taught him to do a few simple repairs, using tools that I knew how to use, and we did some painting and built some storage units. I gave him responsibility for making our lunches and cleaning up after all meals. When the girls came home, I made him read and study from any books I could find. I discovered that he had no religious training, so I had him read some of my favorites in philosophy and psychology, and we discussed it on our morning walk. Thinking was good for him.

For the first few weeks, he was allowed no social life of his own, except for family. And his entertainment time was kept to a minimum. Every day, I tried to find a 'large muscle' chore that would tire him out so that he would sleep. Snow was a blessing, since shoveling in the cold air exhausted him. It was hard for me to get a lot done, since I felt I had to keep a close eye on him, so the extra help was doubly welcome. I had to do my deskwork while I watched him out the window or after he went to sleep.

The good life seemed to agree with him. He did well. We also did a lot of talking and listening on our morning walks, and I used dinner hour as a kind of group therapy, asking the girls to share their day. Kane was routinely asked to talk about how he was feeling about his new routine - from being watched all the time, to having no peers to spend the day with, to not getting high.

We took him to church on Sunday, and my girls were in their glory, as other young ladies hinted around to be introduced to the new kid. I also introduced him to my church friends without going into detail as to why he was with us.

I took him over to the junior high one day to let him see the building and for us to get some teaching materials from my friends who taught his grade. I wasn't sure exactly what grade he'd place into, but I figured we'd better do something with math, at least.

And he and I took some days and went shopping. I had him help with the groceries and with carrying the heavy things when we went warehouse shopping. And a few times, I took him skating again and swimming at a local college, in place of his afternoon run. All in all, we got to know each other a little better, but I still couldn't read his moods, and I never knew what he was thinking. I was still always very apprehensive about what would happen next with him.

*　　　*　　　*　　　*　　　*　　　*　　　*　　　*

It was a few Sundays after New Year's, and he seemed kind of quiet that morning. I tried to speak to him about it, but he was distant and did his best to act as if it were nothing. Looking back, I realized that I should have just made us late to church and had the girls sit down with me and keep hacking at him until he talked. But my girls also had obligations at church, and it wasn't fair to hold them up.

I took Kane to a Sunday Bible class, taught by my friend Jim. It would keep Kane busy while the girls were occupied elsewhere. I sat in on the class with him. One of the students asked him who he was, and he nodded toward me and said, "I'm staying with my aunt."

At that point the other boy turned and recognized me and said, "Hi, Mrs. Wilson!"

The teacher was ready to start the class. He introduced us as visitors and said that Kane was from California. I had told Jim a little about Kane's background, but, of course, Jim wasn't going to make that public. Kane would take care of that...

I watched Kane throughout the class. He was polite and well behaved, but he seemed preoccupied and distant, as he had been at home. I was concerned.

After the Sunday School classes, we proceeded to the auditorium where our services were held. On the way, Kane asked to stop at the bathroom. I thought this was good idea. I didn't want both of us to have to walk out during the service. We then went in and took our seats.

Hannah sat next to me, as she always did. She would get bored during the service and work in a Bible Stories Workbook that we had just for church. I had always tried to make church a pleasant experience, taking into account ages and attention spans as the kids grew up. Of course, they were never allowed to play with toys or do anything that would disturb this very precious quiet time for anyone else, but I also didn't want them to associate church with unpleasantness. So I would bring church-related, quiet activities for them to do. Kane sat next to Hannah, with Dana on his far side.

The beginning of the service required that we stand and sit a lot. I was at the end of the pew, facing toward the minister, so I wasn't looking directly at the children. But during the first hymn, I glanced over, as mothers have a habit of doing, to be sure that they were all standing up. And I happened to catch Dana's eye.

She had an expression that said, 'Check this out', and glanced at her cousin. I looked at him, and he seemed fine to me. I shrugged my shoulders and looked perplexed, as if to say, 'What? I don't see anything.' She again gave me a look that said, 'Don't say I didn't warn you.' I looked more closely at Kane, and he concentrated harder on reading the hymnal. I figured I would give it a few minutes. None of us was going anywhere. We finally finished the hymn and sat down.

I tried to concentrate on the service, looking over at my nephew as inconspicuously as possible. I didn't want to cause a scene in church. And, besides, I couldn't see anything wrong. But my daughter was better tuned in to kids than I was, and I was not going to ignore her concern.

It was a short time until the next hymn and time to stand up again. This time Kane didn't stand up right away. I moved Hannah in front of me and switched places with her. Kane didn't seem to notice. I caught Dana's eye and motioned that she should help me stand him up. As soon as we both grabbed a hold of his arms, he seemed to come around and stood up on his own. I tried to look at his face, but he turned away, busying himself with trying to find his place in the hymnal.

I leaned over and whispered to him. "What's the matter with you?"

"Nothin'." He kept his head down and tried to follow along.

"Look at me." My mind was racing. He was with me all morning. When could he have taken anything, and where could he have gotten it? The bathroom. I let him go to the bathroom by himself. But what could he have taken? He hadn't been out of our sight since the incident with the police. We never had anything in the house. Where could he have gotten anything?

At least he was obedient. He finally looked me in the eye. Whenever I saw eyes like that my own started to burn and tear. He was definitely on something. I looked at Dana who had a, clearly readable, 'I-told-you-so' look on her face.

This was no place to interrogate him. I could either try to leave the service, taking a chance that he'd actually be able to walk, in what appeared to be an increasingly disabled condition, or I could take a chance that he would make it through the service somehow.

We sat back down again. By this time, Dana and I had to prop him up between us. He was becoming more and more groggy. Looking back, I guess I should have been more concerned. But I was so astounded that this was all happening that I just sat there. I was praying that we could get him out of there without too much embarrassment and trouble.

The service went on, and Kane dozed off. I could hear that his breathing was regular, so I wasn't too worried. He just seemed to have fallen asleep.

When the service was finished, several of our friends came over to greet us. I thought that they might be concerned about Kane, but they only commented that that was what *they* sometimes felt like doing during the service! When they left, and while Dana and I were trying to decide if we could carry Kane out to the car, my friend, Jim, the Sunday School teacher, came over with the minister.

"Tara, can we help?" the minister inquired.

"I don't know what he took. He seems to be breathing okay. I don't want to overreact, but I don't want to be irresponsible either."

"Listen, I have an idea. There are enough of us here, who stay for Fellowship, that we can buy you a little time and see what happens. Maybe he took something short acting, and it'll wear off in a little while. How about we move him over closer to the door into the other room? He can sleep on the pew. We'll take turns watching him."

"That sounds like a good idea," I said.

My minister and I took first watch, with my friend promising to return, with a cup of coffee, to relieve us.

"Tara, how long have you been taking care of this boy?"

"About three weeks. He ran away from home Christmas Day and showed up in New York that Monday night." Again, I ran briefly through the story of Kane's arrival. "He seemed to be doing so well, but I guess I just don't understand how to manage this whole thing."

"Well, if it makes you feel any better, nobody does. I'm going to see if I can get any information for you. There isn't much around for kids his age, but we might be able to find some kind of self-help group that he could attend."

"He's going to hate that."

"I know, but if he keeps messing up like this, with all the good care that I know you must be giving him, he's going to have no choice. You don't want to see him spiral down and eventually kill himself."

"I know you're right. I've been on his case twenty-four hours a day."

"I'm glad that you realize how important it is to monitor him. So many parents try to sweep this under the rug. Before they know it, the kids have lost years of growing up. It's hard enough raising kids through the normal crises of life, when they're going through them at the appropriate growth stages. To have to take a full-grown, young adult, and then to have to artificially re-create, like they do in the therapeutic communities, all those adolescent experiences, so that they can learn to deal with them, is a real challenge..."

"I know," I said. "It's like a child who never crawls. They miss forever all the neurological benefits that the body gets from the 'crawling stage'."

The minister looked up at that moment. "Here's Jim. I have to see a few people before they leave. I'll let you know what I find out."

"Thanks."

"How's he doing?" Jim came over with decaf and pastry. I took the decaf, but skipped the sugar. That was, unfortunately, my 'drug of choice', and I fought it as hard as Kane was going to have to fight his.

"He's still out," I said.

"Look, I'll sit with him. He knows me a little. Go take a break. If he wakes up, I'll talk with him until you get back."

"Thanks. I won't be long. I just have to touch base with a few people and let the girls know what's happening."

17. Confrontation

I returned in a few minutes. I didn't feel comfortable leaving Kane alone for too long. I sat down in the pew with him. Jim was sitting in the pew in front, turning to face both of us. We sat in silence for a few minutes. All of sudden, I felt overwhelmed. I could feel the tears welling up in my eyes. Jim noticed right away.

"Are you okay? He's going to be all right, you know. This is not all that uncommon."

"I know," I replied. "I've just been working so hard with him, and I guess I feel like a failure every time this happens."

"Every time? How long has this been going on?"

"He's been getting high for two years that he admits to. This is the second time since he's been with me."

"I see. Well, how often was he getting high at home?"

"I don't know, probably every day, from little things that he said, and that my sister said."

"And how long has he been with you?"

I could see what he was going for. He was trying to make me feel better. "I know. He seems to be doing a little better. But the problem is still there, big time."

"Of course it is, Tara. You've worked with this before. You're letting the fact that it's your own family get in the way here. You know that a drug habit is often unstoppable, and, at best, it takes a long, long time to reverse it. When was the last time he got high?"

"New Year's Eve," I said.

"Oh, he and the rest of the population!" I looked at him. This wasn't helping. "C'mon. Give yourself a break! He's young. And he's been clean for three weeks. I'd say those are positive signs."

"I know. I guess I'm just tired. It keeps you under such a tension, not knowing when or where they're going to lose it, and what's going to happen to them."

"You really love him, don't you?" Jim said.

"Of course! He's my nephew! He's a complete stranger, but he's my nephew."

"But you've started to bond with him."

"Well, we spend every waking moment together. Sometimes it feels more like drill sergeant and draftee." I tried to make a joke, but my heart was still heavy.

I reached down and pulled Kane's hair back from his face. He really should have a haircut. I remembered that a lot of guys used long hair to maintain their drug image. It gave them a kind of 'wild thing-little boy-vulnerable rebel' look, and a lot of guys wound up hiding behind it emotionally. I didn't totally understand it, but I could see that it would be appealing to enablers. I wanted to be really careful that I didn't fall into that trap. So many women never outgrow that teenage girl thing where you just want to mother these adorable, pathetic, Peter Pan types. I wanted this child to grow up. He needed my help in learning to *not need* me, or anybody *else* for that matter.

I pulled one last, stubborn shank of hair back off his face and noticed that it was wet. I looked up at Jim and back down at Kane. I put my finger to my lips, to signal Jim not to say anything.

I went on. "I just don't know if living with me is good for him. If he keeps doing this, I'm obviously not doing a good job. They're not going to let me keep him at home without schooling, and I know that if he can't handle church, he'll never make it in school. I care about him a lot, but I'm not sure he cares enough about himself, or about me for that matter, for me to make a difference. I really don't want to have to put him out… unless of course that's what he wants. Maybe he doesn't want to be with me, and that's why he's pulling stunts like this."

I knew he was listening, and I was hoping that, even if he were still a little high, he would get my message. I knew that I was manipulating him a little, but I was hoping to make some kind of impact...anything.

Finally, I motioned to Jim to make an excuse and leave me alone with him. Jim took the hint. "Well, Tara, I need to speak to a few people. It's getting late. Give me a call if you need me."

Jim left, and I sat quietly with Kane for a while. I expected him to lift his head then, but he didn't. I guessed that he was too embarrassed. I knew that he was awake.

Finally, I, too, got up and went over to the door. Jim was waiting there, knowing that something was up. I whispered, "I think he's awake. He just needs to pull himself together."

Sure enough, a moment later, I could see Kane lift himself up on his forearms and then push himself to a sitting position. He didn't look up. He just grasped the pew in front of him, with both hands, and rested his head on his arms.

Dana came up at that moment to see how things were going.

"Jim, would you keep an eye on him? And, Dana, would you get his jacket and get him ready to leave? I'll go get Hannah."

I had to get out of there. I could feel my emotions building. I had already expressed my sadness and my frustration, but now that I knew he was okay, I was getting really angry. I got my youngest, said my goodbyes, and went back in to help Dana.

Dana and Jim already had him standing up and were making their way to the back door. I followed after them, and then said I would go ahead with Hannah and bring the car around. They sat him back down in the back of the church while they waited for us to return.

*   *   *   *   *   *   *   *

We lived just a short distance from our church, so the ride home was brief. I said nothing the whole way. I could feel Dana looking over at me, but she didn't say anything until we were alone again.

When we got home, I gave Kane instructions to wait for me in the living room. He was, by then, able to make it on his own.

"Sit on the couch and don't get up!" I told him.

I watched him follow my directions and then went into the kitchen to sit for a few minutes before dealing with him. Dana made sure he did what he was supposed to. Kane had come to trust her and, apparently, didn't mind her helping him. Then she came in to see me.

"Mom, what's the matter with you?"

"Why? It's been a normal morning!"

"You don't usually get so upset with us."

"Uh, Dana, Kane is hardly 'us'."

"You know what I mean, Mom. Surely David and Danny must have pulled stunts like this when they were Kane's age. Why are you so angry?"

"Your brothers, at their very worst, never behaved like this. I just can't believe he did that. And in church! I am… so...furious."

"But why? You know what he's dealing with. He's actually been doing okay, Mom. I see kids in school. They are stoned every single day. Without fail."

"Weren't you embarrassed, Dana? Don't you think, after all the time this family has spent on him, that he owed us more than that?"

"Mom, he's just a kid…a screwed-up kid. You know he's really unstable now. If you were worried about appearances, I wouldn't think you'd take him to church. And besides, church is supposed to be for people like Kane, people who have problems and who are working really hard to solve them. Mom, you know that he's working hard on this, don't you? He's really trying. I know he is."

"I know. I know that everything you're saying is right. But why am I feeling so angry?" I paused, then teased, "C'mon, Dana, tell me!"

"Mom!"

"I'm only kidding. I don't know myself." I sat and thought for a minute. Dana was right. I couldn't confront him with my anger when I didn't know why I felt that way. And then I got a very strange thought, and I said it aloud, "I wonder if it's *his* anger."

"What?"

"I wonder if it's *his* anger I'm feeling. Something has been wrong with him all morning. I was thinking that we should've confronted him before church. But I didn't want you girls to sacrifice again for Kane, so I let it ride. I wonder if I'm sensing his anger about something. Sort of a 'contact... low'." I played with that thought for a few minutes. Then, I said, "Okay, Dana. I'm ready. Let's go."

"Are you sure, Mom? I wouldn't want you to lose your temper with him. He could use that as an excuse to go get loaded. People like Kane do that."

"No, Dana. I'm okay. Go set up two of the dining room chairs facing each other."

Dana did as I asked, and I took a deep breath and followed her. Kane had been slumped back on the couch, but he sat up when we came into the room.

"Kane, how are you feeling? Are you up to a little talk?" I asked him.

"Yes, ma'am. But – But can I try to explain?"

I looked at Dana and then back at Kane and then back at Dana. I wasn't expecting that. And I wasn't sure I wanted to listen to another of his whiny excuses about how he was sorry and how he couldn't help himself. I knew all that. What I wanted to find out was *why* he couldn't help himself. But Dana seemed to be on his side, so I figured I could wait. I sat down on one of the two chairs that Dana had set up.

"Okay, Kane. Shoot!"

"I was thinking that church was going to be really boring, so I had this pill that I got the night of the party..."

"What party?" I interrupted.

"New Year's."

"You've been holding drugs in this house for three weeks?" Oh, good, no trouble holding on to my anger through *this* discussion.

"It was only one pill. I swear I don't have any more," he said.

"Go on."

"It was supposed to just mellow me out a little. I just figured it would help me get through the hour without being restless."

"But you've been clean for three weeks, so it had a bigger impact on your body than you expected."

"Yeah. That's what I was thinking."

"Okay, come over here, and sit down in front of me."

He could tell that I was not thrilled with his story, and he was a little hesitant to comply with my directive. He looked up at Dana, and she nodded to him that it would be all right. He got up slowly and made his way to the chair.

"Here are the rules," I said. "I am really, really angry with you, and I am going to let you know how I feel. But no matter what I say, I still love you and care about you very deeply. When I'm done, you can say whatever you want to me. You can say anything you want, as long as we're sitting here in these two chairs. I can lie. You can lie. You can use whatever language you want to express yourself, and so can I. But after it's over, we go back to the house rules. When we leave here, everything that was said is forgotten, by both of us, and we go back to the relationship we had before, okay?" He looked confused but nodded. "Didn't you do this in the lock-up?" I asked.

"I don't know. I don't remember."

"You don't remember? It was only last summer."

"I don't remember because I was 'out of it' most of the time."

"They gave you drugs?" I couldn't believe what I was hearing.

"They didn't give 'em to us. We just got 'em. From the other kids."

I looked at Dana and rolled my eyes, and then went on. "Okay, one more thing. I will never lay a hand on you, no matter how angry I seem. And you can't touch me in anger."

" 'No physical violence', right? I remember that."

Dana spoke up then. "Mom, do you want me to leave?"

"No, I want you to stay. Kane trusts you. Right, Kane? And I think someone else should be here. But I would appreciate it if you would just listen and not join in. This is our conversation. All right with you, Kane?"

He nodded.

"All right, then." I took another deep breath. I hated this. It was a game. I hated games. But he needed me to do this. As usual, 'If it's easy for the mom...'

I started slowly, in a very nurturing voice. "Kane, you know, I like it when you get high. Seeing you loaded and helpless, it makes me feel needed."

I had really caught him by surprise. "What?" he exclaimed.

"Yeah, when you're all bleary-eyed and can hardly stand up, I feel like you really need a mommy. Your mom must have loved having you that way for two years. It must have been like the best time of her life." I said this as sincerely as I could, carefully avoiding any tone of sarcasm.

"What are you, nuts? My mom hated what I was doing. She threw me out of the house when I came home loaded. She never wanted to be anybody's 'mommy'." He paused. And I waited. "I'm only thirteen years old..." He took a deep breath and his eyes started to water, as more anger crept into his voice. "...And she let them put me in a lock-up. I *hated* that place! ...And I hate *her*! ...And she hates *me*."

Well that didn't take much effort. I was pretty sure that someone had done this with him before. He was definitely holding a lot of anger, but he was already starting to let it out.

"Now, Kane. How could your mother not like you? All that excitement with the police and the courts and your acting tough in front of their friends... Remember the Christmas party when you got drunk and caused a scene? You know a mom's life is pretty routine and boring. We live for this stuff. I'm sure she loved being your mommy." I let just a hint of sarcasm slip in, just to keep it real.

He was getting into it. I could feel the rage building. "She was never my '*mommy*'! She was the biggest bitch going. And my father was no better. They deserved each other. They never even took care of me when I was sick."

"Sick? You call what you're doing 'being sick'? Yeah, right!" I half-laughed. I was starting my adversary role here.

"I WAS SICK! I was. I needed them, and they were too damn busy with their work and their parties. And when I got into their liquor cabinet and was pukin' on the floor, they left me in it! And then they made me clean it up the next morning!"

"Aw, poor baby." Okay, we're getting near the edge here.

"YOU DON'T CARE EITHER! I thought you cared about me!"

He stood up to leave. But I had seated him with his knees in between mine. So, although I had promised that I wouldn't touch him, it was a little awkward for him to walk away.

"Sit." I said it in a normal tone of voice, but he was still so wrapped up in his emotions that he didn't hear me. "SIT!" He looked down at me, as if hearing that for the first time. "It's only a game. Sit down." He seemed to pull himself back together and sat down again.

I was relieved. I knew I was playing with fire here, and I wasn't really good at it. I had only played this game myself a couple of times. If he split before I was finished, I could do more harm than good.

He rubbed his face with his hands, and I gave him a minute to compose himself.

"Okay, look at me again," I continued.

"I don't want to do this anymore."

"We're not finished." I made it clear by my tone that this was not over. "You owe me big time. You embarrassed me today." It was time for a new spin. "How dare you pull a stunt like that in front of my friends? How dare you embarrass me in front of nice people?" As I spoke, I realized what I was saying. Thank you, God.

"Oh, what! ...and I'm not nice people!?" He was catching on to the game. Now I was sure they had done this with him in therapy.

"No, you little piece of scum. I take you into my house, and I treat you like one of my kids, and you pay us back by getting loaded in church!? Like you couldn't sit through one hour? No, you're not nice people. You're an embarrassment."

"Now you sound like my mother! You're just worried about how you look to other people. You don't care about me. All you care about is yourself."

Great! Just what I was going for! I had him now... And now for another spin!

"Don't compare me to your mother!" I shouted. "Your mother is a piece of crap. You're right. She always *was* out for herself. She never should have had kids. You were just a stumbling block in her career."

"Don't talk about my mother!"

"She's my sister. I can talk about her any way I want to. I've known her longer than you have. What do you know? She's one cold woman. She never loved anybody."

"YES, SHE DID! SHE LOVED ME!"

"She didn't love you. You said so yourself. She only loved herself...and maybe your father. Once.

"She loved me. It was my fault. I started screwin' up. She couldn't handle it. She didn't know what to do. She and my dad would fight about me all the time. Once I started gettin' high, I just couldn't stop."

I didn't want him to go down that road. Talking about his drug use was not going to help him. We had to get out some more of this emotional garbage. A lot of this was just 'adolescence stuff' that he had thrown out of whack by introducing chemicals into the mix. I was sure that his drug use had not done much to help his parents' stressful married life, but that was not the issue here. The issue was to help him deal with all the thousands of emotional ups and downs of adolescence, and adult life to follow, without trying to even them out with drugs. I kept going. We were both yelling at each other at this point.

"Listen, if your mother loved you, why isn't she here? Why didn't she call and demand to see you or take you home? Huh? Answer me that! It's been about a month for God's sake."

"Because... Because... Damn you!'"

Bingo. We have a winner.

Kane covered his face with both his hands and tears flowed freely. We could both feel the catharsis. I let him just sit for a few minutes. I wanted him to feel the relief of really feeling his emotions.

Then we would sort them out.

Finally, we both pulled ourselves together. Dana brought us both a box of tissues then backed away again.

I continued. "Can you talk?" He nodded his head, still trying to catch his breath. "Do you know what just happened?"

He nodded his head again. He was a smart boy and, as a young child, had been very verbal.

"I love my parents… but I hate them at the same time."

"Okay…" I encouraged him.

"I feel bad for what I've been doing… But I hate that they didn't help me."

"They didn't know how," I explained.

"I know. But I thought that parents knew everything. I thought they just didn't wanna help me. I thought that they just didn't care enough."

"They do care. We all do."

He looked up toward the corner of the room, tears streaming down his face. "I know you care. What I said before, I didn't mean..."

"Hey, I told you. It's a game." I reminded him.

He looked down at his lap. He was avoiding eye contact with me.

"Kane, why aren't you looking at me?"

He kept looking down. "I'm too embarrassed."

"Why, because of church? It's over." I knew that that wasn't it. He still hadn't asked the key question. "Kane, give it up. You know what's screwin' you up. Put it into words. Right now."

"You said it already."

"What did I say?" This was harder than I thought it was going to be. If he didn't spill, I'd have to start all over again. "C'mon. You can do it."

"If- if my parents still love me, why *haven't* they come to look for me?" He completely broke down again.

Finally.

"Kane."

"Yeah?" The tears were still flowing down his face. Hard as this was for him, this had to be so much easier at home, with family, than in some 'junior prison'.

"Kane, do you trust me?" I asked.

"Yeah. I guess so." He wiped his eyes with his hands.

"Do you trust that I know what's best for you, and that I'm willing to go the distance to help you straighten things out for yourself?"

"I don't know if anybody can do that," he said quietly.

"Well, maybe not. And maybe I won't be able to either. But do you trust that I'm giving it my best shot? And that everything I do for you is well thought out and in your best interests?"

"Yeah. Yeah. I do. I really appreciate what you're doing. I know I'm a..."

"Hey!" I held up my hand to silence him. "You're a kid with a problem. That's all. And there are thousands of you. I'm sorry, but you're not all that special."

He looked at me and caught the twinkle in my eye. He was still upset. I couldn't decide whether or not it was a good time to tell him about his parents. I decided that maybe he did need to know something. I was taking a chance.

"Kane, your parents love you and care about you. Both of them. The reason they haven't talked to you is because... I wouldn't let them."

Kane looked at me in amazement. I had to decide what spin I wanted to put on this information. He was extremely vulnerable. Whatever I said to him now would have great impact. I needed to use his relationship with his parents, or lack thereof, to further his recovery, if we dared to call it that.

I decided to say nothing more. I would let him ponder the idea, and let him ask me questions when he was ready.

"C'mon, kids," I said, finally. "Let's get some lunch." We both pushed back our chairs and Kane helped Dana put them back at the dining room table, wiping his eyes on his sleeve as he went.

As they headed toward the kitchen, Dana put her hand on her cousin's back, giving him a gentle pat. "You 'done good', cuz."

I could hear a little smile in Kane's voice as he replied. "And I thought Hannah was tough!"

I chuckled to myself. I guessed that his relief, at not being punished for church, canceled out his anger at me, for having put him through all that. We called Hannah for lunch, and nothing more was said about the 'game'. And, until Kane brought it up again, I wasn't going to say anything more on the subject of his parents.

18. About the Parents

Kane was really good that week. We followed the routine that I had set up for him, and he didn't give me any trouble at all. He had a lot to think about.

One night, about a week or so later, he came into my room at bedtime. I was reading in bed, and he asked if we could talk. I patted the bedcovers, and he sat down at the far end. His back was to me.

I had taught all my kids to look people in the eye when people spoke to them, so I had to ask, "Kane, are you ashamed of something?"

"No, ma'am."

"Did you do something wrong?"

"No, ma'am."

"You got 'bad eyes'?"

"No!" At that he finally turned around. He had been working so hard to stay clean that he was beginning to resent any implication on my part that he wasn't.

"That's better. It's polite to look people in the eye when you talk to them."

"Oh, sorry." He shifted his position so that he was facing me. Then he added, "I'm never gonna learn everything."

"You're doin' all right," I reassured him. "Now what did you want to talk about?"

"Well, can I ask you about my parents?" I knew this was coming. I changed my position. I knew that he'd be able to tell from my body language that he was on thin ice. He changed his tone and spoke more quietly. "It's okay. I guess I don't really wanna know."

"No... Go ahead and ask. I don't want you using your imagination to make things worse than they are, and getting yourself messed up again."

"Can you just tell me how they're doing and... and whether they ever ask about me?"

"What do *you* think is going on?"

"I don't know." He got off the bed and started to pace back and forth. My son used to do that, and it made me dizzy, trying to follow him while he talked. But I knew he needed a tension release, and it was better than other things. So I just closed my eyes, when I could get away with it, so it didn't make me sick. "I'm just wondering if they're divorced yet or if they maybe got back together..." He thought a moment, then added, "...like that's ever gonna happen. And I just wonder if they ever worry about me. I don't want them to be worried. They don't deserve that, after what I put them through. They... they do know I'm okay, right?"

"Are you okay?"

"You know what I mean. They know I'm here, right? And that I'm tryin' to clean up?"

"Look, could you sit down? You're making me really nauseous walking back and forth like that."

"Yeah, sure." He sat down on the bed again.

Now, I had just talked to his mom and dad a night or two before. I had e-mailed them to set up a time when I could talk to both of them at once. I also wanted it to be at a time when I could have the girls keep Kane busy elsewhere.

I told them about my encounter game with Kane, and how he had gotten high behind his feelings about them. They wanted to rush right out and see him.... both of them. Although I thought that was a great sign, I nixed that pretty quickly. *They* needed a lot more time, and *he* was still on the edge. I was not going to waste all the work we had done at our end. And besides, at that point, he still wasn't sure how he felt about them. I wouldn't want them to get all the way out here and then have him take off because he couldn't handle the reunion.

My sister and brother-in-law were working very hard to work things out. They both agreed that their workaholism was a disaster for their family life. And they both agreed that they had a responsibility to carry through the family life that they had started, boring or not, basically to save their son's life. I took every opportunity to remind them of the seriousness of what Kane had been doing. Best of all, they had started in a counseling group, together with other families that had kids acting out with drugs. It wasn't always that the drug use had anything to do with the parents, but it gave the parents a common ground for mutual support. Drug use by a family member usually affects the whole family.

I just had to decide now what part of my conversation with his parents I needed to share with Kane. "Kane, your parents have a lot of work to do." He hung his head. I knew what he was thinking, and that he had taken my comment the wrong way. So I went on to clarify. "They need to work on their marriage, on their parenting skills, and on taking adult responsibility for you and your behavior." At this, he looked up, and I could see a little glimmer of hope in his eyes. "I don't know how they're going to do with all that, but, until they show some promise, and some progress, I don't want them to come near you."

"Do they ask about me?"

"If I agreed to call them every day, they would gladly pay my phone bill. But they don't need to know every detail of your struggle. You need some space. It's bad enough you have to go through this here, in front of your cousins and me. You don't need to deal with your parents' frustration and guilt while you're trying to clean up. At least here, we don't expect much from you. So, when you screw up, we just roll with it, and let you pick yourself up and try again."

I was totally serious, but Kane stared at me with his mouth open. "Are you runnin' a game on me again?"

"No, why?" I wasn't sure what he was getting at.

"'Cause you guys go berserk when I screw up. You expect more from me than the Pope, for Christ's sake! 'Roll with it'?!... If this is your idea of rolling with it, Aunt Tara, I'd hate to see what happens when you get *really* mad!"

I just sat and looked him in the eye. I almost laughed, but thought better of it. "You're right." I said. "You don't *ever* want to see that!" He just sat quietly then for a few minutes. I could see the wheels turning. But I was way ahead of him. "Kane?"

"Ma'am?"

"If you screw up again, you're not going back to your parents."

"What do you mean?"

"Just in case you were thinking about it, you're not gonna get home by getting in trouble here. By staying *out* of trouble, you may earn a visit from your parents, or even a chance to go *home* for a visit... *if* your parents get their act together. But getting in *more* trouble is not going to get you anywhere... except maybe back into the lock-up."

"I'd never get in trouble on purpose."

"I hope not. But I want you to understand something. You're young, and I've taken responsibility for you, so a lot of people are cutting you a lot of slack around here. But you know what you've done, and where you've been. Just because nobody's throwing it in your face every day doesn't mean it's forgotten. Did you ever see that old movie, The Truman Show?" I knew that his mom had always been a big movie buff.

"Yeah, I did. I remember that."

"Well, you're living on a movie set here, in my house, with my family. You step off the set, and you're in the real world. And in the real world, you're a runaway, you have a record with the local police, you've got a record at home, for drugs and petty theft, and so on and so on. And your parents, much as they love you, could actually lose custody of you, since they can't seem to control your behavior. Do you understand what I'm saying?"

"Yes, ma'am."

"Good, because I run my house for my children. My children do not deserve to live in a lock-up or under harsh rules and unrelenting discipline. They are growing up and learning to live under their *own* discipline. If the rules, that I make for them, prove to be too loose for you, and you keep getting into trouble, you know what has to happen."

"I'm outta here."

"And into something more restrictive...not back out on the street. You're welcome to submit to my authority, just as my kids do, because I'm the adult in charge. But I'm not going to institutionalize my home just because that's what you need." He nodded his head. "Of course, I will continue to discipline you every time you break the rules, for as long as you can take living here."

"Got it."

"Go to bed. And if you're gone in the morning, remember we love you and always will."

Kane said good night, and I prayed that I'd said the right things to him. Only time would tell.

19. School

It was the beginning of February, and I was running out of things for Kane to do. We had done as much to the house as we could do in the winter. I had started studying with him every day. The school had set up a home schooling program for him and, at my request, was able to get him some tutors. He was a good reader, and his math seemed up to par. He was also doing well in general. He was pretty open about what he was thinking and feeling. He knew the score with his parents and had made his peace with that situation. But I was beginning to feel that, if we were going to get him back up to speed completely, I was going to have to enroll him in school. I knew that I was asking for trouble, but I also knew that if he couldn't handle the normal world of an average teenager, he wasn't going to make the kind of progress that he needed to make. My brother-in-law, my husband's brother, told me later that this was what was known as 'precipitating a crisis'. Good name for it.

I made arrangements for Kane to meet with his new guidance counselor one afternoon in February. My plan was for us to go in about an hour before school let out. He would talk with the counselor for the first half-hour, while I filled in the enrollment forms and met briefly with the principal (an old friend of mine and my current boss). Then I would join Kane and the counselor to make sure that she understood the situation. Then we would try to see some of his teachers before they left for the afternoon.

Kane was very nervous and was very quiet on the way to the school. When we finally got to the parking lot and were about to get out of the car, he turned to me and said, "Wait."

I stopped and closed the car door again. I knew that he was very apprehensive, and I wanted to hear what he had to say. "I don't think this is a good idea. I don't think I can handle this."

"I don't think so, either," I said.

"Then why are you taking me?!"

"Kane, remember I told you that I think things through very carefully before I do them?"

"Yeah?"

"Well, if I keep you home this whole year, you might have to go into the eighth grade again next year. You're already too mature for the eighth grade. By next year, you'll feel very uncomfortable." I knew that he would like that I said that he was mature. I continued, "Also, you've been doing really well with your recovery. But I'm keeping an eye on you all the time. You need to see if you can be trusted on your own a little."

"But school? Look at this place. It's huge. I'm never gonna be able to stay out of trouble here."

"You're going to have to learn how. And that's why you need to get started. The longer you avoid dealing with people and everyday situations, whether it's by doing drugs or hiding out at home, the further behind you'll be in growing up.

"There are plenty of kids here who are doing what you've been doing. They're a mess, and they're getting further and further behind every day. But there are more kids here who are learning to deal with life, learning from each other, from their counselors, from their teachers, and letting every day and every situation be a learning experience. I'm going to set you up with as many safeguards as I can. But I know you; you can outwit every one of them. Your biggest challenge, Kane, is yourself. You've got to do this. You have to buy in and outwit yourself." He took a deep breath. "Ready?" I asked.

"No, but you're not gonna let me get out of this, so let's do it."

He started to get out of the car, but something made me reach out and pull him back in. "Wait a minute."

"What?"

"You can do this. You have to do this. You have to beat it, out here, where the stresses and the temptation are the greatest. It's not going to be easy for either of us. In fact, if it makes you feel any better, I'm guessing that this is going to bring us a lot of new problems. But, as your grandmother says, 'Kids do things, so that adults can teach and correct them'. You need to keep moving forward. You have a lot of catching up to do...without relying on escapes. 'You catch my drift?"

"No gettin' high in school."

"You have this wonderful way of summarizing a concept."

*　　　*　　　*　　　*　　　*　　　*　　　*　　　*

We went to the guidance office first. The young woman who was to be Kane's counselor was new, and I hadn't met her. Right away, I was apprehensive. I was afraid that she wouldn't be savvy enough to handle his problems. We made introductions all around, and I excused myself to go fill out paperwork and to fill in my principal on the 'gift' that I was bringing him.

When I had completed my 'to do' list, I returned to the guidance office and knocked on the counselor's door. They were just finishing their discussion, and she welcomed me in.

"Kane has been telling me a little bit about himself, his interests, and his old school," Miss Williams began.

"Has he told you *everything* about himself?" I stressed the word 'everything' and looked at Kane as I asked the question.

He looked up sheepishly from his lap, looked me in the eye, and said, "No..."

We didn't have a lot of time, so I decided to lay out the ground rules myself first. "Miss Williams, Kane's relationship with you needs to be spelled out very clearly. He has been in some very serious trouble, and he and I have been working very hard to save his young hide. He and I just spent ten minutes in the car discussing the tremendous risk we're taking by putting him in school here. I need to know everything that goes on with him. And I need to know about any problems immediately. You can't have confidentiality with him from me. Anything he tells you needs to be repeated to me."

"Oh," she interrupted, "I don't know if I can do that."

"Oh, you won't be doing it. Kane will be doing it, on the phone, from your office, with you standing here. Don't worry. He knows that it has to be like this. Right, Kane? Tell this lady what you need from her."

Kane looked over at me. I nodded my head, and he began. When I gave Kane the floor, I expected to have to prod him along to get him to tell this counselor what she had to do for him. But for the next few minutes, I got the surprise of my life.

"Miss Williams, my aunt's right. I'm not a kid any more. You can't let me come in here and make excuses to you and whine about my life and try to get out of things.

"I've been on the streets for two years. I've been doing a lot of drinkin' and druggin'. And sometimes both at the same time." He paused and looked at me. Then he went on. "One time, I was so out of it that I decided to kill myself, and I almost did." He took a deep breath. That part was still hard for him.

"I'm smart, so I was able to waste a lot of time in school, but my aunt says she doesn't think I'm too far behind. You've gotta put me in the hardest classes you have." He stopped to think. Neither the counselor nor I said a word. I was so impressed with him.

"I've been in trouble with the police, and I was in a rehab lock-up for three months last summer. I've also been in trouble with the police here, and Officer Link... you know him?" The counselor nodded. "Well, he was really nice to me, but I know he won't be so nice the next time. I also stole money from my parents to get out here.

"My parents are probably getting a divorce..." He looked over at me, but I didn't give him any more information in that regard. "I know it's not my fault, but it sure felt like it, and my aunt has been working with me to get me through that...which is why I want to tell you that what my aunt says, for you to do, is okay with me. I can't hold guilt. I get off behind it. If I come and tell you something and ask you not to tell my aunt, you can't listen to me. I'm good. I can make you feel real sorry for me. And I can con most people. You gotta be tough with me or I'm not gonna make it here." He paused and then added, "And I have to make it here."

He seemed to be finished. I looked at the counselor and waited for her to say something. But Kane spoke again, this time to me. "Was that good, Aunt Tara?"

I wasn't going to tell him that he impressed the heck out of me. "Yeah, Kane. That was fine."

I turned to the counselor again. "He's still getting high. He's cleaned up a lot, which makes everything he takes that much more potent. I'm *very* concerned about him being here. But as I explained to him, he has to learn to deal with the real world... and without using drugs to *do* that. I'm hoping to speak to each of his teachers to let them know what to watch for with him, but you're going to have to be our key person. Can we count on you?"

Miss Williams had listened attentively to both Kane and me. She had a very determined and stern look on her face, and I was afraid that she wasn't going to give us the 'non-traditional' support that we needed. But the day was full of surprises.

"Mrs. Wilson, I have been thinking about this case since you spoke to me on the phone. I was wondering if I could handle it. You see, I used to have a little brother. He died of a drug overdose when he was fifteen. My parents never saw it coming. I was away at school and had no idea. Even if I did, though, I wouldn't have known what to do then. When I became a counselor here, I had hoped to prevent other kids from winding up in serious trouble... or like my brother.

"As it turns out, most kids who are really into drugs, at least at this age, never talk to counselors about it. Most of my work here has been with testing and schedules, little adolescent spats between classmates, and complaints about teachers. But, actually, I haven't minded, because, you see, I haven't seen a lot of success in my profession with drug addiction. I find it most discouraging."

I didn't think that she should be talking like this in front of Kane. The last thing that he needed was to be depressed about his situation. I was about to say something, but she continued.

"But I have to say, I am most impressed by this young man and by what you are asking of me. I have a good feeling about this. Both of you seem to know exactly what you need to do, and I would be proud to be involved in this boy's success. And I can tell you right now that he's got the best chance of anyone I've ever seen. I will do anything that you think will be helpful."

Well, *now* I was impressed with the *counselor*. Maybe she was going to be okay for Kane after all. I just wanted to get a few more things straight. "Kane, wait outside."

"Yes, ma'am." Kane got up and went into the waiting area. I watched to see that he sat where he was supposed to. Then I told the secretary that he was not to leave the area for any reason and asked her to let me know immediately if he did.

Then I spoke to the counselor. "You seem to understand that there is a lot at stake here. I hope you'll honor my requests, as absurd as they may seem to be at times. If this doesn't work out, I'll need to home-school him again. But I really want to try to put him in some positions where he has to stand up for himself and reject his old lifestyle. He's come a long way in the past few weeks. But, even though he's still young, I'm not so naive as to believe that a little TLC and some conscientious parenting are going to turn him around. But you know, better than I, that there just aren't enough 'beds' for all the kids that need therapeutic care. And, even if you can get your kid in, it costs a fortune if your insurance doesn't cover it. I love this kid, but we don't have a lot of options."

"I meant what I said in front of Kane. I'll help you. He reminds me a lot of my brother," said the counselor.

"You know, I hate to say this, but I hope that won't be a problem. I think you'll probably agree that he's adorable. Every girl in this school is going to want to mother him. And every boy is going to want to see him thrown out. The last thing he needs is adults who think he's 'cute'."

"Don't worry. I'm new here. But I have ten years experience in the field. A lot of it was in group homes and special schools for young people at risk. I've heard it all and cut through most of it. I have an excellent 'crap detector'."

"That's great! You've made me feel much better. By the way, what did Kane talk to you about before I came in?"

"Ah, you're testing me, aren't you?"

"Yes, I am."

"Well, you would have been very proud of him. He actually told me, on his own, most of what he told me in front of you. Actually, I think he'd been rehearsing it. He hadn't mentioned the suicide attempt though. I don't know whether he forgot it the first time or if he just needed you here in order to get through that part."

"Yeah, that was hard for him. That happened the night that he came to me. When the reality of what he'd done finally set in, I thought we might lose him again. He could barely face himself, let alone a family of near-strangers. His family has been living in California, and we hadn't seen him in years." I paused then. I was checking the time. I could hear the students passing in the halls.

Miss Williams also glanced at the clock. "Why don't we bring Kane in for a wrap-up," she suggested, "and then I've taken the liberty of asking his team teachers to stay for a brief meeting after school. That way, everybody is on the same page when he comes in tomorrow."

"That was a great idea. Thank you."

"I'll get him." She went to the door and motioned to Kane to come in. "Take a seat, Kane." He sat back down where he had been. "I've just told your aunt that I've arranged a team meeting, with all your teachers, in a few minutes. This way, you'll be able to introduce yourself, and they'll be expecting you tomorrow."

If Kane was upset by that, he was hiding it. He knew that he'd be starting the next day, but he hadn't expected to meet all his teachers at once.

He nodded, but didn't say anything.

I looked at the floor and sat still. The counselor picked up immediately that something was amiss. I turned and looked at Kane and didn't say a word. He knew what I was waiting for.

"It's okay. I'm cool with it," he said, unconvincingly. I continued to stare at him. He wasn't being honest. "Okay. I didn't expect that. What do I say? How many people will be there?"

We answered all his questions, and I was finally satisfied that he was indeed 'okay' with this. I told him that I would do all the talking if he wanted, and that I would invite him to add on if he felt like it. Or he could just jump in if he had something to say. He nodded in agreement, and we left for the meeting.

20. First Lesson

When we got home, I put Kane to work cleaning the downstairs bathroom, and I went upstairs to call my friend.

"Hi, it's me Tara."

"Hi, Tara. How's it going? I haven't heard from you in weeks. Are you still babysitting?"

"Oh, yes. It's been a real adventure."

"Well, fill me in. What's been happening?"

I gave her a brief rundown on the events of the past weeks and on Kane's progress, or lack thereof, as I saw it. "But I have to tell you what he did today."

"Uh oh. Bad?"

"No, not really. Although he's scrubbing the bathroom for it."

"Oh, one of those. My kids always hated that. Even though it was always part of our cleaning chores, somehow, when they got it as a punishment, it seemed worse than other punishments. So what did he do?"

I told her about enrolling him in school and about our conversation with the guidance counselor and how the counselor set up this meeting with the teachers. "So, we get up there and, of course, these are all my colleagues, and they can't believe I'm using my year off to nursemaid this kid."

"As can't I. Go on."

"Well, we sit down, and I know Kane is really nervous, but I lay out the facts just like I told him I would. We ask the teachers that, if they suspect any drug or alcohol use, or even if he just doesn't act right or behave himself, to call me immediately. Then I ask Kane if he wants to add anything, and he's really polite, and he thanks them for taking the time to meet with us. He tells them he's really trying to clean up his act and to do what he has to do.

"Now he's sitting there, looking like Joe Teenager, but being really polite and obedient, and one of the teachers says, '*I have a few questions and concerns. I wonder if we can ask Kane to step outside for a few minutes.*'

"So I turn to him and tell him to go out in the hall and close the door. He gets right up and does as he's told.

"Then the teacher, who had spoken up says, '*He's such a sweetheart! It's hard to believe that this polite, adorable boy could possibly have been in so much trouble.*' I looked over at the counselor, who was already looking at me, and we both assured her that, indeed, we were not making this up. Somebody else was concerned that, with a child who was so polite and quiet, it was going to be easy to miss him, in a big class, sitting there 'spacing out'. Someone else was afraid that they wouldn't be able to get to a phone on time.

"I knew they were all just really nervous about this, so I did everything I could to assure them that they were not all that responsible, that we just needed their support."

"But Tar, you can see where they would be afraid that if they missed something and, God forbid, he OD'd, or worse, that they would be, or, at least, feel, responsible."

"Well, yeah, but I wasn't really concerned about that happening. I was more afraid of him starting a daily habit again, where I couldn't see it, and where no one else would be picking up on it. I just needed more eyes on him while he was in school. I don't think they would be responsible in any way unless they deliberately withheld information from me. And I made it clear that I knew they had jobs to do and that they weren't there to kid-sit Kane. After all, these were my peers."

"Okay, so what happened then?"

"Well, it was time to call him back in and the counselor goes to get him. I have my back to the door, and I notice this weird look on everyone's face. I turn, not knowing what to expect, and I notice he's bouncing in with a kind of swagger as he walks. I'm thinking to myself, 'What is this now?'

"He comes over, yanks out the seat that he had been sitting on, swings it around, straddles it, and plops himself down. All attitude. I don't acknowledge this at all. All I say to him is, *'Okay, Kane, we're pretty much set for tomorrow'*.

"He starts to stand up then and says, *'Great, let's go.'* My mind is racing here. I can't believe it's possible that he somehow did something while he was out in the hallway. But this change in him is not to be believed."

"You're not going to tell me that he got high while he was waiting in the hallway!?"

"Well, as it turned out, no. But, remember, I had only seen him high on three occasions, and all three times he had essentially put himself to sleep. This was a whole new ball game. So, anyway, I say, *'Sit down, Kane. We're not finished.'*

"He sits down again, puts his chin on the back of the chair and says, *'Yeah, whatever.'*

"Now I still can't figure this out at all. So I go on, trying to buy myself a little time. So I say to him, *'Your teachers aren't sure that they'll recognize your drug use or that they'll be able to notify me in time, to come and check on you. 'Got any ideas?'*

"So he says, in this really tough, sarcastic voice, *'I know! How about I just tell 'em when I'm loaded? And you can give 'em all cell phones. That should do it. Now can we get out of here?'*

"That was it. I had never seen him behave like that, and I was certainly not going to ignore it. But I also didn't want to lose control in that situation. If that was how he was going to behave in school, he was right, he wasn't ready. And neither was I! I just stared at him for a minute, and I didn't say a word. Neither did anyone else. We were all just too dumbfounded.

"Then, all of a sudden, he looks at me, turns his chair around, sits down, and says, *'I'm sorry'*. Just like that. Back to normal... well, at least to what I had come to *believe* was normal.

"Holding myself together, as calmly as I can, I say to him, with as much attitude as I can muster, *'I'm sorry? Did you just go out and score outta some kind of punk bag? What was that all about? You don't talk to these people like that. I thought you knew better. Maybe you're not ready for this. They don't need this kind of behavior in their classrooms. They're here to teach you something, not to put up with your attitude.'*

"Then he says, real softly and obediently, *'I know. I'm sorry. I just wanted to show them...'*

"And I cut him off, because I'm so mad. *'Show them what!?'* I say.

"And he lowers his head, all apologetic, and he says, *'That's how I usually act when I'm high, Aunt Tara. I wanted them to see me, so they'd know.'* And then he looks up at them and says, *'You seem like really nice people. I wasn't sure that you'd know what my aunt was talkin' about. I know a lot of kids act tough every day. Maybe they're like I am. Maybe not. I just wanted you to know that if you see me acting like I just did, I'm in trouble. And you need to call my aunt.'*

"Well, then, of course, I feel like an idiot. And I'm thinking what a great idea that was, and then I'm thinking how easily he could fool all of us. Just like that, he could make these teachers look like fools, in front of their classes. High or not, he could be a handful. I was sure they were thinking the same thing.

"So I say to him, *'You bet you're in trouble. Don't you ever do that again, play-acting or otherwise.'*

"Again, he apologizes and says, *'But they really needed to know.'* And he looks me right in the eye, and says, *'You needed to know'.*

"So I say, regaining my composure as quickly as I can, *'Okay, you made your point. Do you have anything else to say, or do, before we go?'*

"He's all quiet after that, and I run over a few last things with the teachers, we get a list of supplies, and we stand up to leave. I say my goodbyes to everybody, make sure Kane does the same, and we're walking out. And then Kane says to me, *'I'm gonna get punished for that, right?'*

"And I say, without looking at him, *'Big time.'*

"And then we're starting to walk down the hall, and he's quiet for a while. And then he looks at me and says. *'But you have to admit it was a good idea, right?'*

"And I look over at him and I don't say a word. And then he looks away, and he looks down at the floor. And then I say, *'Very'.*

"And then this big grin comes across his face. I very seldom see him smile. But I don't dare smile back. There's no way this can come off as a joke, because we're still fighting for his life here. Then he gets real quiet and we're makin' our way out of this big building. And there are all these girls in the hall, and they're looking at him, and he's not even noticing them. And then he says, *'But I'm still punished, right?'*

"And, of course, I reply, *'Definitely'.* And he seems satisfied with that! And we go home and he gets right to work, without a word from me! Do you believe this?"

"You know, girlfriend, I never believe *anything* in your life. What would I do without you to keep me on the edge of my seat? So, do you think he's going to be able to handle school?"

"Honestly? Not a prayer."

21. The Wedding

I had planned it so that Kane started school just before the February vacation. That would give him a chance to get his feet wet and for the teachers to get a look at his work. And then, when we came back from vacation, he could really get started on catching up.

The week went smoothly. I took him in and picked him up every day, since I didn't want to deal with the bus right away. I could see the bus as a source of a lot of potential problems. Riding in the car is always a good time for moms and kids to talk. This way, I also had time to talk to him without my girls around. In the car, there's no need for eye contact, and things get talked about that might be too uncomfortable in another setting.

I had been looking forward to this vacation as much as the kids. Danny and David came home the first weekend and took Kane skiing, giving me two whole days relatively free. They promised they would stick to him like glue, so that he wouldn't get into trouble.

During the rest of the week, we found other things to do. Kane had been doing well, so I had no problem with planning things that I thought he would like, including two 'day trips' into New York to see the sights.

All in all, it was a good week…until the second Saturday.

On Saturday afternoon and evening, we were invited to a big, fancy wedding. The parents of the bride were old friends of our family, and all six of us were invited.

The ballroom was huge and filled with people. I had not thought to say anything ahead of time and realized, too late, that all the seating was by age groups. I was thrilled to be reunited with old friends of mine from my husband's and my college days. But I had not anticipated that the kids would all be separated from each other, and that I would not even be able to keep an eye on Hannah, let alone Kane.

My friends actually thought this was funny, since all *their* kids were grown. Those of their kids who came were seated with Danny and David. They admired Dana, but were obviously amused by the fact that I, also, had an eight-year-old. And they couldn't believe that I was 'volunteering' to take on an adolescent boy. This apparently triggered a group nostalgia thing on when their boys were in the terrible teens.

Meanwhile, I was totally distracted trying to keep an eye out for my kids. Finally, I excused myself and went to speak to each of them. I reminded Hannah that she was not to leave the ballroom, even to go to the bathroom, without telling me. And I reminded her to keep an eye out for her cousin, and, if she noticed anything, to tell me right away.

I then found Danny, David, and Dana and told each of them my concern. I told them that they were there to have fun, but I asked that they also keep an eye out for Kane. They assured me that they would, and commented that they also felt that the seating plan was not a good idea for him, considering. I complimented them on their maturity at even thinking about such a thing, and went to look for the 'young teens' table.

I found Kane at a table with what appeared to be twelve- to fifteen-year-olds. There must have been about twelve of them, boys and girls, and each one was more stylishly dressed than the next. I was glad that we had gone out and gotten Kane appropriate clothing.

He was talking to a beautiful girl, who was probably about his age, but who, like Kane, looked to be at least a year or two older. I didn't want to embarrass him, so I asked if I might speak to him privately. He excused himself (clothes do seem to do wonders for a young man's manners), and he walked with me a short distance from the table.

He spoke up before I had a chance. "I know. No drinking, right?"

"Right. And, you'll notice that I'm sitting quite a distance from you."

"Yeah I noticed. Hey, thanks for trusting me."

I debated as to whether I should correct him, but then thought 'total honesty', and said, "I had nothing to do with the seating. But I *am* trusting you. I'm not making you come and sit with all the old people at my table."

He smiled a little, knowing that I was putting myself in that category. I then went on. "You can enjoy the food, the company, and the dancing, but absolutely not a drop of alcohol."

"I know. By the way, what do I do with the champagne? It's on the table."

"It's for the toast to the bride and groom. You lift your glass like everyone else, and then put it down. If you want, you can make believe you're taking a sip, but I'm warning you, you don't want to go there."

"I'll try."

"Try? Uh-uh. As Yoda says, 'Do or do not; there is no try'! If you don't think that you can handle this, you come and sit with me right now. Or you could go and sit with the boys. Your choice."

Kane looked over to where the older kids were sitting. He knew that his cousins deserved time with their own friends. After all, they had been nice enough to include him in a ski weekend, about which his aunt would never know all the details… he hoped!

"I'll be okay. I promise." Thinking about the weekend before made him remember how good it had felt to party again. He missed feeling that way, even if it did always get him in trouble.

"All right." (His aunt was talking to him again.) "We'll give it a try, but I want you to come and touch base with me every half-hour."

Kane looked at the clock. It was five o'clock. "Okay", he promised.

I had a really bad feeling about this. He was thinking about something that he wasn't telling me about. I could tell that he was hiding something. But I assumed that he was just anxious to get back to this new girlfriend, and I left it at that.

He was good for about the first hour, and then, I guess, I got distracted and didn't notice that he hadn't come over. It was Dana who came and sat beside me at about seven o'clock.

"Mom, can I talk to you?" I excused myself from the group and stood up to talk with her. "Have you seen Kane recently?" Dana asked.

All of a sudden, reality set in. I looked at my watch. "Uh oh, what happened?"

"He's wasted."

"Are you sure? How do you know? Where is he now?"

"I just bumped into him, literally, on the dance floor. He was hanging on to some girl. I swear she was holding him up. When I accidentally bumped into them, I said, 'Excuse me', and when he looked up, he was all flushed and watery-eyed. He looked at me as if he didn't know me."

"How long ago was that?"

"Just a few minutes. I didn't want to be rude to my partner, so I waited until the end of the dance. Then I didn't see him on the floor, so I'm guessing they went back to their table. I did *not* want to be the one to confront him."

"I understand. Why don't you go back to your friends? I'll look around for him."

I made my way to the table where he had been sitting, but he wasn't there, and neither was the girl he'd been talking to earlier. The other kids said that they hadn't seen them since they got up to dance.

I decided to look around a little. I made my way to the far end of the ballroom, which was not as well lighted as the part where our tables were. I was about to go out an end door, into the hall. Then I noticed that the wall, in this part of the room, curved around and didn't make a right angle to the outside wall. I peeked around this curve and, sure enough, there they were.

Kane was going at it, but the girl seemed to have had enough, and, as I appeared, she was trying to push him away from her.

I could hear her saying. "Kane, get off me. I don't want this. I don't even know you, and besides, you've had too much to drink."

He seemed to be barely able to talk, but I could make out a plea for her not to leave. Once again, this boy was full of surprises. As far as I knew this was relatively new in his repertoire of activities. I could see we were opening a whole new chapter. Oh, I was really not ready to go through this again. Girls were just so much easier to raise than boys.

I guess I should have been happy, in this day and age, that they both still had their clothes on, but I was furious. I was furious at myself for not watching him more closely and furious at him for obvious reasons. I could feel my adrenalin racing, and I knew I'd better be careful.

My first concern was for this girl, of course. I stepped around the bend of the wall and reached out and grabbed Kane by his hair and by his left arm - the hair to yank him back off her and to get his attention, and the arm to steady him so he wouldn't fall over when she stepped away. "I think you'd better go back to your table now," I said to her, in the calmest voice I could manage. Gratefully, she stepped aside and headed back into the ballroom.

Meanwhile, Kane was protesting at the top of his lungs. I was so happy that the band was really loud, even at this end of the hall. "No, Mom, please. I need her. Please don't make her go away. Aw, come on. It's a party. I' been good."

As the young girl slipped away, she almost walked right into my older son, who had gotten the word and found us at just the right moment. She excused herself, went around him, and hurried off.

"Here, Mom. Let me help you." Danny got around behind Kane and grabbed him under his other arm. Kane was still protesting. Danny took over. "Shut up, Twerp." I was so angry that I didn't even correct him. Together we half-carried, half-dragged Kane out into the hall and into a small lounge with a couch. We sat him down and propped him up against the wall.

"Danny, will you watch him? I have to walk away from him. I am too angry."

"Sure, Mom."

I made my way into the hall and out into the lobby. I just needed to calm myself down a little. 'Wait a minute,' I thought to myself, 'Did Kane just call me 'Mom'? And Danny called *him* 'Twerp'. Danny hadn't called his brother, David, 'Twerp' in years.'

*   *   *   *   *   *   *

Danny waited until his mother left and then went after his little cousin. "What the hell were you thinking? We let you off the hook for last weekend and then you pull this shit again. Did you even tell my mom about last week?"

Kane was in no shape to answer rationally, let alone tell the truth. "Yeah, I tol' her." Kane was slurring his words.

"You did not. You're lying. Why didn't you do what we told you?!"

"I couldn' tell her… She was so happy that I was doin' good in school… and she took us places. I couldn' tell her… Please don' be mad at me, Danny. I couldn' help it. It was right there… Please help me out here. I don' feel so good."

"Mom trusted you. We all did. You're pathetic."

"I'm sorry!" Kane started to cry, as he was apparently prone to do when he drank.

"All right. Don't start bawlin'."

"I can' help it. You guys ha' been so good to me, and I keep screwin' up."

"Well, then knock it off! And tomorrow morning I'm not leaving here until you tell Mom the truth about last weekend. Come on! Stand up! You better start walkin' this off. Mom's not gonna be real happy if we have to carry you out of here."

"I don' think I can stan' up." Kane was swaying where he sat.

"You better! Come on!" Danny hoisted Kane up off the couch and put one of Kane's arms over his shoulder. He started to walk with him out of the lounge area. His plan was to walk him up and down the hall. But as they stepped out into the hall, they ran right into…Mom.

*   *   *   *   *   *   *   *

Danny was surprised to see me. Kane could barely focus his eyes on anything.

"Oh… Mom. How long have you been standing there?"

"Long enough to find out that there's something I need to know about last weekend, Daniel!"

"Uh, sorry, Mom. Kane was supposed to tell you during the week. We thought it was something *he* should tell you."

"Son, you're young. The way it works is, you make him tell me, but *you* tell me first, without him knowing."

"We didn't think that would be honest."

"We? I suppose David was in on this, too."

"Well, yeah."

"Go and sit *him* back down. I want to talk to you."

Danny took Kane back to the lounge and sat him down on the couch. "You're gonna owe me big time, Twerp. Now you got *me* in trouble."

"I'm sorry!!" By this time Kane was a complete mess, unable to stop from crying and barely able to sit up on his own.

"Yeah. I know. You said that! You always say that!"

"Please, Danny. Don' be mad me. I'm sorry."

I waited in the hallway for Danny to come out. I could hear Kane crying at whatever Danny had said to him. My eldest son also needed some 'schooling'.

"You made him cry?!" I said to Danny, when he came out. "He's a baby, for Heaven's sake. And he's sick, partly because of *you*. He worships you, Danny...and you made him cry?!"

Danny just stood in the hall and looked at the floor. "I'm sorry, Mom. I'm new at this. I didn't know what else to do." I didn't say a word. I let him think through what was happening. "I guess if we had told you, you might have been able to stop this tonight, right?"

As always, I was impressed with my children's ability to take responsibility, and I told Danny so. I also explained to him that he had made a very common mistake.

"Danny, when you're an adult, responsible for a kid, you can't help that kid hide things from *other* adults who are *also* responsible for him. Lots of mothers think that they can keep secrets, with their child, from the child's father. And fathers think that they're being cool when they tell their child, 'Let's not tell Mom' or 'Mom doesn't have to know about this.' That kind of deception confuses kids and makes them feel really guilty. And some people, like our Kane, just can't 'hold guilt' without getting into trouble."

"Well, I guess you need to know, then," said Danny, "that he got real drunk last weekend. He gave us the slip and found some girls who had beer and wine. We made him pay for it, but I guess it's like you said, the guilt caught up to him."

"That, and the fact that he now had a strong, recent, memory of how good it felt to be high again! It was only natural that he'd want to repeat the experience if he got the chance. And, unfortunately, this was his chance."

"Again, I'm really sorry, Mom."

"It's okay, Son. After all..." I paused until my son, obviously distressed, looked up at me, "...he *is* a little twerp!" I concluded.

Danny caught the twinkle in my eye. He knew that the lecture was over and that I had forgiven him. This was tougher on all of us than I thought it was going to be. And I was beginning to suspect that Kane's problem might be a lot more deep-seated than we thought. I didn't want my son to feel responsible for something that might be way beyond the control of any of us, including my nephew himself.

"I know! I can't believe I started calling him that. Remember? I used to always call Dave that, when he was about Kane's age, and he kept doing stupid things?"

"Yes, I do remember. And I think I just heard Kane call me 'Mom'. I'm afraid this whole family is bonding to him."

I heard something behind me at that moment and turned to see Kane standing behind me, holding onto the wall. I looked at Danny and raised my eyebrows. We were becoming a whole family, an extended family, of eavesdroppers.

"Ma'am?" Kane said.

"Kane?"

"I don' wanna be in trouble again."

I looked at Danny and then back at Kane. I wondered what he meant by that. "I don't think you have a choice at this point," I told him. "I'm afraid that what you've done is done."

He tried very hard to stand up straight. "I can try, can' I?"

I looked at Danny again. "Son, do you want to handle this? Since you did sort of start it."

"What do you want me to do with him, Mom? I can try walking him up and down. Or I can sit with him out here while he sleeps it off."

Kane chimed in again, "I wanna go back inside."

I reacted immediately. "Not a chance, Buddy! Do you think I'm gonna let you go back in there, with that girl and all that alcohol all over the place? Do you think you deserve to go in and sit with those kids again?" I was furious at him, and I let him know it, even if he was pretty incapable of really feeling anything, at that moment.

But then he looked up at me, obviously straining to hold himself together, and said, "No, I-I need to sit with *you*." I knew that he was a smart boy. Was it possible that he knew a lot more about what was going on with him than we were giving him credit for?

"Come on, Mom. Give him a chance. None of us wants to leave yet, and you shouldn't have to leave your friends because of us kids."

I knew that Danny was right. We didn't get to go to that many social functions, and it wasn't fair to the girls either, especially since this was, in no way, their fault. But I also didn't want my friends to have to watch their conversation because of my thirteen-year-old at the table.

Finally, I said to Danny. "Go and get your brother and bring him out here."

I sat with Kane while Danny went to get David. Kane tried really hard to act sober. For one fleeting moment, before I began to try to figure out what I was going to do with him, I actually felt sorry for him. He finally put his head down in his hands, unable to hold it up any longer. David and Danny finally returned.

David took one look at Kane and then at me, and he knew he was in trouble. "It was all Danny's idea," he said.

"Yeah, right!" Danny retorted.

"Cut it out, you two. David, I want you to see the results of allowing someone like Kane to hold guilt."

"Geez, kid. What did you do?" David said. Kane tried to look up at his cousin, but his eyes rolled back in his head, and I had to grab his shoulder so he wouldn't fall over.

"The same thing he did last weekend," I told him.

David looked at Danny. "Did he tell her?"

"Apparently not. I had to," his brother replied.

"Whoops." David knew that, now, they were *all* in trouble.

"Yeah," I said, "well, tomorrow morning when this one can feel something once again, we will all sit down and go over all the details. Until then, the two of you will either take turns sitting with him out here, not letting him out of your sight for a millisecond, or you may take him back to your table and babysit him for the rest of the night. Because I am going to go and enjoy the rest of my evening."

And with that, I got up and left them to take care of their cousin. If Kane was going to be part of our family, his 'new brothers' were going to have to learn to meet his needs, just as the rest of us did for each other.

I went back to my seat and resumed my conversations with my friends. When they asked where I had been, I explained that my kids needed some lessons in watching out for each other and left it at that.

I could see the boys' table from where I sat. Apparently, Kane convinced the boys to let him sit with them. But, after a while, I noticed that they put some chairs together and laid him down to sleep. I was proud of the way they were handling the situation, though I was frustrated that it had gone as it did. It annoyed me that this kid had to be watched so closely. I again questioned whether his living with us was good for him... or for us!

*   *   *   *   *   *   *   *

The next morning, as I had promised, I asked them all to sit with me in the living room. The three boys sat on the couch, my two on the ends, with Kane between them. The girls were invited as well.

"Okay," I began, "the floor is open."

Nobody said a word. Kane looked very intimidated. He was smart enough, by now, not to go for the sympathy angle, although he did not look at all well.

Finally, Hannah, of all people, spoke up. "I'm angry that Kane got Mommy angry and spoiled our day out." Kane winced and hung his head in obvious shame.

"It's not all his fault, Hannah, " added David. "We didn't tell Mom that he messed up last weekend. If we had, he might not have done it again."

"Yeah," said Danny, "I'm the oldest, I should have made sure that Mom knew, even if we had told Kane that he was supposed to tell her himself. We shouldn't have expected him to handle that."

Dana was next. "I was angry to have been put in the position of having to tell Mom, when I saw Kane drunk on the dance floor."

"My turn." I wanted to add my feelings to the rest. "I'm angry with myself because I didn't, first, insist that Kane be seated closer to me, and, second, that I was enjoying myself so much that I forgot my responsibility and lost track of time. If I had gone to look for him an hour earlier, when he first missed reporting in, I might have caught him in time."

Kane sat very still during all of this. He still had his head down. It occurred to me that he might have 'fallen out' again. I glanced around at the kids, and everybody was looking at each other. It was obvious to all of us that it was Kane's move. Of course, we all knew the game, and he didn't. But we assumed that he would figure out that he was now supposed to speak up and take responsibility for himself.

We waited another minute or two. I wasn't sure what to expect. I wasn't sure he could handle this. Danny shifted his position and, without Kane being able to see him, held up one hand and mimicked punching it with his other fist. His expression clearly said, 'Should we let him have it?' He meant verbally, of course. We didn't allow any physical violence in our family.

I shook my head. Finally, I said, "Kane, do you have anything to say?"

At first, he shook his head slowly, but didn't look up. At least we knew he was awake. Then he spoke. "It's nobody's fault."

"Excuse me? " I said, suddenly feeling really angry. "Could you put your head up when you speak to us?" If he were going to dodge responsibility for this, and let us all take the rap for him, then, by God, he was at least going to do it to our faces!

He raised his head up slowly. His face was covered with tears. He wiped his face on his sleeve. "It's not any of your fault. I appreciate you guys trying to take the blame for me, but this was all my fault. I don't know what happened. I didn't mean to spoil everybody's time. Before I knew it, it just happened. I'm really sorry.

"And, Aunt Tara, I was supposed to tell you about last weekend. The guys were great to me. They included me in everything, and they took turns watchin' out for me. They didn't even make me feel like a little kid who needed to be watched. I just met some girls, and they invited me over that night. It happened real fast, and the guys didn't hear them ask me. I sneaked out while they thought I was in the shower. They would have never found me, except that I got so drunk that the girls got nervous and threw me out of their cabin. If Danny and Dave hadn't been out looking for me, I could have frozen to death!

"But they punished me good. They just made the mistake of letting me take the worst punishment on my own. Telling you. I promised them I would do it, but I couldn't. Then you were so nice to me, and I felt guilty for not telling you and then having such a good time…"

I glanced over at Danny, and he gave me a look that said, 'I get it.'

Kane went on, "I guess when I had the chance to party again last night, I figured that I was in so deep now that it didn't matter. I figured, 'What the heck. Go for it. How much worse can it get?' I know now I was wrong. And sittin' here listening to you take the rap for me makes me feel like..." He choked up then and couldn't go on.

I was satisfied. "Danny, David, would you take Kane upstairs to his bedroom? Then you two come back down. Girls, you can be excused."

I needed a few minutes to think.

* * * * * * * *

"Okay, guys. Ideas for consequences for this?"

"Aw, Mom. He really feels bad. He was apologizing all over the place upstairs."

"It's not enough. He needs to do something to feel that he's made this up to you. He knows I'm putting most of the blame on you guys, and that's what's got him. He respects me, but he admires you. We can use that to help him. Danny, go upstairs and check that he's not listening to us. I don't want him to hear this conversation."

Danny went to the top of the stairs and came back down. "He's sitting on his bed, where we told him to sit."

"Okay. Listen. I'm beginning to get a little worried about just how far along Kane is, in his drug and alcohol use. It's beginning to look like he's beyond this being just a discipline thing."

"Do you think he's addicted, Mom?"

"I don't know. I wish I knew more about this. He seems to be able to stay away from it, for periods of time, without it bothering him. But, then, all of a sudden, he loses control, without intending to.... I don't know.

"But, anyway, for right now, let's think of your worst jobs around the house. Make me a list. These would be things that I would ask you guys to do when you were home for a vacation. That way, he's basically doing *your* work. He has to pay you back for what he did to you."

The boys came up with a list of tasks that would serve as Kane's punishment. I also had some other things in mind. I couldn't afford for him to get too comfortable. This pattern of 'screw up, cry, apologize, get forgiven' was not a good game plan, regardless.

"Okay, Mom. Do you want us to take this list up to him?"

"No, you guys have to get ready to travel. I'll go over the list with him during the week. Besides, I want to talk to him first. But I do want you to say goodbye to him before you go, and let him know that you love him. I don't care how you do it; he just really needs to know that."

"Sure, Mom." They each gave me a hug and went off to pack up. I went upstairs to speak to Kane. I knew he had to be hurting.

I knocked on his open door and asked if I could come in. I could see him stiffen a little, but he nodded. I went and sat next to him on the bed. "How are you doing?"

He shrugged and stared at the floor.

"Your punishments have been set," I told him. "You'll start tomorrow."

"Aren't you throwing me out?" Kane asked, surprised.

"No, I'm not throwing you out. You did really well this morning."

He looked up at me, totally bewildered. "What do you mean?"

"Well, you spoke up and took responsibility for your bad self."

"Well, I couldn't just sit there and let you guys think it was *your* fault!" He was very quiet for a minute, and then he looked at me again. He was thinking. Finally, he said, "But then you knew that! 'Cause you set me up! Right?"

I smiled at him, and nodded. "What we *didn't* know was whether you'd be man enough to step up." I paused a moment, then continued. "You know, my kids and I have a big problem with you."

"I know." He hung his head again. "I can't believe you've put up with me this long."

"Our problem with you is that we love you."

At that, he turned and looked at me. "How can you even say that?!"

I put my arm around his shoulder, and he turned and gave me a hug. This was the first time that he had initiated any display of affection, of any kind, to any of us.

I was always told that, when you hug a child, to let the child be the first one to let go. Kane hung on for a very long time. I stroked his hair and rubbed his back. I bet it had been years since he'd hugged anyone. Finally, he let go and sat up. He wiped his eyes and stared at the floor again.

"Thanks, Ma'am."

"Kane, why do you keep calling me 'Ma'am'? It sounds so formal. I am your aunt, after all."

Kane sat quietly for a few minutes. "A long time ago, I heard about this kid, who was a foster kid or somethin', and he used to call his foster mom 'Ma'am', 'cause it sounded like `Mom'."

"I see. Do you remember calling me 'Mom' yesterday?"

He looked surprised and a little embarrassed. "No. I-I was drunk. I'm sorry."

"Well, while you're here, you can call me whichever you want. Under the circumstances, I don't think your mom would mind."

"Thanks."

I stood up to take my leave. "The boys will be up to say goodbye."

I turned around to look at him again from the hallway. He had slid back against his wall, his knees drawn up to his chest. He had his arms folded over his knees and his head down. I wished I knew where we were going with all this. Would he ever get better?

22. Back to School

I knew that school was not going to be easy for Kane, and that I was inviting problems by sending him. There were just too many temptations. But, if he were ever going to make progress, he had to challenge himself.

One day, in early March, I received a phone call from the principal.

"Tara, I need you to come over here right away and pick up Kane. I'm guessing pot and probably some alcohol."

'Here we go again,' I thought to myself, and sighed. "Where will he be when I get there?"

"On the bench in the front office."

"So then he's not passed out?" I confirmed.

"No, not this time."

"Okay, I'll be right over."

When I entered the school office, I saw the five boys sitting on the bench. Kane was the closest to the door. He was sitting with his elbow up on the armrest, shielding his eyes from the light. As I opened the door, he looked up briefly, then changed his position, elbows propped up on this knees, hands covering his face.

'Yeah, you'd better cover those eyes,' I thought, and then looked up to see the principal. He was just coming out of his office to gesture me in.

"Kane," he said, "you wait out here. We'll see you in a minute."

I started to go into the principal's office, when I heard one of the boys say to Kane, "Is that your mother?"

"'Might as well be," he answered.

"'You gonna be in trouble?" the same kid asked.

"Shut up!" Kane snapped at him.

I could hear a tone in Kane's voice that I didn't like, and I said to the principal, "He needs to come in now."

He agreed, and I went back out, took Kane by the arm, and led him into the principal's office. Kane was already starting to stumble.

"If you want to speak to me privately," I suggested to the principal, "we can put him somewhere else. I just think that, if you leave him out there, you'll have a fight on your hands. And with the shape he's in, I don't think anyone would want to see that."

"No problem," he said. "I was just going to fill you in on what we suspect happened. Perhaps, Kane can verify the details for us."

I looked over at Kane and thought to myself, 'Or perhaps not.' He was trying to sit next to me with attitude, but was having trouble just sitting up. The other boys on the bench seemed to be all silly and giggly, like you'd expect with weed. Kane wasn't.

"I don't think that's going to happen," I said. "I think I'd better get him home. I'm assuming five days suspension?" The principal nodded. I continued, "I can bring him over here tomorrow morning, if you want to speak to him and tell him yourself. I think that would make a bigger impression than anything you say now, or that *I* tell him. What do you think?"

"Well, I can see that there's no use in talking to him now. What do you think he took?" the principal asked.

"I really wouldn't know just by looking at him. There's just too much out there these days. And, heck, they mix four and five things together! I can't imagine how even the drug counselors keep up!"

We made arrangements for the next day, and I told Kane to stand up. Someone had brought his stuff from his locker. I put his jacket around him and told him *again* to stand up. He looked at me as if I were far, far away. Finally, I reached down and practically lifted him to his feet.

As we made our way out of the office, the other boys called out, "Hey, Kane!" He didn't even try to answer them.

We made it out the front door. Then he started to reach out his hand, to support himself on one of the columns, to the right of the entrance.

"I'm gonna be sick," he said.

He managed to lean over a grassy area, off to the side of the front entrance. With one hand on the column and me supporting him on the other side, he became violently ill. I just held on to him. I thought he would never stop. I was just thinking about calling for help, when he finally leaned his head against the column, and it seemed like the worst was over.

He was very weak, and I could hardly hold him up. I pulled some tissues out of my pocket and wiped his face and mouth. He was sweating and breathing heavily, and I was hoping he wouldn't pass out. If I could just get him into the car... I was parked at the curb about twenty feet from where we were standing, but it felt like miles away.

Just at that moment, the school nurse came out the front door with a wheel chair. My mouth fell open in disbelief. "I heard him out my window. I thought you might need this," the nurse said.

"Oh, you are a godsend. Thank you!" I replied.

The two of us managed to get Kane seated in the chair. The nurse was a nice lady, and she was aware of Kane's problems. We had decided to put her on our team at the very beginning, just in case something like this were to happen.

We stopped the wheelchair beside the van, locked the chair wheels, and I opened the side door. But when the two of us went to pick him up, he pushed us back. "I can do it!"

He was a little too nasty for my taste, and I was embarrassed that he was rude to the nurse, who was trying to help us. She could tell by my expression that I was about to say something to him, but she put her finger to her lips. She was right. There was that defiance that I had seen in him before. We should let him try to help himself.

He kicked at the footrests and tried to get them up. We just stood there. Finally, with great effort, he managed to push himself out of the seat and stumble the one or two steps to the car. He could barely make his legs move. He held on to either side of the open door and stood there for a minute. I looked at the nurse. She motioned to me to wait. He couldn't figure out how to get himself turned around and onto the seat.

The two of us waited. If he wanted help now, he was going to have to ask for it.

He finally put his hands down onto the seat and leaned over it. I hoped he wasn't going to be sick again… in my car!

But he just stood there, slowly shaking his head, and mumbling. Then, finally, he shouted, "I CAN'T DO THIS!"

Good enough for me. I looked at the nurse, and she nodded. Together, we stood him up and turned him around and got him into a seat belt. He looked so pathetic and so sick. Why *did* he keep doing this?

"Can you take care of him at home?" the nurse asked me.

"I think I'll just stay with him in the car until he comes down. We have a heated garage."

"Good deal. Let me know if I can do anything."

"Believe me I will. *I* have absolutely *no* trouble asking for help!" I leaned his seat back and covered him with a blanket that I kept in the car. He had started to shiver.

*   *   *   *   *   *   *   *

When we got home, I pulled into the garage. I was going to just leave him sleeping in the car. I went back to the passenger side, just to check him once more, but as I did so, he opened his eyes and started to try to get out of the seat.

"Do you think you can walk into the house?" I asked him. "Because, if not, we can stay right here for a while."

"No. I'm comin' in," he said. It was interesting what a different personality I was seeing.

He was very independent, and I let him try to walk on his own. He held onto the car and then onto the doorjamb, as he pulled himself up the two steps into the kitchen. He actually made his way across the kitchen and into the living room.

"I'll just stay here on the couch," he mumbled.

He dropped himself onto the couch and stayed there.

I could feel that I was not handling this well, so I just left him alone. I didn't speak to him; I didn't help him. I just left him there, face down on the pillow, his feet still hanging off the front of the couch.

I did go and get some large plastic garbage bags to cover the floor and the edge of my furniture. I then tucked some towels under his elbow, for absorption, and brought in a bucket to put on the floor next to him. I had to smile at myself for being more concerned about my couch and my floor than about my wayward nephew. I knew I was very much on the edge.

He stayed on the couch the entire day. I must have walked past him a dozen times, and neither of us said a word. When the girls came home, I cornered them in the kitchen and explained the situation. I suggested that they go on about their business, and not get 'into it' with him for any reason. They shouldn't try to engage him in conversation, ask him any questions, volunteer to get him anything, or even make comments to him. I wanted to see what he was going to do about this.

At one point, he hauled himself off the couch and went into the downstairs bathroom, which was about ten feet away from him. I did watch to make sure that he didn't fall. He was unsteady, but he made it fine. He did throw up again, though.

I wished I had been able to talk to the other boys about what they'd been using. I was thinking that, with all the junk that Kane had taken in the past, he should have been able to handle this better. I was, of course, thrilled that he couldn't. I wanted him to get so sick that whatever high he had gotten from this would vanish. I left the room before he came out of the bathroom, so he wouldn't think that I particularly cared about him at that point. He *really* needed to start caring more about himself.

*   *   *   *   *   *   *   *

Kane made it back to the couch and fell back down. This was not going well, and he knew it. He hadn't felt this sick in a long time. He wondered what those kids had given him. He was stupid to go along with them. He was guessing now that they had put something in the beer that they gave him. He knew he could handle the weed. And when they dared him to chug the beer, he didn't think he drank that much. He just made it look that way, to impress them. Although why he wanted to impress them he had no clue at this point.

But he just didn't feel right. He was way too out of it, even for him. Maybe this was how God was answering his prayers, by making it so bad that he wouldn't want to do it again. Then he figured, nah, they probably laced the beer with something. He vowed to get them back...that is, if he could ever lift his head off this pillow again.

And now he was in trouble at school. He thought he remembered something about suspension, and even his aunt wasn't speaking to him. How could he be such a fuckup? He wasn't going to cry any more. He was past crying. He was numb. He had to start doing something...but what? He had tried rehab. Of course, they forced him into it, and he was determined that he wasn't gonna let them get to him. But now he was thinking that maybe he should have. He couldn't keep doing this. He really felt like crap.

It was getting dark, and he could smell supper being cooked. He had to get up and be sick again. What the hell had they given him?

His aunt came in to the darkening living room, some time after that, and put on a light. She came over to him and said, "You wanna eat?" The way she said it made him feel even worse. It was like she *had* to ask. He was scared to death that one of these days she, too, was going to give up on him.

Kane shook his head and kept his face buried in the pillow. He didn't want to eat. He didn't want to face her. He was pretty much down by then. At least he thought he was. But he didn't know what to do. He didn't think he could even make it upstairs by himself. How pathetic was that? He couldn't even put himself to bed. And he sure wasn't going to ask for help. What if she ignored him? He knew he couldn't handle that right now. Even his cousins hadn't said a word to him. So he just lay there.

* * * * * * * *

It was getting late. The girls had gone to bed. I watched TV as long as I could, but I really needed to get to bed myself. I just didn't know what to do about Kane. Sometimes, he seemed to be asleep, and then other times he seemed to be watching the TV. At least, he seemed to have stopped vomiting. He never said a word to me, though. I wondered what he was thinking, if anything.

At eleven, I got up and went to turn out the light to go upstairs.

Finally, he spoke. "Permission to go to bed?"

I recognized the phrase from my work, years before, in a detention facility for boys. The boys always had to ask permission to do everything. They always shortened it to, 'Permission to...(whatever).' It was strange that he should use that right now. Obviously, he was feeling the distance that his behavior had put between us. I thought maybe it was a good thing.

"Go!" was all I said.

I made an extra trip to the kitchen to lock the back door, which I had already locked, just to give him a chance to get up the stairs. I stalled to make sure that I saw him get up safely. I shut off all the lights and followed him. My room was to the left and his was to the right. As I reached the top of the stairs, I glanced down his way, just to be sure that I saw him in bed.

He was still in the hallway. He had stopped part way and was leaning against the wall. I could see that his knees were starting to buckle. I hurried down the hall and put my hand under his arm to support him.

"I can't believe you're not over this by now. What did you do?"

"I'm gonna kill those guys. I don't know what they gave me. I swear I never did anything that made me feel like this."

So, I was right. This wasn't 'just' beer and weed. But he wasn't going to get off the hook for this. "And did they *force* you to get high with them, Big Shot?"

He knew that he was still in trouble. He also knew that his aunt did not expect him to answer that question...because they both already knew the answer.

130

*　　*　　*　　*　　*　　*　　*　　*

The girls had already left for school, and I was finishing my breakfast, when Kane came into the kitchen. He was showered and dressed, and I was impressed. "How are you feeling this morning?"

"Like I got pushed around by a bulldozer."

"Good." I handed him some breakfast. "Your appointment with the principal is at eleven."

"I figured. But I'm probably suspended, right?"

"Right."

"How many days?"

"He'll tell you."

"You're really angry at me, aren't you, Aunt Tara?"

I took a deep breath. "Let's just say that I'm really angry." I paused and thought for a minute. Kane ate his breakfast in silence. "I'm angry, first, that your problem exists at all. And I'm angry, secondly, that there doesn't seem to be any way to fix it...at least none that I can come up with."

Kane was quiet for a long time. Then he said very softly, "Maybe that's because it's not your problem."

I had started to wash the dishes and hadn't caught what he'd said exactly. I *thought* I heard him, and I hoped he wasn't being a 'smart mouth', so I asked him to repeat it.

"It's *my* problem. I'm the one that has to do something about it. Aunt Tara, you guys have been great to me. I really like being part of this family. And I want to earn the right to stay here. But… it's really hard." He paused. I guessed that he still wasn't feeling very well. "When I first came here, all I could think about was myself. I figured that, if I could just get away from my parents, things would be better. And if they *weren't*, so what? I could just party all the time, and if I killed myself, who cares. But yesterday was bad. I don't know what those guys gave me, but I never felt like that. I was just trying to show them that I wasn't a wimp, so they'd think I was cool and leave me alone. I didn't plan to get wasted."

I gave him a look that clearly said, 'That's a load of crap!' He caught it.

He looked down at the table and didn't say a word. Finally, he spoke. "I'm sorry. I screwed up… It was totally my fault. I wanted those guys to like me. But I also wanted to get high… I knew what could happen… I was really out of it, wasn't I?"

"Oh, yeah."

I finished the dishes, and he finished his breakfast. I was about to go and do my other chores, when he spoke up again.

"Aunt Tara."

"Yes, Kane."

"I need a haircut."

I paused. Knowing his background, I just couldn't resist. "Do you want me to yell at you and punish you... or take you to the barber?"

He looked at me, half-smiled, and said, "Yes."

23. Aftermath

Mr. Spencer was quite impressed with the young man before him. Kane presented quite a change from the kid that the principal had seen just the day before. Clean, alert, and smart looking, although still a little hung over, Kane was polite and straightforward, as he entered the principal's office to take his punishment.

"I can see you've gotten a haircut," the principal commented, with obvious approval.

"In more ways than one, sir." Kane glanced over at me.

The principal also looked at me, and just a trace of a smile crossed his face. He and I were of the same generation. When he turned back to Kane, the smile had completely disappeared. "Oh, I see. Well, in that case, you know what we're here for."

"Yes, sir. I know I'm being suspended. I'm sorry for what I did. It was stupid and dangerous, and I take full responsibility."

The principal was further impressed and glanced over at me again. "You know the standard punishment is five days out of school?"

"Yes," I said, "and we will make good use of the time, believe me. We plan to pick up his work today, and I'll stop by each day to get the rest of his work so that he doesn't lose the progress that he's made. Kane knows that he has a serious problem. He also knows that he's not going to beat it unless he can beat it here, among his peers. We've been talking about finding him some kind of a support group. We looked into one over in Smithtown. It's just that they're pretty full up. We all know that this problem is not just Kane's."

"I am well aware of that," Principal Spencer agreed. "In fact, I just met with the parents of the other boys this morning. They had no idea what their sons were doing, and, to tell you the truth, I don't think they left here any more enlightened than when they came in. Either they don't want to hear about it, or they are just so overwhelmed that they can't comprehend how serious it is."

"Well, believe me, *we* know." I glanced over at Kane, and he was nodding his head as well. "I never realized that it would take so much time to treat. Just when I think we're making some progress, he has a setback like this." Then, being aware that Kane was listening, I added, "But he has to keep trying. It's a matter of life and death... and my kids and I don't want to lose him. He's been working so hard. We're very proud of him.

"But speaking of the other boys, just so you know, Kane

believes that they slipped him something, other than what they *said* they had given him. Not that this makes any difference in what Kane's done, but you should know what's being brought onto this campus. Marijuana and alcohol are bad enough, but he was very, very sick yesterday… much more so than he would have been just taking either of those, or even those two in combination. Just so you're aware that this kind of risky behavior is going on. These kids could have just as easily slipped something into somebody's lunch."

"Point well taken," the principal commented. "Now, I'll let you two get over to Student Services and get Kane's work. And Kane, we'll see you back here next Tuesday."

"Thank you, sir, and, again, I'm sorry."

We started to leave and the principal added, "By the way, Kane, I don't expect to find out that you've retaliated against these boys in any way. We don't want any further incidents. If they cause trouble for you again, you're going to have to let someone know about it: either your counselor, or one of your teachers, or your aunt, or myself. I know that's a tough thing for a guy your age to do, but you can't take matters into your own hands."

"Yes, sir," Kane answered. I nodded in agreement, and we left.

24. Uncle Joey

Kane did okay, during his first week back, after being suspended. I had put him in advanced classes. I figured that, that way, there was a better chance that he would not be associating with kids who were out to interrupt the teacher and hold the class back. The last thing he needed was to be distracted and bored.

There was only one minor incident his first week back, and Kane handled it himself. It seemed that the girl, whose family party he had crashed on New Year's Eve, finally decided to confront him face to face. I was guessing that she was actually interested in him and didn't know how else to approach him. When I picked him up after school, he told me that she had brought it up in front of a whole bunch of kids. He said that he just admitted to it, apologized, and then went into class. Apparently, the girl was so surprised that she didn't say anything more, and nobody brought it up again.

I asked Kane what he thought of the whole incident.

"Well, at first, I was really embarrassed. I think she thought that I was gonna deny it. And then she was gonna make a big deal of it and tell everybody the details. When I copped to it, I think it really threw her off."

"Do you think she likes you?" I glanced over to see his reaction.

He shrugged. "I dunno."

"Did you mention this to your counselor? You know, it was probably because of that girl that those guys decided to help you get yourself in trouble."

"No. I really didn't get any time to go to her. Should I?"

"I think you should stop and see her tomorrow. Tell her that you spoke to me already and that I suggested that she should know."

He was quiet for a minute. Then he said, "But I handled it myself."

"Yes, you did, and I'm proud of you. But you have to know how things work in this town. Word is going to get out, to parents, who you are and what you've done, and people could make trouble for you. Once parents think you're a problem, their kids are going to feel that it's 'open season'. They could make a *lot* of trouble for you."

He looked at me with interest. He was beginning, probably for the first time, to see the world outside himself and the impact that his behavior could have on a whole community. I didn't want to overwhelm him, but he needed to start understanding some things, if he were ever going to start taking responsibility for himself.

"But how is what *I* do *their* business?" Kane asked.

"Whoa! Think about it," I said. "Let's start with the tutors you've had for the past few months. This town pays for that. This town pays for police protection through our property taxes. While the police officers were babysitting *you*, on New Year's Eve, they weren't free to help everybody *else*, or to protect their homes or belongings. If you should decide to misbehave in school, and disrupt a class, you are taking time from their kids' education, which they are paying for with their school taxes."

"But, Ma'am, just this week, I've seen plenty of kids who are high in school, and they disrupt big time."

"In your classes?!" I paused, and then continued, "Did you just hear how I reacted when you said that?"

"Yeah…"

"See, I'm already outraged that somebody should be cutting into *your* learning time," I explained to him.

"Well, no, not in my classes. Well, maybe some of them, but not mostly. Some of it is just kids trying to get attention. But I've walked by some classrooms, during passing time, and I can tell that those kids have to be high to talk to the teachers like that."

"Then you know what I mean," I replied. "And, finally, these people don't want the influence of a known drug user, and juvenile delinquent, in classes with their children."

Kane had a lot to think about. He was very quiet. He hadn't even asked me why I picked him up early from school. In fact, we were a long way from home before he even asked where we were *going*!

"I want you to meet somebody," I told him, when he asked.

"Who?" I could tell that he had his guard up.

"My kids' Uncle Joey."

"What does he do? Wait a minute. Is he the guy who runs the TC? Aunt Tara, please. I'm doing the best I can. Please don't give up on me yet!"

"Relax! I just need to ask him some things, and I want you to meet him and him to meet you."

"But, why?!" He was starting to get really upset.

"Kane, I told you from the beginning that I didn't know if I could handle this. I know you're trying, as am I. But what we have here is a chronic disease. You're young, and you've already been dealing with it for, what, almost three years now? I want you to have the best care and information available, so that you can learn to manage this disease for yourself, as you get older. My brother-in-law is the most informed person I know, and he said he has some information for us. I want you to know what you're dealing with, and I want you to start as soon as possible."

"So I can still keep living with you?" Kane asked.

"As long as we can both manage...but I think there may come a time when you need to learn management skills that I can't teach you, and that you can't practice in a regular family setting. I want Joey to know you, so that, if we reach that point, he can help you find the best care for yourself."

Kane threw his head back against the headrest. "Man, I have really messed up my life."

"Kane, I know kids with Juvenile Diabetes, Epilepsy, and Depression, and kids who are deaf, blind, and with all kinds of physical challenges, and they had to learn to face and deal with these at a young age. I think it's time we faced the fact that your condition, in some ways similar to theirs, may not go away. It may never be 'cured'. The best we can do, at least for right now, is to try to manage it. And it may very well be that your predisposition to it is not your fault. It could be genetic. But that doesn't mean that you have an excuse not to do something about it."

"Are they gonna give me drugs?"

"No!" I fairly yelled at him and then regained my composure. "At least, if they do, it'll be over my dead body. Why do you ask that?"

"Well, for some diseases, they give you medication."

"Trust me. Not for yours."

It was a long trip, and Kane managed to get in a short nap before we got there. He awoke as we pulled in the driveway of the residential treatment center, where my brother-in-law had been working for as long as I could remember.

We stopped at a reception desk, just inside the front doors. I hadn't been there in years, but it still looked pretty much the same. Just the faces had changed. A pretty, young girl looked up and asked if I was Mrs. Wilson. I said, 'Yes', and she said that Mr. Wilson was waiting for us, and would be right out, but that he had just received a phone call. Would we please have seats in the waiting area?

As we sat down, she said, "We all admire your husband very

much."

She confused me for a moment. And then I said, "Oh, your Mr. Wilson is my brother-in-law. My husband, his brother, passed away some time ago."

I could tell that she was very embarrassed. "Oh, I'm so sorry," she said. "It was presumptuous of me to say that." I knew that she was a resident and that she was afraid that she had made a mistake for which she would be reprimanded. (I could also tell that 'presumptuous' was probably a Word of the Day.)

I hastened to reassure her. "No, it was very sweet of you to say something nice and to try to make us feel comfortable. Anybody could have come to that conclusion. It's nothing. In fact, this is my nephew, my sister's son, …and everybody assumes that he's mine. Trust me…you were very polite."

She seemed to relax a little. The phone rang, and she had work to do, so we seated ourselves. But, at just that moment, Joe came out of his office.

"Tara! How are you? I am so glad to see you." He gave me a big hug. "How are the kids? You should have brought them."

"Joe, I'd like you to meet Kane."

"Kane, my man." Joe lifted his hand, palm down, and Kane responded, with his hand out, to be 'slapped five'.

"Hi." Kane replied.

"Kane, I haven't seen you since... never. I've never seen you." Joey smiled at his own joke, and Kane had to smile, too. But he still looked very uncomfortable.

Joey turned to the receptionist and told her to get 'Lisa'. We then chit-chatted for a few minutes. I explained that the girls were in school until much later than Kane, so Dana, now seventeen (he couldn't believe it) would be getting Hannah off the bus. And of course David was away at school and Danny was at work in the city. "Joe, you really have to come and visit us more. The kids miss you."

"I know. I really should. It's just that it's hard to find people to staff this place, and we have a crisis a minute. I really find it hard to get away."

"I know. But everybody deserves a vacation. You have to learn to *delegate*." I gave him a look that I knew he would understand. That was a phrase that Joey used to always throw at me, when the kids were little. I desperately needed help, and he had come to 'play' with his big brother. He remembered and grinned. Then he got quiet.

"Geez, I miss Teddy," he said.

"I know. We do, too."

Just at that moment, Lisa appeared. She was an attractive young woman of about nineteen or twenty. Joey stood up, and I motioned to Kane to do the same, although I was pleased to see that Kane was already about to stand. His parents must have taught him something, in those early years.

"Lisa, this is my family, my sister-in-law, Tara, and her nephew, Kane."

"It's nice to meet you. I hope you had an easy drive. You come from upstate, right?"

"Yes, about two hours north."

Joey interrupted our niceties and gave Lisa instructions. "I would like you to give Kane a tour of the facility, and have him sit in on a session or two. Then get him some dinner, and bring him back to my office by six."

Then he turned to me, "Is that timetable okay with you, Tar?"

"Sounds good."

I gave Kane a look that, very clearly, said, 'Behave yourself!' and he nodded back.

$$* \quad * \quad * \quad * \quad * \quad * \quad * \quad *$$

Joey and I had so much to catch up on that the time flew by. He insisted that we talk about Kane, however, as he knew that *that* was my main reason for coming.

"Now, you filled me in on the phone about his background, and what he's been doing, and what you've been doing. What can *I* do to help you?" Joey asked.

"Well, first of all, I'm not sure I have any business trying to handle this kid on my own. He was in a lock-up program in California, supposedly to teach him a lesson, but I think it did more harm than good. I think he's proud that he 'survived it'. I'm kind of afraid that, if it comes to him *really* needing treatment, he won't go, or it won't work for him, because of that experience.

"I'm afraid that he's going to get comfortable with my discipline, Joey, and start trying worse and worse stuff, feeling that there's no 'bottom line', no final consequences."

"Wait, Tara. Does he *act* like he thinks you're too soft?"

"No... He's usually very sorry after he's done something, and he takes his punishment. It's just that he doesn't seem to have a lot of control, and I can't watch him every minute."

"He's young," Joey reminded me. "He's going to be a handful no matter where he is. But I'm telling you, right off, there are very few residential facilities for adolescents. And you have to convince the insurance companies, if you can *get* him insurance, that he really, really needs to be there. I would think that a kid like Kane would do better in a family setting, like yours. Heck, he looked scared to death just sitting out there. What have you been doing to him?"

"I've just been using some of the techniques that Teddy learned from you, back in the day, plus some old-fashioned family pressure."

"Oh, poor kid! We don't use a lot of that old encounter stuff any more," Joey grinned, thinking, no doubt, about what I must have done to poor Kane.

"Oh, now you tell me!" I grinned back at him. Then I added, "But the kids and I give him a lot of support and TLC, too."

"Now, see, that's what he needs. You know, a lot of kids mature out of all this. I think you're doing fine."

"And," I continued "he's scared to death that I'm going to leave him here."

"Here? Are you kidding? Did you tell him that? They'd eat him for supper here."

"I never said anything of the sort," I assured him. "You know I'd never make threats that I wasn't prepared to carry out. He just came to his own conclusions. And I let him. Besides, I wasn't sure that he'd be eligible for a place like this. And I guess it turns out that he's not."

"Well, you know…I was just thinking. If it makes you feel any better, he could come and visit me, as my 'guest', once in a while, if you thought it would do him some good...or even if you just needed the threat of a visit to keep him in line."

"Thanks, Joey. That might be nice for me to have in my own head, at least. Sometimes, it's easier to come up with alternatives when you know you have a back-up plan. I'll keep that in mind."

Joey had called for dinner, for the two of us, and it arrived at that moment. We set out the trays on a low table that he had in his office. The conversation turned lighter after that. We talked about the wedding. He said that he knew the people but didn't know them well enough to be invited.

On the dot of six o'clock, there was a knock at the door. "That would be your nephew. Have we discussed everything that you wanted to?"

"I think so. You answered a lot of my questions. And I appreciate the vote of confidence and especially the offer of back up."

"Great!" He turned and shouted, "Come in!"

Lisa opened the door and gestured to Kane to go in ahead of her. "Here we are!"

"Any problems, Lisa?"

"Not a one. We caught two groups in session. Jacob's and Randi's. They both let him sit in, but they went easy on him." She winked at Kane, and he smiled. "We had dinner, and here we are. Mrs. Wilson, your nephew is a perfect gentleman."

"Thank you, Lisa."

She turned to Joey then. "Will there be anything else?"

"No. Thanks." Lisa excused herself and left the three of us alone.

"Well, Kane. What do you think of our facility?" Joey asked.

"It's okay."

"Your aunt tells me that you were in a lock-up in California. What was that all about?" I knew that Joey wanted to see how Kane handled himself when he talked about his past behavior.

Kane hesitated. He didn't know Joey, and he sure didn't know what we had been talking about. He could come clean, and make himself sound really bad, and risk having to stay in this place. Or he could lie, and play down what he had been doing, and try to convince them that he'd be okay at home.

I figured that I'd help him out. "C'mon Kane. We don't have all day. You and I have to get home to the girls."

He looked at me with relief and then proceeded to answer Joey's question. "I was really messed up back home. I got in a lot of trouble. I was gettin' high every day. I cut school, and the kids I was hangin' out with robbed a store. They caught us, but the guys who took the stuff had dumped it already. They wouldn't have proved anything, except a couple of the other guys were holdin'. They got sent away for two years. I only just got three months, because I was so young."

"And stupid," Joey added.

"And stupid," Kane repeated. Joey looked at me in approval.

"And so you came out here so your aunt could help you."

"Well, not exactly."

Kane was about to tell Joey the details of his arrival, but Joey stopped him. "Yes, you did. You didn't know that that's what you were doin'. But somethin', way down inside you, underneath all the shit, led you out here. And, I'm telling you, kid, you better get down on your knees every night, and say a prayer of thanks that that part of you was still alive and pullin' for you. 'Cause I'm telling you right now, if things hadn't worked out like they did, if this lady here didn't have the generosity to take you in and the guts to take you on, I guarantee you... no hesitation...how long you been here…?

Kane looked at me. "About eight weeks." I answered for him.

"Eight weeks at your age on the streets of New York City... I guarantee you that you'd be *dead* by now or, if not dead, damn sure *wishin'* you were."

Joey let his words sink in. Kane sat very still. I could see that Joey intimidated him a little.

But, finally, Kane looked up at him. He looked him right in the eye and said, "I know. I've been on the streets. I was lucky. I had a home to go back to. The other guys weren't so lucky. I saw a lot of things that kids my age have no business seeing. When I was pretty sure that my parents were gonna throw me out for good, I knew that I had to go someplace else. There was no way I was gonna go back out there. Then, when I got here, I was so afraid that my aunt wasn't gonna want me that I thought maybe everybody would be better off if I just died. I guess I'm real lucky that I even screwed that up."

He looked down for a moment, and Joey looked over at me and nodded. I could tell by the look on his face that he felt that Kane was sincere. Neither of us said a word.

Kane continued, "I've messed up just four times in the past eight weeks. I know that might sound like a lot, but that's good for me. And I didn't get away with it. And I took my punishment. I think I can make it, if I stay with you, Ma'am."

At the word 'Ma'am', Joey looked over at me.

"It's sounds like 'Mom'", I explained. I suddenly had an itch right under my eye.

Joey nodded and then sat and waited again. His very demeanor seemed to make kids like Kane feel like spilling their guts. I envied people like that.

"Please don't make me stay here," Kane said. The plea was directed to me, but Joey answered him.

"Listen, Kid. Your aunt has raised four children…on her own. You're number five. And from what I know of her kids, you're more trouble than all of the other four put together. Why do you think she should keep you on and keep puttin' up with all your shit?"

Kane was quiet for a minute. Then, hesitating, said softly, "Because she loves me?"

"What!? Speak up, boy. I can't hear you."

"Because she loves me." Kane was embarrassed, but did as Joey told him.

"Do you know that? How do you know that?"

Kane hesitated. "Because she *told* me," he said finally.

"Just because she told you? Didn't your parents tell you that?"

"They used to...until I started screwin' up." Poor Kane looked so uncomfortable.

"And what about your aunt?" Joey went on. "Don't you think that she's gonna run outta patience with you, too? Do you think that when a person loves you that that love should be tested over and over again, like you've been doin'?"

"No. But she knows that I'm tryin' and that I just can't control it yet. She stood by me every time. And she bothered to punish me and talk to me and, and...and take care of me. She bothered to find out *why* I was messin' up, when I didn't even know myself. I don't know. I can just feel it. She cares about me."

Joey softened his tone then. "You're feelin' it because it's true. Your aunt *does* love you. And your parents love you, too. But there's such a thing as 'tough love'. Not all people can parent a kid like you. Just like not all people can play the trombone or ski down a mountain. Your parents had to let you go, because whatever they were doing was obviously *worse* for you than forcing you to do something for yourself. It usually doesn't happen to kids at such a young age, but obviously, you're different," Joey said, with just a hint of sarcasm. He paused to let that sink in. Then he went on. "But you know, Kid, I think you might make it... as long as you keep lettin' your aunt kick your butt."

Kane looked at him and then over at me. Then he said to Joey, "My aunt's good. But Hannah, now there's someone you don't wanna have to face."

Joey looked over at me. "Hannah's good, huh?"

"The best," I said, smiling.

"Really. Well, listen, Kid, I want you to stop screwin' up 'cause I got a kid of my own comin' up, and I may need your Aunt Tara, myself, one of these days. I don't want her worn out because of you." He said this rather lightheartedly, and I made believe I was fainting from the thought of ever having to raise another one of these kids.

But, then, Joe's tone turned serious, and Kane responded immediately. Joey could sure work a room. "Listen, Kane. I've told your aunt that if she can't handle you, or if she feels that she needs a break, or if you start getting worse and you need more help than she can give you, I'll take you in here, or find someplace else for you. I know that she loves you, and that she wants to stick by you. But I love *her* more than she loves *you*, and I'm not going to let you do anything to even upset her, let alone hurt her in any way. Kane do you know what you have to do when somebody really loves you?"

"No, sir."

"It means you owe them. Love is not about getting. It's about giving back in return. When someone loves you, you have a responsibility to them. You have a responsibility not to hurt them, not to keep testing that love, not to give them grief. Get it?"

"Yes, sir. I think so. I'm tryin' my best. But I'll try even harder."

"Anything this lady tells you to do, you do it. Anything she tells you not to do, you don't go there. Remember, you owe her your life. And, I know her, she's not gonna settle for anything less than the best you've got."

"Yes, sir. Thank you, sir."

Joey stood up then. It was time for us to go. He had given us about three hours of his time. I gave him a big hug and whispered, "Thank you". Then, aloud, I said, "Please try to get away and come up and see us. If you let me know when you're coming, I'll try to arrange for the boys to come home the same weekend."

"Well, you know, now that I've gotten a line on this one, maybe I'll just come up and surprise you to see how he's doing." As he said that, he shook Kane's hand. Then he added, with a grin, "I wanna see little Hannah kick his butt!"

"I'll be there." Kane said, and we left.

25. Another Phone Call

Talking to Joey made a big impression on Kane. Here was somebody else in his life who was pulling for him. It was important to him. I told him that he could call and speak to Joey whenever he wanted to...under one condition. If he wanted to establish a relationship with Joey, he would also have to call and talk to him when *I* wanted him to. He said he would think about it. I knew how he was feeling...someone else to cop to when he screwed up again. He wasn't sure he wanted that.

But I was thinking long-term. We still didn't know how things were going to work out with his parents and where he would be living in the future. Would he stay with me? Would he go home? If he went home, would he be staying with both parents or with only one? And which one? Would they be able to help him to control his behavior? We still had lots of rocky road to cover before Kane was out of the woods.

He finally settled into school. After their initial fascination with him as the new kid, the other kids finally backed off. I felt that his getting a haircut was a smart move. There was something about the long hair image that was not good for him. He finally became just another student...at least to the kids.

The teachers were still very good about being vigilant with him. They were very apologetic about the last incident and explained that they had had no advance warning from the kids (usually somebody blabs). But the reason that they found the boys at all was because the support staff was notified as soon as Kane didn't appear in his scheduled class. Teachers usually wait until a free period to report class absences. I was very grateful that they showed such concern for Kane. And I made him go and thank them for turning him in. And I went *with* him, to be sure that he didn't chicken out.

*   *   *   *   *   *   *   *

Kane's birthday was March 23rd. On March 20th, about eleven o'clock at night, the phone rang. I was already asleep. I grabbed it quickly so it wouldn't wake the kids. It was my sister. I whispered to her to hold on. Then I said aloud, "I'm sorry. There's no one here by that name. What number did you want?" I paused. Then I said, "No, this is 2964." I paused again and then said, "No problem. 'Bye."

Then I got up and closed myself in my closet.

"What was that all about?" my sister asked.

"If the kids are listening, they'll assume it's a wrong number. Now what's up?"

I could hear my sister take a deep breath. This did not sound good. "Well, Paul and I wanted to call Kane for his birthday later this week, and we wanted to know what would be a good time."

I noticed right away that she wasn't asking me whether or not she should call.

"Do I hear Paul on the extension?" I asked.

"Yes, Tara. How are you?" Paul joined in.

"Oh, I'm fine, considering. Your kid keeps me on my toes."

"Well, that's something else we called to talk to you about."

"Oh, really?" I had an increasingly bad feeling.

"Yes, Kate and I have been working on our relationship, and we're back together now."

"Oh, that's great, you guys. How long has this been?"

"Well, just a couple of weeks, but we feel that things are going really well."

"...And?" I knew before they said it what was coming. Or at least I thought I did.

"And we'd like to have Kane come home for Easter."

"You mean for Easter vacation? Why don't you guys come out here first? I don't think it's a good idea to disrupt his routine for one week like that."

"Oh, we didn't mean for one week. We meant for him to come home permanently. We just figured that it would be nice to have him home by the holiday."

I was dumbfounded. I knew that they were going to ask to *see* him, but I had no idea...

"Oh, now wait a minute," I said. "Are you thinking about what you're saying? Kane can only go a few weeks at a time without relapsing. He is in no way ready to be on his own yet."

"Oh, he won't be on his own. I'm sure that our solving our problems will make Kane feel much more secure and that he'll be fine."

Most of this conversation was between my brother-in-law and me. I couldn't believe that my sister was going to go along with this. "Kate, are you going to quit your job?" I asked.

"No, of course not. Why do you say that?"

"Because your son requires a tremendous amount of supervision, at this point in his recovery. I've already been trying to figure out what I'm going to do with him when I go back to work next year."

"Well, now you won't have to worry about that!" My brother-in-law chimed in again, and I began to see what was happening here. I was becoming more and more concerned.

"Paul, Kane still has some very serious problems. I've put together a large support network here to help him out, and he's trying very hard, but he needs a lot of attention."

"Look, Tara. I really appreciate what you've been doing, but I want my son home."

I didn't want to make things any worse than they were, and I certainly didn't want to jeopardize my relationship with Kane by alienating his parents. I had to bite my tongue.

"Paul, I can understand how you feel," I said. "You have to do what you think is best. I just want you to know that I also love your son, and that I will always be here for all of you. I just want you to think about something. When Kane was six years old, you didn't teach him to read; you sent him to school. When he wanted to play baseball, you didn't start your own team; you found him a league and got him a coach. I'm not trying to take your son away from you, any more than his first grade teacher or his baseball coach did. He needs some special help right now, and he's getting it here. If you take him home and things don't work out, will you please, please, promise me that you'll consider letting him come back here?"

It took all I had not to tell him that I would be hiring a lawyer and taking him to court for custody of my nephew. I knew it was late at night, and I was tired, and I didn't want to say anything that I would regret. But I knew that what was happening was something horrible... But what could I say?

"Sure, Tara. Now that he's gotten to know his cousins, I'm sure that he'll want to visit a lot more often. And he's old enough now that he can actually fly out by himself... Well, we know he can do *that*, don't we?" He chuckled at his little joke. I wanted to throw up.

I kept thinking how this man was talking like an idiot. Did he have any idea what his son had been going through in the past three months? Did he have any idea what my family and I had been through, on his kid's behalf?

I had to say something. "Paul, you do realize that Kane has a serious drug and alcohol problem, and that he's in the very, very early stages of recovery? He's just learning to manage his own behavior, and he's very unstable."

I knew that my sister knew what I was talking about, but I could hear the denial in Paul's voice. "Oh, come on. He's fourteen years old. You're talking like he's some thirty-year-old junkie."

I didn't say anything more. I thought that maybe my silence would have a greater impact.

My sister finally spoke up. "Paul, maybe we're being too hasty. We haven't seen Kane in three months. Maybe Tara's right. Maybe we aren't doing the right thing for him."

"Nonsense! He's our son, and he should be with us. Now that we're back together, everything will be fine."

We talked for a few more minutes and set up the birthday phone call. We still had about three or four weeks until Easter break. Maybe Paul would change his mind.

I hung up the phone and quietly opened the closet door. In the light from the hallway, I could see Kane lying across my bed, face down, resting his head on his folded arms. He turned his head to look at me.

"What are you doing up?" I asked.

"That was my parents, wasn't it?"

"How much did you hear?"

"Enough to figure out that they want me to come home and that you know I'm not ready."

"How do you feel about that?"

"About what? About going home?"

"All of it."

He sat up at that point, sitting cross-legged on the bed. "All this time, I would have given anything to know that my parents wanted me home. And I'm kind of happy that they do now. Except, now I'm afraid."

"Afraid of what?"

"What you said..."

"Look, I'm sorry. First of all I didn't know that you were listening, but you have to know that your dad has no clue about what's been going on with you. He was actually joking about the fact that you made it out here on your own. I'm afraid he thinks that your behavior is some kind of macho thing that he can be proud of. I wonder how proud he'd be if you had accidentally killed yourself."

I knew that I shouldn't be saying these things to the kid. He was already scared to death of himself. My anger at his father was leaking out, and I was too tired to watch very carefully what I was saying.

He sat quietly, and I was afraid that I'd upset him needlessly. But then I realized that he was just waiting for me to finish. Finally, he said, "No, I meant, what you said about my using. You were right."

"But you're committed to recovery, right?" I had to try to reassure him. "And you're learning more and more every day about how to manage your problem. We just have to make as much progress as we can, in the time we have left together."

"How much time is that?"

"Your parents want you to come home for Easter."

"When is that?"

"It's mid-April this year. So we have about four weeks."

I couldn't see his face in the dark, but I could hear him start to sniffle. Tears were pouring down my own face, at that point, so I couldn't say much to comfort him. I went over and sat on the bed next to him and put my arm around his shoulders. I could feel him shaking.

"I'll never make it," he said.

"You will make it. You have to. Something will work out."

"I can't go back there. I know they're my parents and all, but they just can't handle this. I know them. And if they can't handle it, what am I supposed to do?"

"I will always be here," I assured him.

"Right. You'll be here. And I'll be 3000 miles away. Isn't there anything we can do, Aunt Tara?"

I had to pull myself together. I had to get way above this, for his sake. I had to take charge of this situation and do whatever I could. But for right now, he just needed not to fall apart.

"Look, Kane. You need to learn from this, the same way you have from all the other setbacks that you've had. I have watched you from the moment you arrived here three months ago. I've watched you pull yourself up and gain strength and self-respect that I never thought I'd see in you. You have a Power in you that can help you. I want to see you get past this despair that you're feeling. I want you to have a great month and, if your parents want you to go home, I want you to go standing on your own two feet. And I want you to *stay* on your own two feet."

Kane nodded his head. I gave him a tissue and he wiped his face. He got up to go back to bed.

"Kane..."

"Yeah, Mom?" I could feel myself start to cry again, but I fought back the tears.

"You are not going to use this as an excuse to get high. You are not going to misbehave on purpose so that your parents will change their minds. And you are not to slack off in the progress you've made in school, or with me, because of this. Do you understand that?"

"Yes, ma'am," he sighed.

"I am going to be harder on you in the next month than I've ever been, so watch your step."

"Yes, ma'am."

He went off to bed at that point, and I tried to sleep. It was useless. I got up and tried to read. I was looking for inspiration as to how I could make this all work out right. I had a terrible feeling about the whole thing.

26. Fourteenth Birthday

Kane's birthday was on a weekend, so the boys came home to help celebrate. We took him to a pizza place, with a video arcade and rollerblading and laser tag. The kids made cards for him, and we gave him gift certificates for clothing stores, as he had outgrown most of the clothes that his mother had shipped out over the winter. And at eight o'clock that night, his parents called. He asked me if he could take the call in my room, and I told him 'Yes', but that I needed to listen in. He agreed.

"Mom?" Kane started the conversation.

"Kane, Sweetheart, it's so good to hear your voice."

"Kane! It's me! Dad! I'm on the extension. Happy Birthday, Son! How are you?"

"I'm doing much better, but I still get in trouble a lot."

"Well, Aunt Tara says you're doing great, and so are we," his mother assured him.

"That's good news, Mom."

"Yes, Son, your mom and I have mended our differences, and I'm living back home again." Kane's dad picked up the conversation at that point.

"I'm happy for you guys."

"Son, I don't know if your Aunt Tara mentioned it, but we want you to come home. We want us to be a family again."

"Yeah, she told me."

"Well, you don't sound too enthusiastic. We thought you'd be thrilled."

Poor Kane, to be pulled in so many different directions! I hated that he had to go through this. What were his parents thinking? Obviously, whatever it was, it involved *their* needs more than *his*.

"I can't wait to see you guys," Kane reassured them. "I really love you both. It's just that I still have a lot of problems, and I don't know if I can handle them out there."

"Don't be silly. You'll be fine. You'll be home with us, Kane. We'll handle them together. We're going to work harder at being a supportive family."

"Thanks, Dad. I'm just really scared. I've been doing better here, and I don't want to go back to where I was."

"We understand, and we're with you one hundred percent."

"Thanks," Kane repeated. He looked over at me, and I

shrugged.

His dad continued, "Now, Kane, tell us what you would like us to send you for your birthday. We wanted to wait until we talked to you to see what you really wanted. How about some music? … maybe something with earphones, so you don't blast your Aunt Tara out of the house?"

"Aunt Tara doesn't let us use those… especially me."

"Now, why is that?!"

"She wants to hear the lyrics that we're listening to."

"Oh, I see. Well, how about in the privacy of your own room? A young man's got to have some time to himself."

Kane and I looked at each other. Then Kane tried to set his father straight, "No, Dad, I'm afraid not. See, that's what you don't understand. I'm not like other kids."

I caught Kane's eye and shook my head. His father would not understand, and he was only going to start a problem.

"Oh, come on, Son. You sound so serious. You're only fourteen. When you come home, we're going to make up for lost time. You'll see."

"Okay, Dad."

They talked for a while longer. They got to hear each other's voices, at least. However, I could not believe how out of touch Kane's father was. Or how quickly he had forgotten about the seriousness of the problems that his son had been having. Maybe *he* was using drugs! Then again, it was probably just denial. Not many parents can handle the possibility that their kid might be an addict. Our brains have a wonderful way of protecting us from unpleasant realities.

They finally ended their conversation, and we went downstairs, where the kids finished the evening with cake and ice cream. Hannah gave Kane a big birthday hug, and he said it was the best gift he could have gotten. Everyone turned in early.

It was my custom, from when the kids were little, to go around and talk to each one as I tucked them in for the night. This nighttime ritual gave each child private time and a chance to share any last minute worries, or concerns, that might disrupt sleep or get worse in the dark of night. At some point, I had started including Kane in my rounds, and he seemed to look forward to this bedtime debriefing as much as the others. Tonight, I was particularly concerned that we talk about the phone call. "So, how does it feel to be fourteen, the most difficult year in a boy's life?"

"Is it really?" Kane asked.

"I don't know. That's what they say. Although, I think you took yours a year early."

"Yeah, I'm glad thirteen is over. It was *not* a good year."

"How about we just think of it as a turn-around year? You've certainly turned your life around," I told him.

"'You think so?"

"Yeah, I do. So, how was it talking to your parents?" I changed my tone, as I asked this question. I could hear myself go from 'mom' to 'counselor'.

"I'm scared. You're right. They're clueless...especially my dad."

"Did you feel any anger toward them? Remember, when you came, you were very angry with them."

"I think I just feel sorry for them. They didn't know what to do with me." He was quiet then, and I knew that he was thinking about something. I waited. "I'm really tired. I guess I'll go to sleep."

"Not so fast. What did you just think about?" I asked him.

"It's nothin'."

"Kane…"

"Okay! I'm really pissed that they're making me go home. They don't know anything about me, or what I've been through, and they're acting like it's all just gonna go away. Aunt Tara, I'm really afraid of what's gonna happen to me when I get home, 'cause I can tell they still just don't get it. They just want everything to be 'nice'. I'm afraid of what they're gonna do if it isn't."

"I think you're right on target. I think that the way that you're feeling is exactly the way you *should* feel under the circumstances. And, with that, you've earned the right to go to sleep."

I knew that we should have talked more about that. I knew that we would have to talk about possible situations that he might encounter and what he should do in each. But I was feeling so guilty about not being able to 'fix' this for him, that I just had to get out of there.

"'Night, Mom."

"Good night, Kane."

The month went by way too quickly. I tried on several occasions to change their minds, but Kane's parents were determined to have their only child back at home. I guess a part of me couldn't blame them.

I guess I should have been looking forward to my future freedom. After all, a whole year off from work should be a source of never-ending pleasure. But I was terrified for Kane. I was actually afraid for his safety.

He did very well in school for the whole month. One time, he fell asleep in his English class. The teacher called the nurse, and the nurse called me. But it turned out that he had just fallen asleep, having lain awake all night worrying about his return home.

I had him speak to a number of support people, including Joey, regarding his fears. Joey was very supportive of Kane, but when he got *me* on the phone, he went nuts. How could I let them do this!? I told him that I didn't know what else to do. He said that I should have gotten legal custody when they were happy to get him off their hands! *Now* he tells me!

I explained to him how Kane's father felt, and that I really had no legal rights. He finally had to agree. Then he gave me what turned out to be some very valuable suggestions. He told me to make sure that Kane was allowed to call me whenever he wanted and that I had various ways to get in touch with his parents. He suggested that I get cell phone numbers, work numbers, and names and numbers of places they frequented. If Kane were to contact me in an emergency, I would need to get in touch with them immediately.

The day of Kane's departure was approaching, and I could hardly believe that it was actually going to happen. I purchased a plane ticket for him and packed all his stuff. I had to do it while he was at school so he wouldn't see how emotional I was getting over this. I didn't want him to have my feelings weighing him down with everything else.

On the day he was to fly home, the kids said their goodbyes in the morning. I would take him to the airport while they were at school.

Once we had checked in and were in the waiting lounge, I asked him for his carry-on bag. I went through everything he had. He just sat there and never said a word. Then I asked him to give me his jacket. I checked it over. Other passengers, bored with waiting, were watching us with interest. Finally, I said, "Pockets", and he stood up and proceeded to empty out all his pockets. I checked through his wallet and then gave everything back to him. I was so preoccupied with my own thoughts that I didn't notice that he was standing there grinning at me.

"What?" I said, noticing, then, that he hadn't sat down yet.

"I'm gonna miss this."

I finally had to grin myself, although the tears were pushing themselves out of my eyes. "Sit down."

He plopped himself back down beside me, and I noticed the other passengers smiling. I was a little embarrassed, but how were they to know? I looked over at him. He looked so innocent…and so healthy! I was so proud of the progress we had made. I prayed to God that he would be all right.

28. Trouble

Kane called me when he got home. I spoke to both his parents and reminded them that the reason he looked so well was that I kept an eye on him every minute. They had to be vigilant with him. He still needed lots of help and supervision. I tried to pour out all my advice and wisdom in a few words, but I knew that I couldn't do anything more. I would just have to trust that he would be all right and that he and his parents would learn to survive together.

I received calls every few days after that. Mostly, they were from Kane, but his mother would also call. I don't remember his dad ever initiating a call, although I did speak to him on the extension on various occasions. They seemed to be happy with Kane's progress. For some reason, though, I kept thinking about Helen Keller, when she first returned to the big house, after just a short time in the garden house with Annie Sullivan. I hoped I was wrong, but the fear just wouldn't go away.

It was mid-April when Kane went home. My own kids and I tried to make up for lost time. We went to movies on the weekends, went skating, and went for long hikes. We needed time together so that we could talk and catch up on each other's lives. My girls agreed, though, that, even though they missed having me all to themselves, they felt that our family had done something good for Kane. We had all learned to appreciate our lives and each other more, because of him being with us.

I asked them how they would feel if he ever needed to come back again. Without hesitation, they said that they already missed him and felt like he was their brother. I teased them then and said, "Yes, and *knowing* that, I would like to know if you would ever want him to come back and live with us again!"

They got the joke, and Dana added, "Mom, you stuck us with two brothers already, what's one more?"

Then Hannah asked, "Why did he have to go home, Mom? He was getting much better, wasn't he?"

"Yes, he was. And I didn't think that it was a good idea for him to go home. I want you to know that I tried very hard to get Aunt Kate and Uncle Paul to change their minds. But Kane is not my child, and his parents have a total right to do whatever they want with him."

"Would you have done that if it was one of us, Mom?"

I had to think how to answer that. It was not a simple 'yes' or 'no' question. "Hannah, your Dad and I talked a lot about how we wanted to raise you kids, especially knowing that there were drug issues on both sides of our family. You know that the tendency to use drugs often *runs* in families. So, we did everything we knew, or could learn, to give you kids the best chance to avoid those problems.

"So far, things have gone pretty well, but the world can be a tough and dangerous place, and things are always changing. Parents have to be very vigilant, always watching and listening. If one of you kids were to have a serious problem, and I felt that what we could do at home wasn't helping you, I guess I would have to look for help elsewhere. I know that if I ever found something that helped you, I would try my best to put my personal needs aside and do what was in your best interests, even if it hurt like crazy."

"So, if you were Aunt Kate and Uncle Paul, you would have let Kane stay here?" Dana asked.

"Yes, I would."

I changed the topic after that. After all, we were trying to catch up on our own lives. We had spent the past four months on Kane's. I was sure that my daughters had other things on their minds, and I insisted that they talk about themselves for a while: the new boy in school, the latest craze on the playground, the prom, their favorite new musical groups, the list went on and on. Kids' lives are so full and complicated that, given the littlest opening, all kinds of neat stuff starts pouring out. A parent needs to listen attentively to all the good stuff, so that, just in case there's some not-so-good, some scary, or some downright bad stuff in there, it doesn't go unnoticed and un-addressed.

*   *   *   *   *   *   *   *

It was a Thursday night, about the second week in May, when the phone rang in the middle of the night. It woke me out of a dead sleep. I looked at the clock. It was one a.m. I really hated wrong numbers in the middle of the night. I always thought that it was going to be news that somebody had died or had been in an accident. My heart always started pounding before I even answered the phone.

"Hello?" It was sheer habit that enabled me to speak. I was so sleepy.

The voice at the other end also sounded sleepy. I couldn't quite make out what they were saying.

"Who is this?" I asked, trying to wake myself up.

"Mom?"

Then I was awake! "David is that you?"

"No, it's me."

"Danny?" It didn't sound like Danny. It didn't sound like David either, though, and I was running out of sons.

"It's me. Kane."

"Kane! How are you?"

"Not so good."

By now I was wide-awake. "Not so good? Why? What's happening?"

"I'm really tired."

"Well, it's late, Sweetie." Then I realized that I wasn't thinking clearly. It was late for me, but it had to be about, what, ten o'clock where he was. I began to get nervous. "Why are you tired? What have you been doing?"

"I haven' been doin' anythin'." His words sounded a little slurred.

"Kane, are your parents there?"

"Nah, they wen' out."

"Out where? Do you remember?"

"I think..." He stopped.

"KANE!" I fairly shouted into the phone.

"Wha'?" Thank God he was still there.

"Where did your parents go?" I tried to calm my voice.

"Out... to eat... But they... lef' me... food." His speech was slowing down. Dana came into my room then.

"Mom, what's the matter?" she whispered.

I mouthed to her to get the portable phone and come back. "Kane, have you been drinking?" There was a long silence on the other end. My hands were starting to sweat. Dana came back with the phone. I repeated my question. "Kane! Have you been drinking?"

"Nooo... I jus' took...a couple o' these."

Dana covered the mouthpiece and whispered, "He sounds bad, Mom."

I nodded. "Some of what, Kane? What did you take?"

Again, a long pause… "Some of these....li'l....pills."

My heart was racing. I had to think fast. "Kane, your cousin Dana is here. She can't wait to talk to you. I'm going to put her on the phone, while I try to call your parents, okay?"

"Italian... They wen'... for... Italian food."

Bless Joey. I grabbed the list of phone numbers that my sister had given me. Since Kane was tying up our line, and we couldn't afford a cell phone, I had to go to a neighbor.

"Dana! Keep him talking!"

She nodded. As I grabbed my coat, I heard her asking Kane if he had any more of the pills left. "Hey, Kane, I bet you can't throw those pills and get 'em into the waste basket." Bless her heart. She was so good with kids, even in a crisis.

I raced out of the house and jumped over the low hedge to the neighbor's yard. My neighbor, Fred Townsend, is a minister and quite used to people calling on him at all ends and hours of the night. He and his wife, Mary, both came to the door when I pounded and rang the bell.

"Tara, come in. What's the matter?"

I was breathless. "I need to use your phone. I'll pay you back."

"No problem." Fred picked up a cell phone from the hall table and reached it to me. "Here!"

I tried calling my sister and my brother-in law on their cell phones, but both went straight to voice mail. I then called the restaurant that they'd given me as one of their favorite dining spots.

"Pray for me, Fred. They've got to be at this number." I got the Maître d' at the restaurant. "Please, sir, this is an emergency. I'm calling from Connecticut. I must talk to Mr. or Mrs. Paul Winter. I know they eat there frequently."

"One moment, please."

I thought I would die waiting on the phone. The Reverend and his wife were watching me with great interest. I started to explain, "Remember, my nephew, Kane...?"

"Hello?" It was my sister's voice on the phone.

"Oh, my God, Kate. Is that you?"

"Tara? What's the matter?"

"I just got a call from Kane. Kate, I think he's overdosed. I'm at a neighbor's. Dana is trying to keep him talking on the phone. You have to go home right now."

"But, Tara..."

"Kate! You have to trust me on this one, and if Paul doesn't go along with you, you go yourself. Now listen to me. Call your 911 right now, or better yet, give your address to the Maître d' and have him call for you. Have the paramedics meet you there. Please, Kate, go home right now!"

"Tara, how can this be?"

"Please, Kate, trust me. If I'm wrong, I'll pay for the ambulance. But listen, as soon as you know where they're taking him, call me and give me the name of the hospital. I'll be out as soon as I can. I won't leave home 'til I hear from you."

"Wait! You're coming out here?!"

"Go, Kate! Call 911. Go home and find him. Call me as soon as you know where they're taking him. Oh, wait. Take this number, just in case our line is tied up." I looked at Mary and she nodded. I gave my sister the Reverend's number. I was afraid that Kane might pass out without hanging up the phone and would tie up our line. "Now, go. And don't let Paul talk you out of this."

I hung up before she had a chance to say anything else.

Fred was already up and running before I got off the phone. "Take our cell phone with you, Tara. Go home and get your stuff. I'll take you to the airport as soon as you hear from your sister."

I raced home. Dana was in tears in my bedroom. "I think he...he..."

"Did he drop the phone?"

"Yes, I was talking to him and then I heard a thud and I couldn't get him any more. Mom, do you think he...?"

"It will do no good to imagine the worst. Let's pray that he just fell asleep. I got Aunt Kate on the phone. She's going to call the paramedics and get home. Listen, Dana, I'm going out there."

"Where?! To California? Now? Tonight?"

"Call your brother Danny. Tell him what's happened. Tell him that we need him to come home this weekend. I'm just going to put a bag together, and Reverend Townsend is going to take me to the airport. You can handle things here, right? You can get Hannah off to school?" Dana nodded, and I continued talking to her while I started to pack my things. "You can stay home if you want, although I don't think it will do much good. I shouldn't get out there until almost lunchtime, our time, and I probably won't have any news until the time you get home from school anyway."

Dana was great. She dried her eyes and calmed herself down. "I can do it, Mom. We'll take care of things here. I hope he doesn't die." Then she started to cry again.

"Stop! We have too much to think about." I picked up the phone and listened, I could hear nothing. I realized that if we kept listening maybe someone, my sister or the paramedics, would think to talk to us when they found him."

"Dana, go wake up Hannah. I need her to stay on this phone. Then take this cell phone and call your brother. Be fast, in case Aunt Kate tries to call us back on that line."

We moved fast. I explained to Hannah that if she heard any noise at all, on the other end of the phone, she should call me immediately. I got dressed quickly, grabbed my suitcase and my purse, and packed whatever I could find. Dana got Danny, and he said he would take a day off and come up on the earliest train.

"We'll be fine, Mom. I'm sorry I got so upset."

I stopped what I was doing and gave her a hug. "I love that you care, Sweetie."

"Mom! Mom! I hear something." I threw myself across the bed and took the phone from Hannah. I could definitely hear voices.

They were muffled. God knows where the phone wound up. But I could hear them.

"He's in here!" It was a man's voice. I assumed it was the paramedics. God bless my sister for having the guts to follow through on this.

"Is he breathing?" It sounded like the same man again.

"Yeah, but it's a good thing somebody called us when they did. Let's get him stabilized and into the truck."

I didn't want to distract their attention from Kane by making any noise on the phone, so I just continued to listen and wait.

"Is he going to be all right?" I could hear my sister's voice. I decided that now was a good time to distract somebody. I started to whistle and shout into the phone, and my sister finally picked it up.

"Tara?"

"Kate! You did it. I heard them say that he's still breathing."

"Oh, my God, Tara. I can't believe this is happening."

"Hang on, now! Don't 'lose it' on me. I told you that he was a full time job. Just ask them what hospital they're taking him to. Can you do that?"

"Yes, I'm okay. I'm going to be okay."

"Okay, then. Ask them."

I heard her speaking to the paramedics. "My sister is coming out from Connecticut, and she wants to know what hospital we're going to."

"Tell her Davis Memorial, in Clear Ridge. Any taxi driver will know."

Kate turned back to the phone, and I told her that I had heard what he said. I repeated it back to her, just in case. "Look, Sis, I probably won't be out there until about nine in the morning, your time, but I'll be there."

"Are you sure, Tara? Can you leave the girls?"

"Danny is coming home to be with them. And remember, Dana is almost eighteen. And Hannah was the one who stayed on the phone until we heard the paramedics. So they'll be okay. They'll take care of each other." I said this as much for my girls' sake as I did to explain things to my sister.

"I think I'm beginning to see why Kane did so well out there," Kate said. "Tara, I'm so sorry. If we had listened to you, this wouldn't have happened."

"Sis, we'll have plenty of time to talk when I get there. Don't beat up on yourself. I told you that Kane has a very serious problem. I was never sure that we were doing the best for him here, either. Maybe this was all just part of the plan for you to better understand what he's been going through and what he needs. Is Paul there with you, at least?"

"Yes, he's helping the paramedics. He was the first one up here."

"Oh, then that was *Paul's* voice I heard first." I prayed to not feel good that Paul would finally see what I was talking about. No father deserves to see his son in that condition. Although I was still angry with him for not listening to me, I didn't want to think that I would use this near-tragedy to avenge my pride. "I'll see you in few hours. Go with Kane in the ambulance, and let Paul follow in the car."

My sister was certainly competent enough to figure that out for herself, but I knew she needed to have things to do. She couldn't afford to think too much about this right now.

"Will they let me do that?" she asked.

"I think so. It can't hurt to ask," I told her.

"Thanks, Sis. I'll see you later."

"I'll see you soon, Kate."

29. Close call

I was so relieved to be able to make the cross-country flight knowing that, at least, he hadn't died. I knew that he was probably in serious trouble, but at least he was still alive. I didn't know how I could have sat for five hours in an airplane not knowing if I was going to a hospital or a funeral parlor.

I arrived in Los Angeles at eleven o'clock in the morning, my time. I was able to get a taxi with little trouble. And the driver was familiar with the hospital. So, even with the rush hour traffic, we made it in good time. At least, that's what the driver said. I had other things to think about.

By the time I found my sister and brother-in-law, it was noon, my time, just as I had predicted. Kane had been moved out of the emergency room and into ICU. I didn't know much about hospitals, but I guessed that was a good thing, at least as far as intensive care could be a good thing!

My sister spotted me before I saw her. She came up to me and hugged me. Paul was right behind her, and, much to my surprise, also gave me a hug.

"Thank you for coming, Tara. When Kate told me you were flying all the way out here for Kane, well..." He started to choke up, and I interrupted him.

"I love your son. I feel like I've been through so much with him. I had to be here. Besides, this may be a long siege. We're all going to need each other. And speaking of need, I need some food!"

"You go with her, Kate. You two probably have a lot to talk about. I'll come and get you right away if there's any change."

Kate and I went to the cafeteria. All we could manage was some soup, but it tasted good.

"How does he look, Kate?" I asked her.

My sister shook her head and could hardly speak. "He looked like he was dead." She started to sob and then regained her composure. "He was pale and hardly breathing. I was so frightened. They wouldn't let us stay with him in the emergency room. I'm guessing they pumped his stomach. Do they still do that?" I shrugged my shoulders. I just didn't know much about medical things. My sister went on. "We got to see him when they put him in ICU. They had an IV in his arm and oxygen tubes in his nose. He just looked so young to be in such bad shape."

"He *is* so young to be in such bad shape." I said. "It makes me crazy. What's happening to our children?"

Kate looked up at me. "Your kids are okay, right?"

"I didn't mean my own children. I meant America's children. There are thousands and thousands fighting Kane's battle. It's just so hard to raise kids now. It's so dangerous. And so many kids are not making it. I just don't get it."

"Well, we know how it is in our house... "

"Look, Sis, I know I've given you a hard time about this. But the truth is, I watched Kane like a hawk, and he still got by me a number of times."

"But you have to admit, Tara, he did much better when you were on his case all the time. I guess not all adults can do that for their kids."

"I just don't know any more, Kate. I don't think adults should *have* to do that for their kids… at least not to the extent that I had to watch Kane! Maybe some kids are just easier than others. What I don't understand is what makes the difference. I thought that it was all the effort that we put in when they were younger, but both my boys tried getting away with things. It wasn't all that easy with them, either."

I allowed myself to ramble on. I hoped it would keep both our minds off Kane for a while. "I just think that maybe there are more temptations out there now, and adults have to be that much more vigilant with regard to their kids. I know that puberty has a major impact, but how come some kids find healthier outlets for their energy? And all this is coming at a time when our culture is telling us that we moms need to 'take more time for ourselves'! I'm afraid that, instead, it's going to be pretty much full-time parenting until our last kid turns, like, twenty-five."

We talked for a while more and then made our way back to ICU. Paul was sitting right where we had left him. We assumed that there was no change. I wondered if I would be allowed in to see my nephew. Kate said she would ask the nurse. She thought that they would allow in one family member at a time. But whether or not it had to be *immediate* family, she didn't know.

Kate came out a few minutes later and brought the nurse with her. Kate introduced us and explained to the nurse that Kane had been living with me for most of the winter, and that I was the one that he called when he overdosed.

The nurse was very amenable, but I think it was the fact that I had flown in from the East Coast 'just for the occasion' that actually got me in the door. The nurse led me down the hall to a private room right across from the nurse's station. The room was dimly lit. She went in ahead of me.

"Kane, your aunt is here to see you. She came all the way from Connecticut. You must be one special kid." She turned to me. "I believe in talking to them whenever I can. I think it seeps into their subconscious, and they know that there are people around pulling for them... especially the young ones! They really need their parents, and the parents are only allowed in for short periods of time."

"You are a good person," I told her.

"Thank you. And so are you to come all this way. He really must be a special child."

"He's had such a hard time with this drug and alcohol stuff. It just gets such a hold on them."

"Tell me about it. We see it too often in here. But this one is so young. How old is he?"

"He just turned fourteen."

She shook her head. "Well, let me give you a few minutes alone with him. I'll be right outside if you need me."

"Uh, can I touch him?"

"Of course. If we're going to pull him back from wherever he is, he needs all the contact and support he can get. Just be careful of the tubes."

I stood and looked at him for a minute. He looked terrible. Ironically, his hair had grown long again. I couldn't believe what he had done to himself in one month. He must have been doing something before this incident. I bet that his parents just weren't picking up on it. I could kick myself for not being more forceful in making them leave him with me. But, who knows, maybe something like this would have happened with me, too. I had no answer.

I went over closer to him and picked up his hand. "Kane! Wake up! I want to talk to you!" I knew that he couldn't hear me, but I, like the nurse, believed that you had to try to get in there somehow.

But, then, I didn't know what to say. As far as I knew, the role that I was used to playing with him was not appropriate any more. It wasn't my place to talk about discipline or consequences, or even his future, for that matter. I was suddenly just a relative from far away. The tears welled up in my eyes, and I said nothing. I massaged his hand like I used to do when he had headaches. Then I reached up and pushed the hair off his face. I remembered the morning that he put himself to sleep in church. I wished that he were faking now, the way he had been that morning just before he 'came around'.

Finally, I thought of something to say. "Kane, it's okay to wake up now. We're all here for you. Your parents and I love you, and we'll work out something so that you won't do this to yourself again. All your cousins are praying for you. Danny came home to stay with Dana and Hannah, so I could come out here. And I'm sure they've called David at school, so he can pray for you, too. We love you, and we want you to get better. So, you can come back from where you are. We're ready for you."

The nurse came in then and said that I had to leave, but that I could come back again later. I thanked her, and she gave me a tissue. I thanked her again.

Kate came up to me as I walked back into the waiting room. She could see that I'd been crying and was immediately concerned. "Is he worse?"

"No, but I am! He looks terrible. I guess just that 'one time' can really do a number on you." I tried to keep it light, but I was also fishing for information. At that moment, I saw Kate and Paul exchange glances. I guessed that they hadn't intended for me to see, but I did. "What?"

Neither of them said anything.

All of a sudden, I realized that I had been right. His appearance was not the result of this one incident. Again, I didn't know what to say.

They knew that I had figured it out. I walked over to the window and stared out into the parking lot. I couldn't believe this.

Finally, Paul came over to me. "You were right. We didn't know what to do. He looked so great when he first came home. Then, right away, we noticed things, little things, his attitude, certain old behaviors returning. We were hoping that he was just testing us, that if we kept our cool, and if Kate and I stuck together and spent more time with him, he would get over it."

I just kept staring out the window. I wanted to just disappear. I wanted to go someplace else. I could feel my heart crumbling in my chest.

I had worked so hard for this child. And they took him away from me, just when he had a real chance of pulling through. And then they see him falling apart again, and they don't even tell me…until it's almost too late. What if he hadn't called me? What if I hadn't had the number at the restaurant? What if they hadn't been there? What if they hadn't taken my advice and gone right home?

I stopped then. I forgot about my brother-in-law standing there. I forgot about how angry I was at them. I suddenly realized what an incredible, *blessed*, chain of events had led me to this place at this moment. I felt a wave of gratitude pass over me. All of a sudden I knew that everything was going to be okay.

I turned to Paul and smiled. "It's okay. Everything will work out."

At that moment, we could hear a doctor being paged to ICU. Before we could panic, our friend, the nurse, stuck her head in the waiting room and said, "He's coming around. The doctor has to see him first, but we'll keep you posted."

Kate and Paul hugged each other and then came over and included me.

"Let's sit down," I said. "I'm sure they'll want to check him over thoroughly before they let us in to see him."

Finally, after what seemed like an eternity, the doctor came into the waiting room. "Mrs. Winter?"

"Yes?" I could see that my sister was still very worried.

"Your son wants to see you. He's not totally awake yet, but he keeps asking for his mom."

My sister was so relieved that I thought she was going to collapse. Paul held on to her until she could regain her composure. The doctor held open the door so she could go in. Then he turned to Paul and me and said, "Sorry, hospital rules. I can only let one of you in at a time."

We nodded, and the doctor ushered Kate past him, into the ICU hallway. As they left the room, I heard him say to her, "Does he always call you 'Ma'am'. That seems so formal."

I shot a glance at Paul. He'd heard it, too. I tried to act as if I hadn't noticed and went to sit down on one of the sofas. "So how long do you think they'll keep him here, Paul? I'll bet the insurance companies have already figured out the average length of stay for drug overdoses." I tried to make light conversation in what had suddenly become an even more uncomfortable situation.

Paul stared at me. He didn't say a word. Finally he came over and sat down next to me. "Tara."

"Yes?"

"What did Kane call you when he stayed with you?"

"Aunt Tara."

"What else did he call you?"

"Well, one time when he got really, really drunk, he called me 'Mom'. But he was really embarrassed later and apologized. I told him that if it made him feel better, he could call me that once in a while. I told him that his mom probably wouldn't mind."

"And did he?"

"Did he what?"

"Did he call you that?"

"Not usually."

I could see why Paul was the head of his company. He was patient and persevering and, when he wanted something, he didn't give up.

"What did he call you... usually?" Paul continued.

The game had been fun, but I was tired of playing. I looked him in the eye. "'Ma'am'. He called me 'Ma'am'."

"I see." Paul stood up and walked over to the window. It was his turn to stare at the parking lot.

After some time, the doctor returned with Kate. He motioned to Paul to follow him next. Paul turned to me and waved toward the door. I shook my head and said, "No. He needs to see his father now."

"You're the boss," Paul said. And he followed the doctor in to see his son.

'No,' I thought, 'Springsteen's The Boss.' I knew then that I was losing my mind.

Kate came and sat next to me. "How is he?" I asked her.

"He's still pretty groggy, but the doctor thinks he's going to be okay. If what he took was what was on the prescription bottle, it was a mild sedative. We just don't know how many he took or what he took prior to that. They said that he was 'out of it' for longer than he should have been."

"Where did he get the pills?" I asked.

She hesitated, then said, "The name was torn off the bottle. He probably got them on the street."

"In which case, there could have been *anything* in the bottle," I added. My sister nodded in agreement.

"The doctor said that he has to run some more tests, but he was pretty sure that we got him soon enough so that there won't be any brain damage." At that point, Kate broke down and sobbed. "Brain damage! Can you imagine? That bright little boy! How could I ever forgive myself?"

"Hey! He said *no* brain damage, right?"

"Right."

"Well, then, what are you getting so upset about? He's going to be okay."

"I know, but, what if..."

"Hey, listen. He's okay and that's it."

We both sat very quietly for a while. Finally, Kate spoke, "Tara?"

"Yes?"

"What does Kane call you?"

Here we go again. I really didn't want to hurt my sister's feelings. "Kate, I lived with your son for almost four months. I know that Kane loves you very much. After all, you're his mother. He just associates me with the times when he loses control, and I give him an anchor. The fact that he called out for me now, in the condition he's in, doesn't count for all that much. And besides, I had just spoken to him, and my voice was probably in his subconscious."

"Tara, the fact that he called out for you now, in the condition that he's in, counts for *everything*! He needs you now. For whatever reason, he obviously feels that you're someone who can help him with this."

I stared at my sister. Did I detect a change of heart? "So what are you saying?"

Just at that moment, Paul returned with the doctor. "Who's next?"

"Well, I would be, Doctor," I said. "But I think it's more important right now that the three of us talk to each other. Any chance I could get a rain check?"

"Sure. Just let me know when you're ready. He could probably use a little break now anyway. Two parents are enough for any kid."

We smiled, and then I turned back to my sister. Kate looked at her husband then, and said, "Paul, I was just starting to tell Tara what we were discussing."

"Oh, good. Well, what did she say?" Paul asked, looking at me.

"I didn't really ask her yet," Kate told him.

"Ask me what?" My heart skipped a beat.

"Well, we know we have a lot of nerve to ask you this," Paul said, "and we'll understand if you say 'no'. After all, the stakes are that much higher now…" He paused.

"What? What?! WHAT?! You guys are driving me nuts! If you don't ask me to take this boy back home with me, I'm gonna kill myself right here and now. 'Cause if I come home without him, my kids are gonna kill me anyway." Kate looked up at Paul and started to cry. Even Paul's eyes filled up with tears. "That *is* what you were going to ask me, right?" I added.

Kate nodded her head and sobbed, "Yes, yes. We don't want to lose him. If we have to give him up to keep him, then we have to learn to let go!"

I guessed that made sense somehow. I didn't care. I was so happy. I leaned forward and hugged both of them. "Thank you! Thank you!" Then I stopped. I had been so afraid for Kane and wanted so badly to protect him. But all of a sudden, I realized what I was taking on again. I stood up and walked around the room. Kate and Paul watched me. They knew that something was bothering me. "Look, guys. You understand. I will do my best. I am not a miracle worker. What Kane did last night was the most serious thing he's ever done. Nobody fully understands this behavior. I don't know if what's been working for Kane, these past months at my house, is going to continue to work. You understand that, right?" They both nodded. "Has either of you told Kane that I'm here?"

Kate answered first. "No, I didn't. He was still so out of it that I pretty much just sat with him and held his hand. But I did figure out that it wasn't 'Mom' he was asking for."

Paul added, "I didn't say anything. And he really didn't seem to want to talk to me either. He wants *you*, Tara."

"I guess it's possible that he sensed that I was there, when I went in before. No matter. What I'm really concerned about is that he's going to think that just by going home with me that everything is going to be fine. That could be a dangerous idea for him to have in his head right now. We know that there's no geographical cure for drug use.

"And I also don't want him to think that, because he did this, he's somehow being rewarded, if what he *wanted* was to come back with me." I needed to think. "Listen. How would you guys feel if I went back to your house and slept for a while? Remember I'm jet lagging here. I've been awake since one o'clock this morning, thanks to your little tyke, and it's now seven p.m., 'body time'. That's like eighteen hours on three hours of sleep. I really need to think this through before I talk to Kane, and I need some rest."

It was decided that Paul would take me home and get me settled. I also needed to call the kids before it got too late. They would be very relieved to hear that Kane was going to be all right.

I had fully intended to do some serious thinking that evening, but, after I called home, I fell right to sleep and didn't awake until early morning. I had some pretty weird dreams, but I was even too tired for those to disturb my sleep.

30. Starting over

Still being on East Coast time, I awoke, fully refreshed, at three o'clock in the morning. I thought I heard someone downstairs and went to investigate.

"Paul, is that you?"

"Yes, Tara. I wound up going to bed early also, and now I'm wide-awake."

"Why don't we just go back to the hospital? I'm sure Kate would appreciate the company."

We headed back to the hospital and arrived about four-thirty. I remembered reading to my children, when they were little, about hospitals. The hospital was 'the building that never sleeps'.

We went up to ICU, but couldn't find Kate anywhere. Finally, a nurse spotted us and asked who we were. We explained, and she said that Kate was sleeping on a cot in the nurse's lounge. We decided to just wait and not disturb her. At about five-thirty, Kate came in and was both surprised and happy to see us. "How long have you guys been here?"

"Only about an hour. We didn't see any point in waking you."

"How's Kane?" she asked us.

"Sleeping, I guess. We didn't want to disturb him either."

At that point a nurse came in to talk to us. I guessed it was a slow time. Either that or this hospital was particularly user-friendly. "Your son is sleeping peacefully. Just in case you go out and don't see him when you get back, I wanted you to know that we'll be moving him to the second floor sometime this morning."

"What's the second floor?" Paul inquired.

"It's just regular patient care. He's well enough to leave ICU."

"Oh, that's good."

"He should be ready to go home tomorrow," she added.

"Oh, that's what I wanted to ask you about," I remembered. "How soon after he's released would he be able to travel, like to fly?"

"Well, of course, the doctor would have the final word on that, but, strictly off the record, I don't see why he wouldn't be able to travel right away. It's not like he has wounds to heal or internal injuries, or anything like that."

I nodded my head. "Thanks."

"But you have to ask the doctor, and don't say I told you anything. Okay?"

"Sure, no problem." The nurse left us then, and I started thinking. I had to get back to my own kids.

Finally, Paul said, "How about we all go and get some breakfast. I think there are some things we need to talk about, all together."

We found the cafeteria and ordered a light breakfast. We did need to iron some things out. And fast.

I started. "Look, guys. We don't have much time. I need to get some things straight. First of all, you haven't changed your minds, right? You're going to let me take him?" They looked at each other, and then both nodded. "Then I'm going to need his paperwork: birth certificate, social security card, insurance info. And I'm going to need to have legal custody of him. Can you have something drawn up?"

Paul spoke up then. "I'll get my lawyers on it this morning."

"Paul, it's Saturday."

"I'm the CEO. No problem. Consider it done."

"I'll need them by tomorrow," I reminded him.

"You'll have them," Paul assured me.

"Kate, you'll need to pack his things, spring and summer," I continued. "I want us to leave right from here."

"We will get to say goodbye to him, won't we?" Kate asked.

"Of course! You'll be driving us to the airport." I smiled at her. I couldn't imagine how hard this must be for my sister.

We worked out a few more details. Paul would also get his people to make our flight and limo arrangements. I wished I had people! Then we went back up to see Kane. At least his parents would see him. I wasn't quite ready yet.

When we got up to ICU, the nurse told us that they had just moved him downstairs. We went to find him.

I said that I would wait in the waiting room until they had a chance to see him themselves. "But, guys, don't be surprised if he's not very nice."

Kate stopped and turned back to me. "Why do you say that?"

"He should be pretty clear-headed by now. He's going to realize what's he's done, and he may be scared and angry."

"Angry with *us*?"

"Well, mostly with himself, but he may take it out on you. He's going to blame *you* for this, even though, and you've got to remember this, *it's his own fault*! If he doesn't take responsibility, if you act like *you're* guilty, he's never going to grow up."

Kate came and sat on the couch next to me. "I don't know if I should go in."

"Well, now you know why I'm *sitting* here!" I said, smiling.

She looked at me, as new insight crossed her face. "How should we approach him?"

"Again, I repeat," I said, "now you know why I'm sitting here!" Paul had been listening and now he, too, came and sat beside us. I had to smile again. "Well, *somebody* has to go in!" Then, I stopped and thought for a moment. "Look, let's give him a chance. Just go in and ask him how he's feeling. Don't tell him that I'm here, and don't discuss our plans. Above all, don't ask him what *he* wants to do, or how he would feel about going home again with me. The last thing he needs right now is to feel that he has any control in what happens to him. He just needs to know that there are adults in control, and that he will be taken care of. Hang tough! Remember, he may be coming out of a real creep bag..."

"What do you mean by that, Tara?"

It seemed that whenever I was around this issue, the old slang found its way back into my vocabulary. "Well...you remember Teddy's brother, Joey, right? Well, Joey used to believe that when guys would smoke from a particular bag of marijuana, they would behave in a particular way. Sometimes they would be nice and mellow, and other times they would be nasty or act like a 'creep'. So, when Joey would talk about people, he would describe their personality as if it were coming from the effects of smoking a particular bag of marijuana... in this case, a 'creep bag'." I paused and thought back to those days so long ago. "I felt like I had to learn a foreign language when I met Joey. It's so long ago now and the slang has changed, but some things just stick in your head and become part of you." I paused again, lost in my thoughts about my husband and the world that we grew up in. But we were the adults now, and we had work to do..."Anyway, guys, we're stalling here."

"But how should we act toward him?" my sister asked again.

"Let him know that you love him and that you'll deal with this misbehavior, and don't let him be nasty or disrespectful to you. If he's not polite and respectful, just say that you'll come back later. And then walk out."

My sister took a deep breath. "I can't believe that I need instructions on how to deal with my own child."

"Believe me, he's not... well..." I stopped.

"I know. He's not a child. And he's not totally mine anymore."

"Right," I agreed. "Once the drugs get a hold of them, they're fighting something that you can't protect them from. They need us to support them, but they're pretty much out there on their own. It's not easy on anybody... But, go! Show him that you love him. It will come to you what to say."

Kate and Paul went in to see Kane, and I sat and waited.

*   *   *   *   *   *   *   *

I had to get my attitude back. Kane and I had parted company on much better terms than we'd started. But now we were back to square one. We were back even further than square one. I had to be prepared once again to be really tough with him. Tough and distant. After all we'd been through together, I didn't know if I could play that role again.

At least, when he came to me the last time, I had the advantage. If this were going to work again, he was going to have to give that authority back to me. What he had been doing these past weeks at home would definitely have an impact on how we related to each other. The last time, he had hit bottom and was making his way up. Now he had been let loose again. I wasn't sure whether the events of the past few days were another bottoming out for him or whether he was just going to see himself as invincible now... or, worse, give up on himself. I was becoming more and more curious, and more and more anxious, about what attitude he was going to have.

At last, Kate and Paul came out of Kane's room. They did not look happy.

"Well, what's his attitude?" I asked.

"You were right," Paul said. "He's not nice. He turned away when we came in. He wouldn't answer us when we spoke to him."

"Was he being nasty, or was he just ashamed?"

"I think it's what you said. He's angry, and he's going to blame us. We were very careful about what we said to him."

"Did he say *anything*?"

"Not much. He asked when he was getting out of the hospital."

"What did you tell him?"

"We said, 'probably tomorrow'."

"Didn't he ask if he was going home?"

"No, as a matter of fact, he didn't. He *did* ask if he was going to get in trouble for this. We weren't sure what we should say, so we just said, 'What do *you* think?'"

"That was good."

"Then he asked if we had called you. Again, we were evasive. We said, 'Did you want us to?' He didn't answer, but then, after a while, he said that when he was 'out', he dreamed that he heard you talking to him. Then he said he was really tired and could we leave. The whole conversation was very formal."

"That's okay. He has a lot to think about, and he probably doesn't want to. I think we'd better keep a close watch on him until we get him out of here."

"Tara, aren't you going to speak to him?" Kate asked me.

"I'm thinking not. I think I might just show up tomorrow to take him home. In the meantime, though, why don't I stay out here, as a representative of the family, while you guys go and take care of business? I'm really going to need those papers, and the tickets, and Kane's things."

*   *   *   *   *   *   *   *

My sister went home to pack, and Paul went to call his people. I sat on a bench in the hallway, a short distance from Kane's door, for the rest of the morning. I knew that hospitals were always short-staffed, and I was not going to take a chance that he would slip out on us. I knew this boy.

I found a magazine to read, and the nurses put in a lunch order for me. I spoke to them regarding my concern about Kane, and they were glad that I would be an extra set of eyes. I asked them if he shouldn't be up and around and getting ready for discharge the next day. They agreed, but said they just didn't have the staff to handle him. They had to be careful that he would be completely steady on his feet.

Finally, one of the nurses said, "Are you the one he calls 'Ma'am'?"

"Yeah, that would be me. How did you know about that?"

"Well…when we're dealing with kids, we try to find out all we can. Someone must have told the nurses. They said upstairs that he was calling for you again in his sleep last night, and that you were here, but you hadn't gone in to see him. What's that all about?"

"He probably calls for me in his sleep because I'm his worst nightmare," I said, smiling.

"Why do you say that?" the nurse continued.

"I have four kids of my own," I explained. "When Kane ran away from his parents, just after Christmas, he came all the way to Connecticut to find me. He almost OD'd on me that night, and I swore that this kid was not going to come into *my* house and influence *my* children. Well, he wound up staying until Easter. I hit him with as many DIY therapy and child-rearing techniques as I could come up with. And he was doing much better.

"When his parents insisted that he come home, I was beside myself. I knew he couldn't do it. It was too soon. But I sent him home anyway, on a wish and a prayer that he would do well. I sent him off with encouragement and a positive attitude. Obviously, it wasn't enough." The tears were welling up in my eyes, as I recalled how I had felt giving Kane *up*. I could admit to myself now that I had really felt that I was giving *up* on Kane.

The nurse was a real sweetheart. She was an older woman, and I knew she understood how I felt. "Soo… now you don't know what to say to him? Is that why you haven't gone in?" she asked.

"Well, not exactly. His parents are desperate. They're sending him back home with me tomorrow. We have to start all over again. But now, I guess, I'm not sure how he feels about me doing that. I don't know if he'll buy into my authority again. He trusted me the last time and…" I could feel myself starting to tear up again, "…and I feel like I let him walk right into this. I knew he wasn't ready, and I let him come back here anyway. And he could have died."

The nurse listened attentively. She put her arm around me. "But he didn't. God has given you both another chance. Sometimes bad things happen for a reason. That little boy needs you. But he needs you to be strong. Very strong! The fact that he survived this tells me he's a handful."

"Oh, you got that right. And cunning. Do you know, one time he got high on me in church? In church! Can you believe it? And another time, I took him to a wedding, and he was supposed to check in with me every half-hour. Well, didn't he find a way to get himself loaded! And then he started making out with this girl, in a dark corner! And I had all four of my kids keeping an eye on him!"

As I talked to the nurse, I began to regain some of my strength. As I told her what we had been through, I could feel my determination start to build. I was not going to give up on this child. I was not going to let some chemical substance beat out my love and concern for him.

And I didn't care how he felt or what he thought, I was going to push my self-doubt aside, and I was going to do for him what he needed me to do.

By the time we finished talking, I felt much better. The nurse could see it, too. "I knew you were a strong woman," she said. "I know you'll do right by your nephew. He does desperately need you."

I had been looking at Kane's door, and, at that very moment, I saw him look out into the hallway, prepared, so it seemed, to make his way down the hall.

"I can see that," I said, as I nudged the nurse. She looked in the same direction. He was wearing sweatpants, a tee shirt, and sneakers…probably the clothes he was wearing when they brought him in. If we hadn't been sitting there, he might have passed for a visitor. "Kane! Get back in bed!" I fairly shouted down the hall.

He had been looking in the other direction from where we sat. When he heard my voice, with all the command in it that I could muster, he turned quickly and almost lost his balance. I could see why they said he was not quite ready to be walking around on his own. He stared at me and blinked his eyes. He grabbed the doorjamb to steady himself, and then he turned and went back into his room.

"Do you want to go in and see him now?" the nurse asked me.

"Nope! That did it. I'm satisfied. I think we'll be okay."

The nurse smiled and patted me on the knee. "Then I'll go in and make sure he got back in bed." She paused, and then added, "And I'll make sure he doesn't think he's hallucinating." She winked and chuckled and went off to check on Kane.

I turned back to my reading. I'd let him think about that for a while.

*   *   *   *   *   *   *   *

"Kane, Love, you heard your aunt. Now let's get you back into bed."

Kane was standing, holding on to the end of his bed, when the nurse came in to check on him.

"Then that *was* my aunt. How long has she been here?"

"She's been here since the morning after you came in. She flew in all the way from the East Coast, I hear. You must be somethin' really special." She made him lie down, and she covered him over.

"No, I'm not. I can't believe she flew all the way out here.

What about my cousins? Are they here?"

"I'm sure I don't know. I haven't seen any youngsters. Just your parents and your aunt is all."

"Has she been in to see me? I've been so out of it, I don't even remember. I did have a dream that she was here, but that was a long time ago."

The nurse stood listening to him. Then she said, "You know what? On second thought, you two need to talk to each other." She proceeded then to get him back up out of bed. "And besides, the doctor wanted you to start getting a little exercise, before you're discharged."

"Discharged? They're letting me go home?"

"Well, now, I don't know about that."

"Why? What happens to kids that... you know?"

"I really don't know, son. You have to talk to your family about that."

        *   *   *   *   *   *   *   *

I had a feeling that she was going to bring him out. I just kept reading my magazine, trying to figure out what I would say to him. Finally, the two of them stood in front of me.

"I think the two of you need to talk," said the nurse. "When you're finished, he needs to practice walking a little."

The nurse helped Kane to sit down on the couch next to me. He sat very still and didn't look at me at first. I didn't say a word.

Finally, he said, "I can't believe you're here."

"You called me," I reminded him.

"I did?"

"Yes, you did." I paused to give him time to think. "Whaddja want?" I meant to lighten the mood a little.

He started to laugh, and then he started to cry. "I'm sorry. I'm still a little out of it."

I didn't know what to say to him, so I just sat and waited to see what he had to say.

Ironically, he said exactly what I was feeling, "I let you down. I'm *so* sorry."

I looked at him. "But, on the other hand, you're *so* not dead."

He looked at me and nodded. He wiped his eyes on his sleeve. "Can we walk a little?"

I helped him up, and we started down the hall. "Kane, I expect you to pay me back for this."

He stopped walking and looked at me. "What do you mean? What do you want me to do?"

"Well, for now, keep walking. You're going to need all your strength." We continued slowly on down the hall.

"My parents are sending me away, aren't they?"

"Yes, they are. They realize now that they can't help you. Don't you agree?"

He looked at the floor and nodded. "I' been gettin' high for weeks. They never even noticed."

"I figured. Have you looked at yourself in the mirror lately?"

He shook his head. "So where are they sendin' me?"

When I didn't answer, he knew enough not to repeat the question. I let him have his own thoughts for a while.

Finally, I said to him. "Kane, you realize that I had to leave my children to come out here."

"I'm really sorry, Aunt Tara. But I really appreciate you bein' here."

"Danny came home for the weekend to watch Hannah."

"Oh great. I don't even live there any more, and I'm still a pain in the butt to him. I bet he was mad."

"Oh, no. I'm sure he wasn't mad. He loves his sisters. But you know, with my kids home alone for the weekend, my house is going to be a wreck."

Kane half smiled. "I'm sure they'll pick it up before you get home, Aunt Tara. Your kids are like that."

"Oh, no, they won't." I told him.

"Why not?"

"Because I told them not to."

"What? Why?"

"'Cause I told them that would be *your* job."

Kane stared at me in disbelief. "You mean it? You're takin' me back? But I thought you said that my parents were... Oh!" He got it.

I changed my tone then and made it as serious as I could. "Kane, we're not picking up where we left off. What you've done is really serious. You've broken trust, and we're way back where we started."

He was very quiet. I was sure that he was relieved and happy, but he knew what I was talking about. We had a lot of work to do. And he had to know that, in the end, I might not be able to help him after all.

"You might have to go to counseling, or to meetings, to deal with your drinking and drug use," I continued. "I may need you to be accountable to other people besides me."

"I don't care. I'll do whatever I have to." He took a deep breath. "Thanks for not giving..."

He started to sob again, and I pulled him close to me and gave him a hug. I was happy that he seemed genuinely receptive to getting some more help with this. That alone was a good sign. He held on to me for a long time. I turned and saw the nurse watching us from down the hall. I mouthed the words, 'Thank you', and she returned a 'thumbs up' sign.

When Kane had calmed down a little, I told him he needed to keep walking. We went up and down the halls for a while and, when I felt that he was tiring, I took him back to his room.

"I think you should rest now," I said. "I'll be in the waiting room. You are not to leave this room without permission and an adult with you. 'You got that?"

"Yes, ma'am."

"Oh, and when your parents come back this afternoon, you are to be a model son. You are to hug them and thank them profusely for giving you this chance. If they hadn't approved, it wouldn't have happened."

"Yes, ma'am, I will."

"Good boy. Now, get some rest."

I went back out in the hall and found the nurse and gave her the biggest hug I could muster, which wasn't a lot since I was totally wiped out.

31. Where we came in

He said that he could quit.
"I can stop whenever I want to."
But he knew what he couldn't, and wouldn't, do
Was ever want to want to.
                    -L. Dell

Kane was very agitated the next day. I assumed that it had to do with some sort of depression state, brought on by what he had gone through. He managed to be civil to his parents, however, and gave them a proper goodbye.

I didn't expect too much of him and watched him closely. His dad held on to him for most of the transport from the hospital to the airport. Kane was pretty strong by then, but we were being careful. He didn't seem to mind the whole thing. His agitation was from inside, not from events going on around him.

He said goodbye to his mom in the waiting room, and his dad helped me get him on the plane. They gave each other an awkward hug, and Kane and I were both relieved when the farewells were over and we were on our way. I put him by the window, and I sat on the aisle. We had requested an empty middle seat, if at all possible. We explained that he had just gotten out of the hospital and might need to lie down during the flight.

The stewardesses were very cordial and very attentive. After all, even in his present condition, Kane still had that appealing 'little boy lost' look. Unfortunately, it was the look that appealed to women of all ages and, even worse, often turned them into enablers. Back in the day, such women and young ladies were referred to in the TCs as 'mother-lovers'. (The similarity to another term was not accidental, since this was not a healthy relationship, especially for teen, or young adult, males.)

The stewardesses stopped by regularly to see if he was feeling all right and if he needed anything. He tried to sleep, but wasn't doing so well. I was beginning to wonder what kinds of drugs he had been doing since he left me. I prayed that it wasn't something harder than he'd been using before. I tried to concentrate on my immediate plans for him when we got home, but his restlessness was driving me crazy. Finally, I had to say something. "Kane, what is the matter with you?"

"Aw, I think it's the rebound."

"Rebound? From what? Did you take something since you went

into the hospital?"

Kane looked at me somewhat in disbelief, "I may be stupid, but I'm not crazy."

"Then this is a rebound from the pills you took the other night? I don't get it."

"I don't know. That's what my mom always said when it happened. She would get all irritable and said it was a rebound from something she had taken."

"Your mom?"

"Yeah." Kane obviously didn't realize what he was telling me. He was very preoccupied with his own discomfort.

"'You wanna lie down?" I asked him, finally. "You can put your head on my lap, if it would be more comfortable."

"Okay." He shifted his position so that he could lie down. "Man, drugs can make you feel like crap. They oughta be illegal."

He wasn't trying to be funny. He just wasn't thinking. I didn't even bother. We put up the armrests, and he laid his head down in my lap. "If I rub your back, will it help, or will it make you feel worse?"

He shrugged his shoulders. When Hannah was little, and she didn't feel well, or when she was overtired, I would rub her back to help her go to sleep.

I didn't say anything for a while. Soon, I could feel him start to calm down a little. I knew he was still awake though, so I asked the question that I had been mulling over in my mind for the past several minutes.

"Kane?"

"Yeah?"

"Do your mom and dad do drugs?"

"No more than anybody else's parents," he said.

"*I'm* 'somebody else's parents'," I reminded him.

"Yeah, but you're different. You're older. No offense."

"None taken. But you know I'm not that much older than your mom and dad."

"Really?"

"Really."

"Well, they don't do drugs in front of me," he went on, "but their friends smoke, I know. And one time, I came home during one of their parties, when they thought I was staying at a friend's house, and I know there were drugs there. I don't know if my parents used them or not, or if somebody else just brought them."

At that point, he rolled back to look up at me. "I thought all adults did drugs and alcohol...except like, you know, you and Joey."

"What do you mean 'like us'?"

"You know, like some people can't handle it, and they get addicted. So they don't do it any more."

"Kane, I never did illegal drugs. And neither did your Uncle Teddy. Joey was one of the lucky ones. He figured out what was happening to him early on and got himself into a program. But not all adults do drugs!"

"Well, most of my friends' parents do." He thought a minute and then added, "And so do most of my parents' friends."

I left it at that. I was looking forward to my next conversation with my sister! What kind of people was she associating with?!...Or becoming?

After a while, Kane actually dozed off, and I rested my head back. The stewardess came with a blanket, and we covered him up. Very quietly, she whispered to me, "How is he?"

I shrugged, and said softly, "We'll see."

Then she mouthed the word, 'Drugs?'

I was surprised, but I guessed that he *did* have that wiped-out look. I nodded. She shook her head slowly. I didn't think it was that easy to recognize. Does it take one to know one? Now I was starting to wonder about *everyone's* drug use!

When we arrived in New York, Kane was awake and feeling much better. He was able to walk off the plane by himself and even to help get the luggage. Then we went to look for our limo service.

Much to my surprise, our driver was the same man who had driven Kane up to our house at Christmas time. He took our bags and loaded them in the trunk. He didn't seem to recognize us.

Kane was very excited about seeing the lights of New York City at night. I always thought it was a spectacular sight. I pointed out the Manhattan Skyline, with the Empire State Building, and the various bridges. Seeing as how he had missed all this on his last trip, I was happy for him that he was in better shape this time around... at least at the moment.

We finally left the lights of the city and headed up the Interstate toward our home in the northern suburbs. He settled down then, and we talked about what we would be doing when we got home.

The driver had checked his destination list and had been watching us in the rear-view mirror. Finally, I said to him, "Do you remember us?"

Kane looked at me and then at the driver. Kane wouldn't remember *him*, of course.

The driver made eye contact with me in the mirror. "I thought you looked familiar. Is this the young man that I drove up to your place the last time?"

"Yes, it is," I answered.

"Well, it's certainly good to see him so, so…"

"Alive?" I filled in for him.

"Well, yes, now that you mention it. That's a good word."

"Well, he hasn't had it easy, but he's still hanging in there." Kane looked at me like 'Who is this guy?' "Kane, this is the driver that drove you up from the airport when you showed up here last Christmas."

"Oh." He had to think about that. "Oh, thanks. That was a real bad time for me."

"So I noticed." I knew that the driver was dying to say something else, but he was too professional.

"Kane, why don't you tell this gentleman a little about yourself?"

"Do I have to?"

"No, I'm sure Hannah will be waiting up for us."

Kane threw his head back against the seat. "And so it begins again." (I had to smile… but just a little!)

Kane stopped to gather his thoughts for a moment and then started in. "All right. I've been usin' drugs since I was eleven." He glanced at me. "…Okay, ten. I came out here to my aunt to see if I could clean up. She put me through hell. I was just startin' to get a handle on it, when my parents decided that I should go back and live with them in California.

"My parents are not the greatest role models. And they're not very observant. I started gettin' high again right away. I fooled them for a long time, actually. I do pretty mild stuff, mostly weed and alcohol. And sometimes I did pills, if I was pretty sure I knew what it was. There're a lot of rip-off drugs in California.

"But one night I was feelin' really down, and I took some prescription pills that I found in my mother's bedroom. I got scared that I was gonna overdose, 'cause I had done some other stuff earlier in the day, and I didn't know if I was down from that yet. So I called my aunt in Connecticut. She called my parents and they got me in time. I was pretty messed up, and I had to spend a few days in the hospital. Now, I gotta try to clean up all over again. So that's why I'm here in your limo… Again."

The driver was quiet for a moment, apparently waiting to be sure that Kane was finished. Finally, he spoke. "Well, thank you for sharing, son, even though that's a whole lot more than I think I ever wanted to know about anything in my whole life."

I had to smile.

"Sorry, but my aunt makes me do that. It's part of her weird idea of therapy."

I just shook my head. It was going to be a long spring.

*   *   *   *   *   *   *   *

We were quiet after that. I was really tired, since I hadn't napped on the plane. It was about seven o'clock body time, eleven o'clock local time, and it would be almost midnight by the time we walked in the door. I assumed that the older kids would wait up, but I hoped that they would put Hannah to bed.

We still had another hour to go. I glanced over at Kane. He was looking out the window. He was starting to bite his lower lip, something that I noticed he did when he was uneasy.

"What are you thinking about?" I asked him.

"Uh, nothing."

"I'm baaack." He tried to manage a smile at that. But I could tell that something was bothering him. He put his hands through his hair and then wiped his palms on his legs. "Look, whatever you're feeling is all psychological," I told him. "If you didn't go through some kind of withdrawal in the hospital, you're not gonna go through it now."

"I know. I just feel like I really need something."

"Hang tough, Kid. This is a total abstinence kind of program." I was watching him closely now. "You better not have anything on you."

"I don't." He was taking deep breaths.

"Give me your wrist." I just wanted to take his pulse, but he looked at me indignantly.

"I don't do needles, I swear. That shit is way too sick for me."

"Just give me your wrist and watch your language."

He put out both his wrists and mumbled, "Sorry".

But, now that he had brought it up, I was going to check him over. Although it wasn't really dark out, I put on the overhead light. His wrists looked clear and so the did the insides of his elbows and between his fingers. "Take off your sneakers." He looked at me like I was crazy, but I noticed that he had started to calm down and to breathe more regularly. This turned out to be a good distraction.

I checked his feet and made him pull up his pant legs so I could check the backs of his knees. If nothing else, I was reassuring him that I cared and was ready to go the distance for him.

"Now, let me check your *pulse*, like I was going to do in the first place!" I was going to add '…you paranoid little twerp', but it was hardly the time to lighten things up.

His heartbeat seemed normal now, but he was still breathing a little heavily. He had his head back on the seat, and it seemed like he was trying to calm himself down. I knew very little about 'things medical', but 'anxiety attack' came to mind. Whether it was a result of his recent self-abuse or something on his mind, I had not a clue.

"Okay, Kane. Let's go back to my original question."

He put his fingers through his hair again and this time leaned forward, elbows on his knees. Like a typical mother, I'm thinking that, first of all, he needs another haircut, and secondly, if this guy stops short...but I say nothing.

"What was I thinking about?" He looked over at me. I nodded. He thought for a minute, then said, "Everything."

I'm thinking that this is about as revealing as 'Nothing', but I wait.

"I'm thinking about everything... my parents, your kids, school, if I can stay clean this time. I never thought I would get so messed up that I couldn't just stop whenever I wanted to." He sat up and looked at me then. "I'm real happy that you're doing this for me. But I know I'm gonna hate you when you try to stop me from doing what I wanna do. How am I gonna love you and hate you at the same time?"

I smiled over at him. "Kane, I'm a mother. It comes with the territory. All kids feel that way from time to time. Thankfully, it's not always about such serious matters, but we moms get that 'love / hate' thing from our kids all the time.

"Look, we've been here before," I continued. "You're stuck with me. I'm not giving up on you. If it gets too bad, we'll try something tougher. But I will still be there pulling for you. And so will your cousins. We love you, and we know that this is what you really want, and we're going to help you. This *is* what you want, isn't it?

Clean and sober?"

Kane nodded his head, then slumped back in the seat. "I just know it's gonna be so hard."

"Maybe not."

"What do you mean?" He looked over at me.

"Maybe it won't be as hard as you think. You did it before, and now that you know how easy it is to get caught off guard, you have even more reason to want to learn how to handle this. Maybe it'll be easier than you expect. Have a little faith in yourself."

"But all the other guys talk about how awful it is when you really need to get high, and you can't get anything."

"Maybe that was because they really *wanted* to get high. If we can figure out your triggers, maybe we can set you up so that you don't relapse so easily. If there's nothing making you want to get high, you'll have a better chance. I hope you're telling me the truth about not using anything that's more physically addicting… like heroin?" I ventured.

Kane shook his head, "No way! That stuff is a death sentence."

"Well, back in the day, kids were doing barbiturates. After a while, everybody knew that you had to go to detox to come off those. If you tried to stop by yourself, you could actually die.

"Now, some kids now are fooling around with research drugs, and unidentified stuff, coming in from other countries... Not even the doctors know how *those* work.

"As much as I won't tolerate you doing *anything,* Kane, I would be real happy to know for sure that this little episode you're having is just anxiety."

"I'm not strung out. I swear. I'm just really tired. And nervous."

"Well, I guess we'll know soon enough, won't we?"

He really did seem much better after that. Thoughts can really do a number on the body. And I was sure that he was *very* worried about what would happen to him in the next few months.

32. Home Again

When we pulled in the driveway, the outside light came on. Kane and I got out, and I saw him look up at the house.

"The guy comes tomorrow to put the bars on the windows," I said. Kane looked at me in confusion. "I'm joking! Help the driver with the bags."

Just at that moment, Danny opened the garage door. "Hi, Mom! Welcome home! Kane, man, we're real glad to have you back."

Kane mumbled, "Thanks."

Danny looked at me as if to say, 'How's he doing?'

I shrugged, and then said, out loud, "Kane's got a lot of work to do over the next few months. I told him that we're all behind him, no matter what it takes."

"She's right, Kid. We don't want to lose you."

Kane nodded his head and then walked into the house with the bags he was holding, with Danny and me right behind him.

Dana had come down to the kitchen. When Kane put down the bags and looked up at her, she put her hands over her mouth to stifle a gasp. The flip side of Dana's being able to openly express her feelings was that she was not able to hide them very well.

Kane looked at her, then put his head down and shifted his weight from foot to foot, obviously feeling very uncomfortable. Finally, he said, "That bad, huh?"

Dana went over and put her arms around him. "I'm so glad you made it. I was so afraid for you." Tears welled up in her eyes as she remembered, I'm sure, that night on the phone. It was a terrifying experience that I had hoped my kids would never go through. I thought about how my husband had worried so much about his brother, and, now, Joey was still here and Teddy was gone. I secretly felt that it was the stress of worrying that killed my husband.

At that moment, a sleepy little Hannah came through the kitchen door and gave her mom a big hug. "Hi, Momma. Is Kane here? Is he okay?"

"Hi, Baby. Yes, Kane is right here. He's fine."

Hannah went around me and went over to her cousin. "Kane, you look terrible. You better get to bed." She reached up and hugged him around the neck. He had to bend down to hug her. He used to be able to pick her up. He was too weak now. He buried his face in her hair to keep, I'm sure, from crying. I heard her say something to him then, and he pulled back and looked at her. "Can you give me 'til tomorrow? I'm pretty tired tonight."

"All right, but no excuses."

"Hannah, get back to bed," I said. "In fact, all of you go to bed. I'm going to need your help tomorrow, and I don't want everybody to be tired. Danny, would you help Kane take his stuff up to his room? Did you take care of that little matter that I mentioned on the phone?"

"Yes, Mom."

*　　*　　*　　*　　*　　*　　*　　*

Kane followed Danny upstairs. When they got to his room, Kane noticed that there was no mattress on his bed.

"Boy, she's really gonna make it hard on me."

Danny looked at Kane and followed his gaze to the bed. He started to smile. "Nah, she's making you sleep on the floor in her room. You better not try to sneak out. She hears everything. Believe me, I've been there."

"I guess I deserve this."

"It's not so bad, except that she lectures you while you're going to sleep! I think she thinks it'll stay in your subconscious better." Danny noticed then that Kane was really down. "Hey, Twerp, you scared us majorly. Mom blames herself for this because she let you go home."

"I know. I was just thinking how tough this is on everybody. And, besides, she didn't have a choice about sending me home."

"No, she had no legal right to keep you here, and I guess your father was pretty hard-nosed about it. But, when she thought you were going to die, she was really upset that she had let you go home.

"So, listen," Danny continued, "I know you young kids are just gettin' into this drug thing, but I've seen guys doin' it for years. They pretty much don't go anywhere. Most of them are still living home, when they should be out on their own. They're still hiding their stash from 'Mommy', because they can't hold a job, and they can't afford an apartment. It's sort of embarrassing.

"My mom and all of us are giving up a lot for you. The other kids and I have talked while Mom was away. If you're not serious about this, we want you to come clean, and tell us. We know that cleaning up will be hard for you, even if you're really trying, but if you're just 'shuckin'', we won't let you hurt our mom like this again."

"Look, I'm sorry. I really appreciate what you guys are doing for me. I know that sometimes it might not seem that way, but I wanna *be* here," Kane assured him. "I have a chance here. Your mom is smart. She makes me feel like she really cares about me, and she seems to see everything…" Kane paused, "and she sees *through* everything!"

"Well, remember, she has lots of time logged in."

"Didn't you guys ever get high?" Kane asked Danny.

"David and I have both done some stupid things, but we have this whole family thing going on. And we managed to find enough friends, so it wasn't so hard. I can't imagine how it is for you."

Kane sat down on the box spring. "I told your mom about my parents gettin' high. Well, I sorta did. I wasn't sure how she'd react, so I just slipped it in."

"Wait! Aunt Kate and Uncle Paul use drugs?!" Danny said.

"Well, you know, it's a California thing. There's a lot of social pressure at parties."

"But your mom is a lawyer. She could be… debarred, or whatever they call it."

"I know. Everything was getting so screwed up. I just couldn't handle it any more. I was the one they were supposed to be watching for drugs. I shouldn't have had to watch *them*. And then, when it started gettin' too heavy for me, I couldn't *go* to them, because, what were they gonna say?... or do? When I had to go back there, I started to really not care about anything."

"Why did you call Mom?"

"Just luck, I guess. I went out with my friends, and we were doing some shit...stuff, and when I got back, my parents weren't home… as usual. I went up to my mother's room to watch TV, and she had these pills by the bed. I was pretty out of it already, so I wasn't thinkin' too straight, so I took a couple. I don't really know how many.

"Then, I started to feel really sleepy. I panicked 'cause I thought they might be sleeping pills, and I remembered that I had made *that* mistake once before! Somehow I managed to get your mom on the phone just before I passed out.

"It turned out they were some kind of sedative or something, but whatever I had taken before didn't mix too well with them. Luckily, it had been a while since I dosed the first stuff. But it still knocked me out pretty good. Man, when I woke up in the hospital..." Kane shook his head in disbelief at his own stupidity.

I had purposely given the boys time alone together, but I

wanted to get things finished up. I was very tired. I tapped on the open door to alert them that I was there.

"Danny, no war stories. I don't want him rehashing his drug use."

'No pun intended', I thought, but didn't say it. Did these kids even know what hash was? I shook my head. So many years! So much junk! ...So much trouble!

"Okay, Mom, sorry. We're finished in here."

"Kane, change into your sweats. Danny, I need you to help me move these beds just a little."

"Sure, Mom. 'Be right there."

I headed back for my room, but I could hear Kane say to Danny. "How does she do that? It's like she not only knows everything we're talking about, it's like she knows what I'm thinking! One time, she even knew that I had a dream about my dad, and she came in, in the middle of the night, to confront me about it! How weird is that?"

"I told you. She's good. Now, you better go and do what she told you."

"Thanks for talkin'. Will you be here in the morning?"

"*I'll* be here. *You're* the one we're not so sure about."

Kane smiled. It was good to be here. Hell, it was good to be *any*where.

33. Settling Back In

I kept waking up all through the night. Kane had a lot of trouble sleeping. Making the decision to abstain is pretty heavy stuff. You have 'drug dreams' and nightmares that you messed up. And you keep waking up to check that you're okay. At one point, I awoke to see him sitting up, holding his knees against his chest.

"Are you okay?" I rolled over to look down at him.

"No! Are you sure I can do this?"

"Absolutely positive," I assured him.

He rolled back, and over on his side. I kept thinking of the Bible references to 'rending of garments and gnashing of teeth.' I watched him for a while, but he seemed okay, so I went back to sleep.

The first thing I did when I woke up in the morning was to make sure that he was still there. He was sprawled out on his stomach, sound asleep.

I climbed out of my bed and moved it away from the door. I wanted to say goodbye to the girls before they left for school. Dana was just coming up to see if I was awake.

"How's he doing, Mom?" Dana said quietly.

"I think he'll be all right. He had a hard night, but he's sleeping now. He was still weak when we left the hospital, and then we traveled right away, and now he has to buy into this clean lifestyle again. It's a lot to deal with at any age, let alone fourteen. It's just the age when you want to be free and enjoy growing up. What a bummer!"

"Mom. No one says 'bummer' any more."

"Oh, sorry!" I laughed, gave her a hug, and met Hannah at the top of the stairs.

"Mommy, can I say goodbye to Kane?"

"He's still sleeping, Sweetie. Let's let him rest."

Just at that moment, I saw Hannah look past me. I turned and saw that Kane had gotten up after all. "Bye Han! See ya', Dana!" Then he turned to me. "Can I come down?"

"Sure."

We all went down to see Hannah and Dana off to the school bus.

When they left, I started Kane on a new diet. No sugar, healthy carbs, lots of protein, vegetables, and fruit. I had tried a similar one with him before, but I hadn't been that concerned about the sugar, since he didn't have the symptoms of sugar addiction. But I had been thinking about my own problems with sugar, and doing some more reading about it. Since it is an addictive drug, and a gateway drug for most of the planet, I thought maybe it might be a trigger for Kane's drug use. And since sugar cane is in the Grass Family, along with all the grains, from which almost all alcoholic beverages are made, I decided to take him off the grains, as well.

It was worth a shot. I had been pretty careful, but I upped my vigilance, getting canola mayo and sea salt, since the regular kinds were laced with sugar, and being extra careful to read labels on things.

Danny came down to breakfast and slapped Kane on the back. "Good, you're still here."

Kane lurched forward in his seat. I was just about to reprimand Danny, for being too rough with him, when Kane jumped up from his seat and lunged at Danny.

Danny was surprised, but countered his attack. He twisted Kane into a headlock, then got his arm and twisted it behind his back. "Ho! I guess we're feeling pretty good this morning!"

Kane shouted in well-deserved pain. Having raised two boys, I just watched in silence as they went through this little bonding ritual.

Danny kept holding Kane as he pushed him over to his seat and sat him back down. "Now, eat your breakfast like a good little boy."

Kane was going to go for it again, but Danny was ready this time and clamped his both hands on Kane's shoulders, pinning him in the chair.

"Hey!" Kane needed somebody to clip his wings, and despite his protest, I knew that he was loving every minute of this.

"Now stay there!" Danny commanded.

I could see that Kane was beginning to see Danny as someone older and wiser than himself. He needed to build those support networks. He was starting to reach higher than his own screwed-up thinking.

"Mom, if it's okay with you, I'd like to come home more often to help you keep this one in line," Danny offered.

I just smiled and nodded. Boys!...'gotta love 'em.

34. A Constant Struggle

The next few weeks were not easy. The second time around lacked the momentum of the first. Failure was an everyday feeling that Kane now had to deal with. I didn't allow him to go back to school right away, and that bothered him. Whether he needed the freedom, or whether he just felt that he had worked so hard to gain that privilege the first time, and now resented that it was being withheld, I didn't know. And I didn't care. I had to follow my gut on this one.

Kane was also now six months older than he was the first time that he had lived with me and was now well into puberty. When he was off the drugs, his sex drive came back with a vengeance. I kept him as physically and mentally active as I could and suggested that he try to control his thoughts. After all, that was where *every* battle was won or lost.

I told him that, until he had himself straightened out, he had no right to involve anyone else in his life. If he wanted to start dating or just going to social functions, he was going to have to prove that he was willing to relate to people as himself. If he didn't have the courage to relate to girls without being high, he was going to have to wait until he could.

I had always preached abstinence to my kids. There was no reason that they couldn't wait until they were married to have sex. And there were lots of reasons why they should. Did anyone ever wonder why our culture required marriage licenses preceded by blood tests? Does anyone ever wonder why we have so many children without fathers to help raise them?

I, for one, was in no hurry to have grandchildren, or a grandniece or grandnephew, for that matter. A nine-year-old has no business getting behind the wheel of a car, and a fourteen-year-old has no business messing with the reproductive system. Maybe I'm just very old-fashioned, or very practical. But I didn't feel that this child had any right to be skipping ahead to responsibilities that involved other people, before he had learned to be responsible for himself.

However I would deal with it, it definitely put a new "wrinkle in wrehab"…Okay, losing it again…. I was beginning to feel a real need to renew my own personal subscription to 'A Life'…Sigh.

Danny was true to his word and gave me a lot of his time to try to help out with Kane. I got a family membership at a health club, and that did wonders. They spent many weekends there, and I took Kane a

195

few days a week to work with a trainer. I needed to have him personally supervised, and the trainer was very understanding. And that gave me some free time, some exercise, and some time with other adults.

David came home for the month of June. He had technically graduated, but would be returning to school to continue with his Masters, starting in their summer program. Having both of the older boys home made it so much easier to share the responsibility for Kane.

But where there's a will, there's a way. And even though we believed that Kane truly wanted to get his act together, there was a certain something about adolescence that made the fight particularly difficult.

It was a Sunday night at the beginning of June. The girls still had school and, so, had gone to bed early. Dana was starting review for final exams, and Hannah had an inter-school field day the next day. They both wanted to get a good night's sleep.

Danny and David had taken Kane hiking for the day, and Kane had come home complaining that he was exhausted. So, Kane, too, had decided to go to bed early.

I think it was about nine o'clock when the three younger ones turned in. The older boys and I were watching a movie and were totally absorbed in the film. We had no idea what was happening elsewhere.

35. Same Old Same Old

Security officers, Joe Mullaney and Bill Thompson, were patrolling the upstairs of the mall. The upstairs was closed now to customers, but, since the movie theater was still open downstairs, occasionally they would find people 'out of bounds'.

The two of them stopped to rest for a minute against a movable kiosk that was unrented and had been pushed over to the wall, partially blocking a service door. The two had been discussing their teenage sons, both of whom were active in athletics.

"But you still have to keep an eye on them. Sometimes, it's the jocks that wind up with the biggest drinking problems."

"Yeah, I hear you. I try to have the parties at my house, whenever possible. My wife gets lots of food and soda, and we make sure that there's a lot for the kids to do. I usually invite a few other couples to help us out. We make our presence well known, and the kids have gotten used to us. I guess the ones that don't want that know better than to come, and the ones that come, deep down, I think they appreciate it."

"Yeah, I know what you mean. It's easier for them to stay out of trouble if they can 'blame' their good behavior on the adults around them."

"I always tell my kids to blame me for anything they don't want to do. I give them permission to make me out as the biggest ogre on the face of the earth. I tell them to tell the other kids that I'll beat their hide and hang it up to dry in the garage, if they step out of line. Of course, my kids know that I'm always there for them, but the other kids don't have to know that!"

The two officers, both youth workers during the day, earned extra money by working the mall on 'school nights'. It was usually quiet and gave them the weekends free with their families. They were both about to move on, when Joe stopped short.

"What's the matter?" Bill asked him.

"Did you hear that?"

"No, what?"

"Listen." Joe turned to look behind him. He could hear a low moaning coming from somewhere behind the kiosk. He looked toward the service doors and motioned for Bill to back him up. He went cautiously over and put his shoulder against the door to push it open. But as he did so, he glanced down at the floor.

Between the back of the kiosk and the door, was a narrow space, just big enough to hide a person. He shined his flashlight into the space and discovered a young boy. Wearing a sweatshirt, with the hood pulled over his head, and a pair of tattered jeans, the kid appeared to be asleep, but was moaning softly. In his hand was a paper bag.

"Hey, Bill! Look at this."

Bill came around the corner of the kiosk and looked down to where Joe's flashlight lit up the space.

"I'm gonna take the bag. Watch him." Joe reached down and took the bag out of the boy's hand. The kid didn't stir. His hand slid down to the floor beside him. The bag contained a bottle and Joe carefully brought it up to his nose. "Whew! Smell this. Strong stuff."

"Much too strong for this half-pint."

"We'd better get him out of here. 'Think we can carry him?"

"Sure."

The two men rolled the kiosk away from the door so that they could get a better grip on the boy. They each put one of his arms over their shoulders and hoisted him to his feet. "Come on, Kid. Help us out here."

The boy was barely aware of what was happening. His eyes fluttered open briefly, and then he slipped off again. The two men had to practically carry him back to the mall security office. When they arrived, their dispatcher, sitting at the window, immediately jumped up and opened the door, so that they could take him inside. They sat him down on a bench, and, right away, he started to slide down onto the floor. They grabbed him and moved him to another chair, where they could lean him up against the wall.

Joe stayed with the boy while Bill went in to get the Chief of Security.

"Did you search him for ID?" the Chief asked.

"We wanted to make sure that we had witnesses before we did that. He's very young," Joe replied.

"Well, okay, let's do it." They took off the boy's sweatshirt, patted down his jeans, and went through his pockets. They found nothing. "Hmm…'Almost looks like he planned this, doesn't it?"

"Yes, sir. It sure does."

"Well, let's give him a little time to sleep it off. Maybe he can tell us something in a while."

"Should we leave him out here, sir? We could lay him down in the staff room."

"Nah, I'd feel better if he was sitting up. If he vomits, he could choke, and we wouldn't be aware of it. Leave him there." He turned to Sadie then. "Sadie, can you keep one eye on him?"

"The one in the back of my head, sir?"

"Yes, Sadie, that would be the one."

Sadie was a character. Her job was to man the window, as people came with problems and inquiries. The kid was seated directly behind her. But Sadie was the motherly type, and the chief knew that she would keep an eye on him.

Bill and Joe were released to go back to their patrol. As they left the office, Joe commented, "Don't you wonder what kind of parents would let a kid, that age, get in that kind of shape?" Bill just shook his head.

It made no sense to send the boy anywhere, with no identification. He could just as well sleep it off where he was as he could anywhere else. The Chief did call and report the incident to the local police department, just in case there should be inquiries. Since the mall was surrounded by many small towns and communities, there was no telling where this boy had come from.

Left alone, the boy slept through most of the night. The security shift changed, and the new people were briefed on what had gone on overnight. It was agreed that they would let the kid continue sleeping until such time as he would be able to tell them something himself.

At about eight o'clock in the morning, the boy began to stir. He opened his eyes slowly and looked around him. He knew that he was in an office, but he had no idea where the office might be. His head hurt so badly that he thought he was going to be sick. His neck was stiff from where he had been leaning against the wall all night. He tried to change his position, but every move sent knife blades through his skull. He heard himself moan, and it echoed and reverberated through his head. Just about the time that he knew he was going to be sick, a person sitting in front of him, turned to him, and put a wastebasket in his hands. He thought his whole body was going to turn inside out.

"I been waitin' for that!" It was Sadie. She had decided to stay on, to watch out for this poor child.

"Excuse me?" The boy was barely able to hold his head up, and he couldn't believe that this woman was talking to him.

"I figured you tied on a good one. I was thinkin' you was too young to handle it." The boy was still too sick to defend himself.

Another wave of nausea just proved the woman right. She got up from her post and came over to where he was sitting. "You poor baby. What could have gone so wrong to drive you to this?" The boy just sat there, involuntarily rocking back and forth. "'You think you're finished?" He nodded, and she took the bucket away from him. "Hey, Tim! Come take this and dump it, will ya'?"

Another officer appeared and, although not thrilled with the assignment, did as requested. Sadie took a blanket from a nearby chair and put it around the boy's shoulders. He had started to shiver. "Hey, Kid. Don't you think it's time you went home?" she asked him. The boy had leaned his head back against the wall, but at this question, he sat up again. Sadie watched his face. "You do have a home, don't you?" He looked like he was thinking really, really, hard. "How about telling me your name?" she said, finally.

He looked at her long and hard and then shook his head. "No. No. I've got no place to go now." He sat very straight and very still. His eyes were closed, and Sadie thought that he seemed to be fighting the urge to be sick again.

Sadie had sons of her own, and she knew how boys could be. She made sure he was safe and then turned back to her desk. "Okay, suit yourself." She knew that there was probably no use pushing. He needed to figure this out for himself, in his own time. She was perfectly content to just do her job and wait it out. She also figured that his folks ought to be missing him about now, and that, eventually, somebody would call for him.

But this boy had no intention of being found by his family. He was too ashamed. He needed to go somewhere else. "I'm gonna be leavin' now," he announced after a short while.

"Tim!" Sadie called out. The officer appeared almost immediately. Before Tim could ask her what she wanted, Sadie tilted her head back in the boy's direction. And before the kid barely had a chance to stand up, and discover that he couldn't, Tim had grabbed him and sat him back down again.

"Whoa, young fella. I don't think you'll be goin' anywhere for a while…at least not until the Chief comes in. He's gonna want to talk to you before you leave."

"You can't keep me here!" the kid protested.

"Who can't keep you where? I'll take it from here, Tim." The Chief of Security appeared just at that moment. "Come with me, Son." He grabbed the boy under the arm and escorted him to another office.

From where he was seated in the Chief's office, the boy could see out through a window to where Sadie was manning her information window. The cobwebs were beginning to clear from his brain. He knew he was in deep trouble. His family had no idea where he was. If he refused to talk, maybe they would just let him go, and his aunt wouldn't find out what he had done. He shook his head. He finally had enough experience to know that it never worked that way. Why had he done this?! Why did it always seem like a good idea at the time?!

"Now, Son. Tell me. What's your name, and where do you live?" the Chief was talking to him again.

"Why does everybody always want to know that?!" He knew that he shouldn't have said that. He should just tell the man and face the consequences. But he couldn't. He just couldn't. Not again.

"Look, Son. What's the worst that can happen to you? Will your father beat you for this?"

"What?! No! Nobody beats me."

"Then what are you so afraid of? Why are you afraid to go home?"

"I'm not afraid to go home."

"Oh, come off it! Why else wouldn't you tell us who you are? You're sick. You're shivering. I'm sure that you'd rather be home than here. Why don't you just give us your phone number and let us call your folks."

"I can't."

"Okay, suit yourself. I give up." He leaned over his intercom. "Sadie, could you come in here a minute, please?"

The boy could see Sadie get up from her desk and come toward the office. "Yes, sir?"

"Sadie, take a guess at where you think this boy comes from, and get their local police department on the line for me, will you?"

"Okay, sir. I think I'll start with Wellmore."

"No!" The boy practically jumped out of his chair. "No, no, please don't call the police."

"Sit down, Son!" The Chief was getting tired of this game.

The boy did as he was told. "Please. I'll tell you. Please don't call the police."

The chief turned to Sadie. "Give us a few more minutes, Sadie. I'll let you know if I need you to make that call."

Then he turned back to the boy. "Okay, so who are you? And

how do I get in touch with your parents?"

Feeling totally defeated, the young man leaned forward in his chair, buried his face in his hands and began to cry. What was the matter with him? He knew that he was tougher than this. He had never cried when he was younger and the police picked him up. He was actually a little proud of it back then. What was happening to him? He felt so bad. And it wasn't the drink. It was deeper than that. He felt...

"Come on, Kid. I haven't got all day."

The boy looked up at the security officer. He wiped his eyes and tried to choke back the tears. The officer handed him a box of tissues. "Sir, would it be okay if I made the call? You can talk to my aunt afterwards, but would it be okay if I told her what hap… what I did?"

The officer nodded and handed the boy the phone.

He fought back the tears as he entered his aunt's phone number. He didn't want to cry on the phone. She picked up immediately. "Hello?"

"Aunt Tara? It's me, Kane. I'm in trouble. Can you come and get me?"

"Where are you, Kane?" His aunt didn't sound surprised this time. That made him even more nervous.

"Uh...I'm gonna put somebody on the phone who can tell you all that." The boy handed the phone to the officer and sat back in his chair. He was far from proud of himself, but he did at least try to take some responsibility. He still felt like crap. He was starting to really hate when things like this happened.

"Hello, ma'am! This is the Chief of Security at Stanbridge Mall. Are you familiar with our location?"

"Yes."

"We have a young man here who spent the night in our Security Office. He's asked me to allow *him* to give you the details when you get here. Can you come right over?"

"Thank you, Officer. I'll be right over to pick him up. Do you need me to bring anything?"

"He called you 'Aunt'. Do you have some type of guardianship papers? He looks to be pretty young."

"Yes, of course. I'll bring them with me. By the way, did you *make* him call me?"

"No, he insisted that he be allowed to call you himself."

"Good. That's very good. I'll be right over."

36. Hard Decisions

Before I left for the mall, I put in an emergency call to Joey.

"Tara, what's up?"

"Joey, I'm heading over to our local mall. Kanc just called me from their security office. He spent the night there."

"Loaded?"

"I'm guessing. He asked the officer if he could be the one to tell me the details when I got there."

"That's good."

"Joey, I have to go back to work in a couple of months. Am I doing the right thing trying to handle this myself? Do you think I should look for residential care for him? We didn't even know he sneaked out last night. How irresponsible is that!"

"Now, Tara. Remember what you're dealing with here. They need you to stand by them, no matter what, through all the ups and downs. If you send him away now, you could do more harm than good in the long run."

"I don't know, Joe."

"Do you want me to drive up there today?"

I stopped and thought about that for moment. "I haven't seen him yet. But if he sees you here, he's gonna freak."

"Well, I have a perfect right to visit my family whenever I want. If *you* want me there, that's all that matters."

"Thanks, Joey. I don't think it's necessary for you to come up, but I would like you to do me a favor."

"Anything."

"Would you make some phone calls for me? I'd like to know what kind of residential treatment we have around here for his age group... even if his parents have to use his college fund, or their retirement accounts, to pay for it! Remember, he's fourteen."

"Sure. But are you sure you want to go in that direction?"

"No, but *he* might."

"You *think*?" Joey sounded *very* doubtful.

"I can't believe that he's not getting pretty fed up with himself. One time, he even said that maybe he should have let them help him, the last time he was in. I have a feeling that he's coming to the conclusion that he can't handle this. I would like him to be close, though, so that we can visit him when they allow it. And I want him to know that he can come back here, when he's more stable. If he chooses this option, I just want to be ready."

"You really think he's gonna *ask* to go into treatment?"

"Am I being stupid?"

"No! I just think that you don't realize what you're saying. Very, very few people go voluntarily...especially at Kane's age. I don't think he's going to let you off the hook that easily."

"What?"

"Come on, Tara. Face it. You're scared. You're not sure you can handle him, and you're looking for an option."

"Joey, I just don't want anything to happen to him."

"You can't protect him. All you can do is stand by him. You know what they say, 'It's like carving Mount Rushmore. You just gotta keep chippin' away at it.' He's trying to solve the Great Life Problem. You just have to stand by him until he finds his way. Eventually, they all grow up and take on the responsibilities of adulthood."

"Or they kill themselves," I added.

"Or they kill themselves," Joey agreed. "But, ultimately, you don't have control over that. You're not his God. All you can do is keep lighting the path. If he doesn't pick up his bed and walk down it, that's not your problem. And, believe me, Tara. I know you. If you let it *become* your problem, then you've got an even *bigger* problem."

I sighed. "I know. Why do I care so much?"

"You're cursed."

I had to smile. "Well, at least you've made me feel better. I'm gonna go get him now. Do you think I should suggest that he call you?"

"Let *him* suggest it. Let's see where he's going with this. He may have some ideas of his own this morning that may surprise you. He's a smart boy. He knows that this is not good. That's why he asked to call you and to be the one to explain this. Just make sure that the security officer, who knows the real story, is sitting right there when you talk to Kane. Don't give him an opportunity to hold guilt."

"Oh, I know. We've been down *that* road before."

"Good luck, Tar. Let me know what happens."

"Okay, Joey. Thanks."

"Wait a minute, Tara. One more thing."

"Yeah?"

"When you were down here, I forgot to ask you how your brother's doing?"

"Tom? Oh, he's..."

"No," he interrupted me. "Not Tom... Jayce." He caught me off guard. It took me a minute to answer him. "Tara? You there?"'

"Yeah, Joey. I'm here. You just surprised me. Nobody ever asks me about Jayce any more. And I guess that's a good thing, because I have no clue! I haven't heard from him in about a year now. I haven't seen him since his college graduation, and that was like a decade ago!" Geez, I missed my kid brother, but I tried to be philosophical about it. "I guess people, even family members, are put in your life for a while, you do your best to be there for them, and then you have to let go." I could feel a lump forming in my throat as I spoke. I hoped Joey wasn't going to push me any further on this one. I *did* miss my little brother.

"Well, I'm sure he's okay," Joey said. "He's probably just too busy conquering the world."

"Yeah, right!" I wasn't so sure about that.

"Well, I'll let you go. Just let me know what happens with *this* one."

"Okay. Thanks, Joey!"

I hung up the phone, but Joey's words stayed in my head. 'Let me know what happens with *this* one.' Joey was a wise man. He knew what I needed to hear…even if he had to make me say it myself.

37. Helpless

I went to the window at mall security and told the woman on duty there that I had come to see the Chief of Security.

"So, what's his name anyway?" she asked me.

Well, that caught me by surprise. "Excuse me? I don't know his name."

"No, I mean the boy. I've been trying to guess all night. I'll bet it's not Rumpelstiltskin."

I didn't know what she was talking about, so I just stared at her.

"Come on in." She got up from her seat and opened the office door for me. "I'm assuming you're here for the boy. I was assigned to babysit him last night."

Finally, I began to realize what she was getting at. "Oh, I'm so sorry. Thank you. He's my nephew. He's been having a really hard time of it."

"So I noticed," Sadie replied.

"His name is Kane...Kane Winter."

"Oh! I would never have guessed that one in a million years. Have a seat. I'll tell the boss you're here."

She went down the short hallway and returned almost immediately with the Chief Security Officer. I stood up to meet him.

"Mrs...?"

"Wilson. Tara Wilson. How's he doing?"

"Not so good. I just wanted to tell you that he's very, very nervous about speaking to you. He had a really bad night. I told him that I would run interference for him, but he wants to tell you about it himself. He's very young. Is this the first time he's done this?"

"No! Not by a long shot. He has quite a history. My family and I have taken him in, to try to help him, but he keeps messin' up like this. I'm afraid I've just about lost all confidence in my ability to protect him from himself."

"Maybe that's what he's worried about. Ever since he spoke to you, he's been a wreck. I could hardly keep working in my own office! Between him trying to sit up straight and his muttering to himself, I thought I would go out of my mind in there."

"Well, shall we go and put both of you out of your misery?" I suggested.

The officer led the way back to his office. Kane was seated in a hard-back, wooden chair. He had a blanket still wrapped around him.

When we entered the room, he tried to stand up. He pushed himself up out of the chair, but held on to one of the arms. I could see that his knuckles were white.

"Sit down, Kane." I didn't want him to fall, and I assumed that he was standing for my benefit. The officer pulled another chair over in front of his desk so that I could sit facing my nephew. The officer then took his seat behind the desk.

"Son, your aunt has come to take you home. But before I release you, she needs to know what happened here last night. I can fill her in, or you can tell her. Do you still want to do this?"

"Yes, sir." Kane tried to get comfortable in the chair. I could tell that he still wasn't feeling well, but he looked determined to handle this.

"Then go on, Son."

"Aunt Tara. I sneaked out last night. I'm so sorry! Some guy bought me a bottle at the liquor store, and I came in here to drink it. I knew I'd be safe in here. I just needed to get away was all. I'm really sorry. I always forget how it's gonna turn out."

He stopped and waited for me to say something. I had nothing to say! I had no idea what to do with him next.

"Aunt Tara, I know that it's no good to say I'm sorry. I'm so sick of doin' this, but I keep doin' it. I don't want you to give up on me, and… and… I want to keep livin' with you. But I know you have the right to send me away. If you need to send me someplace else now, I'm okay with that. I'll do whatever you need me to do."

The tears were pouring down his face at this point. I could tell that he had been doing some hard soul-searching, but this was not the time or the place for us to be having this discussion. He was still drunk, and it sounded like what he was saying was just a peace offering...like it was the only thing that he could think of to say.

I still couldn't decide what to say to him. I just sat staring at the floor. The words wouldn't come.

"COULD YOU JUST LOOK AT ME?!" Well *that* got my attention! I looked up at him. He had startled himself! "I-I'm sorry! Could you please just say *something*? Please? Anything?"

I stared him right in the eye. I had nothing left. I just couldn't think of anything more to say that I hadn't said a dozen times before. I felt so sorry for him. I was really out of ideas. I didn't know how to help him any more.

I stood up and went over to him and helped him put on his

sweatshirt. I didn't say a word. I just took care of him.

We had given him lots of opportunities, while he was with us, to stand on his own two feet and to do for himself. We had insisted on competence and self-reliance, all the time supervising and teaching. But, obviously, there was still a part of him that was extremely needy, that still needed to be taken care of, to be 'babied'. After all, he was only fourteen, and he'd just lost his mom and dad out of his life again... and it was all his own doing. Maybe that was it. Maybe, when he felt that he needed to be babied, he made himself helpless.

I zipped up his sweatshirt for him, and he sat and sobbed. I wondered what had brought this on. What was it that he 'just needed to get away' from? I tried to think what had been going on with him just prior to this. He'd only been back with us a short time. Of course, he could have just been trying to get away from something in his own head. I knew better than to think that I could ever completely understand this.

I finished his jacket and turned to the officer, "If you're done with him, we'll be going now.'"

"If I could just get you to sign this report..."

I took care of the remainder of the paperwork, then went and stood beside Kane, who was sitting with his head down. I put my left arm around his shoulder and my right hand under his right arm. I gently pulled him up to a standing position.

We left the Security Office and went out into the hallway. When we reached the food court, just outside the security area, he stopped walking.

"Could we sit down for a while?" he asked. I nodded and guided him to a table. "Aren't you ever going to speak to me again, Aunt Tara?"

"Are you hungry?" I asked.

He shook his head quickly, then grabbed it with both hands. Ouch. "No. No, I don't want anything."

Again, I sat and waited. We had no place more important to be than right here. I sat back in my chair and looked around the mall. There weren't many people. Some salesgirls were taking a coffee break, and a young family was enjoying their baby boy. I glanced back over at Kane and noticed that he, too, was watching this little family.

Finally, he spoke again. "Thanks for taking care of me in there." I nodded. "Thanks for...well, for everything you did...and everything you didn't do...like, for not screaming at me or anything."

I nodded again. "You're welcome."

"You know, I was thinking." He paused. "I think I miss my parents." I raised my eyebrows and just looked at him, in a kind of amused surprise that he would say that. "I don't mean my parents the way they are now. I don't even know if I mean my parents at all. I just miss..." He looked again at the young family seated near us. The parents were feeding the child and talking to him and enjoying being a family. "I miss that. I don't remember if I ever even had that."

"You miss being a little kid? ...and being taken care of by your parents?" I asked.

He thought for a moment. "Yeah, I guess." He sat quietly for a few minutes. "Am I being a baby to want that?"

"No. Every kid deserves that," I said. "Not every kid *gets* it. And not every kid gets as much as he *needs*, for as long as he *needs* it. But just because you're big doesn't mean that you're not loved, or that you can't receive love from those around you."

"Oh, I know that you guys care about me. And I know my parents do, too. It's just not the same. I don't know. It's not like you can be little again."

I couldn't tell if this was really an issue for Kane, or if he was just still a little melancholy from the alcohol.

I took a chance. "But when you're totally helpless, Kane, and you can't even stand up on your own, and somebody has to hold your head for you while you puke, does that come close to being treated like a baby again?"

Kane stopped looking at the family at the next table and looked at me. "Is that what I'm doing?"

"I don't know. You tell me. Is it?"

"I don't know. I never thought about that before." Kane looked down at the table. When he lifted his head again, he had his eyes closed, and he looked like he was suddenly in great pain. "Can we go home now?"

"Just one more thing," I added.

"What?"

"I want you to look at that family again." He glanced over once more to the people he'd been looking at. "You're looking at that baby, right? And you're thinking about how you used to be." He nodded, and I continued. "Well, I'm looking at the father, and I'm thinking about who you're *going* to be. And, you know, it takes a long time to learn to do that job well. I think maybe you need to stop crying about the past and start preparing for the future."

    I knew that he heard what I was saying. I also knew that he was only fourteen. He was supposed to have years before he had to grow up. He was supposed to be having fun. I could tell by the look on his face that he was not having fun.

    Once again, I helped him stand up, and I held on to him as we walked to the car. He was pretty much walking on his own, but he didn't pull his arm away from me.

    *   *   *   *   *   *   *   *

    The kids had known, before they left for school and work, that Kane had not come home the night before. When he and I arrived home, there were messages from the older three, saying that they had called to see if he had gotten home safely. He was obviously surprised and touched by their concern.

    "They are going to be so angry with you," I commented.

    Kane looked at me in surprise. "Really? Why?"

    "Why? Why? What is the matter with you!? Don't you get what it means to love somebody? …and to be worried that something bad is going to happen to them?"

    "But I..."

    "But you what? You still don't get that this is risky behavior, do you?" I looked at him in wonder that he could still be so dense about what he was doing. "I guess it's just your age. You know that kids your age think that they're invincible, right? They think that nothing can ever happen to them, that they're somehow immune to death."

    "No. I know that. I've had friends die."

    "Really, Kane? Real friends? People you counted on? …as more than a supplier?…people you really loved and cared about for who they were? I'm guessing not." Either he understood what I was saying better than he wanted to admit, or his head hurt so much that he was willing to concede the argument. He didn't reply. "Why don't you go upstairs and work on your schoolwork?"

    *   *   *   *   *   *   *   *

    When I went to his room to check on him, a few hours after our return home, I found Kane asleep on his schoolbooks. I stood in the doorway for a few minutes and just looked at him. I thought of

Shakespeare's quote about sleep knitting up the raveled sleeve of care. Not so much in this case, I wagered.

I guessed that Joey was right. All my life, I always wanted to fix things. I was the peacemaker. I was sure that if I could just figure out the problem that I could solve it. It was finally dawning on me. With people, I was not the one who was going to do the fixing. Oh, I could be 'a receptionist in the front office', perhaps, but I was not 'The One' that they needed to see.

I determined, at that moment, that, although I was going to stand by this child for as long as he needed me, at the same time, I needed to find a way to turn over his spirit to the only Power that could really help him.

'Provide for him, Lord,' I prayed, silently. 'I love him dearly, but I just don't know how to help him.' Tears started to fill my eyes, and I wiped them away.

I turned to go. I was going to let him sleep. But at that moment, he must have sensed my presence. He stirred and lifted his head and turned to the door.

"Aunt Tara?"

I wiped my eyes again and turned back to him. "I came to see if you want some lunch."

"Oh. No. Thanks. I guess I messed up my stomach pretty bad."

I nodded my head. "Well, you come downstairs when you're hungry."

"Okay."

38. Breaking and Entering

As a man thinketh in his heart, so is he.
-Proverbs 23:7

It was a couple of weeks after the incident at the mall that I felt, for the first time, that I was making any headway, at all, in talking to Kane. We were out for our morning walk, and the both of us were feeling pretty discouraged. He had managed to stay clean for about two weeks, but he wasn't happy. Next to being high, everything else paled by comparison. Whether it was the effect that the drugs had on the chemicals in the brain, or his fascination with his drug-induced state, or that he just hadn't yet discovered something better in life, Kane found little joy in everyday living.

I remembered reading a quote, once, about heroin that said, 'It's so good, don't even try it once.' I knew, from my own experiences in life, that there are some things that off-balance the system so much that they're not worth doing. It's like 'for every high, there's an equal and opposite low.' If you don't want to have to go through the low, then you don't want to even bother to go for the high in the first place.

I knew that true joy and peace could only come from inside oneself, through a power that many call 'God', and that no human being could give that to another. But I also knew that, in order to receive these 'gifts of the spirit', one's thoughts had to be in the right place. Our thinking had to be aligned with basic principles that *worked*, according to what human beings have learned through the ages.

Ideally, that thinking is taught and nurtured throughout the life of a human being. But I also knew that it was accessible to anyone at any time. And I knew that it was my job, as a thinking adult, to try to prepare Kane to be receptive. We never know what positive thoughts or experiences the Universe, God, Life itself, might throw to us, at any moment, as a lifeline out of our own screwed up thinking.

We walked in silence for a long time that morning before I felt that I had anything to offer him. Finally, I just decided to start and see where it went.

"Kane, I want you to know that when I look at you, you look the same to me as any other kid who does not have your issues." Kane just shrugged his shoulders. He was pretty down on himself. "Am I right that you've decided that abstinence, that is, no drugs at all, is the way to go for you?"

"Well, I know that I can't do just a little. Once I get started, I'll be right back where I was and worse. It's just that some days are so hard, and, no offense, but life is so boring." He was quiet again, then, but I knew that he wasn't finished. So I waited. "Did you know that some of those guys at Jocy's spent like thirty years strung out, and they're still having trouble staying completely clean? Man, I don't wanna do this shit my whole life." He glanced up quickly, "Uh, sorry."

"We'll consider this walk-time to be like a game," I told him. "Anything goes. I want to hear how you feel about everything, 'in your own words', as Hannah says." We were both able to smile when we thought about our wise, little Hannah.

We walked in silence again. I wasn't sure where I was going with this, and I was waiting for thoughts to come to me. "Okay, so let's go back to what I was saying. From the outside you look just like any kid who isn't using. So the difference must be on the inside. You could have a body chemistry that predisposes you to drug use, but we know that that can be managed without using illegal substances…"

"Yeah…?"

"So the need to use must be based in your thoughts."

"Okay. So what thoughts do I think that somebody else doesn't think?"

"Or, how do others direct those thoughts into more productive activities?" I restated.

He looked at me with just the slightest trace of amusement on his face. "I don't think I know what we're talking about," he said.

I had to smile. "Well, let's think back. When you first came out here in December, how did you feel about your parents?"

"I was pissed."

"Okay, anger. Then New Year's Eve?"

"I was bored and a little...uh..."

"Go ahead."

"A little horny."

"Okay, boredom, and in need of sexual release." He looked at me in amusement. I ignored him and went on. "Church?"

"Boredom," Kane responded quickly.

"Not exactly. Remember? That's when you were hurt, because you felt like your parents didn't care about you, and you didn't know that I had been in touch with them."

"Oh, yeah, and then I was really angry with you because you didn't tell me about it."

"Really? Now, see? You managed to sit on that anger without acting out on it. As I recall, you made a joke about the whole thing and let it go. You know, all of us have to do that a lot of the time. Every day of our lives comes packed with lots of opportunities for hurt, fear, anger, and all kinds of other negative emotions. We have a choice about what to do with them. You can get stoned and forget about them and bury them. Or you can learn to handle them and grow from them. The collective wisdom of our human culture has a lot to teach us about dealing with all the hurts and stresses of life."

"How do you mean?"

"Well, you were angry at your parents, for example. Adolescents are often angry at their parents for a lot of very important reasons. And, by finding out about those reasons, you begin to understand more about yourself and about growing up.

"Just throwing a temper tantrum and digging in your heels, like you did when you were two, or going out and chemically beating yourself over the head, like you've been doing, isn't helpful.

"Our human wisdom tells us to honor our parents and to respect the wisdom of our elders, in the family and in the community. Adolescence is a time to sit down with your parents and talk about your family's values, to explain to them your need for a little more freedom, and to give your parents a chance to trust you a little more. You promise them that you'll take the punishment if you screw up, you *don't* screw up on purpose, and you show them that you can follow the new rules."

"But what if your *parents* are screwing up, and you really can't depend on them?"

"Then you have to start learning from people you can trust. In the olden days, Kane, kids were considered adults, and out on their own, at thirteen and fourteen. In our culture, we still have kids answering to their parents when they're in their twenties and thirties, because they can't get out on their own yet. Our culture is complicated enough that you *can't* be totally on your own at your age, but, on the other hand, you're old enough to be getting started, by learning from the people who care about you."

"So what am I supposed to do?"

"Listen. And ask questions. My kids and I have discussed lots of things since they were very little. They know how I feel about things and why. They know that, as they grow up, the rules change. And the rules will *keep* changing until my kids are out on their own, and making their *own* rules. That's something pretty exciting to look forward to, and it makes them want to stick around for what's coming next."

"Like what?"

"Well, let me think…. Ok, when my kids were little and we went out in public, they always had to hold my hand. I never let them 'run free' or run ahead of me. At first, it was a safety issue. As they got older, there were places where they could run and play as long as they didn't leave the area, and I would be watching them every moment, from a distance. As they got older still, they were allowed to go with friends and the friends' parents, as long as I trusted that the other adults were going to watch them.

"My kids were never allowed to be 'mallies', but as they got older, they were allowed to go on school-sponsored trips, where there would be responsible adults nearby. Then, when David was in high school, for example, he was able to go on a trip out of the country, with a travel group. The kids earned their freedom as they learned responsibility… gradually, little by little."

"Wait a minute. What are "mallies"?"

"They're kids that hang out in the malls, without any adult supervision. It's like hanging out on street corners, for city kids."

"Oh, okay…I know. "

I stopped myself from saying 'I'll bet you do!'. I was beginning to feel that he now deserved more respect than that. I admired him for what he was trying to do.

"So," Kane said, thoughtfully, "you're saying that, if you let yourself be bossed around when you're a kid, by people who care about you, then you'll be able to boss *yourself* around better later on."

"Very good. You always manage to say things so simply." I could see that he appreciated the compliment.

"What about drugs?" he asked then.

"What about drugs? The only way to avoid having problems with drugs is to avoid using them. However, let me rework your question. Let's say you asked me, 'What about using drugs to solve life problems like anger, boredom, and hurt feelings?'"

"Yeah."

"Once again, when you're a little kid, you run to Mommy and Daddy with everything. It's up to Mommy and Daddy to teach you how to deal with each thing as it comes up. Now, you'll notice that we don't use very much medicine around here."

"I thought you just hid it from me."

"Well, what little we have, I *do* hide from you." I smiled at him and went on. "No, we pretty much believe that, if you treat it well, your body will do a lot of its own healing, and that medicines, even over-the-counter ones, just put extra stress on a body that's already struggling to heal itself.

"And we treat emotional pain the same way. We believe that you can, through your thoughts, find healing for all kinds of problems, without using drugs that affect your mind."

"But what if you have like an accident or something?"

"Well, everybody has accidents once in a while, just like everybody has problems that they need help with. But we have found that if you keep yourself straight and calm and try to take care of business in an orderly way, every day, you have fewer of both of them. And, when you do need special help, you get back on track more quickly."

"Is that why you have me doing all this work around the house, to keep me busy so I don't start thinking about things that I shouldn't be thinking about?"

"Yes, partly. And partly because you're my fifth kid, and I'm getting too old to keep up to it all!" He smiled, and I went on. "My husband and I also found that when we talked through problems with our kids, it taught them a line of thinking, a way of reasoning things out, that they could then use themselves. We started when their problems were small, and we kept working with them, as they got older, and as the problems got more complex.

"For example, we taught them that when someone hurt their feelings, they needed to realize several things. First of all, it could be the *other* person's problem. The *other* kid might be jealous, or frustrated with something that *they* couldn't do or handle. Or maybe they're angry about something *else*, and lashing out at *my* kid, when it had nothing to *do* with my kid!

"Or maybe it was something that my kid was *sensitive* about. Sometimes people make fun of us for things that we can't change, and we have to learn to deal with that. And sometimes our God makes use of other people to alert us to things about ourselves that we *do* need to change. Maybe my kid needed to take a good, hard look at himself first, to see if there was something that he needed to talk to us about.

"In any case, every problem gave our kids the opportunity to learn to mature as healthy human beings. Can you see what they would have missed, if they had spent years covering up those feelings, with alcohol or other drugs?"

"Yeah, I guess… My parents never talked to me like this. Whenever I went to them with things, they started yelling at me for something. I never really got to the important part."

"But, admit it, Kane. Now think back. Didn't you usually start off the conversation by telling them about something that you knew would tick them off? Then they would yell at you, and you'd have an excuse not to talk to them about the difficult stuff?"

Kane was silent then. He was thinking. Thinking was good. "Yeah, I guess maybe I did. But I think maybe I did that to kind of check their reaction. You know, like, if they were going to blow up over something that I knew was no big deal, then I could pretty much guess how they were gonna react to what I *really* had to tell them. I never got to tell them about the stuff that I was really worried about… I don't know… Maybe I'm just making excuses."

"No, I understand. It's scary being a kid. And a lot of adults forget that. Of course, *not* going ahead and telling them *anyway,* was your real mistake."

"You know, Aunt Tara, I don't understand how people can be so comfortable with themselves. I always feel like I'm doing or saying the wrong thing. After everything I do, I feel like I screwed up, I said the wrong thing, or I should have done something else. How can anybody live like this? When I'm high, I just don't even care. I feel like, 'Hey, I'm cool'… and nothing else matters."

"I know. It's tough," I told him. "But pretty much everybody feels that way, if they really think about it. And our society is so diverse that there's no one 'way to be'. If you fit in with one group, you're a 'loser' with the others! After a while, you figure out what all the old philosophers were talking about. 'Be yourself!' 'As a man thinketh, so is he.' 'To be a man is to be a non-conformist.' 'If you can talk with crowds and keep your virtue, or walk with kings nor lose the common touch…'"

"What is all that? Where did you learn that? I've never heard that before." Kane actually seemed interested.

"Well, I guess you could say they're battle scars, what was left behind after fighting many good fights."

Kane nodded thoughtfully. Then he looked up at me and said, "You know, I'm getting hungry."

I smiled. "You know, me too. Let's turn around and head back home. But before we end our discussion for today, I want you to think about something for tomorrow."

"Okay, sure."

"Now this is a little more difficult. Are you ready?"

"Shoot!"

"Okay. Did you ever see one of those pictures that you can tilt back and forth and see two different pictures in the same place? You tilt it one way and you see one thing; you tilt it a little in the opposite direction, and you see something totally different?"

"Yeah, like a hologram."

"Okay, now forget that for a minute. Now I want you to think of yourself as a mirror, placed so that it reflects the sky and the clouds and the birds flying overhead. And when people look at you they see a reflection of all the very best things in the Universe. In this mirror, they see Love, they see our love for you; they see life and all the beautiful things in nature, including yourself; they see intelligence, and all the ideas that I make you think about, and so on. You are a mirror reflecting all of the most incredible things in the Universe. And it is going to be your job to watch your thinking and your actions, every day, to be sure that what you are reflecting, what people are seeing when they look at you, is only what is good and healthy. Are you following me?"

"I think. But what about all the shit I've been doing?"

"Well, do you remember that picture, that we just talked about, that could be tilted so you can see two pictures in the same place?"

"Yeah?"

"Well, your *mirror* has been tilted so that it's reflecting a lot of *junk* that's been in your life. And when the world looks at you, that's what it's seeing. It's seeing "junk thoughts" like anger, sadness, and defiance, and lots of bad behavior that's coming from those thoughts. You've been allowing a lot of things in your life that aren't serving your purpose."

"Which is...?"

"To reflect to others the very *best* that there is, for you and for them."

"So what if I flip back and forth like the picture?"

"The more you reflect the positive view, the more fun and rewarding it will be. You'll be able to maintain that reflection and have no interest in returning to the other. In fact, the other will eventually disappear. In drug programs, they call this 'acting as if'.

You have to try to always act, think, and behave like the person you want others to see, like the person you want to become.

"Of course, you're going to need help doing this for a while. And that's why I'm keeping you here, with me, for as long as I can, provided, of course, that you're willing to do your part."

"Do you talk to your kids about this reflecting stuff?"

"Of course. We all need to fill our lives with uplifting thoughts, to take nourishing care of our bodies, and to keep secure and happy people around us, as much as possible. That way we can be positive when we interact with others. After all, that's our purpose.

"At first, when your cousins were little, I taught them these ideas to protect them. As they got older, it became the foundation for their relationships with friends, co-workers, and even strangers that they meet. And they understand that it's the basis for their real purpose in life."

"But isn't that, like, lame, being good all the time?" Kane asked.

"It's not about *being* good, it's about *reflecting* good. The rest of the world is dying for it. It has like 'magical power'. It protects *you*, while making the world a better place to be. Don't you like being with my kids?"

Kane nodded and thought about that for a while. It was so hard to explain some things, let alone try to understand them, especially when you're only fourteen. I figured that I had overloaded him for the day, and that he was just being polite by pretending to think about this.

But then he said, "Okay, so like, when I was messed up, I was like a mirror reflecting all the messed up stuff around me: my parents, my drug friends, the drugs I was taking, my own fucked up thinking. Everybody thought it was me, but it really wasn't the real me. 'Cause the real me also had the choice to show, or *reflect*, as you say, all the good stuff around me, like I'm trying to do here, like doin' healthy things and talkin' about good stuff and actin' right."

I stopped him right in the middle of the sidewalk and turned him around to face me. Wow. 'Act as if'! He had actually gotten that powerful concept.

"Exactly!" I said. "Now I want you to hold onto that thought for as long as you can, and tomorrow, I want us to talk about it some more, okay?"

"Okay."

I watched Kane's face carefully as we walked the rest of the way home. I had never seen such genuine brightness and peace shine out of this child's face before.

It had been a kind of 'pinball conversation', as we went from one topic to another, and from example to example. But it had pretty much reflected the thinking patterns that I was used to, among our family members, especially the guys.

But, more importantly, I felt that points had been made, and understood. And Kane had had a very important insight. He was beginning to see that change was possible and that he had choices. And most of all, he was beginning to grasp that all the things he'd been doing weren't really part of his true nature. He could redefine himself as a 'reflector of good' and let go of his concept of himself as a 'bad person'.

I wanted to get him to the point that he felt that he could lay claim to all the good in the world, and that maybe, just maybe, his life had an important purpose after all. Heavy stuff for a young kid! Well, I guess, not so young.

39. Reach for the Sky

Sometimes, when the house got too noisy, I would go into the downstairs bathroom, where I could still hear the kids in the living room, and sit on the toilet lid and read.

It was one of those Sunday afternoons. Hannah had gone on a play date. David was out. And Dana and Kane had a loud, raucous movie on, in the living room. I closed myself up in the bathroom and tried to read.

It was pretty hopeless, since the kids were into the movie and were shouting and laughing along with the action. I was about at the end of my patience when I heard Dana give out a loud shriek.

I counted to ten slowly before I said anything and then shouted myself, "Dana! Please don't scream like that! It makes my heart pound!" I then went back to my book.

I started to read again, but then realized that it was too quiet. And Dana hadn't said a word in response to me. At least, I'd usually get a 'Sorry, Mom.' or an 'Okay, Mom, it won't happen again.' Something. She would always say something. Actually... *not* to respond was rude, and I found myself feeling a little annoyed!

Finally, after hearing nothing from the two of them, for another thirty seconds or so, I opened the bathroom door and stepped out.

What I saw was not to be believed. My two kids were standing in the living room, their backs to me, and their hands held high above their heads. Facing me, with his back to the front door was a strikingly handsome, rugged-looking man, with a gun. The gun was pointed at the ceiling, but my kids, obviously, were not taking any chances.

"What's going on here?" I asked.

Dana chanced turning to look at me. "Mom, quick, put your hands up. He has a gun."

"Well, I can see that he has a gun." I smiled at my daughter.

"Mom, please. Don't smile at him. You might make him angry. Just put up your hands."

Meanwhile, the gunman didn't move and didn't change the expression on his face.

To humor my daughter, I put my both hands up in front of me. "But, Dana..."

"Aunt Tara, she's right. If we just stay calm and go along with him, it'll be better." Kane was obviously shaken. Apparently, he hadn't been on the receiving end of this kind of treatment before.

I stood still and looked at the gunman for another minute, while my children stood frozen. Finally, feeling like Katherine Ross, in <u>Butch Cassidy and the Sundance Kid</u>, I spoke to the young man brandishing a gun in my suburban living room. "Uh, you'd better put that away before a neighbor peeks in and shoots *you*!"

He spoke then for the first time. "Don't worry 'bout me, lady. I' just come for the kids."

Unable to resist playing along, I put on my best, distressed voice, "Oh please, kind sir. Don't take the children, for they are just ignorant teenagers and surely would be of no use to you. Why, they don't even recognize their own Uncle Jayce when they see him!"

I had to laugh. And at this, the 'gunman' broke into a smile, put away his weapon, and came over to give his big sister a hug.

"Jayce, I can't believe this! What in the world are you doing here? I had no idea you were coming stateside. It is so good to see you!" I hugged my long-lost, wayward 'little brother' as tears filled my eyes. It had been so, so long…

Dana and Kane were standing dumbfounded, watching the two of us. Finally, Dana found her voice. "Uncle Jayce?"

Jayce turned to her and swept her up in a big bear hug. "Dana, you're beautiful! I haven't seen you since you were like, what, seven. And this must be Kane." Kane reached out his hand, and Jayce took it and gave him a hug with his other arm. Then, in a serious tone, he said to Kane. "I been hearin' about you."

Kane looked at me, and I shrugged my shoulders. But to make him feel better and to even out the playing field a little, I said, "Kane, meet your counterpart from the last generation."

My brother smiled sheepishly at me, then turned to Kane, and, with a no-nonsense tone, said, simply, "We've got some talkin' to do." He turned back to me then and said, "But I *did* come for the kids. How about we go for some good old-fashioned American pizza and ice cream?"

"Sure," I said, "but you're not leaving *me* out! You kids go get ready. And you, Jayce, you go lock that gun in whatever baggage you have with you, and I never want to see it again! You got that?"

"Yes, ma'am!" He feigned obedience to me, his 'big sister', and then reassured me, saying, "You know I wouldn't bring a loaded gun into your house, Sis."

"Yeah… that's what they *all* say!" I teased him, as I turned to go get ready.

"There have been *others*?" he quipped, calling out to me, in mock disbelief, as he followed me to the foot of the stairs.

I sighed and thought to myself, 'How *did* I get born into this family...?'

Dana and Kane took off to change clothes. Jayce then disappeared back outside, to put the gun away. He soon returned and plopped himself down on the couch, where I joined him, while we waited for the kids.

"How did you get here?" I asked him. "How did you get in? You scared the kids half to death!"

"Aw, you know me. I've been around the Pacific for the last few years, so I stopped off at Kate's house on the way in. She loaned me your key, and I made her promise not to call you. I rented a car at the airport in New York."

"You imp!" I teased. Then, on a more serious note, "So, you know what's going on with Kate and Paul, and why Kane's here?"

"Well, I got their side of the story. I'll have to get yours later. I have a proposal for you, but I don't want to discuss it in front of the kids."

"Okay." He had piqued my curiosity, but then Dana and Kane reappeared at that moment, so we postponed our discussion.

I went to get out my keys, but my brother stopped me. "I'll drive, Tar."

"I don't know, Jayce."

"Hey, I'm a grown-up now," he grinned. "I'll be careful."

I looked at him warily. I knew my brother. I couldn't believe that he would *ever* be a grown-up. But I nodded, and we took off in his rental car.

40. Neophilia

Neophiliac: one having the (DRD4) gene for
novelty-seeking behavior.

Now, Jayce was my baby brother. I was eighteen and leaving home for college when he was born. I didn't get to spend much time with him when he was little. But during his teens, he gave my parents such a hard time that they sent him to live with Teddy and me for a few years. My boys were only six and three at the time, and Teddy wasn't crazy about having Jayce live with us.

Jayce was a wild kid. He was always in trouble with somebody. I wasn't supposed to know that he was drug-involved, although I was there when he came home drunk once or twice. Teddy said that Jayce didn't want me to know what he was doing, so I played along, letting Teddy handle him, when my brother lost control. We were hoping that that might cut down on his use a little. But he was a daredevil and a prankster and always stirring things up.

But Jayce was bright. When he finally went away to college, he discovered that he was a genius with business and computers. He made a fortune by the time he was in his late twenties, invested it incredibly well, and stopped working shortly thereafter! We had been in touch, first through letters, and then through e-mail, over the years, but there were long periods of time when I didn't hear from him.

From what I could piece together, he had decided to learn a lot of very specific skills, like marksmanship, flying, SCUBA, and foreign languages. At first, I was sure that he had become a drug runner, and I was terrified for him. But then my sister saw him briefly in California and told me that he was, what she, laughingly, called, 'a mercenary for Jesus'. He had decided to devote his time and talents to religious organizations that needed to get help to their missionaries, in the field, in various locales.

Apparently, he worked for 'God, in general', not favoring one religion over another, and he would make himself available for the most difficult missions. My sister said he was doing things like flying missionaries out of dangerous situations, air-lifting supplies into areas that other rescue groups were having trouble getting into, and actually finding ways to free those who had been wrongly imprisoned for 'spreading the word on things spiritual'.

I was proud of my brother, not so much for what he did, but for how he made use of who he was. I was very curious, and not a little apprehensive, about what kind of ideas he had in mind for our nephew, and Kane's all-too-familiar behavior profile.

  *   *   *   *   *   *   *   *

Later that evening, after David and Hannah had come home, and had time to visit with their long-lost uncle, I finally sent them all off to bed. I told them that I wanted Uncle Jayce to myself for a while.

The kids reluctantly said good night, after reassurance that their uncle had promised to spend a few days with us.

I made Jayce some hot chocolate, his favorite in any season, and made myself a cup of herbal tea. We settled down for a long chat.

Over pizza, Jayce had filled us in on his personal exploits, pretty much confirming what my sister had told me, and regaling the kids with tales of his most interesting missions. Though he was never one to talk about his own faith or religious beliefs, I could see that he had developed a strong personal philosophy of life. He, apparently, had found a God that loved him, protected him, and forgave him for his 'screw-ups'.

"So, Jayce, what really brings you home this time? Besides a craving for pizza and hot chocolate?"

"I missed you, Sis."

"Aw, you are so sweet! But really, what are you doing here?" He threw his head back and laughed. I thought I caught a glimmer in his eye. Then I panicked for a moment. "You're not sick, are you?"

"No, nothing like that."

"You're getting married!"

"No, Sis, 'fraid not. Not yet, anyway. But, I promise, you'll be the first to know."

I stopped talking then and decided to just wait and listen.

He was quiet for a minute and then started to talk. "Well, you know I've been working for various religious groups, mostly Christian missionaries from different churches. They're all basically alike, I guess. You know, I see these people in some pretty dangerous situations, and I admire them, and I'm glad I can help them out."

Typical of my brother's thought pattern, he then headed off in another direction. I always suspected that Jayce, like my son Danny, had ADD. His 'pinball thinking', in addition to his risk-taking behavior, was typical of young men with un-medicated, Attention

Deficit Disorder.

He continued. "You know, Sis, you and I have always been a lot alike."

"Oh sure," I interrupted him, "I make three meals a day and do five loads of laundry, and you fly helicopter missions into war zones."

He grinned and went on, "Do you remember when I was living with you, and we watched a movie together called The Mechanic?"

"Yes, I do, with Charles Bronson. I remember that Teddy was upset that I let you see that, because he was afraid that you'd get the idea to become a hired assassin." I paused for a minute. "You haven't, have you?"

"No! Come on, Sis! I'm one of the good guys now, remember?"

I reached over and patted his arm. "Sorry, Kid. Old habits do die hard."

"Well, remember how, after the movie, we talked about how cool it was that Charles Bronson was able to do all those things? He flew a plane, rode a motorcycle, rode horseback, was an expert with a gun, did SCUBA diving…?" I nodded my head. I remembered that conversation. "Well, then you told me that *you* had learned to do a lot of those things, before you got married and had the kids. So, I decided that, if I ever got the chance, I would learn to do all those things, too... and I have!" He paused.

I had been thinking about what he said about the two of us being alike. "Well, now that I think about it," I said, "I guess we both had restless spirits. I just reigned mine in a lot tighter, and a lot younger, than you did."

"Restless?! Admit it, Sis. I was totally out of control for a long time. I guess I still am, a little, sometimes." He stopped to think. "But, as I got older, I decided that I wanted to use all those 'Charles Bronson skills' to help people, especially people who use their lives to help *other* people. I just thought it would be a cool idea." He took a deep breath then, and I could see he was blinking back tears. I had no idea why.

I waited until he was ready to go on. Finally, he continued, "Well, remember, I was talking about these missionaries? Well, a lot of times, in the middle of all the chaos that we were in, they would insist that we stop and pray! It used to drive me crazy! I was running on this incredible adrenalin high, risking my neck, and they were stopping to pray!

"Well, after this happened a few times, I got used to it, and I began to think about it. I was putting myself in these dangerous situations for a high. They had chosen to work, in the same dangerous situations, with people who *had* to live in those conditions. And they were trying to bring them peace from it. I felt really weird about that. They were praying to their God for safety, and here I was gettin' off on the danger." He wiped tears from his eyes and looked at me. "I don't know if I'm explaining this very well."

"No, it's okay. Go on." As usual, I had no idea where he was going with this, but I could see that it was very important to him, and *he* was very important to *me*. But I couldn't remember ever seeing him so emotional.

He continued. "Then, I kept thinking about something that Mom used to always say. She used to say, 'Charity begins at home'. I kept thinking about that. I didn't know why, but it kept popping into my thoughts. I knew 'charity' meant 'love', like love for your family and those in need, but I couldn't figure out why I kept thinking about it.

"I happened to mention it one night to this missionary guy, on a long flight out of the jungles somewhere. I told him that I felt that, to be happy, I needed to live the life I was living. I told him that, as ungrateful as it sounded, I felt that the peaceful, safe life, 'back home', was so incredibly boring that I would go out of my mind.

"He told me that our thoughts are often God's 'angel messages' to us, and that I should pay attention to them. Then he started asking me about my family, and I told him that I had no family, 'cause I thought he meant like a wife and kids. But, when he started to act all sorry for me, I realized that he meant like you guys. So I started to tell him all about you and Teddy and the kids; and Kate and Paul and Kane; and Linda; and Tom and Slade; and Mom and Dad.

"Then he told me that I should pray about two things. First, he said that I should think about whether I was right with all of you, if I owed you anything, thanks, apologies, like that." He took a deep breath. I was beginning to guess why he'd come home. "Secondly, he said that I should pray to know if there was anything that you needed from me. Like here I was doing this great work for total strangers, out in the world, but that maybe my own family needed me for something. And then he said something really interesting. He said, *'Jayce, when we prayed back there in the middle of all that chaos, do you know what we were praying for?'*

"And I said, 'Well, I assumed for safety and an end to the chaos. And I guess, a painless death, if it were going to end that way.'

"And he said to me, *'Well, I guess those would have been good things to pray for, but, you know Jayce, the missionaries that you help are a lot like you. We like the danger and excitement that this life affords. If we didn't, we all could have chosen much safer walks. No, when we pray, Jayce, we're listening for directions from our Commander-in-Chief. We're listening, for ideas that we need to apply in that situation, right then, whatever those ideas might be. It's very exciting, Jayce. We never know what He's going to ask us to do next. And you know, from the time I got the idea, as a young man, to go into this line of work, God has spoken to me in all kinds of places, and His ideas are always the most astounding, exciting ones I could ever imagine.*

'He speaks to each of our needs, including the needs of those of us that walk, shall we say, 'off the beaten path'. After a while, Jayce, even the craziest of us run out of crazy ideas. You know that old song, 'kicks just keep gettin' harder to find'? Well, God never runs out. And, if you want to live your life on a roller coaster, Jayce, just 'log on' with Him.

'But, Jayce, remember what I said about your family. God wants your whole self. He doesn't want you to have any unfinished business, guilt, or preoccupations that are going to block His channel to you. I think maybe He's telling you that you need to get in touch with your family, and just check things out at home. Maybe it's nothing. But maybe it's the answer to prayer. Maybe not even your prayer, but somebody's.'

"Well, I didn't really know how to pray, so I asked him how I should do that. He said, *'Just watch and listen. God will speak to you through everything and everybody around you, as well as through your own thoughts. You'll hear a line from a song on the radio. You'll see someone going through something that you've been through, or need to go through. You'll be reading a newspaper, and a headline or a sentence will jump out at you. You'll get the message'.* Well, we hit some trouble about that time, so I didn't get to think about it again until quite a while later.

"I knew that I hadn't been in touch with you all in a while, and I started to ask myself why. I was going to e-mail you one night, and I stopped and realized that the most important thing that I wanted to say to you was something that I wanted to say in person. And then, I thought about Mom and Dad, and I realized that, well... I guess I've been growing up a lot lately."

He stopped talking and the tears were rolling down his cheeks. I moved closer to him and put my arms around his neck. He rested his head on my shoulder for a minute.

Then, he sat back and wiped his eyes. "How are Mom and Dad? Are they…?"

"They're fine!" I reassured him. "They will be so happy to see you, you Prodigal Son you! The kids and I go up about once a month in the good weather and help them with work around their house. They spend the winter in Mexico now, with Linda. In fact, they've just come home recently, so we'll be going up there pretty soon. They don't like the computer, and they hate spending money on long distance calls, so I depend on Linda to let me know how they're doing while they're away. They're really doing quite well, considering all that we kids have put them through."

He smiled through his tears. Then he said, "Wait, I'm getting ahead of myself. 'First things first'! God! I can't believe how much of Mom rubbed off on me." Again he stopped to compose himself.

I could feel his emotions as I sat there. "This is really hard for you, isn't it?" I commented.

He nodded. "That missionary guy *told* me that there were things more scary and gut wrenching than fighting and risking my life! But, let me do this." He turned and faced me then. "Sis, I want to thank you, with everything I've got, for all you did for me growing up. You not only took care of me, you understood me, and you fought for me, when everybody else had given up, including me. And I know now, knowing how much alike we really are, what a sacrifice you were making. Not only were you tied down, raising kids of your own, but then you took *me* on, with all my problems. I want you to know that I love you, and I appreciate everything you did for me. And I hope you'll forgive me for being too chicken, for the last ten years, to come and tell you that before."

Now the tears were streaming down *my* face. I reached over again and hugged him. I loved my brother so much, and I wanted the best that God had in store for him. All my work and all my years of praying for him were not in vain after all. I silently whispered a little prayer that I prayed a hundred times a day, 'Thank you, God'.

"Jayce, God told me to take care of you. Like you said, I was a young mother with small children. It was a pretty important, but a pretty tedious, job. When God told me that you should live with us, I was overwhelmed. All I could think of was another three piles of laundry a week. But you taught me more about parenting than I could have learned from a hundred books. And you gave my life the real challenge that God knew I needed. Believe me, oftentimes, after dealing with you, a boring day of laundry and food shopping was a welcome blessing!

"And, because of you, I realized that taking care of God's children, young and old, was a greater adventure for me than all the hang-gliding, river rafting, and mountain climbing that I could ever squeeze into my life. It's not everybody's calling, and certainly not everyone has the temperament to do this kind of work, but I love the fact that God has also put you in a position to help others, albeit in a very unusual way."

"Thanks, Sis. I wasn't sure what you would say to me. I was afraid that you would resent all those things that I did back then, and all the times that my problems took you away from your family." He paused for a minute, then added, "I'm glad I came home."

"'God's emphasis is always right'. And 'God is Love'. No matter what I would have said to you, He would have given you the strength to hear it and grow from it."

"I love you, Sis."

"I love you, too, Jayce."

"So, tell me about our nephew Kane. Is he as bad as I was?"

"Jayce, he's done things you wouldn't touch."

"Really!?"

"Well, things you wouldn't touch at his age. Of course, I wouldn't know what you did after you left me, and I don't think I want to know. But Kane has really given me a run for my money; police, overdose, suspension from school...you name it."

"Whoa, overdose. Kate left that out."

"Yeah, I guess she would. I think they were her pills."

"Geez, I guess I *have* been away a long time."

I just smiled at him. "'You want me to give you the condensed version?"

He nodded his head, and I was just about to begin my story, when I heard a noise from the upstairs hallway. It sounded like somebody crying. I figured it was Hannah, having a nightmare after a too-hectic day. "Give me a minute, Jayce. I'll be right back."

I jumped up from the couch and scooted up the stairs to the

upstairs hallway. As I turned right, to Hannah's room, I almost tripped over Kane, sitting on the floor, with his back against the wall, knees drawn up. He had his head down, and I thought he was asleep.

Still thinking that I was headed to Hannah's room, I reached down, touched his shoulder, and said, "Hey, wake up, you little eavesdropper, and get yourself back to bed." When he looked up at me, tears streaming down his face, I realized my mistake. I crouched down on the floor next to him, and he put his arms around my neck.

"I'm sorry," he sobbed. "I'm so sorry."

"What for? What are you talking about?"

"What he said. That's me, too!"

I held on to him and pushed his tear-soaked hair off his face. This boy's hair grew faster than anything I had ever seen. Just at that moment, Jayce came up the stairs.

"Is everything okay? Can I do something?" Jayce asked.

I stared up at him, the light beginning to dawn in my thought. Suddenly, I knew exactly why Jayce had been sent home. I didn't know the details yet, but I knew the reason. I looked from Jayce's face back down to Kane's. "You know? I'll bet you can. Come on. You two definitely need to get to know each other better."

Jayce got around the other side of Kane and helped me lift him to his feet. The three of us went down into the living room, Kane vigorously wiping the tears from his face. I motioned to the two of them to sit on the couch.

It was only about eleven o'clock. "Kane, you can stay up and talk to Uncle Jayce until he's finished with you. Then you can show him to Danny's room and get to bed yourself. I'm trusting you. Do you think you can handle that?"

"Yes, ma'am."

"Good, because I'm going to bed." I kissed both of them goodnight and headed up to my room. I said a really short prayer that night, because God already knew what was in my heart. 'Thank you!'

41. Paying Back

The next morning, the girls left for school. The school year was almost over, and the girls were down to half days. David took Kane to the gym, for his regular session with the trainer. We had planned some family time for that afternoon, but the morning was free for me to talk to my brother, Jayce, about Kane.

"So, without breaking any confidences," I began, "what have you learned about our nephew?"

"Wow, you were right. He's got it bad." Jayce said.

"I know. But you've got an idea, haven't you?"

"Well, yeah. It came to me while I was visiting Kate and Paul. I even went so far as to ask their permission, but they made it really clear that you would have the final word on this."

"So, what is it already?"

"Well, before I tell you, I'd like to know what you've been doing with him. He told me some things, but I need to know from you."

I took a deep breath. I had tried everything that I could think of. How to sum it up...

"Well, Jayce, I did all the 'mom things'. I loved him; I took care of him; I rescued him when appropriate. I punished him. I pushed him. I made him recognize and confront his feelings. I put him in positions to have to deal with all the responsibilities of life. I gave him good food, clean clothes, a good night's sleep, exercise, and recreation. I took him to church, I sent him to school. That was a disaster! I gave him a limited social life. That's one area that we haven't quite built up enough trust for yet. And, together, we made some progress in cutting down his AOD use."

"AOD?"

"New catch phrase. Alcohol and Other Drugs."

Jayce nodded. "But you haven't been able to eliminate that entirely, right?"

I shook my head. "It's a tough one. You know, I think with Kane, it's not that his life is so bad that he's trying to get away from it. I think it's that the drugs are so good that even the best life, that I can give him here, pales by comparison."

Jayce nodded his head and continued to look at me for a while. I could tell that he was thinking this through. Finally, he said, "Okay… So, does he have down his basics? He can get himself up in the morning? Makes his bed? Takes care of personal hygiene? Can do basic food, cleaning, and laundry chores? Understands household expenses? Can 'work, pray, study, and play'?" I smiled. That last one was another one of Teddy's…

"Yeah, he's been really stepping up," I told him, "although I think it's more out of boredom than any kind of enthusiasm for the work!"

"What about getting along with people, respect and tolerance?"

"Well, I think our community, the neighbors, church, our friends, represent a pretty diverse group. I've never seen him exhibit any attitudes or behaviors that would make me think that he has a problem in that area."

"So what have *you* thinking about for his future?" Jayce asked.

"Well, up until just recently, I was thinking that it looked pretty bleak. But then I had this insight last night, when the three of us were in the hallway. I think that I really hit on something when I said that you are Kane's counterpart, from your generation. I'm wondering if Kane's drug use is an indicator that, like you, he's meant to live a life that's just a whole lot more exciting and stimulating than the one he's had so far… aside from his drug-related escapades, of course.

"Kane is a great kid," I continued, "and he's risen to every challenge that I can come up with. He doesn't fit the profile that I'm used to seeing in young drug abusers. He actually realizes, at age fourteen, that he screwed up by starting to get high. And I've had him set things right with his parents, which is really hard for an adolescent. But he's still just not happy. His life is joyless. He does what he's told. As I said, his AOD use is down. But there's something major missing.

"I know that we parents can't expect kids to be happy all the time, or even a lot of the time. Life just has too much 'housekeeping and homework' for that. But, even when he's playing by all the rules and really trying hard, Kane is lacking that basic inner joy that we should be able to expect for our kids. His spirit is, I don't know, suppressed."

"What do you think's gonna happen with him?" Jayce asked.

"I don't know exactly." Then I remembered that one time, on our morning walk. "He did have a good insight, though, not too long ago. We were talking about purpose in life, and he seemed to understand that he can just as easily reflect the good that's around him as he can the bad, and that he has the power to change."

"Well, that's major!" Jayce remarked.

"I know," I said. "I was really happy about that. And so was he. It gave him a kind of ground zero to look at himself and his potential in a whole new way. I could actually see a light in his face that morning."

"So, then, he *is* searching."

I nodded my head. "My heart aches for him. He's like us, Jayce. He wants more out of life. He's tried the things that the world is offering, and they blew up in his face."

Jayce finally picked up the conversation at that point. "He's lucky in that. A lot of people spend their lives going from one 'cheap thrill' to another, wasting years, health, and resources, only to find out too late, that all those things just don't do it. The saddest ones are the ones who go to their graves thinking, 'If I could've just had more money, a better car, a bigger house, a more attractive woman, I would have died a happy man'. All the time, they're thinking about what they *wanted*, for themselves, instead of what they could *do*, or *be*, for somebody else…maybe just by listening for directions from their own Commander-in-Chief."

"Commander-in-Chief?" I asked.

Jayce laughed. "Remember? That's what that missionary guy called God - his 'Commander in Chief'."

"Oh, right. So, Jayce, you've found some peace and joy in your life? You're listening to God and having the courage to trust that what you're hearing will be good for you?"

"Well, I'm just gettin' started, but I think it's a good plan, Sis."

"I do too."

I resisted mentioning to him that I had discussed this very concept with him years before, but that he hadn't been ready to hear it. I guess, as a wise, young man once told me, 'A guy's gotta figure it out for himself.' I sighed and smiled. If only you could be sure that they wouldn't accidentally kill themselves while they were working on figuring it out!

"I know what you're thinking." Jayce interrupted my thoughts.

He took me by surprise. "No you don't," I retorted.

"Yes, I do."

"Tell me then."

"No, I'm not telling you." Jayce knew his part in this old game.

I picked up the couch pillow and threw it at him. Some relationships are classic. "You twerp, you have no idea what I was thinking about!" All of a sudden, I gasped and put my hand over my mouth. "Oh, my gosh!"

"What? What's the matter, Sis?"

"I can't believe it. I can't believe I just called you that!"

"You used to always call me 'Twerp'."

"I know! I just remembered! Danny and I were just talking about that the other day. Danny called Kane a 'Twerp' once, when he was angry with him for screwing up. We talked about how I used to always reprimand him for using that term with David. Now I know where he got it from! Oh, dear! I can't believe it. Now I have to apologize to my son!" I had to laugh at myself. But then I remembered the real purpose of our conversation. "But, Jayce, I want to know what you're thinking about for Kane. Do you really have an idea for him?"

"Yes." He got serious then. "I want to take him with me, Tara. I'm doing a special project this summer. I was asked by a coalition of religious organizations to train some young men to do what I do. And I've agreed. Most of the trainees will be in their late teens and twenties, but I called the guy in charge, and he said that I could bring Kane, if I would take responsibility for him.

"It's here in the States. We'll be at an old military base out west. It's for six weeks, starting right after the Fourth. It won't cost anything for Kane. I'd really like to do this, Sis. It would be good for me, as well as for him."

Whoa. I had to think. "These are Christian guys?"

"Well, let's just say they're all affiliated with God-based religions that have outreach programs in less-than-posh locations."

"What will you be teaching them?"

"Personal survival, self-defense, some language. There will be licensed flight instructors and other trainers as well. Just because I can *do* some things doesn't mean that I can *teach* them."

"I understand. And I respect that *you* understand that. There will be no drugs or alcohol tolerated?"

"Definitely not."

"And you'll personally watch out for him, as if he were your own kid?" Jayce nodded. "Aren't there things that he's too young to learn, I mean that require permits and such? He's only fourteen."

"I know. I'll take care of that."

"God doesn't protect you if you lie."

"No, I know. Really, Sis, there's plenty for him to learn."

"Well, I guess there're only two things left to do then."

"What's that?"

"Get to know him a little better, to make sure you want to do this, and then ask him."

"Thanks, Sis. Your confidence in me means a lot."

"Don't thank me," I smiled. "I am not the Commander-in-Chief! *He's* the one who sent you here!"

42. Preparations

David and Kane came home from the gym about 11:30.

"Hey, Mom! When's lunch? Where's Uncle Jayce?"

"Lunch will be at one o'clock, when the girls get home, and Uncle Jayce is sleeping."

"Sleeping? Why?"

"Well, he just did a lot of traveling, he was up late last night talking to Kane, and he has some important business to take care of this afternoon. So, I suggested that he get some rest."

The two boys looked at each other and then burst out laughing.

"What?!" I said.

They were still laughing.

"What are you laughing at?" I was getting annoyed with them.

Finally, David spoke up. "Mom, Uncle Jayce is like this world famous, really tough, hero kind o' guy, and you..." He started laughing again.

"David!"

"...and you sent him upstairs to take a nap!"

"I did not!"

"Yes, you did."

"Oh, go and get washed, you little..." I snapped the dishtowel at them and sent the two of them 'off to the showers'.

When the boys were gone, I took the phone and went out to the backyard. I had to do something that I didn't feel good about. I had learned that sometimes, as adults, we're faced with dilemmas like that. Usually, I found it easy to figure out the right thing to do, because it was usually the *tough* thing. But when two right values stood opposing each other, sometimes it was a lot harder to choose between them. We had to hope that we were right, and that consequences would be equal, whichever path we chose. I needed to call my parents and let them know that we would be visiting that afternoon...and that Jayce would be with us.

My parents were elderly. They had raised five, very strong-willed, children, and they were old and tired. As much as I knew that Jayce wanted to handle this on his own, I also knew that my parents might not be able to stand the shock of seeing their youngest son, for the first time in many, too many, years.

"Hello, Mom?"

"Tara? How good to hear from you."

"Welcome home, Mom! The kids and I are coming up this afternoon. Don't worry about food. We're taking you and Dad out to dinner. Is that okay?"

"Oh, fine, dear. We've been so looking forward to seeing you. You know we always love to have you come. But aren't the children in school?"

"Just the girls, Mom. And they have half days all this week."

"Oh, that's lovely, dear."

"Mom, is Dad there?"

"Why, yes. Did you want to speak to him?"

"Yes. Please."

My father got on the phone then. I could feel my pulse race faster. I hoped this was going to be okay.

"Tara?"

"Hi, Dad. How are you?"

"I'm great. You're coming up?"

"Yeah, I'm bringing the kids. And Dad, I'm bringing someone else along, too."

"Oh?"

"Yeah," I paused, saying a silent prayer. "Jayce is here." I could hear silence on the other end of the line. "He doesn't know that I'm calling you. He wants to come and make his peace with you and Mom. Dad, you know how much I love Jayce. This is really important to him, and I'm sure he can handle whatever you have to say to him. But, Dad, if this is not going to be a pleasant reunion, then I'd rather not be there for it. I'll drop him off and take the kids and drive around the block or something." There was no sound on the other end. I began to panic. What had I done? "Dad! Are you there?"

"Oh, Tara! Oh, Sweetie, you can't imagine what a wonderful gift this is." I felt my whole body relax at once. I thought I was going to faint. "Tara, your mother and I have prayed for this day for so many years, well, you can't imagine. We hold no animosity toward Jayce. We were worried that he would never forgive *us* for not being able to parent him. Here, you tell your mother."

"Wait, Dad. There's one more thing. You know that Kate's son, Kane, has been living with us..."

"Oh, yes! Linda told us a little bit about that. We were hoping that you'd be able to bring him up at some point. We always look forward to seeing *all* the grandkids."

"Well, Dad, I've been noticing how much Jayce and Kane are

alike..."

"Ah, yes, from what Kate has told us, the three of you are like three peas in a pod."

With that, I took the phone from my ear and just stared at it. 'Really?' I thought. I gathered my composure again.

"Well, I think it will be real important to Kane, Dad, to see how you and Mom handle Jayce's return. I think it will be a model for his own reconciliation with his own parents some day. I just wanted you and Mom to be aware that Kane will be watching this reunion with great interest."

"Ah, Tara. You do take care of your children. Don't worry. All will be well."

"Thanks, Dad. I love you so much. Now I'll talk to Mom."

My mother was all excited when she got on the phone. "Oh, Tara. You can't imagine how we have prayed for this day!"

"Now, calm down, Mom. I'm calling so that you and Dad don't have heart attacks when we get there. Please don't go and have one now!"

I heard my mother laugh. "How is your brother? Is he well?"

"He's great, Mom. He's 'healthy, wealthy, and wise'. I'm so proud of him. And you will be, too."

"Where is he now?"

"He's taking a nap. He and Kane stayed up talking, late into the night, and I wanted him to be rested before he saw you."

"You're still taking care of him."

"You're still taking care of *me*, Mom!"

"Oh, go on. You're a competent, grown woman."

"I'll always need you! And even after you're gone, I'll be using what you taught me to take care of the younger ones. You know that that's what it's all about."

"Oh, stop, now. You'll have me in tears."

"I love you, Mom. And so does Jayce. I'm so happy that he's decided to do this. And now I'd better get going or we'll never get up there."

"'Bye, Sweetie."

"'Bye, Mom! See you later.

I hung up the phone and breathed a sigh of relief. 'Whew!'

43. Home at Last

The ride to my parents' house always took us about an hour. The kids were good in the car. They always brought something to do. Jayce sat in the front seat with me. I could see that he was really apprehensive, but I didn't want to talk about it in front of the kids. I also didn't want him to guess that I had called our parents. We drove most of the way in silence.

But, finally, I couldn't stand it any more. I was never one to be able to hold guilt. "It's gonna be okay, Jayce."

He nodded his head, but didn't look at me. Then, all of a sudden, he turned to me. I knew that he knew. We *were* two peas in a pod.

"You called them, didn't you?" I just stared at the road. "You didn't have to do that. I'm a big boy, Sis. I can handle my own life now. You don't have to run interference for me any more."

I could tell that he was annoyed. He was also using this as an opportunity to vent his anxiety... at my expense, I might add. Then, suddenly being aware of the kids in the back, he stopped. But he was still fuming a little. I gave him a chance to get over it.

Finally, I said, "I didn't do it for you."

At Kane's age, Jayce would have snapped back at me at that point, but he *had* grown up. He just looked at me. I glanced over at him and then back at the road. I couldn't stop the tears from flowing down my face. I was absorbing his emotions, as well as feeling my own, and all of this was a little overwhelming.

"Aw, I'm sorry, Sis. I didn't mean to upset you. I guess this is a whole lot harder for me than I thought it was gonna be."

"And just what effect did you think it was going to have on Mom and Dad? And me? Mom and Dad are old now, Jayce. We all try to make life as calm and peaceful for them as we possibly can, which, unfortunately, often means shielding them from the exploits of their children and grandchildren!

"I know you're worried about how they're going to receive you," I continued, "but did you give any thought as to what the shock of seeing you again might do to *them*? I felt that I had to prepare them." I glanced over at him again. He was staring down at his hands. "I know that they love you, Jayce, and I know that they're good people. But they're my *parents*, too, and parents don't tell their kids everything that they're feeling. If they were going to turn you away..." I could barely continue. I reached into my purse for some tissues. "...I didn't want to be there. I just couldn't take that." I wiped my eyes and regained my composure then.

"So, Jayce, as much as I respect your confidence, and as much as I know that a man has to face his own demons, I also have responsibilities to other people besides you. I hope you can understand that."

I glanced over at Jayce again. He was looking out the window. I guess there *were* things in life a lot scarier and more gut wrenching than the daredevil behavior that 'my boys' had engaged in.

I glanced in the rear view mirror and noticed that Kane, who was seated way in the back of the van, had been watching Jayce and me. Although I assumed that he couldn't hear our conversation, exactly, I knew that he sensed that something was going on. He looked concerned.

When we got to my parents' house, I parked in the driveway. Then I said to the kids, "Let's let Uncle Jayce go first. Go ahead, Jayce. We'll unload the car."

I watched my brother get out of the car and slowly walk toward the house. He was still dressed in jeans and boots and a tee shirt. At thirty-two, he still looked twenty-four. He was fit, healthy, and smart. And I was sure that the younger generations would see him as 'cool' and 'tough', as well. I couldn't help but think about how much emphasis our culture puts on outward appearances, and how well we learn to hide, or bury, what's going on inside of us.

"Hey, Mom! Can we get out now?" The kids were anxious to get out of the car.

"No." They knew, when I used that tone, not to ask again. I waited. Finally, I saw the screen door open and Mom appear on the porch. With arms open wide, she gathered her youngest to her. The tears were streaming down my face. My father appeared then and put his big arms around both of them. I watched as my brother Jayce hugged both of his parents at the same time, something that I never, ever, thought I would see in any of our lifetimes.

I turned to my kids then, and said, "Look, I want you to do as much as you can around here today to help out, and I especially want you to make sure that Uncle Jayce has as much time alone with Grandma and Grandpa as possible. Understand?"

The girls and David said, "Sure, Mom. Can we get out now?" It was getting hot in the car.

"Yes. David, would you take out the tools we brought, and, Girls, make sure all the groceries get put away." I noticed, at that point, that Kane hadn't answered and was leaning his head against the seat in front of him. "David, is Kane feeling okay?"

"Yeah, I guess. Kane, 'you okay, man?"

Kane nodded his head, without looking up, and mumbled, "Yeah."

"He says he's okay, Mom."

I wasn't so sure. He was acting funny. David and the girls got out and started to empty the car. I got out of my side and leaned in the back door. I reached back and put my hand on Kane's shoulder. "Come on." Kane shook his head without looking up. I climbed into the seat in front of him. "What's the matter?"

Again, he shook his head. I sat and waited. I had a feeling that I knew what was bothering him.

Finally, he spoke. "How old is Uncle Jayce?"

"Thirty-two."

"How old was he when he came to live with you?"

"A little older than you."

He was quiet then. I wanted desperately to speak to his need, but I wasn't sure how. I waited for the right thoughts to come. Finally, I said, "Come on."

"No, I don't want to." I tilted forward the seat in front of him. I took his arm and gently started to pull him out of the van. It was really hot in there, and he knew he couldn't take it much longer anyway, so he went along with me. I started to walk him toward the house. "Where are we going?" he asked. I didn't answer him.

I led him to the house, up the porch steps, and into the front hall. I heard voices coming from the kitchen. I listened to be sure that we wouldn't be interrupting at a crucial moment. I heard talking and laughing, and decided that it was a good time to go in.

Kane started to pull back, but I tightened my grip on his arm. Both of us knew full well that if Kane didn't want to do something that I couldn't physically make him do it, so I knew that he just needed some help with this.

When we entered the kitchen, Mom was taking some cookies out of the oven, and Dad and Jayce were seated at the kitchen table.

Dad saw us first. "Tara, Kane, come on in!" I hugged both of my parents in turn. Although I was never able to get up to visit them as much as I would have liked, I really felt their absence when they were away for the whole winter. It was good to have them 'home' again.

My mother was thrilled to see her 'West Coast grandson' and gave Kane a big hug, which he graciously returned. "Hi, Grandma."

"Well, look how you've grown! I am so happy to see you, Sweetheart!" It was still so obvious that Kane was just not used to expressions of affection. But he was learning.

At that point, I turned to my father and my brother. "Listen, I am really, really, sorry to interrupt you guys. I promised myself that the kids and I would stay out of your way and give you time alone together. But I'm afraid that there's some more healing that needs to be done in this family between sons and their parents…" Using as many facial expressions as I could to hint at my meaning, I continued, "…and, even though I am blessed to have witnessed this miracle today, I am not the one to offer reassurance that future such miracles can also occur." I was hinting my heart out! And they finally got it.

Dad and Jayce looked at each other and, at almost the exact same moment, reached to pull out the kitchen chair, that was between them, and invited Kane to sit down.

I turned back to my mother then. "Mom, how about you and I put those cookies out on the porch and see how many children we can lure in?"

I had never seen my mother look happier, as she handed me the pitchers of lemonade and picked up a big platter of my kids' favorite cookies.

As she passed by her son and her grandson, she bent over and kissed each of them on the top of the head. "We'll be sure to save some for you gentlemen!"

I would have liked to hear the conversation that my brother and my dad had with Kane, but I knew that my role, in that instance, was simply to bring them together. Those were my 'orders', obviously given on a need-to-know basis. I was proud to be able to just do my part.

We stayed at my folks' house until really late. Jayce explained to our parents about his summer plans and reassured them that he would be back to see them before the end of the summer. The kids were around, so he didn't mention his idea for Kane. We could fill them in later, if it, indeed, became a reality.

On the drive home, I was the only one awake. Jayce had gotten all the kids involved in a soccer game after dinner, and everyone was tired. I was wise enough to know that, when everyone else was exhausted, the mom would still have to carry on, so I had sat out.

It had been good to just sit and talk with my folks. It made my heart sing to see them reunited with Jayce. He had been such a challenge growing up. I knew that they could never quite understand why they had had such trouble with him. There are times when it, very clearly, seems that love cannot conquer all. As a teacher, and as a parent, I had lots of experience with personalities that were difficult to deal with. And I could see why other adults might not understand how hard it must be, especially for their own kids, to *have* one of these challenging personalities!

My mind wandered from topic to topic as I drove. I missed Teddy right then. He should be driving, and I should be resting. But, as much as I missed and loved my husband, I seriously doubted that Kane and Jayce would be making this ride with us if Teddy were still alive. Life is so strange and unpredictable. But, I guess, truth be told, that was one of my favorite things about it.

I thought, then, about the next day. Jayce and I would have to talk again about his proposal for Kane. I had suggested that Jayce use these few days to get to know him, before he took him *on* for six weeks! I wondered how Jayce was feeling, now that he had had a chance to observe Kane for a while. I also had to think about the *logistics* of this upcoming trip. I was sure that there would be paperwork, and specific gear that we would need to gather or buy.

In what seemed like no time, we were in the driveway and waking everybody up, so that they could all be sent to bed! The girls still had school, and David would be working for some friends of ours the next day. Needless to say, after everyone else had gone to bed, I was still up packing lunches and setting out dishes for breakfast. A woman's life could be so routine.

44. Rising to the Challenge

There is no shame in being in recovery. Rare is
the adult who is not recovering from at least
one of the excesses of adolescence.

-Unknown

"How did you sleep?" I asked my brother, the next morning.

"Better than I have in years."

"Well, considering where you've been sleeping for years...!" I teased. My brother had come down to breakfast early. The girls and David had left already. Kane was still asleep.

"You know what I mean, Sis! I'm so happy that I got a chance to patch things up with Mom and Dad. I didn't realize how much I needed to do that. I always figured it was just teenage nonsense, and that everybody should be over it. I didn't realize how deep the bonds are between parents and kids."

"I can't wait to see what kind of kids *you'll* be given to raise."

"Oh, now, I don't know..." my brother protested.

I just smiled at him. I wasn't sure that I knew Jayce's God, but I knew that *mine* had a great sense of humor. And justice!

I decided to change the subject. "So, what have you decided about Kane?"

"I'd still like to do this for him. What do you think?"

"He likes you, and he admires you. That's a good start. But the hard part in parenting, even surrogate parenting, is if they respect you enough to submit to your discipline. You do realize that you're going to have to discipline him, and that he might not like you for it, right?"

"Yes, ma'am. I sure do." He looked at me with a twinkle in his eye, and I knew that he was remembering back.

"And especially with Kane. If hc doesn't submit to your authority, you're going to have to have a plan in mind. Because, if you don't, he's gonna lose it! And you're gonna have one difficult, little stoner on your hands. And, with the personal stake that you seem to have in this program of yours, I don't think you're gonna want to be put in that position, Jayce."

"You're right. What do you suggest?"

"Well, I think, out of respect for your position in the program, that Kane should know that he gets no second chances. I think that you should tell him, up front, that if he drinks or gets high at all, you'll send him right home. Immediately. No discussion."

"Do you think he can handle that?"

"Do you really think that you can handle anything *else*? Look, when he drinks, he drinks until he passes out. When he gets high, he's a real brat. When he does the two together, which seems to be his preference, there's no telling what's going to happen. I don't think you can cut him any slack on this. When he's here at home, we're better prepared to deal with slip-ups. But the program that you're describing doesn't sound like it will allow for that. And I don't think that *you* should allow that."

Jayce sat thinking for a few minutes. I got up from the table and started to fuss with the dishes. I had something else that I had to say to him, and I really didn't want to look him in the eye when I said it.

"Jayce, you're a grown man. Your lifestyle is none of my business. But I've worked really hard with Kane, and even *he* knows what's best for him, regarding his drug use. Even though he's young and immature, and he slips up more than either of us would like, he knows that he can't 'chip'. So, if you're using, to any degree, I would like you to think very seriously about whether you want to set yourself up as a role model for Kane right now."

There, I said it. It had to be acknowledged. I had sent Kane off into the 'jaws of death' once before. I was going to try to avoid making that mistake again.

Jayce didn't say anything for a long time. I busied myself with the dishes for as long as I could, until, finally, I had to confront him. "Well? Can you set a good example for Kane, or not?"

He nodded his head, slowly at first, then with more determination. Finally, he spoke, partly to himself. "Geez, when God sends you to spill your guts, He certainly goes all the way." He looked up at me briefly and then back down at the table. "I had no intention of telling you this... Maaan!..."

He got up and started pacing across the kitchen. 'Oh, no,' I thought, 'not another pacer! What is it with this family?!' I averted my eyes to keep from getting nauseous.

"Tar, I wasn't going to tell you this, but, obviously, I am now." He stopped and looked at me. He looked more nervous than he did when we went to our parents' house! "I've been clean and sober for ten years. You didn't know it, but I was doing a lot of junk while I was living with you. Ted knew. He used to try to talk to me and punish me, but he couldn't stop me. Nobody could.

"But I was able to hold on to one little bit of control. I was really careful to never let you see me that way, except for maybe once or twice when I drank too much." He was watching me intently for my reaction. "And I never brought anything into the house. I would never, ever, put the kids in danger." He was wringing his hands, now, and watching my face.

"I used to do it, mostly, at night. I would sneak out when you thought I was sleeping and then sneak back in, loaded, and sleep it off. I used to get high at school a lot, but the teachers didn't really recognize it in those days. Except once, I got caught, and I convinced them to call Ted at work. He saved my neck. I guess he's someone I'll never be able to put things right with... at least not in this lifetime." He stopped for a minute and took a deep breath. "But Teddy knew how important it was to me that I didn't lose your respect...even though I couldn't control what I was doing."

He stopped talking and turned to go out of the kitchen. With both hands up against the door, he stopped, thought better of it, and then turned back to me. "I'm not hiding any more. I'm going to stand here and hear what you have to say to me. So, shoot!"

"No, you finish first. How did you clean up?" I asked him.

I surprised him with that. He thought for a minute. "Well, remember when I got into college, and you guys were so surprised?" I nodded. He came back and sat down at the table. "Well, I found out later that my high school counselor had taken a special interest in me, because I was so smart... and yet so stupid..." He stopped to reflect and then went on. "Well, when I got to college, they gave me about a week to hang myself. And then my profs, my advisor, my roommate, my RA, and my high school counselor did an intervention!

"They confronted me on my drinking and my drug use. They told me that my scholarship would be on the line. And then they set up a plan to watch me in every class, and they took turns at night taking me to all kinds of meetings. They would make me study while I was listening. They said they knew that I was smart enough to do both."

He smiled, remembering, and then got serious again. "I didn't know what was happening! Except for you, nobody else ever seemed to care what I did. Oh, I know differently now, but, I guess, back then, I was just too wasted to notice. But then, all this attention from complete strangers just floored me. I didn't know what to do. I actually became totally paranoid. I didn't know who all was watching me!

"They really set me up good. And then, as I cleaned up, they kept *on* me, encouraging me, and giving me support and opportunities, all the way through school.

"When I finally graduated, I got so turned on with my work that it was easy to stay clean. And then, after I made a lot of money, I knew that I didn't want to go the party route again, so I started preparing myself to do what I do now."

He stopped again and stared at the table. I put my hand on his arm, and he looked up at me. I was practically speechless. I was so overcome with pride. But all I could get out was, "I can't believe it."

Jayce looked down at the table again. "I'm so sorry, Sis. I know that this has to be upsetting to you. I was...I was hoping you'd never have to find out."

"No, Jayce, it's not that. As long as we're confessing, I knew about your drug use. Teddy and I never kept secrets from each other. He knew how you felt about disappointing me, and we tried to use that to help you. I also helped set up the intervention." Now it was Jayce's turn to be speechless. I continued, "What I can't believe is that you managed to stay clean all these years. I thought surely, when you never came home, that that's what you were hiding. And now you turn up here, telling me this, just when I have completely run out of ideas on how to help Kane. I just...I just can't believe it!"

My brother just sat and shook his head. *"You* can't believe it?! I've just spent the last decade holding incredible guilt, and being totally ashamed of what I had done to you... and keeping this secret from my entire family!! Now you're tellin' me that it was all just a nightmare! ...and all I had to do was wake up!"

I reached over and gave my baby brother a big hug. It was like something I had always noticed with my students at school. It was the ones who drove you the most crazy, the ones that you had to fight with and discipline the most, the ones that you thought you would be thrilled to never see again, that wound up holding the biggest place in your heart, and whose lives you wound up worrying about for years after they left you.

Then I patted my brother's arm again. "Jayce, I hate to interrupt your great awakening, but I'm afraid that, as they say, you're just gonna have to get over it. We're both adults now, and we have some serious work to do with the next generation. Let's talk about Kane."

My brother looked at me with this incredulous look on his face. He had just confessed to what he felt was the biggest sin of his life, and I was like 'Yeah, yeah, whatever. Let's get on with important things'. He had to smile. He knew how I really felt. He knew what I was saying. This was some homecoming!

I continued, "Kane's gonna be down here any minute. I want us to present a united front on this. After what you've told me, assuming that you're telling me the truth about being abstinent..."

"I swear, Sis. I'll have my sponsor get in touch with you. I have a lot of people who can vouch for me."

"Okay. Well, then, you are the perfect one to work with the kid. I still can't believe this. That missionary guy was right. You are the answer to my prayers. You can relate to him. You know about treatment. You'll recognize if he messes up. You know what? This summer, he's all yours. I know that you, with God's help, will know exactly what to do for this child."

"Are you sure, Sis?"

"I am! Everything that I've done for him up to now has been a 'stab in the dark', Jayce. You can't imagine how I've prayed for wisdom on this one. God sent you to do this."

Jayce threw up his hands. "You got me, Sis. You know I'd do anything for you."

*   *   *   *   *   *   *   *

Jayce and I spent the next hour laying out a plan for presenting this project to Kane. I suggested that we *tell* him, rather than *ask* him, since he would be afraid of any major change in his life right now. I suggested that Jayce not reveal personal information about his own history, unless, at some future point, it seemed like it might be helpful for some reason. We decided to tell Kane that if he used even once, he'd be sent home, but that if he stuck it out, and he liked it, there might be other opportunities in the future.

When we were ready, I called Kane down to breakfast.

"Kane! 'You up?"

"Yes, ma'am!"

"Come on down here. Uncle Jayce and I need to talk to you."

Kane was down the stairs in an instant. I could tell that he liked Jayce and wanted his approval. "'Morning! What's up?" he greeted us.

"Well, I'm glad to see that *you* are!" I replied. "Do you know what time it is?"

"I was studying," Kane defended himself. "I heard you guys down here talking, so I figured I'd wait until you called me."

"Well, that was very considerate," I told him.

"See? I'm learning!"

"Yes, you are. And, Kane, seeing as how you've been doing so well, Uncle Jayce and I have a surprise for you."

"Really? What?"

Jayce picked up from there. "Kane, I'm doing a training program out west this summer. It will train young men, a little older than yourself, to do some of the kinds of work that I've been doing. Some of the training is very specialized, and you have to be older, but some of it is appropriate for your age. Your Aunt Tara and I have made arrangements for you to participate. You'll be flying out with me after the Fourth of July."

"Oh, wow! Aunt Tara, you're really gonna let me go?"

"Yes."

"Cool."

"Jayce," I said, "let's see if Kane can guess the rules without our telling him... Kane?"

"I know. I know. No drinkin', no gettin' high. Follow the rules. Do what I'm told."

I looked at Jayce, and he nodded in approval. Kane was very proud of himself.

I continued. "And what are the rules?"

"No sex, no smoking, no drinking, no drugs, no crime, no gambling."

Jayce covered his mouth with his hand so that Kane wouldn't see him start to laugh. Boy, did *that* bring back memories!

And Kane had picked up the same sing-songy tone that my older kids used when they were mocking me on this. Now that I thought about it, I wondered if my boys had picked that up from their Uncle Jayce when they were little! Anyway, in this case, Kane was totally serious, ...and, I had to admit, the combination *was* kind of funny. But *Kane* would never know that!

"And....?" I went on.

"And whatever else Uncle Jayce tells me," Kane concluded.

"Okay! Good man!" I said, glancing over at Jayce, to see his reaction.

Kane turned to Jayce then. "Hey, Uncle Jay, you're not as strict as Aunt Tara, are you?"

Jayce didn't answer right away. He was playing this very cool. He finally looked at Kane. "First of all, the name's 'Jayce', not 'Jay'."

Kane changed his tone immediately. "Oh, 'sorry, Uncle Jayce!"

"And, second of all, your aunt raised me before she raised you. And, with all due respect to my sister, if you think she's tough now, you should have known her back in the day! You've had it easy, Kid."

"Yes, sir."

To me, it always seemed that boys liked it when the men in their lives (if they were lucky enough to *have* men in their lives!) set high standards for their behavior. They loved it when they could say, 'He makes me do this', or 'I have to do that', or 'I'll get killed if I whatever' or '...if I don't whatever.' There was a pride in their voice that you didn't hear in other conversations. Of course, you could always tell when the younger admired and respected the elder, and that really made all the difference.

I knew that God had sent Jayce to help Kane. Jayce had already paid the price. He knew what Kane was going through, and he knew what Kane needed to understand, in order to get, and stay, clean. But, most of all, I knew that Jayce loved Kane, like he would a son, or a brother. For the first time, since that Monday night, last December, I had a good feeling about this kid's future.

45. Departures

The next two weeks were crazy busy. Dana graduated from high school and was getting ready to go for summer orientation at her college. Hannah had a moving up ceremony, from her primary, K-3, school to an intermediate, 4-6, school, and was getting excited about summer camp. David was getting ready to go back to college for the summer session, to continue his studies. And Danny was in and out, trying to be there for each of his siblings on their special days.

Amazingly enough, Kane held it together through all of this. I was really relieved that I didn't have to deal with any more of his crises, while trying to enjoy these milestones with my other children.

And, of course, there was a lot to do to get Kane ready to spend the summer with his uncle, doing, literally, 'God knows what', with all the ready-for-anything supplies that he would need for that.

I knew that this summer would be good for Kane. I had a long talk with him about using this opportunity to learn as much as he could, especially about himself. If he were going to have to live with himself for the rest of his life, he needed to know how he operated. There's an old saying, 'Know thyself; and then trick thyself!' If anybody needed to know how to outwit himself, it was Kane. And I was now confident that I had found him an excellent teacher, in my brother Jayce.

It seemed like no time before Jayce was back to celebrate the Fourth with us and to pick up Kane, to head out west.

I knew that I was supposed to welcome this break, but I knew that I was going to miss the both of them terribly. I was going to miss *all* of them terribly. I think it's kind of curious, and a little sad, that a mom's job is to make her job obsolete! But I still had lots of parenting ahead, with a 4th grader and high school freshman, still at home. Obsolescence was certainly not in my *immediate* future!

46. Back on Track

Kane had a great summer with his uncle. He learned many new skills and thrived in the structured routine and controlled environment of the training camp. The older guys took a liking to him, and he was everybody's 'kid brother'. They were all young men of character and, so, served as excellent role models for Kane, *and* for Jayce. When Kane returned home that summer, he was healthy and strong, both physically and spiritually. I could see that Kane finally felt that he now had more to lose than he was willing to risk.

It turned out that Kane had been able to finish enough schoolwork, over the course of our year together, to begin the ninth grade with his age-mates that fall. Throughout his freshman year, the most difficult for most boys, he kept in touch with his uncle, who continued to support him in his recovery.

I can't say that Kane never slipped up at all, in the months, or years, that followed that first summer that he spent with his uncle. There are so many things in today's world that can trigger a substance abuse issue. But he was learning to make himself accountable to the people who could really help him.

My brother and my brother-in-law were very fortunate to have had my husband in their lives at a time when they were 'going off the deep end'. And now they had the chance to 'pay it forward' by taking my nephew under their wing. With the help of his Uncle Jayce and my brother-in-law, Joey, Kane found other strong men, many of whom were working their own 12th Step, who were willing to watch him, watch over him, and watch out for him - men who could teach him how to 'put on the brakes' when he was heading for the 'slippery slope'. Even though he was 'just a kid', Kane was very faithful about attending his meetings, working with his sponsor, and reporting to his uncle on a regular basis, all part of Jayce's requirements for Kane's on-going participation in the summer program.

But, most importantly, Kane was learning that, if anything were ever going to change in his life, *he* was the one who was going to have to change it…and that, instead of 'waitin' for the world to change', he needed to 'start with the man in the mirror'. With the help of these men, who were *like* him and who *liked* him, despite his screw-ups, he was able to begin to sort out the Great Life Problem: how to become the person he was created to be, without losing the love and support of those who meant the most to him.

And, as for me, I realized (a little sadly, I guess) that, even though a part of me wanted to be the one to put my arms around him, make it all better, and fix this, that wasn't what Kane really needed from me at this point. As I had learned, 'a man's gotta figure it out for himself.' And I guess we women need to figure out that, although our mothering is very important at the right time, it is, in many ways, a 'limited time engagement'…and that our role needs to change, as our boys become young men… *if* our boys are to *become* young men.

Of course, just like all of us, Kane would always need the love and support of his entire family – but *not* to bail him out, prop him up, and hold his hand! He would need us to continue to teach, encourage, and guide him - in learning how to take care of himself, in preparing for meaningful life work, and in finding a suitable helpmate, whom he could love and encourage, as she would love and encourage him.

Kane started dating Samantha toward the end of ninth grade. Sam was the younger sister of one of Dana's best friends, which was nice, since I already knew the family. But my favorite thing about Samantha was her 'zero-tolerance policy' with regard to tobacco, drug, and alcohol use. And Kane bought into it. He told me that he didn't want to lose her, and we all liked having her around.

When he brought his grades up high enough, I allowed Kane to start a part-time job on the weekends. He told Jayce that he was going to save up to buy a helicopter! I suggested that he, like the rest of the adolescent male population, might just want to start by saving up for a car.

EPILOGUE

As my friend had predicted, shortly after Kane's arrival, Kane *did* wind up staying with us until he graduated high school. And then he entered college at his uncle's alma mater. He is currently a junior and will graduate next spring. He and Samantha are still dating.

Kane spent all his high school and college summers, and some school vacations, training with his uncle. I was never exactly sure of the curriculum of my brother's program. It sounded like the Boy Scouts meet FEMA meets the Navy Seals - without the explosives and weapons, of course - although I think they did do basic firearms training and safety, as the young men came of age. It was an incredible program.

Besides being prepared to do the work that they were originally commissioned to do, these young men could, if needed, become a civilian 'army' of volunteers! The diversity of their skills and training was amazing; from first aid, to food prep, to distribution of supplies, to entertaining young children in emergency situations, to mastering all those 'Charles Bronson skills' that my brother and I had tried to emulate. And the consequent self-esteem was well-earned and well-deserved.

Kate and Paul had to kick in for some of the training costs, but they were more than willing to do so when they saw the strong, responsible, *competent,* young man that their son was becoming.

Kane's parents reconciled, and they keep in touch with Kane on a regular basis. He is now able to visit with them, from time to time, without any problems. However, his plan is to stay on the East Coast after graduation…at least when he isn't working for his Uncle Jayce, 'somewhere or other'!

I know that our family was very blessed with the way that things worked out for Kane, and for Jayce before him. (And for Joey, before that!) Not everyone is so lucky. Substance abuse has plagued our family for generations now. But, strangely enough, it has been, in a way, a blessing… if only in the fact that it has forced our boys to become strong men. It forced them to learn how to look inside of themselves and to discover how to connect with their Higher Power, their God.

And, as for us womenfolk, well… a part of me envied my brother and my nephew their adventures. I guess my dad was right. We were three peas in a pod, Jayce and Kane and I. We *all* had that gene for novelty-seeking behavior…not an easy one to manage, for any of us! Some say that God put women on this Earth to help men with their daily toil. It occurred to me that, perhaps, God put *men* here to keep us women from being bored with *ours!*

As that missionary explained to my kid brother, if you really want to live your life on a roller coaster, all you have to do is open yourself up to doing God's work! And sometimes God's work *is* more scary and gut wrenching than fighting or risking one's own life (…especially when it involves *fighting* for people that we really care about, who may be risking *their* own lives!)

But, often, God only hires us on as short-term contractors. Sometimes we have to have faith that, when the Commander-in-Chief gives us an assignment, and we've used our *courage* to do all that we can, we have to find the *serenity* to let go and trust God to take care of the rest. And, when we do, sometimes miracles *can and do* happen. And some of us get to watch our 'bad boys' turn into strong men, men of character …and that can be a pretty exciting, and rewarding adventure!

ABOUT THE AUTHOR

Laura Dell has been interested in the field of adolescent substance abuse since the early 1970s. When she completed her Master's degree, in 1971, and returned to her hometown to teach, she became concerned about illegal drug use among her middle school students.

In her second year of teaching, in preparation to teach a health class, she took a course entitled "Use, Abuse, and Addiction". Her term paper, entitled "Drug Counseling for the Classroom Teacher", was picked up and published by the Do It Now Foundation (DIN), a publishing house for harm-reduction literature, in Phoenix, AZ.

In 1976, she took a summer job working with DIN, in Phoenix. On the weekends, she "rode along" with Terros, an ambulance service, commissioned exclusively to respond to drug overdoses. She finished the summer with a 10-day stay at Synanon, the "great grand-daddy" of many of our, currently operating, therapeutic communities. As a guest at Synanon, she participated in the community, as far as she was able, and published an article, through DIN, about her experience. ("Synanon: What's It All About?" Drug Survival News, DIN, 1977)

One of the life-changing ideas that Ms. Dell gleaned at Synanon was that Synanon felt that addicts needed to be "re-parented", that they needed to re-learn certain basic life skills in order to become self-sufficient adults. Ms. Dell used this information to create a prevention-based, lifestyling course, for young adults, entitled Omniology: the Study of Everything (c Laura L. Dell, 1981 – currently in revision.) And, then, at that point, she decided to *dis*continue her journey through the world of substance abuse treatment and to do some parenting herself. Ms. Dell is the single, adoptive mother of three, now adult, children, and a grandmother to eight, "bio-adopt" and "bonus", grandchildren.

But, due to what seemed like a worsening of drug abuse symptoms among her students in the late 1990s, Ms. Dell decided, in the year 2000, to re-enter the field of substance abuse treatment and prevention. She had continued to educate herself on this topic over the years, and, so, decided to complete the classwork for the NYS CASAC (Certificate in Alcohol and Substance Abuse Counseling), which she did in 2003. Being required to complete a number of volunteer hours, in a formal treatment setting, she chose to volunteer in the adolescent unit of a treatment hospital.

Braking Kane: the Struggle to Stop was written as the author prepared to *begin* the coursework toward the CASAC. It served as a way for her to consider everything that she had previously learned about substance abuse treatment (much of it from when, as someone so aptly put it, "the substance abuse field was like the wild west!") before she began her training in more current methods of AOD (Alcohol and Other Drug) treatment.

As a middle school teacher for over thirty years, Ms. Dell spent much of her life with adolescents, and, to this day, feels great compassion for those in this very challenging stage of life. It is a time when many young people turn to illicit drug use to deal with turbulent emotions, family strife, personal grief, the unsettling changes and fears of adolescence, the desire to fit in socially with their peers, and the emergence of their own, often unique, personalities.

In the past, even moreso than now, families were on their own to deal with drug and alcohol issues. The face of treatment has changed in recent years; there is now a much broader understanding of this behavior, and many more facilities are available for very young clients. But far too many families are still faced with handling this "at home", with little or no information or experience on how to do so.

Unfortunately, in a way, adolescents are often too young to suffer many of the unpleasant, and more catastrophic, consequences, of the addicted lifestyle - the things that drive others to seek treatment: loss of job and income, homelessness, threat of jail time, loss of family and friends, etc. And parents and teachers, especially those with no personal or family history of drug use, either just don't *see* the "signs and symptoms" in these young people, or they attribute the behavior to other things. In any case, years of habit-formation can go by before parents become aware, are able to break through their own denial, and, finally, begin to seek help for their children.

This is just a story, a "fictional composite of possible realities" (see Disclaimer pg. 4), perhaps a fantasy, perhaps a prayer. But Ms. Dell hopes that Braking Kane: the Struggle to Stop may serve to give a "heads up", to some readers, regarding the very *existence* of the younger drug abuser, and to further, among others, "the conversation" regarding prevention, early intervention, early treatment, and, perhaps, a different kind of education, for our at-risk adolescents and young adults.

59325129R00142

Made in the USA
Charleston, SC
01 August 2016